VAMPIRO

VOLUME II:
THE OBSIDIAN KNIFE

DON W. HILL, M.D.
AND
TOM CAVARETTA

ISBN: Softcover 978-1-953537-56-0
Hardcover 978-1-953537-57-7
Ebook 978-1-953537-58-4

Scripture taken from the King James Version of the Bible.

Printed in the United States of America.

To order additional copies of this book, contact:
Bookwhip
1-855-339-3589
www.bookwhip.com

For my wife

I believe in the best of humankind. Kindness, charity, selflessness, and love are abundant. I have seen these qualities every day since I met my wife.

—T.C.

CONTENTS

INTRODUCTION

The coauthor of this work of fiction grew up in the Southwest as an avid sportsman with a love of bird hunting. He also developed a reverential appreciation for what we now refer to as the great outdoors. While bird hunting with friends in the Chihuahua desert that extended north into New Mexico and far West Texas, he found many Mesoamerican artifacts of great interest. These ancient treasures included seashells, pottery shards, and razor-sharp obsidian that had been crafted into tools such as arrowheads and knife blades. These discoveries confirmed that at one time there were trade routes that originated deep in the heart of Mexico that had been used by the ancients to engage in the very human act of commerce.

During the formative years that the coauthor spent in the Southwest, he also developed a great admiration for the regional Hispanic culture. Evolved over centuries in this hemisphere by a proud and industrious people, this culture's sociological cornerstone has been, and likely always will be, the strong bonds that unite family members. Some Hispanics have been demonized by uncharitable members of our modern society as "illegal aliens," or perhaps *mojados*, or sadly even "beaners" in the recent past. The Latino ethnic group of the American Southwest has historically not been generally acknowledged to possess the same attributes of the various people of predominantly western European ancestry who later migrated to North America: love of God and country, loyalty to family and friends, and the firm dedication to the principles of hard work.

Sadly, there have always been enough miscreants lurking about to have a negative impact on any given society. Of course the various subsets of Hispanic ethnic groups, like any other, have had their fair share of demonstrable sociopathy. As portrayed in this work of fiction, outbreaks of human vampirism occur on a cyclical basis in the deserts of the American Southwest. If such a thing does indeed exist, this author contends that it is a disease process which in and of itself does not necessarily equate to some innate allegiance to dark or evil forces. Among all biological entities, either microscopic or macroscopic, there is a physiological driving force to consume sustenance. The imperative for a living being to feed is not evil; it is nature. If a shark consumes another fish in the ocean, does that action constitute a manifestation of evil by that particular apex predator? After all, how far should we take this line of reasoning? If a vegan consumes a head of lettuce, does it mean that he or she murdered an innocent plant? If that is the case, then perhaps all life-forms on this planet should be considered inherently evil!

If all things in the universe are connected somehow, then all forms of life on this planet, and perhaps elsewhere, are also connected somehow. The one great independent variable in this equation that is clearly capable of disrupting what should otherwise be a fairly harmonious coexistence in this universe is the limitless capacity for evil that humankind has and the evil it is able to perpetrate. In this work of fiction, the gift of free will has been bestowed not only upon the healthy human beings who are walking upon the face of the planet Earth but also upon those infected with the transmissible virus that is responsible for human vampirism. The tendency for some to gravitate toward evil endeavors is beyond the spiritual and intellectual capacity of this author. Perhaps the consequence of original sin continues to reverberate throughout the human condition, much like the background radiation that is still detectable as a consequence of the original big bang continues to reverberate throughout the universe.

On the front dustcover of this novel, there is a warning proclaiming that there is something dangerous out there that might try to slip across the border. Because this is a novel firmly entrenched within the science fiction genre of human vampirism, that statement on face value is likely a given. However, the particular warning on the cover of this work of fiction is also intended to be a multifaceted allegory. This author hopes to intellectually challenge the status quo in the perpetual war on illicit drug use. There are several thematic elements to this novel, and one of them is the focused attention on the tragic consequences of the illegal drug trade that occurs across the border between Mexico and the United States. It is easy to point a finger at Mexico for the never-ending drug problems north of the Rio Bravo. In reality, the issue is driven by the sometimes brutal economics of supply and demand among the haves and have-nots. The conflicts that may arise in this illicit industry are usually settled through the adherence to a modification of the macroeconomic principle of guns versus butter. At a national level, the "guns versus butter" paradigm represents the challenge that a political entity must face in an attempt to balance capital expenditures directed toward perceived militaristic necessities with the basic maintenance and remedial needs of societal infrastructure.

In regard to the large cartels south of the border that now control the drug trade in the Western Hemisphere, the "guns versus butter" balance has a somewhat different connotation, one that may readily be appreciated as follows: the employment of guns to eradicate the various regional competitors in the drug wars versus the dispensation of butter in an overt effort to corrupt politicos and law enforcement agencies. In most simple terms, the "butter" is merely a bribe to entice government officials to literally look the other way when various and sundry nefarious activities that are perpetrated by the drug cartels are actually occurring. As for the majority of the humble and decent people who are living south of the border, they perhaps are more interested in the basic staple of tasty butter to be applied to their fresh dessert *sopapillas,* in addition to a generous tablespoon of wild clover honey.

The border towns south of the Rio Grande are not representative of Mexican culture. Instead, they are the reflection of a market evolution driven by the insatiable gringo appetite for mind-altering substances (including cheap mescal), trinkets, and a good time to be had by all. It may be hard to believe, but a giant sombrero, a papier-mâché Pikachu, nunchucks, and a fat Elvis painted on black velvet are not frequently found in Mexican homes outside of La Frontera! Equally ironic, there are no murders committed by cartel members that occur over struggles for the right to export vanilla extract, *pan dulce*, or *sopapillas* with wild clover honey.

In a large part, the United States is Mexican. The territory of Calafia was thought to be an island at the time that Hernán Cortés showed up looking for new real estate for the Spanish Crown circa AD 1536. In fact, the territory of Calafia is now naturally recognized as California. *Sucesiones de difuntos* is Spanish for "descendants," and the offspring of the original exploratory probe by the conquistadors is still here to this very day. The land that Cortés claimed for the crown, of course, had already been inhabited by numerous indigenous tribes that eventually intermingled and integrated with the European settlers who had come from Spain. This was actually the main contrast between the Spanish migration and the Anglo transatlantic conquest of the Western Hemisphere. Instead of integration, the Anglo settlers were more likely to employ ethnic segregation, if not outright extermination, from time to time.

Before the Treaty of Guadalupe Hidalgo of 1848, most of the southwestern United States was a part of Mexico. As an example, the Nueces River was once the official boundary between Los Tejanos and the state of Coahuila. After the war with Mexico, the United States laid claim to everything north of the Rio Bravo.

This coauthor would like to thank the readers for this opportunity to relay a brief historical overview of the complex woven societal fabric of the American Southwest. Despite the nuances of cultural differences and language barriers, we are, after all, human beings. Let's try to make the best of it, shall we?

As for the *Vampiro* novel set, it was our intent to delicately layer in a biological rationale for the reality of the "eat or be eaten" viciousness of "life on the Serengeti." The readers of these fictional stories should surely expect some thought-provoking clashes to occur as a consequence to the age-old struggles between good and evil. And, as the reader might expect, it will all be served up with a generous portion of *arroz, frijoles,* and en ocasiones, *la picadura de un chile picante*. Enjoy the bite!

—T.C.

1

TURN! TURN! TURN!

It was Monday morning. Blake Barker had received a most distressing telephone call from Mr. I. B. Terdly, who was the owner of the Nuts and Bolts hardware shop. Blake had been informed, in no uncertain terms, that he had miserably failed his probationary work period. At that very moment, Blake was unceremoniously cast into the voracious maw of economic misfortune that is perpetually hiding in the shadows and ready to pounce on any laborious soul who is living paycheck to paycheck. Ever ready to devour the ranks of the unemployed faster than Dudley Do-Right could gobble down a row of green peas that have been strategically and sequentially aligned on the blade of a table knife, the proverbial pink slip confirmed that Blake Barker was now out of a job.

The termination of Blake's employment was a consequence of the incident that had occurred the previous week. In his capacity as the acting store manager, Blake Barker had viciously pulverized a petty shoplifter in the parking lot of the strip mall where the hardware store was located.

"The police are not inclined to file charges against you at this time. Nevertheless, legal counsel from the corporate department of risk management informed me today that we're likely looking at a very expensive lawsuit," Terdly explained. "Blake, I'm forced to terminate you immediately in an attempt to mitigate the economic damages that the company and I will likely face sooner rather than later because of your reckless behavior. To be honest, I'm sorry that I ever hired you."

"Now wait just one minute," Blake countered. "Everything I ever did was done with the best interests of the company at heart."

Mr. Terdly cut Blake off and said, "Enough of your lame line of horse manure. At the end of the day, I'll come by your house and give you your two weeks of severance pay. I'll swing by your home later this afternoon and pick up both sets of shop keys from you at that time. I promise you that I'll behave in a civil fashion when I see you, if you'll afford me the same courtesy. After that, I never want to see your sorry ass ever again!"

To bring more rain down upon what was already turning out to be a perfectly crappy day, Blake would be compelled to feed. At that point in time, Blake reluctantly accepted the fact that he had become a vampire, much like his hated nemesis, Romero Lopes. Perhaps in retrospect, this was not such a bad circumstance, Blake Barker actually concluded. After all, he was now physically equipped to hunt down and eventually exterminate the night crawler that had murdered his wife, Lynne. If Blake's life was now spiraling inexorably out of control, it would be his new mission, for whatever amount of time he had left on the planet, to eventually take Romero Lopes down with him.

On the southern edge of his small farm was the cattle ranch of Prissy Maddox. When it was time for his next blood meal, Blake had already come to the realization that a very odd phenomenon would invariably recur. Whenever he walked out to the fence line, the cows from the ranch on the other side of the barbed wire partition would gather at the property limit to apparently greet him with boisterous bovine bellows.

Although Blake's olfactory receptors were acutely honed to readily detect the pungent odor of manure and cattle urine emanating from the adjacent plot of land, the same could not be said of his deductive cognition, as the vampire was at a loss as to why the cows would behave in such a receptive fashion. Blake would optimize these opportunities to take a small portion of bovine blood from each of the blissful domesticated ungulates on a rotating basis.

As long as Blake was gentle, the cows actually seemed to enjoy the peculiar experience of being phlebotomized. They willingly exposed their vulnerable necks to allow the hungry vampiro to partake of the thick liquid nutrients flowing through their vessels.

Dr. Cloud had gowned up in the biohazard suit before he entered the hospital room of Miguel Pastore. "Do you really think all of this is still necessary?" the patient asked.

"For now, at least," Cloud replied.

"You really don't have any evidence that what I'm infected with is an airborne illness, do you?"

"Not yet," Dr. Cloud admitted.

"Are you ever going to let me outside so I can get some fresh air?" queried the former mortuary diener.

"Maybe at some point," the attending physician answered. "Until we learn more about human vampirism, discretion is the better part of valor, at least for now. I really don't want to know the details, but I understand that Parker Coxswain has been bringing to you what I might euphemistically refer to as unprocessed porcine and bovine nutritional support from a nearby meatpacking plant."

"I don't want to be rude to you," Miguel said, "but perhaps the less I say, the better."

"I respect your discretion in this matter. Truly, I do. In any event, there appears to have been some clinical improvement, as you've now gone several days without needing a packed red blood cell transfusion," Cloud observed.

"What does the rest of my hematological profile look like?"

"You're still spilling blasts into your bloodstream, but fortunately you've not crossed the threshold into a full-blown acute leukemia process," Cloud elaborated. "Tell me, how do you feel?"

Miguel answered, "To be honest, I've never felt better. I was afraid that when I became infected, I would transform into a homicidal maniac. I am happy to report that I have little desire or compulsion to consume human blood, at least for the time being.

It would seem that I'm perfectly content for now to only consume animal blood. For that alone I'm at least grateful."

Dr. Cloud nodded his head. Then in silence he sat down in an empty chair at the foot of the bed of Miguel Pastore and gazed at the ceiling.

"What's up, Doc?" Miguel asked. "Something tells me you didn't come by to visit me right now to talk to me about my peculiar dietary requirements. What's eating you?"

"Miguel, something happened to me a while back when I used to date your sister, Lorena," Dr. Cloud said as he shrugged. "A fundamental change in my very essence must have occurred. I have a confession to tell you: I've *never* gotten over her. I don't know what went wrong between us, but I'm still in love with her. I think I always will be."

"I'm so happy to hear that!" Miguel answered as he flashed his fangs with a broad smile. "I always thought that you and Lorena would be a good match. I've not seen her since I got admitted to this hospital, and I'm currently not in contact with her. To my knowledge, however, she is still working as a domestic for a man named Blake Barker, down in Mesilla. Look, Cloud, do what you must do, and Godspeed to you!"

It was time for Romero Lopes to assess the status of his painful injury. He had to find some way to wash out the maggot-impregnated wound on his right anterior thigh and flush out the fly larvae and the dead cat mung from the gaping chasm that had crippled him. Hidden in the shadows of the tree line, Romero could readily see that his mortal enemy, Blake Barker, was cavorting with the cattle on the property line at the south end of Barker's five-acre spread.

Unaware that Lorena had previously absconded with young Nathan and fled the premises in a clandestine fashion, Romero warily walked up to the front of Blake's house to procure the garden hose that was attached to the home's external water spigot. The evil vampiro could ill afford another encounter with the business end of an obsidian knife blade wielded by the curandera whom he had erroneously believed was a powerful *gran bruja*. Romero quickly and quietly hosed out the writhing decayed organic poultice from his open wound. The night crawler was pleasantly surprised to see that the formerly noted necrotic and gangrenous flesh had been voraciously consumed by the legion of maggots that he had previously ladled into the large cavity in his leg with a spatula.

Because Romero Lopes had lost his rectus femoris and also the greater portion of the vastus intermedius muscle group on the front of his thigh, his ability to extend his right leg at the hip would be forever impaired. Somehow and in some way, Romero Lopes would have to recover the obsidian knife that was now in the possession of Lorena, as it was clearly a powerful bladed weapon. If the vampiro could only get his hands on the obsidian knife, he would relish the opportunity to ambush the curandera someday and return the same *regalo especial* that she had permanently rendered upon him.

Speaking of which, where was Lorena? Where was Nathan? Romero Lopes had been keeping an eye on Barker's farmhouse, and the night crawler didn't remember seeing either the curandera or her young ward return home after they'd driven away with Blake's brother, Cletus. If Lorena and Nathan's mission was only to take Cletus to the airport in El Paso, then she and Nathan should have been home long ago. The vampiro decided to take a peek through Nathan's bedroom window to get a better idea of what might be going on. After all, if nobody was inside the home, and if Blake was currently preoccupied on the south end of the spread for whatever reason, perhaps it would be a good time for Romero Lopes to break into the farmhouse to try to recover the missing obsidian blade.

The virologist Sister Joyce Lipton and the infectious disease physician Andres Reese paid a visit to the hospital room of Miguel Pastore, but this time neither of the medical specialists was wearing the biohazard suit that the patient had become quite accustomed to seeing whenever anybody entered his locked room.

"Whenever medical personnel come into my room, they're always decked out like Buzz Aldrin and Neil Armstrong on Tranquility Base. Aren't you both afraid of getting infected from me?" Miguel asked. "What's going on?"

"Not unless you plan on biting us," the nun replied. "Why don't you tell him the good news, Andres?"

"It would be my honor," the infectious disease specialist answered. "We believe that your illness is a blood-borne disease that can't be transmitted by incidental contact or through airborne dissemination."

"I always suspected that was the case," Miguel said. "What makes you people think so now?"

"We've confirmed the veracity of a peculiar incident involving a vampiro living down in Mexico in the town of Santa Sangre. Apparently this infected individual has been living out in the open there for many years as a community resident," Andres replied. "Reportedly, nobody else in that particular town south of the border has ever been infected with human vampirism."

"So, what does this mean to me?" Miguel asked.

"Your official status has changed. You're a bona fide patient now and no longer an incarcerated prisoner in isolation!" Andres exclaimed.

"I asked the hematology–oncology fellow named J. D. Brewster to take you outside to get some fresh air," the virologist happily reported. "He's been advised to make sure that you stay in the shade to keep your skin from getting blistered."

Miguel was pleased that he was going to get a chance to see the bright blue cloudless Santa Fe skyline. Upon Brewster's arrival with a wheelchair, however, Dr. Reese glared at the subspecialty fellow with obvious disdain. Andres turned to his colleague Dr. Lipton with a specific petition. "Excuse me momentarily, Sister, as I need to have a word in private with Brewster."

Dr. Andres Reese forcefully grabbed J. D. Brewster by his left elbow and pulled him down the hallway.

"What have I done now?" Brewster defensively asked. "You can't treat me like this. I'm a fellow, not a student."

"This past Wednesday when I was in the doctor's lounge getting a cup of coffee, I listened to an inappropriate salacious tale that you were sharing with Parker Coxswain."

"Oh, crap!" Brewster exclaimed. "We were just engaged in a little harmless chatter. We didn't mean to offend you or anybody else. I'm sorry about all that. In retrospect, that story was a bit on the blue side by even my rather marginal ethical standards. Sometimes I can be a jerk, I guess."

"*Sometimes?*" Andres Reese asked. "How about *all of the time*? I certainly didn't appreciate my name being tied to the butt end of some nasty scatological joke. That's exactly how rumors get started around this place. Listen to me very carefully, smart-ass. If I ever catch wind of being insulted by you in such an egregious fashion ever again, I'll file a formal complaint about you with administration."

"Ease up, Dr. Andres!" Brewster pleaded. "Mea culpa. It won't *ever* happen again."

"It better not. Pay attention, Brewster. I happen to be an *infectious disease* specialist, not an *incestuous disease* specialist. Now, you might think that your sophomoric anecdote was nothing more than a juvenile humorous example of malapropism, but I was highly offended. Go ahead and try it one more time. When I get done with you, I'll send you back to Houston in a tin can. You'd be well advised to convey this particular warning to the other alumni, or animals as the case may be, from the University of Texas at Santa Fe. Am I clear?"

"Crystal."

After Joyce Lipton and Dr. Andres Reese had departed, Brewster loaded Miguel Pastore into the wheelchair to take him outside for a breath of fresh air before the patient was subjected to a follow-up CT scan of his kidneys with intravenous contrast. Miguel asked, "What in hell was Dr. Reese all worked up about? I could hear him unloading on you all the way down the hallway. What did you do or say that got him so pissed off at you?"

"Sadly," Brewster replied, "Dr. Reese doesn't have a sense of humor. There are indeed anger management issues to contend with here, or so it would seem."

When the doors opened, Brewster pushed the wheelchair holding Miguel Pastore into the elevator. A young woman was present on the elevator. She accompanied the young doctor and his patient on the trip down to the ground floor. There was music that was being piped into the elevator from a set of speakers on the ceiling of the lift, and it happened to be the electric folk rock song "Turn! Turn! Turn!" by Roger McGuinn and the Byrds.

"Dr. Brewster," Miguel asked, "do you ever have the sense that you're somehow being scrutinized by God and His very universe? I feel that way this very moment!"

"What now?" Brewster asked.

"Don't you see?" Miguel asked. "This classic song is meant specifically for me to hear at this very juncture in time."

"How so?"

"Think about it," Miguel elaborated. "After all, I've personally 'turned, turned, turned,' have I not?"

"Well, I'm listening to the lyrics of this tune," the young woman on the elevator observed, "and they seem quite interesting. I've never heard this song before. I like the jangly sound of the guitar. It sounds like a bell!"

Dr. Brewster, an idiot savant who knew every single hit song from the 1960s, commented, "The sound that you are hearing is from a twelve-string atomic Rickenbacker 360 powered through a compression box with a treble booster. The song was released by Roger McGuinn and the Byrds back in 1965 on the Columbia record label. An earlier version of the song was first recorded by the communist folk singer Pete Seeger, as I recall. The lyrics, however, are straight out of the Bible. Ecclesiastes 3:1–3 to be precise. The melancholy prose was originally penned in the time of King Solomon, circa 600 BC."

"I'm offended that you used the term 'BC' and not something more appropriate to the historical time frame to which you are referring," the young woman replied.

"Oh, is that so?" Brewster asked as he gave the now unwelcome elevator interloper a side glance.

"I'm a human secularist. I find it hard to fathom that a medical scientist such as you, as indicated by the designation on your name badge, is actually a *deist.* How quaint! How unsophisticated! How, well—how charmingly provincial!" the woman said with a rather haughty inflection.

"What did you say?" Brewster asked in anger, raising his voice.

"The particular notation you employed, 'BC,' strongly suggests that you're the type of person who actually believes that a mythical figure now referred to as Jesus of Nazareth actually once existed," the woman opined.

"Did he not?" Miguel interjected.

"The alleged life of this person is purely a fairy tale," the woman added. "Nothing more than an opiate for the masses as far as I'm concerned. The proper terminology you should use when referring to this remote historical epoch in human history is 'BCE.' That's what enlightened people say when they now refer to matters of antiquity."

"BCE, eh?" Brewster asked.

"Just in case you're not aware, BCE is the acronym for 'before the common era.' You should simply make a promise to me that from here on out, you'll try to use more liberal and softly nuanced terminology. If you swear to do so, I'll even let you hold open the elevator door for me upon my departure! After all, you wouldn't want people to think that you're little more than a malodorous conservative Southern bumpkin who shops at Walmart, or perhaps that you're from some dreadful place like Texas, now would you?"

Never one to shy away from a sparring match, Dr. Brewster was quick to pull the trigger. "I disrespectfully reject your bigoted opinion, and therefore my verbiage stands as previously stated!"

"Well, if you don't start using the term 'BCE,' you're going to offend a lot of intellectually advanced atheists such as me!"

In retrospect, the woman should have reined in her arrogance at that particular juncture before her fishing reel got ensnarled in the subsequent vicious backlash that would leave her both bewildered and emotionally traumatized.

Miguel Pastore flashed his fangs as he punched the elevator's emergency stop button and jumped out of the wheelchair. He grabbed the young woman by the collar and then slammed her against the closed doors of the elevator. He forcefully spun her around in a 180-degree arc, and then he easily hoisted the terrified woman halfway up the back wall of the lift.

"Pay attention to what I am about to tell you," Miguel said with a malevolent sneer as he shook the woman by her shoulders. "In every hospital room at this facility, you'll find a Bible that has been placed there by the Gideons. Before you leave this hospital today, you're going to commit to memory Ecclesiastes 3:1–3. There will be a pop quiz on this passage from the scriptures when I find you later today. If you fail this test, I'll rip your throat out, drain every drop of blood from you that's now coursing through your veins, and then I'll eat your liver!"

The woman, who had only moments before professed to be an atheist, cried out in fear. "Dear God, save me!"

Miguel Pastore repeatedly licked the woman's face with vigor before he pried opened the elevator doors with his bare hands. Before the doors automatically slammed shut, the vampiro unceremoniously cast the woman out of the elevator shaft. She landed squarely upon her keister and slid halfway down the hallway upon the linoleum floor near the hospital's intensive care unit.

Brewster, who had been looking upon the frightening scene with apparent casual indifference, pulled a tasty confectionary resin out of the top pocket of his white lab coat and offered it to Miguel. "Gum, señor?"

"Chewing or bubble?" Miguel asked as he pursed his lips and squinted intently at Brewster, considering his magnanimous display of generosity.

"Bubble," Brewster answered. "Trust me, it works better than Valium for reducing stress."

"Dubble Bubble?" the vampiro asked.

"Oh, hell no," Brewster answered as he popped a loud gum bubble against the roof of his mouth. "It's Bazooka bubble gum from the Topps Company. Same guys who make the baseball cards in

Brooklyn, as I recall. I'll have you know, Bazooka bubble gum comes with an excellent cartoon strip, at least in my humble opinion. It's inserted within the outer wrapper."

"Now I remember. Who's the dumb-shit skinny dude in the cartoon strip who wears the red turtleneck sweater all the way up to his eyeballs?" Miguel asked as he jammed the sweet chewy treat into his *boca*. "Is that the guy they call Bazooka Joe?"

"Not even close," Brewster explained. "Bazooka Joe's the little bastard with the eye patch."

"Does he wear the patch over his left eye or over his right eye?" Miguel asked for clarity.

"Over his right eye, but I could've sworn that the little pecker head was blind in his left eye. Well, what do I know? Be that as it may, the guy who always wears the red turtleneck in the cartoon strip is the lanky, cranky ectomorph named Mort."

"What's his story?"

"Who?" Brewster asked. "Do you mean Mort or Bazooka Joe?"

"I'm askin' about Mort," Miguel replied. "Besides the fact that he's an anorectic beanpole, what's the lowdown with that stupid red turtleneck that he invariably wears?"

"I have it on good authority that Mort has advanced—stage IV—head and neck squamous cell carcinoma as a consequence of a long-standing history of tobacco and alcohol abuse that began in utero. Over time, the cancer simply ate away at the poor fucker's face. Right down to the bone, as a matter of fact," Brewster professed. "He now has to wear the turtleneck to hide his hideous mug; otherwise he'd become a social recluse."

"You're full of shit," Miguel said. "You're from Texas, are you not?"

"Indeed, I am. Nonetheless, I'm on the square with you, my jaundiced friend," Brewster replied. "This was all revealed to me once Mort signed over a standard release of information form and I had the opportunity to thoroughly comb through his complex medical records. Sad to say, Mort now has a lethal tumor burden. He signed off on a DNR code status, and he's now finally enrolled into Our Lady of Perpetual Motion's at-home hospice program for symptomatic terminal care. Sadly, Mort's agreed to abandon aggressive cancer management."

"Mort's a friend of yours then, I take it?" Miguel asked with a look of incredulity.

"More of an acquaintance," Brewster answered, "but we're tight. After all, I'm doinking his older sister. She's a chunky-monkey."

"Is she now?" Miguel asked.

"No shit," Brewster answered. "She's an honest-to-God two-ton Tessie, if I may be honest with you."

"Speaking of primates, have you been smokin' any purple monkey shit lately? Frankly, there's something seriously wrong with you, man!"

"No, no, no!" Brewster answered. "I'm just high on life! As a matter of fact, I was thinking about giving you Mort's oversized red turtleneck, just as soon as the scrawny, cachectic, pathetic son of a bitch kicks the bucket."

"Now, why should I wear a stupid turtleneck like that?" Miguel asked. "To hide my fangs?"

"Wrong, again, you bipedal parasite!" Brewster exclaimed. "When you're out and about in public, I want you to be able to hide the fact that you're a beaner. Speaking from my very own personal experience as a virile (or is it sterile?) Anglo male, it would be far more frightening for me to run into a person who's actually a member of a violent Hispanic ethnic subgroup than to cross the path of someone who's become a bona fide bloodsucking vampire!"

"What did you just call me?"

"Don't worry, Miguel. I'll be sure to dry-clean the garment first just to wash the blood, snot, and drool, and any of the residual crusty cancer cells, out of that damned red sweater before you actually throw it on. You'll be stylin', my man!"

"Do you wat me to kick your ass now," Miguel asked with a sly grin, "or should I simply wait until I've had my afternoon siesta?"

"Tsk, tsk, tsk." Brewster laughed. "Such an overt demonstration of hostility is rather unbecoming for any self-respecting mosquito, bat, tick, or lamprey such as you, is it not? Shameful! Was that display of aggression a product of human vampirism?"

"Nonsense, gringo!" Miguel retorted. "I'm as gentle as a lamb!"

"Can't prove it by me," Brewster said. "Perhaps your confrontational nature is merely a consequence of your violent and relatively uncivilized Hispanic heritage."

"*Un momento*, jackass!"

"Dig this," Brewster elaborated. "With a floppy red turtleneck, you might be able to pass for a handsome gringo like me! Incidentally, I just want to let you to know that older, fat, hippy chicks really dig me."

Miguel began to laugh so hard that he started to choke. "Tell me something, Dr. Brewster," Miguel requested. "Just how did you make it this far in life without somebody shaking the holy shit out of you?"

"What makes you think that it hasn't happened already? Maybe more than once, as a matter of fact. Speaking of shaking the holy shit out of somebody, it was hard for me not to notice that you really got worked up into a high-rpm frenzy over that idiotic cretin whom you threw off the elevator just a moment ago. I must say, I truly admired your evangelical zeal whilst spreading the Gospel amongst the godless infidels."

"Thanks!"

"I'm glad you gave that nasty hag a hearty heave-ho," Brewster added. "After all, she turned out to be a rather substantial physiological and existential threat to our very well-being!"

"How so?"

"She was a competing biological entity that would have inappropriately consumed an inordinate amount of the very limited ambient oxygen supply found within the confines of this rather claustrophobic elevator car," Brewster explained.

"An elevator car which we now happen to be stuck on," Miguel added, "that incidentally appears to be descending to the ground floor at the pace of a constipated turtle."

"In any event," Brewster added, "that was rather nicely done, señor. As best as I can tell, that woman has now seen the light. Bravo!"

"I'm truly grateful for your most generous compliment," Miguel Pastore said sarcastically. "I've always tried to live my life as an exemplary model of Christian charity."

"Is that so?" Brewster asked as he mustered a quizzical look.

"You know, Dr. Brewster," Miguel explained, "it's one thing for me to talk the talk, but I believe it's far more important to walk the walk."

Brewster laughed out loud as the elevator doors finally opened up on the ground floor. "Agreed, but nonetheless, there are indeed anger management issues to contend with here, or so it would seem."

"Amen!"

Once the infectious disease service deemed that respiratory isolation was no longer necessary for Miguel Pastore, the research scientist, Booker Marshall decided that it was time to proceed with an off-the-books experiment. Although he had paid visits to the patient in his hospital room on numerous occasions, Dr. Marshall never interacted with the vampiro before without being gussied up in a fully equipped biohazard protection suit.

When the research scientist entered Miguel's room, something extraordinary happened: the patient jumped out of bed, backed up into the corner of the room, and proceeded to extend his arms outward in an obvious defensive manner.

"What's the matter, Mr. Pastore?" Booker asked. "You don't seem particularly happy to see me today."

"Something's wrong!" Miguel proclaimed.

"Relax," Booker said. "I'm here to inform you that the pathology department has sent off your medical records, in addition to a sample of your peripheral blood, bone marrow aspiration, and marrow biopsy specimen to be evaluated at both the CDC and the AFIP. It's time for us to get a second opinion from Uncle Sam."

Although Miguel Pastore was drenched with sweat, he was able to compose himself while he slowly worked his way back toward the edge of his hospital bed to resume a recumbent position. The patient finally replied, "I don't know what happened just now, Dr. Marshall, but for some reason you just scared the holy hell out of me. I'm actually feeling a bit lightheaded just now."

The research scientist asked, "Are you upset that we sent off your material to these federal agencies to review?"

"I most certainly am," Miguel Pastore replied, "as you've just likely put my life in jeopardy. There's a military officer, Captain Morales, who will now probably try to hunt me down and put a bullet in me. Even though I've been friends with this man for years, I know that he'd have no qualms about killing me now that I've transformed into a night crawler. I wish you had simply left well enough alone."

"Your concerns seem unfounded."

"No! The clock's eventually going to run out on me," Miguel said, "but there's more."

"What else?"

"I became frightened and jumped out of bed as you just witnessed," Miguel explained, "but I was totally unaware up until this very moment that you had invited the federal government to stick its nose into my personal business. Something *else* is going on, I tell you!"

"Well, spill it!" Booker demanded.

"The reason I jumped out of bed," Miguel explained, "is because for some reason I'm very frightened of you at this moment, but I don't know why."

Dr. Booker Marshall garnered enough strength to remain standing under his own power. In and of itself, this simple act was a bit surprising, as he previously always made a point of sitting down at the foot of Miguel's bed when he was paying the patient a visit during clinical rounds on the isolation ward.

The frail and chronically ill doctor firmly tugged at his lower lip as he slowly approached the right side of the patient's bed. "Miguel, what I am about to ask you to do may indeed seem a bit odd, but I assure you that there is indeed a method to my proverbial madness. I'm going to extend my right hand in front of your face, and I would like you to place your nose about an inch or two away from the back side of my hand. I want to see if you might be able to detect any unusual odors or other impressions while you smell my flesh. I just need you to promise me that you'll not try to bite me."

"You're one strange duck if I may say so, Doc, but I'm willing to play along with your rather odd request for the time being. You need to promise me that you'll not try to bite me either." Miguel laughed nervously as he placed his nose close to the dorsal aspect of Booker's right hand.

The subsequent reaction that the patient demonstrated was quite astonishing; Miguel began to suffer from acute vomiting, followed by persistent dry heaves.

Oddly, the research scientist did not appear to be surprised at all by the effect that his essence had upon the vampiro. Dr. Marshall picked up the telephone on the nightstand beside the hospital bed and called the nurses' station to request a stat order of the antiemetic drug known as prochlorperazine to be administered to the patient intravenously.

"I'm sorry that I did that to you," Dr. Marshall said, "but I had a theory that a patient afflicted with human vampirism may very well find my personal body odor signature to be quite repulsive."

"Repulsive?! That doesn't even come close to what you smell like to me, Dr. Marshall," Miguel replied. "I don't want to offend you, but to be frank, you smell like you're in advanced stages of decomposition. Are you, well—are you okay?"

Dr. Marshall did not readily answer the patient's pertinent question.

"I have one more request from you, and then I promise I will get out of your hair for the rest of the day. I'm going to set three petri dishes in front of you on this Mayo table. Each of the petri dishes contains blood from three different biological sources. All that I will tell you for now about the origin of each of the blood samples is that they were harvested from a living mammal of some type. I would like you to taste-test all three blood meals, and then I want you to tell me what you think about the flavor of each sample, be it good, bad, or otherwise," Dr. Marshall instructed as he pulled off the transparent top to each of the specimen plates.

Miguel shrugged his shoulders and said, "I'm certainly not opposed to ingesting a midmorning snack, Dr. Marshall. Well, down the hatch."

The patient picked up the first petri dish and licked it clean. He issued his initial impression: "Okay, so far, so good. Shall we find out what's behind door number two?" Miguel Pastore quickly ingested the contents of the second petri dish and added, "Well, so far, so good. Two down and one to go."

Dr. Marshall raised his right hand to interrupt the proceedings. "Tell me something: could you taste any difference between blood meal number one and blood meal number two?"

"No, I didn't. Was I supposed to?" the patient asked. "Both samples tasted exactly the same to me. After all, blood is blood, or so it would seem to me. Would you be so kind to tell me what were the biological sources for the first two samples I just ingested?"

"The first sample that you tasted was beef blood," Booker answered. "The second sample that you ingested was blood that had been harvested from a goat. Frankly, I'm quite surprised that you couldn't discern any difference in the taste. Okay, let's wrap up this little experiment. I want you to taste the blood in the third petri dish, and then please tell me what you think."

Miguel Pastore picked up the third petri dish and brought it within just a few inches of his lips. He again developed symptoms of acute nausea and vomiting. As he bared his fangs, he hurled the petri dish across the room and proclaimed, "Good God, that third sample smells like death itself. In fact, it smells like you, Dr. Marshall! I'm certain that the third petri dish contains your very own blood. I asked you this question once before, but you never gave me any kind of answer: are you okay? There must be something physically wrong with you!"

"No, I am *not* okay," replied Booker Marshall, with obvious sad resignation concerning his own limited projected life expectancy. "I'm afflicted with sickle cell disease, and as a consequence, I'm suffering from life-threatening occlusive vascular complications as we speak. In fact, I'm now blind in my left eye. Nice, eh? In addition, as a particular famous cartoon character once said, it looks like my kidneys made a wrong turn at Albuquerque. They're headed due south this very moment. Your initial impression about me when you smelled the top of my hand was absolutely, 100 percent correct; I'm indeed in advanced stages of decomposition."

Nathan and Lorena were clearly not home, as the young boy had always promised that he would leave his bedroom window unlocked to afford his "uncle" Romero an opportunity to pay nocturnal visits. As the evil vampiro peered through the window, he could readily see that Nathan's wicker basket in the corner of the room, which previously had been filled to the brim with the young child's toys, was now completely empty. That could only mean one thing: Nathan and Lorena would be gone for a long time. Perhaps they went on vacation somewhere together. It suddenly occurred to Romero Lopes that perhaps they would never be coming home at all. If Lorena was gone, she surely would have taken the obsidian knife with her! There was only one thing left to do: he would have to confront Blake Barker in the backyard of the farmhouse and then beat the truth out of him as to where Nathan and the curandera had gone.

Romero entered the backyard through the side gate and quietly approached Blake Barker, who was still at the south property fence line, engaged in some type of peculiar activity with the neighbor's cattle. Romero was perplexed about what was going on, as Blake clearly had his mouth directly upon the lateral neck of one of the cows. "Oh, no, no, no! This can't be!" Romero softly proclaimed. As he got closer, he realized that Blake Barker was enjoying a blood meal. Suddenly Lopes felt that he was quite vulnerable. Blake Barker had become a night crawler!

With the limited mobility that Lopes suffered from as a direct consequence of his right leg injury, there was no way possible that he could physically challenge another vampiro in a fight to the death. That would be especially true if the potential adversary was a newly transformed vampiro like Blake Barker who would be seeking revenge for the murder of his wife. The better part of discretion for

Romero Lopes would be to make a quiet and cautious retreat back into the shadows.

I. B. Terdly had picked a very bad day to pay a visit to Blake Barker's farmhouse to retrieve the keys to the Nuts and Bolts hardware shop. As Terdly pulled up to the front of the home, Romero Lopes was simultaneously making a hasty retreat from the backyard side gate. Sadly, the hardware shop owner misidentified the vampiro as Blake's gardener or perhaps even a farmhand just before he shouted out to get Romero's attention. "Say, boy, come over here. I have a job for you." Once Lopes was near the vehicle, Terdly said, "My name is Mr. Terdly. I want you to go and tell Blake Barker that I'm here to pick up the shop keys that he needs to return to me."

The vampiro had approached within just a few feet of the driver's-side window. Romero Lopes simply stared at the corpulent man. I. B. Terdly was soon to become Romero's very next meal! Suddenly, I. B. Terdly became particularly annoyed at what he perceived to be rude behavior. After all, Romero Lopes had only leered back at the man without uttering a single word.

"God almighty, all you Mexicans are alike. I'll bet that you lazy bastards wouldn't even bother to piss on me even if I just spontaneously burst into flames. Fine, then. Be that way." Mr. Terdly struggled to extricate the wallet from his back trousers pocket. Once this was accomplished, he peeled a dollar bill from his wallet and then proceeded to wave the George Washington note out of the driver's-side window with his left hand.

"I understand the principles of capitalism," the fat man said. "This is more than you deserve, but take this dollar bill and go find Blake Barker like I ordered you to do. Hurry up, boy! What are you waiting for? Tell me, boy, are you a Mexi-can or one of those Mexi-can'ts?"

Romero Lopes pulled the dollar bill out of Terdly's hand, crumpled it up into a small ball, and then stuffed it into the man's mouth. "Listen to me very carefully, you fat bastard. If you stay completely still and cooperate with me, I promise you that I'll make this a very quick and pleasant experience."

The frightened man vigorously nodded his head while Romero Lopes violently avulsed his left hand from his wrist with brute force.

Romero Lopes casually tossed the severed hand into the back seat of Mr. Terdly's sedan and said, "Finger food! I'll save that for dessert. As for now, I am ready for the main course." He placed his mouth over the man's wrist stump and vigorously sucked away at the blood spewing out of Terdly's radial artery as if the vampiro were a teenage soda jerk in a malt shop trying to polish off a thick strawberry milkshake through a flimsy straw.

Although in agony, I. B. Terdly tried to remain calm. He finally mustered up enough courage to spit the dollar bill out of his mouth. "You promised that this would be a pleasant experience!"

"*Pobrecito!* Isn't this a good time, or what?"

"No!" Terdly winced. "Thus far, this hasn't exactly been a trip to Disneyland."

The vampiro briefly interrupted the terminal phlebotomy that was being performed on his victim. He allowed the gushing blood to ejaculate all over his face as if he were taking a hot shower. "You self-obsessed Americans! It's always about you! I am terribly sorry for the misunderstanding, but the comment that I just made to you should have implied that *I* was going to have a pleasant experience, not *you*."

After his bovine blood meal, Blake sat on the swing on the back porch of his farmhouse and cried over the loss of his Paloma. How could he raise Nathen without his mother? His world began to spin with sorrow, rage, and anxiety. He wondered how he was going to be able to financially provide for his child now that he had lost his job. To make matters worse, he had a mortgage payment that was coming up, and currently his homestead didn't meet the necessary requirements to be designated as an active agricultural zone.

Now that Blake was a vampire, he had come to the realization that he would need to suppress his aggressive tendencies in order to blend in with the other members of society at large. He wondered if he should divulge his new predicament to his siblings. Maybe that would be a very bad idea, as he would likely be shunned by his sister, Liz, and brother, Cletus. This was especially true in light of how rude he had been to his own family members at the end of their recent visit.

He intuitively understood that his new biological imperative to feed on blood and viscera would have to be somehow tempered in order to ensure the health and welfare of his son, Nathan. Sadly, if and when Lorena and Nathan returned from their vacation, Blake would have to terminate Lorena, one way or another. Speaking of Nathan and Lorena, where in hell were they? He had expected to hear from Lorena by now, but there had been no word forthcoming. Well, she had previously left a phone number on Blake's refrigerator underneath a magnet that looked like a jalapeño, so Blake thought it would be best to give her a call to make certain that everything was okay.

After Blake Barker had ambled back inside the farmhouse, he flipped on the television. It was now time for the broadcast of the local evening news. Blaring through the television speakers was a cautionary report that a local resident of the town of Mesilla, New Mexico, by the name of Miguel Pastore was hospitalized at the university hospital associated with the Saint Francis College of Medicine in Santa Fe with an apparent case of bubonic plague.

Blake gave voice to his thoughts. "Wow, that's Lorena's brother! Bubonic plague, my ass; I'll bet my bottom dollar he got infected with something a hell of a lot worse than the damned plague! I'll bet Lorena doesn't even know about this. I'd better give her a call."

Blake went back into the kitchen and grabbed the telephone. He dialed the number that he thought would ring the residence of a home in El Paso, but he was surprised by the message he heard from the other end of the line. "Hello, this is the Sun Port, El Paso, Taco Hell. How may I assist you?"

Blake apologized and put the phone back down on the cradle, thinking that he had dialed the wrong phone number. He tried to call the same phone number once again but he got the same response. He was suddenly on a free fall down an elevator shaft as it took him only a moment to realize that Lorena had absconded with his son, Nathan. He called his sister, Liz, in Lubbock, but nobody answered the phone at her address. It was time to call his brother, Cletus, because perhaps he was involved with Lorena in some kind of secret dastardly deed. After all, Blake could not have helped but notice the way that his brother and Lorena previously gazed upon each other with mutual affection.

Blake Barker didn't even offer his brother a superficial cordial greeting once Cletus picked up the phone. "Cletus, this is Blake. Lorena has disappeared with Nathan. After she dropped you off at the airport in El Paso, she never came back to Mesilla." His voice rose in anger. "Don't give me any horseshit, bro. Did she say *anything* to you about any plans that she may have had?"

Cletus feigned ignorance about the entire matter. "All she told me was that she was visiting some relatives in El Paso. You need to relax, Blake. I know that Lorena loves Nathan, and she'll take care of him. You shouldn't worry. I'm certain that she'll be home soon. Cálmate, bro, it is going to be okay. Look, I gotta run. I left an important file that I'm working on back at the office. I have to go downtown tonight and retrieve it right this very minute. It was good talking to you."

With that, Cletus promptly hung up the phone. Blake was certainly suspicious that Cletus knew a lot more than what he was willing to talk about. Blake called him back immediately. On this occasion, the older brother sat perfectly motionless while he simply stared at the ringing phone in anxious silence.

Blake heard the unmistakable sound of a high-pitched scream coming from the front yard. He hung up the telephone, and with caution he carefully opened the front door to see what the matter could possibly be. In the twilight, he saw the shocking image of Romero Lopes physically assaulting his former boss, Mr. I. B. Terdly. Truthfully, there was little, if any, demonstrable concern regarding the welfare of the obese man who had terminated his very own shop manager earlier on that very same day. There was, however, a sudden golden opportunity to dispense merciless revenge upon the vampiro who previously butchered Blake Barker's dearly departed spouse.

The evil ghoul was rudely interrupted from his endeavors to exsanguinate I. B. Terdly when Blake Barker bellowed out, "Romero Lopes! Your ass is mine!"

2
CLUSTER

With only three hundred yards to go, Joe Cephas Smoot had considerable ground to gain if he planned on winning this obstacle course race against the dozen or so other participants who were members of the Special Forces. The remaining challenges included a rope climb over a fixed wall, a crawl underneath an array of barbed wire, and a hand-over-hand traverse across a mud-filled pit.

Dr. Ron Shiftless, having just arrived to the athletic event, was appalled to see that Joe Cephas appeared to be bringing up the rear of the pack. He walked up to Colonel Placard, who was watching the physical training session through a pair of binoculars.

"What's going on here?" Shiftless asked. He furrowed his brow and extended his palms upward in an obvious plea for the colonel to specifically explain the inexplicable. After all, how could the military's prized bioweapon perform so poorly in this race?

The colonel issued a terse, truncated response: "Shut up and watch."

The scientific director of the military's bioweapons division turned his ire toward the vampire from Arkansas, who was now closing in from about fifty yards out. "What in hell is the matter with you? Run faster, you hillbilly sack of shit!" Shiftless bellowed out to Joe Cephas a sharp warning: "Put your foot on the accelerator! I swear to Jesus, if you don't win this race, I'm cutting your dinner rations by one unit of blood! You can starve to death as far as I am concerned."

Colonel Augustus Placard simply sneered at Dr. Shiftless with disdain. "Just watch, moron. Wait and see ..."

Suddenly, Joe Cephas put his head down and went into a dead sprint. He snapped his head sharply toward Dr. Shiftless and blew him a kiss as he quickly over took the men who were in front of him. When the race was over, the vampire had finished the obstacle course forty feet ahead of his closest competitor. Joe Cephas was not even breathing hard when he easily beat the army's finest who proudly sported the green beret.

Completely ignoring Dr. Shiftless, Joe Cephas Smoot walked up to Colonel Placard and warmly shook his hand. "Well, Colonel, this is the first time that you put me through a nutcracker like this. I didn't know what to expect."

"How are you holding up, Smoot?" the colonel asked.

"My legs began to cramp up a bit at the very end, but I was able to push through the pain," the vampire cheerfully answered. "I hope that you're pleased with my efforts."

"I'm proud of you, son, more than you'll ever know." The colonel beamed. "What you did out there was truly extraordinary. I want you to go get cleaned up, and then I will personally introduce you to the bolt-action M40A3 that will chamber a .308."

"Scoped?" Joe Cephas asked.

"Unertl ten-powered optics," Placard answered. "Today you'll learn how to break it down and assemble it with a blindfold so you won't have any trouble working with a rifle like that in the dark, if necessary. In addition, the model you'll be working with will have a muzzle suppressor."

"No joke?" Joe Cephas asked. "Are you going to train me to be a sniper?"

"We'll take it out to the range and see just how steady your hands really are. Uncle Sam would like you to be a long-distance specialist in addition to having the ability to pull somebody in close for a slow dance, if you catch my meaning." Colonel Placard said. "Hit the showers and get cleaned up. I left an ice chest sitting on your bunk that has a liter bottle of anticoagulated beef blood in it. Enjoy the snack."

"Thanks, Colonel. I can't tell you how much I enjoy working with you."

"Feeling's mutual, son," the colonel replied. "I'll see you in an hour."

"I brought you a sixteen-ounce jar of zinc oxide, Smoot," Dr. Shiftless said as he handed a plastic grocery sack to Joe Cephas. "Be sure to cover yourself in this stuff before you come back out into the sun."

"Thanks, Doc," the vampire wryly replied. "I was just beginning to think that you put me in the doghouse for some reason."

After Joe Cephas Smoot trotted off toward the barracks, Dr. Shiftless was furious. "Look, Colonel Placard, I know this creature won the race, but frankly I'm disappointed with his performance today. That pathetic parasite should have won this obstacle course by a country mile."

"That creature has a name," Placard said. "It happens to be Joe Cephas. I suggest that you learn it and start using it. He's not what you think he is. He's a man as far as I'm concerned, and a good one at that. Better than you, in fact. You'd better start treating him with respect. Otherwise, the blood that's coursing through your very own veins might start to look pretty tasty to him over time. As for my opinion, I suspect that your blood tastes like shit, for what it's worth."

"Nice. Is that a threat?" Dr. Shiftless asked.

"Take it any way you like," the colonel replied. "As far as Joe's performance today goes, he *did* win the race by a country mile. You just weren't here to see it."

"What do you mean?" Ron Shiftless asked. "I saw the end of the race, and that's all that mattered."

"You're wrong. When the race was over, it was already the second time he crossed the finish line. Don't you get it? He lapped the damned field when the other men were only halfway through the obstacle course the first time through. Put that in your pipe and smoke it, Dr. Shit Face."

"Sorry—I stand corrected."

"You should be sorry. Tell me something: why weren't you out there getting in some physical training today? You're a member of this team, and at some point you'll be going out into the field with us. We might be cleared to go on a mission sooner than you think. It's time for you to get into shape. I'm serious. You need to lose that gut," the colonel said as he sharply poked the younger man in his protuberant abdomen.

"Hang on, Colonel; I got called up before things took a nosedive in 'Nam. You should know. After all, you were there too," Dr. Shiftless replied. "I'll be able to cut it when the time comes. I just need a tune-up. It's like learning how to ride a bike; once you learn, you never forget."

"Is that so? Enough of your trite clichés; you can't prove any of it to me."

"I'm serious," Shiftless replied. "After all, it was just a few years or so ago."

"Oh, yeah?" Colonel Placard sarcastically asked. "It may have been just a few *years* or so ago, but in your case, I'm certain that it was a hell of a lot more than just a few *pounds* or so ago. I want you to be out at the range in an hour with Joe Cephas. It's time for me to see if you can still hit the broad side of a barn. In fact, you'll have to prove it to me and to our president, Ronald Reagan. He has taken a personal interest in our project."

"I can still dot an *i* and cross a *t*," Ron replied.

"Joe Cephas needs to remain a civilian contracted employee, but as for you, you need to get back down to your fighting weight and reenlist before we go any further. I can petition for you to get your old rank back as a captain. Before you do, you'd better start showing a bit of civility to Joe. After all, he might just end up saving your sorry ass someday."

Romero Lopes wheeled about in time to confront his assailant. "Hold on now, Blake! I don't have a quarrel with you. Besides, you're like me now. You're my new blood brother. Or perhaps I should say that you're my new brother *in* blood."

"You killed my wife!" Blake screamed as he lunged forward and grabbed Lopes around the neck with both hands. "I'm going to tear you apart, and I'm going to do it slowly."

"Oh yeah," Lopes said, "I almost forgot. There was that small mishap I had with your spouse. Sorry about that."

Blake pulled Romero Lopes to the ground and tried to straddle his torso to finish him off, but the younger vampiro gave Blake a head-butt that stunned him. Dazed, Blake fell away to the pavement.

While watching the battle intently, I. B. Terdly was struggling in the front seat of the car, attempting to engineer a makeshift tourniquet for his left wrist to stem the flow of blood that was gushing out of his severed radial artery. The man realized that he only had seconds to pull off this feat before he would likely lose consciousness. He yanked off his necktie with his right hand and threw the tie around his severed wrist. He clenched one end of the necktie in his teeth to anchor it while he used his free hand to fashion a knot and then tighten it over his wrist. He pulled hard with all of his remaining strength. Although lightheaded, the hardware shop manager was buoyed by hope once the bleeding from his severed wrist was under control.

Terdly realized that there was only a small window of opportunity for him to escape the melee. He shimmied back to the driver's seat and turned over the ignition to fire up the motor. He threw the column shifter into drive, hit the accelerator, and fled the scene.

Romero had ripped open the shirt of Blake Barker and was about to extract the liver from his adversary's abdominal cavity when he realized that I. B. Terdly was trying to escape. Romero was forced to make a split-second decision: He could finish off the older vampiro, and thus eliminate him from being a potential future threat, or he could finish off his meal. Because he was getting hungry, Romero chose the latter course of action.

In his rearview mirror, I. B. Terdly was terrified to see that Romero Lopes was limping after him. The vampiro caught up to the rear of car, jumped up on the trunk of the vehicle, and blasted through the rear window. As the vampiro climbed into the back seat of the vehicle and assumed a comfortable position, he interlaced his fingers behind the back of his head. He spoke to I. B. Terdly as if the man behind the wheel of the car was little more than a limousine chauffer. "Thanks, Pops, for taking the wheel. Why don't I let you drive for a while so I can catch my breath for a moment or two back here? I have an idea: let's take a lovely drive out into the desert and have a romantic evening picnic."

Whatever previous spell that Romero Lopes had cast upon I. B. Terdly appeared to be broken. Terdly was not going down without a fight, and he certainly was not going to sit by passively and allow the vampiro to simply suck away at the bloody stump at the end of his left wrist.

"My left hand is somewhere down there on the floorboard around your feet. Find it and pass it over to me. I don't know what kind of ghoul you are, but if you're still in my car by the time I get to the hospital, I'm going to crawl into that back seat and gouge your eyes out," Terdly calmly said. "I still have one good hand, and I'm warning you now that I'm going down swinging."

"My oh my," Lopes said. "I really enjoy it ever so much when one of my meals puts up a fight!"

Lopes began to climb into the front seat when Terdly slammed on the brakes, causing the vampiro to lose his balance and crash headfirst into the dashboard. Before Lopes could gather his wits to finish off the hardware store manager, Terdly, using his right hand, pulled out a sterling silver ballpoint pen from his left front shirt pocket and rammed it into Romero Lopes's left eye. The vampiro howled in pain as Terdly scraped the eyeball out of its socket. The ocular organ proceeded to roll onto the front seat of the automobile.

"What, did you think I was joking?" Terdly asked. Before the store manager could blind Romero Lopes in his other eye, the vampiro reached up and grabbed Terdly around the anterior aspect of his neck and simply ripped out his throat. It was all over.

Lopes dragged the dead body out of the car and stuffed the corpse into the trunk of the sedan before he sped away to consume his meal in peace and quiet on the outskirts of town. Once Romero reached a spot that appeared ideal for an evening picnic, he stopped the car, opened the trunk, and pulled off one of the dead man's shoes to liberate a sock, which he needed to pack into the wound on his own face. Romero wadded the sock into a ball and jammed it into his empty left eye socket. Then the vampiro took the necktie that was tied around the stump of Terdly's left wrist. Romero tied it around his own face to hold the sock securely in the empty eye socket.

Although the knife wound in his leg still hadn't healed, Romero Lopes had no reason to believe that his missing eye was more than a minor setback. He wondered how long it would take for his body to regenerate a new one.

After Lopes finished his meal, he drove Terdly's car north to Santa Fe. Romero fiddled with the dial on the dashboard, looking for some tunes. The fuzz of static gave way abruptly. "Authorities have confirmed the identity of a man recently admitted to the Saint Francis College of Medicine with the bubonic plague. Miguel Pastor, a local ..." Romero Lopes laughed out loud at the report. "The plague? The plague, my ass! I turned that bastard into a night crawler!" The vampiro convinced himself that Miguel would be more than happy to sell out his sister, Lorena, and reveal where she was hiding out. If Lopes could find Lorena, he could find the obsidian knife. If Lopes could again find his beloved obsidian knife and kill Lorena, he would proudly regain his self-given title "El Gran Brujo."

Blake Barker stumbled into his kitchen, where he proceeded to place ice cubes from his freezer into a plastic bag. He used it as a cold compress against his forehead, which throbbed with pain. As the cobwebs cleared, Blake was furious with himself for having let a golden opportunity to kill his mortal enemy slip through his fingers. Blake shook his head in disgust when he accepted the high probability that Mr. Terdly was already dead. Although he held his former boss in utter contempt, he would have never wished such a grim fate upon any man, especially one who was his former employer.

Blake wondered about the whereabouts of Lorena and his son. As he had just learned, Lorena's brother, Miguel, was hospitalized at the Saint Francis College of Medicine's hospital in Santa Fe. Perhaps Miguel knew something about what was going on.

If Blake could find Lorena, he could perhaps find his son, Nathan. If Blake could again find his beloved son and also bring Lorena home, he would proudly regain his self-ordained title as the world's best dad.

The city of Atlanta was beginning to win over John Stewart with its cosmopolitan ambiance. When the nurse hooked him up to the plasmapheresis machine, he leaned back in the reclining chair and wondered what new restaurant he would try out for dinner. The time had come again for the Centers for Disease Control and Prevention (CDC) to harvest his natural antibodies, which were to be recruited for the vaccine project orchestrated by Dr. Blanks.

Although no member of the research team would give John an honest answer to his question of whether or not progress was actually being made, he became suspicious that Blanks and his team were running into a brick wall. After all, why would they subject him to the same procedures again and again? He tried not to worry about such matters, though, as he had a solid contract and was making decent money. What was there for him to be concerned about? In the end, he was naturally immune to the infectious RNA virus that recently had been proven to cause human vampirism. Even if the whole world went to hell, John Stewart was convinced that he would somehow survive a pandemic outbreak of human vampirism.

"I like this city," Stewart told the pheresis nurse. "I can't see why that pig of a human named General Sherman and his goddamned Yankees wanted to burn this place to the ground. I don't know where that son of a bitch is buried, but if I ever find his grave site, I'll yank out my doodle and make a point of taking a leak on his headstone. Say, are you free tonight? Maybe you'd like to have dinner with me!"

"Thanks, but I'm married," the nurse replied as she waved her wedding band in front of the nose of John Stewart.

"So, you're married? I don't care. Get over it," Stewart replied. "You happen to be talking to the man who, without a doubt, has the most powerful immune system on the planet. I'm surprised that women aren't lining up around the block to have a crack at me just on the slim chance that I might be able to convey my immunity to their offspring. So, how about it? Don't put up a fight; just surrender to my boyish charms."

Without a single word, and with absolutely no expression on her face, the nurse stopped what she was doing and briskly walked over to a small potted fern that was on the desk behind the nurses' station. Beside the plant was a plastic spray bottle that was used to water the plant and keep the fern leaves free of dust. She set the spray nozzle on the plastic bottle to "stream," walked back in front of John Stewart, and started to blast away directly into the man's face.

"I'm originally from Texas," the nurse said. "At the Battle of the Alamo, Santa Anna demanded that the defenders of the old mission surrender to avoid any bloodshed. The 'Texicans' answered the Mexican general with a cannon shot. I assure you, Mr. Stewart, you should thank your lucky stars today that I don't have a cannon right about now. Am I clear?"

"Crystal."

The associate director of the human vampire research project was a man named Dr. Kohl. An administrator at the CDC for a decade, Kohl collaborated with Dr. Blanks on the previous outbreak of human vampirism that occurred in New Mexico back in 1979. Fortunately, the associate director arrived just in time to defuse the skirmish that was percolating under the surface between John Stewart and the nursing staff. Because of his no-nonsense demeanor, Kohl had been assigned by Dr. Blanks to be the unofficial disciplinarian who had the unenviable task of keeping John Stewart's rather abrasive demeanor and burgeoning libido under wraps.

"This is the last time I'm going to tell you to quit hitting on the nurses," Dr. Kohl said. "As soon as you're finished with this pheresis run, we need to get back to your apartment so you can pack an overnight bag. I'll drive."

"What's going on?" Stewart asked. "Going somewhere?"

"Field trip with Seth Blanks. He's already headed to the airport, and he'll be waiting there for you. Here's your airline ticket," Dr. Kohl said as he passed over the travel documents to John Stewart. "You'll be flying into Albuquerque, where you boys will pick up a rental car and then make the fifty-mile drive north to the Saint Francis College of Medicine in Santa Fe."

"As long as I have a chance to chow down on some New Mexico red while I'm out there, that's fine with me. It sounds like the team made a breakthrough," John Stewart said. "Are we going to try out our new vaccine back in the Land of Enchantment?"

"No, it's not ready yet," Dr. Kohl answered. "There's a human vampire out there that we just learned about, purely by accident. Some researchers at the medical school sent a sample of this patient's blood over here for analysis. In the requisition they mentioned that they were also sending an identical sample to the AFIP. If that's the case, then the military already knows about this patient."

"Is that a problem?"

"I'll tell you what, John: if the military gets involved at this point, we're screwed!"

"I don't understand. What's the big deal?" Stewart asked. "Whether or not you're talking about the military or the CDC, we're all under Uncle Sam's big happy umbrella, right?"

"One would think," Dr. Kohl said, "but that's just not how the world works."

"Why not?" Stewart asked. "Maybe we should all just stand around the campfire, hold hands, and sing 'Kumbaya.' After all, aren't we all just trying to paddle this boat in the same direction?"

"No! That's the point," Kohl answered. "You boys need to get out there lightning-fast and convince this guy to come work with us at the CDC on our vaccine project before the army gets their hooks into him and drags him off to their bioweapons division in San Antonio."

"Bioweapons division?" Stewart asked. "Sounds hinky to me."

"I'm on the level with you," Kohl explained. "If that happens, the military will turn this poor bastard into a loaded gun. If we miss this opportunity to bring this guy on board with us at the CDC, who in hell knows when we might stumble upon another living, breathing vampiro to work with."

"Well, you have me. I count for something."

"True, but that's the problem," Kohl said. "You're *all* we've got at this time. Tag, buddy—you're it! Our project here at the CDC will only get funding as long as we have at least one infected subject to work with. You are not infected, John; you're immune! If we don't find somebody who's actively infected to work with, Uncle Sam will pull the plug on this entire project."

"The government wouldn't do that, would they?"

"Sadly, it's happened before," Dr. Kohl answered. "I was here when it happened back in '79."

"What in hell do you need me for on this trip to Santa Fe?" John Stewart asked. "I'll be a fifth wheel."

"You're dead wrong there, buddy boy," Dr. Kohl replied. "You'll add a human face to the project. I hope you'll be somebody whom this patient will be able to relate to. He needs to understand that everything we're doing is on the up-and-up. Frankly, it's all for the benefit of the entire country, if not the entire world!"

No matter how long Captain Morales stared at the telephone on the corner of his desk in his office at the New Mexico National Guard, it continued to ring incessantly. After what seemed to him to be an eternity, he was finally forced to pick up the receiver to find out who was on the other end of the line.

"Morales, is that you?" Coronal Placard asked. "Say something, damn it!"

"It's me, Colonel," Morales finally answered in a stilted monotone. "How are things in San Antonio?"

"Shaping up," Placard answered. "I need to know if there have been any more cases of human vampirism that have been reported in your neck of the woods."

"None to speak of, sir."

"I have a mission for you," Placard said, "and this one's off the books. You might not believe this, but Miguel Pastore somehow survived the massacre at the morgue. He's bottled up at the university hospital that's affiliated with the Saint Francis College of Medicine in Santa Fe. My team and I are flying out there to try to recruit him to join the bioweapons division here in Texas."

"Your orders, sir?"

"I want you to go up to Santa Fe and babysit him until we get this sorted out," Placard answered. "I know how you feel about all of this, but no harm had better come to him. Set your personal feelings aside and do as you're ordered. Clear?"

"Crystal," Morales answered, "but I'm on today and I won't be able to head up to Santa Fe until late this afternoon. In fact, you and your team will probably get to Santa Fe long before I do."

"Get there when you can."

Unfortunately, Captain Morales had no intention whatsoever of carrying out this order. He had been given previous instructions from the NSA that superseded any requests from Colonel Placard, or anybody else for that matter. Morales was previously ordered by the NSA that if Miguel Pastore ever somehow reappeared, the captain's duty would be to put Miguel down like a rabid dog.

The NSA was bound and determined to make sure that absolutely no case of human vampirism crossed the border and made it out of New Mexico. If that ever happened, the infection could spread to some other part of the country. There was only one obvious civil defense course of action to be taken, and Captain Morales was now duty-bound.

Morales concluded that this new problem would be dealt with in the same fashion in which he'd handled the Stumpy Wheeler issue after the massacre that occurred at the morgue and Wheeler got infected. Although he had personal misgivings about this ghastly mission, the captain was certainly in no position to disobey an order that came directly from Washington, DC.

Lost in thought, Morales slowly walked over to the armory, where he reluctantly signed out a .45 automatic M1911 Colt pistol for alleged target practice. Once done, Captain Morales climbed behind the wheel of his personal vehicle and took a long and lonely drive up to Santa Fe.

"Look, Dr. Shiftless," Joe Cephas Smoot explained. "I'll be happy to spot you, but don't try to do too much too soon. If you blow out your rotator cuff, Colonel Placard will sideline you."

"Sorry," Ron Shiftless replied as he nestled underneath the bar to try to knock out ten bench press repetitions. Ron felt clearly embarrassed about how deconditioned he truly was. "Well, I know that I can't pump out a thousand pounds like you can. I can't even do two hundred. I'm pathetic."

"Be brave. Let me set it at 120. Now that you have your commission back, would you prefer that I call you Dr. Shiftless or Captain Shiftless?" Joe Cephas asked politely.

"Well, that was very kind of you to ask," Ron Shiftless said, somewhat surprised. Perhaps there was more substance to this misfortunate creature than the scientific director of the bioweapons program was ready to admit. "As we're a clandestine military unit, it would be proper to call me Captain Shiftless, I suppose."

Colonel Placard arrived just in time to dissuade Ron Shiftless from any physical endeavor that would have no doubt resulted in a self-inflicted injury. "This is the last time I'm going to tell you to quit pushing it. As soon as you boys are finished with your workout, we'll be heading out. We'll stop at the barracks first so Joe Cephas can pack an overnight bag. After that, the three of us will drive over to Ron's off-base apartment. You'll need to grab some gear also, Doc. I'll drive."

"What's going on?" Shiftless asked. "Going somewhere?"

"Field trip with me. Here's your airline tickets," Colonel Placard said as he passed over the travel documents to Smoot and Ron Shiftless. "We're flying into Albuquerque, where we'll pick up a rental car and then take the fifty-mile drive north to the Saint Francis College of Medicine in Santa Fe."

"As long as I have a chance to taste a small sample of New Mexico red while I'm out there, that's fine," Joe Cephas said. "For me, that's the saddest part of being of vampire; there is a fairly narrow spectrum of sustenance my gastrointestinal tract will actually tolerate. Although I've never personally tasted New Mexico red, people rave about it incessantly. Do you think it would hurt if I added just a tablespoon of red chili to a unit of blood, Captain Shiftless?"

"Well, Joe, if you puke, I'll be there for you."

"Great! Excellent! It sounds like our team is ready for a mission," Joe Cephas said. "Colonel, are you saying that we're about ready to break out our team back in the Land of Enchantment?"

"No, you boys aren't quite ready yet," Colonel Placard answered. "There's a human vampire out there in Santa Fe that we just learned about, and I assure you it was purely by accident. Clinical researchers at the medical school sent a sample of this patient's blood over here for analysis. In the requisition they mentioned that they were also sending an identical sample to the CDC. If that's the case, then the research scientists at the CDC already know about this patient. If the CDC boys get to Santa Fe first, that would certainly throw a monkey wrench into the works."

"What in hell do you need me for on this trip to Santa Fe?" Joe Cephas asked.

"You'll add a human face to the project," Colonel Placard replied. "I hope you'll be somebody to whom this patient will be able to relate. He needs to understand that everything we're doing is on the level and for the benefit of the entire country."

Before Blake embarked on his trip to Santa Fe, he wrote a message on a piece of paper and taped it to his front door, just on the outside chance that Lorena would return home with his missing son. The message instructed Lorena to call him immediately once she returned home. Barker proceeded to inform her that her brother, Miguel, was hospitalized in Santa Fe. Blake neglected to mention in his memo that he was headed up north to shake down Miguel for the specific details of where she might be hiding out. After all, if Lorena had indeed kidnapped Nathan, Blake would hunt her down to the ends of the earth to find his only child.

Alas, it was a memo that Lorena would never be destined to read, as she was now a refugee who had fled the country. There was, however, one interested party who would indeed find and read the memo. Dr. Cloud had long hoped to someday win back Lorena's affection. The physician had driven down from Santa Fe to the town of Mesilla, and he coincidentally passed by Blake Barker on the road only seconds after the latter had left his homestead.

Upon arriving at Blake's farm, Dr. Cloud found the memo that was taped to the front door. After reading it, he pulled it off the door, crumpled the sheet of paper into a ball, and then threw it upon the ground in disgust. Thinking that he had been duped by Miguel Pastore, Dr. Cloud was furious.

"After all I did for that bastard, and he still lied to me! I wasted a whole day to come down here just to get jerked around!" the doctor said. "That son of a bitch is lucky that my people never adopted the custom of taking scalps!"

Dr. Cloud had never previously met Blake Barker, but the physician thought to himself that if Barker was heading up to Santa Fe to shake down Miguel Pastore and find out where Lorena might be hiding out, he would be standing right there beside him in Miguel's hospital room at the same time to get the story right out of the horse's mouth. Dr. Cloud vowed to himself to find Lorena if it was the last thing that he ever did.

"Where do things stand with the outside pathology referrals?" Miguel Pastore asked.

"Good question," Dr. Booker Marshall replied. "I'm actually somewhat surprised that I haven't heard anything as of yet. Tell me, Parker, did you get any feedback yet?"

Dr. Coxswain was standing at the front door of Miguel's hospital room and stepped inside. He folded his arms defensively as if something were wrong while he fixed his gaze upon the floor. "I had Wanker down in pathology make a few phone calls before I came up here, and he told me that neither the AFIP nor the CDC acknowledged the receipt of the specimens that we sent them."

"How is that possible?" Booker asked. "It was your responsibility to coordinate the shipment of the specimens from our pathology lab."

"Beats the shit out of me," Dr. Coxswain replied. "Don't put this on my head. Check this out: The specimens were sent by registered mail. We already received both of the signed receipts that were sent back to us courtesy of the US Postal Service. This confirms that the CDC *and* the AFIP took custody of the specimens last week. At this time, both institutions claim that they don't know what in the hell we're talking about!"

"That doesn't make sense," Booker Marshall said. "How could the exact same screwup occur at the exact same time at two separate, independent institutions? That seems to be way too strange for a simple coincidence."

Miguel Pastore suddenly felt as if he had a noose around his neck. "Good God, it was no coincidence! I'm screwed! They're coming for me. Hide me, boys! Discharge me! Do something with me! Come on, gentlemen! Do *anything* with me! Before the day is out, either I'm going to get a bullet in the head from Captain Morales or else the regular army will find me and I'll get hauled off to become a glorified lab rat. If that happens, I'll just simply disappear. For the love of Jesus, save me!"

"Now, hang on, Miguel," Parker said. "I think you might be exager—"

It was too late. Parker Coxswain was cut off in midsentence when Colonel Placard and his two associates burst upon the scene. "Miguel Pastore? Allow me to introduce myself. My name is Colonel Augustus Placard, and these two gentlemen with me are Dr. Ron Shiftless and our special agent Joe Cephas Smoot. Joe happens to be just like you; he's infected with the virus that causes human vampirism. I'll have you know that despite his illness, Joe Cephas has become a very valuable commodity to the United States government."

"What do you want with me?" Miguel asked.

"Frankly, Mr. Pastore, we would like to invite you to join our bioweapons research facility in San Antonio, Texas," Joe Cephas said. "I joined up, and I believe it to be one of the best decisions that I have ever made in my entire life."

"I'm going to ask you three men to leave this hospital room immediately," Dr. Booker Marshall said.

"Why don't you just go out and cop a leak, Doc? You really don't have any say-so in this matter anyhow," Ron Shiftless said. Turning to Pastore, Ron made a threat. "To be honest with you, Miguel, you really don't have much say-so in this matter either. You can either come with us voluntarily, or we'll force you to come with us at gunpoint if necessary!"

Hot on the heels of Placard's team were none other than Dr. Blanks and John Stewart. "Don't believe what the army is telling you. You do have a choice. My name is Dr. Seth Blanks, and I am from the CDC. My team is working on a vaccine to try to cure and also prevent human vampirism."

"First come, first served," Placard said. "You don't have any jurisdiction here, Seth. I suggest that you get to the back of the line."

"Maybe you should have let Captain Morales shoot me in the head back at the restaurant a while ago," John Stewart said. "As best as I can tell, you don't have any jurisdiction here either, Colonel Placard. Check this out, Miguel: I happen to be naturally immune!" John Stewart said. "I was previously bitten by a vampiro named Romero Lopes, who's still at large. Not only did I survive, but also I never got infected! Dr. Blanks and his team are trying to engineer a vaccine based upon my immune system. Why don't you come with us?"

Blake Barker and Dr. Cloud had ridden up on the elevator together, but neither of them knew that they were both headed toward the hospital room of Miguel Pastore. Each man tried to push the other aside to enter the room, but Blake Barker wedged into the room first. "Miguel, you know me. I've met you before. Lorena has disappeared, and she has my son," Blake explained. "Tell me where she is right now, or else I'll ask the authorities to bring charges against you for being an accomplice in my boy's disappearance."

"Don't lie this time!" Dr. Cloud chimed in from the entryway, trying to shout over the enclosure of what was now more akin to a can of sardines than to a hospital room. "Tell me where Lorena is right now. I'm looking for her, too."

Dr. Blanks was surprised to see Blake Barker. "Blake, I can tell by looking at you that you got infected! How did it happen? Don't tell me you got bitten by Romero Lopes."

"Hello, Dr. Blanks," Blake said, "it's good to see you again. I ate a bad egg. It must have been infected. Lorena Pastore told me not to do it, but I didn't listen to her. It's my own damned fault."

"Well, fancy that," Joe Cephas said as he extended his right hand to greet Blake Barker. "That's how I got infected! I'm pleased to meet you. My name's Joe Cephas Smoot, but you can call me Joe Cephas."

"Likewise, Joe. My name is Blake Barker, but you can call me Mr. Barker," Blake said sarcastically. "Maybe you and I can go out on the town some night together and drain a cat, or yank the liver out of a goat, or do some kind of evil shit like that. It'll be a hoot."

"You're on, Mr. Barker!" Joe Cephas said. "That sounds like fun."

"Stop right now," Dr. Blanks said. "You need to come with me to the CDC. I might be able to help you."

"Rain check, Doc," Blake said. "First, I have some serious business to attend to, and there's a greater likelihood that I can accomplish my mission if I remain vampire for at least just a bit longer."

"And just what might that be?" Colonel Placard inquired. "You wouldn't be planning on trying to hunt down somebody named Romero Lopes, now, would you? If you join up with my team and become a bioweapon, maybe we can help you accomplish your mission."

"Frankly, that's on the agenda, Colonel Placard, but I've specifically come up here to shake down Miguel Pastore for the real dope about something that has a much higher priority." Turning to Miguel, Blake asked, "Where in hell is Lorena? Why in hell did she take my son?"

"That's a tough question," Miguel answered. It was now his turn to become sarcastic. "Perhaps it was because you turned into a bloodsucking vampiro like me. Other than that, I really wouldn't have a clue, asshole!"

"How could she possibly think that I would ever hurt my own boy? I've got this under control!" Blake answered. "Granted, I've had strong urges to choke the shit out of other people, including my own brother at one point, but I've put all of that in a jar, and the lid is screwed down tight."

"Look, Blake, I'm not looking for trouble," Miguel Pastore said, "but it looks like trouble has found me. I sympathize with your situation, and I truly believe that you should be reunited with your son. If Lorena is not at your house, then perhaps she's gone down to old Mexico. She has a godfather down in Santa Sangre."

When a dark and evil figure forcefully plowed through the doorway, Dr. Cloud and Colonel Placard's entire team was driven down to the floor. It was none other than Romero Lopes! "Santa Sangre? I would have never guessed your sister was hiding out in that nasty shithole of a one-horse town, Miguel. Nice. Rural squalor at its finest!"

"Lopes! You just made my mission a whole lot easier," Blake Barker said as he pulled the extension rod from an adjacent IV pole and lunged at Romero. Lopes simply deflected the blow and rammed Blake Barker's head through the Sheetrock masonry board on the lateral wall of the hospital room.

"Frankly, I'm surprised that you haven't learned your lesson yet about trying to tangle with me, Blake! As for you, Miguel, you should be thankful for the gift that I've given you."

"You think this was a gift? Before I rip your face off, tell me why you're looking for my sister!" Miguel demanded.

"Don't you know? She's a gran bruja in her own right. She stole my obsidian knife. I want it back so I can slit her throat with it," Lopes boasted.

"You better leave Lorena alone, you bastard!" Dr. Cloud threw himself at the vampiro, but when the doctor was swatted away like a fly, he was left with two bruised ribs.

"Don't be rude, you puny squaw," Lopes said.

With nowhere to go, Placard and Dr. Blanks backed up against the wall in fear of what was going to transpire next. John Stewart and Dr. Shiftless were quick to follow suit.

"Who are you?" Joe Cephas asked as he moved forward to confront the violent intruder. Romero Lopes didn't answer the question but simply flashed a malevolent smile and took a bow.

Miguel Pastore jumped out of his hospital bed while Blake Barker jerked to and fro to extract his head from the drywall. Once free, he cleared the debris from his eyes. He cautiously backed up to where Miguel Pastore was standing. The two new allies stood abreast of each other and slowly tried to bookend Romero Lopes.

Miguel Pastore reached out and patted Joe Cephas on the shoulder. The designated bioweapon was now standing to Miguel's immediate left.

"I'll tell you who he is, Joe Cephas," Miguel said. "He's none other than the vampiro responsible for what's now known as the 'massacre at the morgue.' I can't tell you how happy I am to see you, Romero."

Blake Barker took his index finger and jabbed Romero Lopes in his empty eye socket. "What happened to your left eye, dickhead? Did Mr. Terdly put up a fight? Bet you didn't see that coming."

Realizing he was out numbered, Romero Lopes addressed Joe Cephas. "I can smell you. You're just like me. Why don't you join up with me? *Yo soy un gran brujo!* I'll make you *un brujo también.* All you have to do is help me out here."

"Any orders, Colonel?" Joe Cephas asked.

"Yes, son," Placard answered as he pointed at Romero Lopes. "I want you to kill this son of a bitch and then rip his heart out."

"It would be my pleasure, Colonel!"

If it were not for the unexpected arrival of Captain Morales in the hallway, the reign of terror initiated by Romero Lopes would have ended right then and there. "Well, well, well," Captain Morales said as he brandished his .45-caliber automatic. "What do we have here? It looks like I'm late to the party. I want everybody in this room who has fangs to line up against the wall. I should spoon all of you bastards together in the corner, and then maybe I can get by with just one bullet to your brain with a through-and-through shot. I'd like to put all of you animals down at the same time!"

From a biblical standpoint, perhaps the book of Ecclesiastes was missing a specific verse or two that may have been directly applicable to this situation in which Captain Morales had found himself: "To everything, there is a season and a time for every purpose under heaven: a time to talk and a time for silence; a time to awaken and a time to sleep; a time for solitude and a time to mate; and a time to pull the trigger before it's all too late ..."

For Captain Morales, the window of opportunity to exact sweet revenge on Romero Lopes had suddenly closed. Although slowed by his permanent leg injury and the fact that he was now missing his left eyeball, Romero Lopes was nonetheless a formidable adversary. In the blink of an eyeless socket, Lopes reached out and grabbed Captain Morales from the threshold, wrapped his forearm around the officer's neck, and then bared his fangs. "Drop the gun, Captain, before I break your neck." Morales did as he was ordered. "Stand fast, everybody!" Romero Lopes shouted. "I mean it!"

Undeterred and fearless, Dr. Booker Marshall stepped forward and slowly approached Lopes. "Let him go! Do it now!"

"Fine by me!" Lopes said. "I'll take your sorry ass next!" Romero Lopes buried his teeth into the neck of Captain Morales and then cast him aside before grabbing Dr. Booker Marshall. He was about to inflict the same injury upon the research scientist, but some kind of repulsive molecular scent that emanated from Booker Marshall stopped Romero Lopes dead in his tracks. Dr. Marshall was afflicted with sickle cell disease, which caused a violent and unexpected reaction in the vampire. Lopes developed dry heaves!

To escape the noxious odor that was a consequence of Booker's abnormal hemoglobin, Lopes pushed the doctor out of his way. While Lopes was distracted, Captain Morales pulled out his .38 revolver back-up weapon. Before he lost consciousness, he got off a smoking-hot round of lead that pierced Romero Lopes through the chest. As the bullet traveled through the body of the vampiro, the fixed pane of glass in Miguel Pastore's hospital room was blasted into jagged shards.

Although on the third floor, Romero Lopes threw himself out the window. Blake Barker and Joe Cephas, in hot pursuit, jumped out the window after him. Rising above the pain caused by his bruised ribs, Dr. Cloud limped out of the room. Bent at the waist, he pressed his right hand against the left side of his rib cage as he headed straight for the main elevator.

"Where are you going, Cloud?" Parker Coxswain asked, following Cloud into the hallway. "You're jumping into a fight that you just can't win! Think about what you're doing."

"I have to find Lorena. She's in danger!" Dr. Cloud exclaimed. "Hold the fort, boys. I hope to see you again someday. If I get killed doing this, I want to let you know I consider all of you to be honorary members of my tribe. Good luck, and God bless."

As Dr. Cloud hobbled out of the building, he was now a man on his own mission to track down the woman who was the object of his deepest desires.

"Come with me if you want to live!" Dr. Blanks barked out as he and John Stewart grabbed Miguel Pastore and scurried with him down the hallway toward the fire exit stairwell.

"What about the captain?" Shiftless asked, pointing to Morales, who was strewn out upon the floor. "I should stay here and patch him up."

"There are other doctors in this damned place. Let them handle it," Placard replied. "I'm going to put in a call to the National Guard. They need to lock down this campus until we find Romero Lopes and put a bullet in his brain. We'll come back for Morales after he gets stabilized," Placard said.

When Dr. J. D. Brewster heard the commotion, he found his way to hospital room, number 316, which had been previously occupied by Miguel Pastore. Brewster was too late; the smoke had cleared and the battle was already over. The hematology–oncology fellow showed up just after the code team arrived. There was blood, broken glass, and debris scattered about the room.

Captain Morales was quite lethargic, but he became communicative once he was loaded onto a gurney by the code team. As he was being hauled down to the emergency department to have the bloody wound on the lateral aspect of his neck cleaned and dressed, he cried out for an act of mercy. "Goddammit! I got bit. Somebody shoot me. Do it now!"

"Settle down, Captain," Parker said. "We'll make sure that you're as good as new in no time."

Upon the departure of Captain Morales with the code team, Brewster followed Parker Coxswain and Booker Marshall into the hallway. It appeared to Brewster that his two colleagues were in a state of shock. They looked pale, and their glazed eyes were wide open.

The stress that Dr. Booker Marshall had just experienced was already sending him into another acute sickle cell crisis that would warrant hospitalization and additional packed red blood cell transfusions. This new attack from his underlying hematological disorder would result in further visceral end-organ damage to his kidneys, which were only functioning at a modest level of efficiency to begin with.

"What in hell happened in there today?" Brewster asked.

Brewster received a casual reply as if an acquaintance were speaking about something as trivial as the weather. "Nothing," Parker Coxswain answered. "I assure you, not a damned thing happened in there today."

LAMADRE

3

¿QUIÉN ES MÁS MALO?

"You have eyes in your head, you dumb-ass Arky, do you not?" Blake Barker asked Joe Cephas as he pointed to the pavement. "You can see it as plain as I can. Either Romero Lopes sprouted wings and flew away, or he simply disappeared into thin air. In any event, the drops of blood stop right here."

"He must have healed up already from the gunshot wound," Joe Cephas Smoot surmised. "I can scarcely believe it." Joe Cephas took the toe of his shoe and kicked at the blood trail that abruptly ended on the asphalt that covered parking lot at the medical center. "That's the only explanation. He has to be around here somewhere. I can still smell him."

"I can smell him too. Wait a minute—we're a bunch of idiots! What you and I can smell is each other. You're standing far too close to me. You need to get the hell away from me right now."

"You're starting to piss me off, Blake!" Joe Cephas said. "You're not my boss."

"We have to split up. Otherwise, we won't ever find him," Blake said. Pointing to the far end of the parking lot, he added, "Go work the other side of that row of automobiles. Start looking underneath the cars and behind the light pillars."

"Don't be stupid," Joe Cephas replied. "We need to stick together. If Lopes is hiding out here, he could ambush us one at a time if we get separated from each other. I'm getting military training right now. You should know that I'm fully versed in these dangerous tactical conditions. In this kind of situation we should—"

"I don't give a shit, Gomer Pyle!" Blake rudely interrupted. "Do as I say." Blake grabbed Joe Cephas and pushed him into the back of a van. Blake leaned forward and sneered in the face of the younger vampiro. "We have to find this bastard and finish him off immediately before the cops or the National Guard gets here. We need to divide and conquer. Are you going to help me or not?"

"Get your hands off me!" Joe Cephas exclaimed as he raised the palm of his hand to push Blake's face away. You don't have any authority over me or even any jurisdiction here. What's wrong with you? You clearly have problems with anger management, or so it would seem."

"I'll show you anger management," Blake said as he wrestled Joe Cephas to the ground.

Unseen from his hiding position at the far end of the parking lot, Romero Lopes slipped into the sedan previously owned by the now departed I. B. Terdly. The evil vampiro was able to make a hasty retreat just seconds before the police and National Guard arrived and cordoned off the medical complex.

Before he got to the interstate, Romero Lopes realized that he would have to stop at a nearby service station and fill the stolen car's gas tank. After all, it would be a long drive all the way from Santa Fe to the village of Santa Sangre, Mexico ...

"Look, I'm just fine," Joe Cephas told Colonel Placard and Ron Shiftless. As Joe dabbed at a split in his lower lip with a handkerchief, he waved off an emergency room nurse who brought him a plastic bag with crushed ice. "That's truly very kind of you, miss, but I should be okay in no time."

The nurse left the bag of ice on the counter in case Joe changed his mind.

"What in hell happened out there?" the colonel asked.

"Blake Barker and I had a minor disagreement with each other about tactical matters. As a case in point, I was trying to choke the shit out of Blake when he popped me in the mouth," Joe Cephas explained.

"Did you catch wind of Romero Lopes?" Dr. Shiftless asked.

"Damnation if he wasn't within spittin' distance from me!" Joe Cephas exclaimed. "Blake and I happened to see Romero Lopes jump into a beat-up sedan that had the rear window blown out."

"Don't tell me he got away, son," Placard said.

"The last I saw any hide or hair was when Blake Barker jumped off the ground and was in a dead-ass sprint trying to chase down the car that Lopes was driving."

"Well, did you manage to get the license plate number or perhaps catch the make or model of the car Lopes was driving?" Shiftless asked.

"It was a gray four-door, a late-model sedan. I couldn't see the rear license plate because Blake was in the way the whole time. He was partially blocking my forward field of vision. The car was a Ford, but there's nothing else I can really tell you," Joe said.

"The cops are out there on the parking lot right now, and it looks like the entire National Guard from the state of New Mexico has just pulled up on the front lawn," Shiftless said.

"Should I go back outside and tell those boys what I saw?" Joe Cephas asked.

"No! Bad idea, son," Placard said. "The best we can do right now is hope that Blake Barker is able to run down Romero Lopes and finish him off. The very existence of our bioweapon team is a top secret. Nobody can ever find out who we are or what we're doing."

"They're giving Captain Morales a two-unit transfusion right now and a tetanus booster," Shiftless noted. "What he really needs, in my humble opinion, is a rabies vaccination!"

"Very funny," Placard replied. "As soon as the ER personnel finish his red cell transfusion, we need to take him into custody and haul his ass down to San Antonio with us."

"There's no way that he'll get on board with our program," Shiftless protested. "This guy's a dick."

"Look, Ron, he's coming with us. Hell or high water," Placard said. "We have to secure him in cuffs right away."

"What are you talking about, Colonel?" Joe Cephas asked. "Why do we need to use a stick when a carrot might work? In my opinion, we should just ask him to join our team right now. After all, he strikes me as a man of righteous convictions."

"Maybe you're correct," Placard replied. "Sometimes you surprise me, Joe."

"I have my moments," Joe Cephas said. "After all, I might be ignorant, but I'm not stupid."

"He is indeed a man of solid convictions," Placard agreed, slowly nodding his head. "He told me he's going to eat a bullet if he's infected and destined to eventually transform into a night crawler. It's imperative that we convince him otherwise. I'd like to believe at times that I'm a pretty good judge of character, and it would seem to me that you can see the same attributes in this man that I do, Joe. We *need* another righteous man to round out our bioweapon team. I'll see you boys soon. I need to get out to the CDC in Atlanta before I return to San Antonio. I think it's high-time that Dr. Blanks and Miguel Pastore hear the branch creak just a bit."

Blake Barker had little time to spare once he made it back to his home in Mesilla. He stuffed his clothing into a duffel bag, grabbed his two shotguns, and then threw the items into the trunk of his car. There was one remaining valuable item that he needed to take with him if he was indeed going on an expedition to Mexico to find Lorena and his missing son, Nathan. That valuable item happened to be the razor-sharp obsidian knife that he had secretly recovered from the dead hippy named Ruby.

After taking his fill of liquid nutrition from the cattle grazing on the adjacent farm, Blake went back inside his house and washed the blood from his hands and face. When he went to his bedroom chest of drawers, he was furious to find that the obsidian knife was now gone. Lorena must have stolen it just like she had stolen Nathan.

Why would she take it? She already had the obsidian knife that she recovered from the burned-out farmhouse where Romero Lopes lived. Why on earth would she need another? Blake was starting to comprehend the fact that the obsidian knife was something much more than honed volcanic glass. Surely, it must possess some unknown force that is either spiritual or paranormal in nature.

Upon his departure, Blake locked the front door of the farmhouse. He had an unsettling premonition that this would be the very last time that he would ever see his homestead. As Blake stepped off the porch, the pesky county tax assessor, Mateo Levi, was briskly approaching. As the tax assessor walked across the front lawn, he said, "I've surveyed your home yet again, Mr. Barker, and I'm sad to say that your residence no longer meets the criteria for an agricultural zoning designation."

"Do tell."

"Do you know what I have in this envelope?" Mateo Levi asked as he waved a document in front of Blake's face.

"Let me guess," Blake replied. "Would it be your testicles?"

"I, sir, happen to be a public servant. There's no reason to be so rude to me," the tax assessor said. "I have your new property tax bill in this envelope. If this is not paid in full within the next ninety days, the county can and will issue a tax lien against this real estate."

"Listen to me, you little shit weasel," Blake said as he pulled the small, frightened man close to him. "You should thank your lucky stars that I just ate!" As Blake Barker bared his teeth, he repeatedly pimp-slapped Mateo Levi with the back of his hand until the tax assessor collapsed to the ground.

After Blake Barker climbed into the front seat of his car, he turned his head toward the startled tax assessor and said, "If you ever step foot on my property again, I'll suck on your neck until you're as dry as a popcorn fart. After that, I'll go over to your house and eat your wife and children. Am I clear?"

The tax assessor began to tremble when he stood up and brushed the dirt from his britches. "You know, Mr. Barker, it looks like I've made a terrible mistake. I'm quite certain that I'll be able to justify your current agricultural zoning designation. To be honest, I think

I'll be able to lower your property tax quite a bit. In fact, maybe this piece of property should simply fall off the tax roll altogether. How does that sound to you?"

"I'm glad you're starting to see things my way," Blake Barker said just before he sped away. Once he hit the interstate, he turned south for the long drive to the border.

Upon his arrival to Atlanta, Miguel Pastore was immediately taken aback by the utter cold sterility of the CDC. His quarters were more akin to a prison cell than to a domicile. No sooner than when he sat down upon the edge of the thin mattress that covered his narrow bunk did Colonel Placard and Dr. Blanks arrive to discuss the business at hand.

"Miguel, I would like you to have a chat with the man whom I introduced to you in Santa Fe," Colonel Placard said. "I believe he'll turn out to be the keystone to discovering the cure for human vampirism. As you might recall, this is John Stewart. He happens to be from your hometown in New Mexico, of all places."

"You're from Mesilla," Miguel said with a smile, "and it's a small world indeed."

"John was previously attacked and bitten by the vampiro Romero Lopes," Placard explained, "so you might be wondering why John didn't get the infection. That's exactly what Dr. Blanks needs to find out. I'm on my way back to Texas. If the vaccine project turns out to be a failure, rest assured that I'll come back to find you, Miguel. You could still be a valuable tool in Uncle Sam's bioweapons program someday." Placard ushered this unveiled threat with a sneer.

The colonel issued one last warning to the research scientist who was now becoming an adversary. "Keep me posted, Dr. Blanks. Last time I warning you!"

"Scout's honor," Dr. Blanks replied sheepishly.

"Sometimes I wonder about that. Don't hold out on me. As for now, my team will need to saddle up. Neutralizing Romero Lopes may be our very first mission."

Placard glared at Dr. Blanks and Miguel Pastore for what seem to be an eternity without saying a word. Satisfied that he had successfully intimidated the CDC, Placard departed Atlanta to return to San Antonio.

Once Miguel was certain that Colonel Placard had vacated the premises, he gave a sigh of relief as he mopped his brow.

"Dig this; that Colonel Placard fellow and his army goons scare me a hell of a lot more than any vampire," John Stewart confessed. "Nonetheless, if Lopes is still alive, I'm going to hunt down and kill that blood sucking tick someday."

"You'll have to take a number and stand in line," Miguel Pastore reported. "I insist on getting a crack at Lopes before you do, amigo. He was the vampiro that infected me. Up until the time that I was bitten, my life was gravy."

"As John didn't get infected when he got bit, we strongly believe he is naturally immune!" Dr. Blanks said with a broad smile. "John, I'd like you to break the ice with Miguel."

"Well, hell's bells! No need to break the ice, Doc. I actually met this old horse thief a long time ago," Stewart said as he looked Miguel over. "You used to dine at El Chopo Restaurant, where I worked in a former life. Sometimes you'd come in with a pretty girl who appeared to be a bit younger than you. Was she your girlfriend?"

"No, she was my sister, Lorena," Miguel Pastore answered. "I remember seeing you too. I never knew your name though, until you and Dr. Blanks came up to visit me at the hospital in Santa Fe. It's strange, you know? Not only is it a small world, but also everything in the universe seems to be connected somehow."

"Your sister, Lorena, is an industrial-strength major-league babe and a half. Is she seeing anybody steady?"

"No, and don't go there. She doesn't do well in relationships. She was dating a friend of mine who's a doctor from Santa Fe. She blew it, just like every other relationship she's ever been in," Miguel cautioned.

"Well, she hasn't met me yet!" Stewart said.

"Yeah, and she's not about to either if I have any say-so in the matter." Pastore laughed.

"Look, Miguel, I don't want to date her," John Stewart said. "I just want to doink her."

"¡Señor Stewart, *eres cochino*! This is *exactly* why I don't want my sister to date una *comadreja* like you."

"Thanks, Miguel," John Stewart said with a wry smile. "I hope I resemble that remark!"

"I know you're famished after your long flight, Miguel," Dr. Blanks interjected. "Let me get you loaded up on about five hundred milliliters of beef blood. After that, we need to get to work. We'll get some chemistries and a CBC drawn today. I'd like to find out if the stress of your long flight exacerbated your hemolytic activity. We need to keep an eye on your white cell count, also. If it continues to expand, we'll need to make sure that this disease is not evolving into an acute leukemia."

"If that ever happens," Miguel said, "what will become of me?"

"Well—" Blanks hesitated. "I've been yelled at in the past for being too blunt with my patients. Here I go again. Just as a leopard can't change its spots, I can't be anything but blunt with you, even if I tried to sugarcoat things."

"Then spit it out," Miguel requested. "I'm a big boy now. I expect the worst."

"If we're unable to eradicate the virus that has caused you to become a vampire, a malignant transformation will likely occur that will be irreversible. Now, look: I surmise that we might be able to achieve a temporary remission state with chemotherapy if you were to develop leukemia."

"Leukemia. Swell. That's what the boys in Santa Fe were always clamoring about."

"Let me paint you a picture. If we're unable to completely eliminate the virus from your body once and for all, any malignancy of the blood that you might develop down the road, in all likelihood, will come right back to haunt you yet again, even if a remission is successfully achieved. Your prognosis is that a leukemic transformation will be a terminal event," Dr. Blanks explained.

"Lights out?"

"If the infectious disease that you harbor causes a secondary acute leukemia, you'll be having an up close and personal conversation with God much sooner than later."

El Primo and his foot soldier El Gato were both imposing figures. Each man was a 240-pound cinder block of muscular aggression. The local residents would most assuredly give these two henchmen a well-deserved wide berth whenever they were out and about conducting drug cartel transactions in the northern Mexican city of Juárez.

Primo and Gato were given strict instructions by their boss, Flaco, to find the new torpedo that the Calle Vampiro gang had apparently recruited. After all, if the competing cartel was bringing in a new hit man to Ciudad Juárez in an attempt to put the squeeze on Flaco's lucrative enterprise, the interloper had to be found quickly and subsequently terminated in the most violent and vicious of means as could be fathomed.

Flaco was the head of the Routa gang, a subsidiary of the Chihuahua cartel. The Routas controlled the illegal bountiful drug trade in Juárez. There was no way in hell that Flaco would allow his competitors, the hated and feared Calle Vampiro cartel cowboys, or their affiliated gang members, known as the Aztecas, to find an opportunity to establish a presence in the Routas' territory without a fight. If necessary, it would be a fight to the death.

"I'm telling you, Primo, I don't know the assassin's real name," Flaco explained as he scratched away at his new tattoo that depicted a red rose with the phrase LA MADRE emblazoned on the dorsum of his left forearm, just a few inches proximal to his wrist. "Let me tell you what I do know. The toothless old whore met this hombre, and she gave him a hum job. She told me that this stranger couldn't man up. His cojones were shriveled like raisins. She wanted to laugh in his face, but when she looked into his yellow eyes, she was suddenly afraid that he would kill her. In fact, she's still afraid of him. She thinks that he's eventually going to come back, find her, and rip her to pieces. I don't know why she would think that way, but I've never seen the old whore so frightened by a trick before."

"What did this stranger look like?" Primo asked.

"Like a ghoul—pale skin, *ojos amarillos*, and long, sharp, nasty teeth," Flaco answered. "The old whore is a good informant, so I don't want any harm to come to her. Until you and El Gato eliminate this threat, I want you to tell El Segundo to keep an eye on the old whore. He'll be her bodyguard. Give El Segundo the order that he's not allowed to get any hum jobs from her while his cock is on the clock, or else I'll slap the shit out of him. Am I clear?"

"What makes you think this guy is a Calle Vampiro hit man, jefe?" Primo asked.

"Simple. He pressed the old bitch about any information she knew about the Routa gang."

"Maybe he just wants to take a shipment," Primo countered. "I'll wager a peso that he just wants to do business with us."

"Oh, really?" Flaco asked. "Then why did this stranger ask her how many soldiers were in the Routa gang? Why did he want to know the real name of the big dog? No export merchant would personally ask these specific questions if he just wanted to take a load of coca."

"Maybe we don't have to do anything," El Gato surmised. "Maybe he'll just come to us."

"That's just what I'm afraid of," Flaco said. "The old hag asked the stranger if he had a name, and the son of a bitch said he was un gran brujo. He would not tell her his given name, but he called himself Mago. Listen to me, Primo: you and El Gato need to find this pinche *pendejo*. Find him now and take care of him, I tell you."

"What do you want El Gato and me to do to this Mago character if we're actually able to find him somehow?"

"I want you to exercise the Chihuahua cartel's capital punishment protocol number six: cut his penis off while he's still alive and shove it up his *culo*, then drain all his blood. We have to prove our complete loyalty to the Chihuahua cartel," Flaco said.

"Anything else?" Primo asked.

"After you kill this man who calls himself Mago," Flaco added, "cut out his heart and then bring it to me. Leave his dead body in front of the Federale sub-station. Although we have the local policia in our pocket, our enemies, the Aztecas, have a dozen or more of the Federales on the take. We're about to toss a bad taco on that combo platter. We'll need to make an example of this guy, whoever he is."

"*¿Quién es más malo?*" Primo asked with a smile.

"*Yo soy más malo, pendejo.* Don't you ever forget it either."

"I can't find anything to dissuade myself from having these suspicious intuitions. Anytime you gentlemen have smiles on your faces, it's good news for the bioweapons division, but it ends up being bad news for me," Captain Morales said as he leaned back in his chair and stared at Dr. Ron Shiftless and Colonel Placard, who were sitting across from him at a conference table.

"My oh my," Dr. Shiftless replied. "Did you wake up on the wrong side of the floor this morning? Or perhaps you're just feeling a bit more cynical than usual?"

"Don't jerk me around, Doc," Morales said. "I can very well see the physical changes that are now happening to me. Give me the bottom line. Level with me."

"You're infected. What else do you want me to say?" Shiftless asked.

"Oh, I don't know," Captain Morales said. "How about, 'Gee, Captain Morales, we're sorry about your new unfortunate circumstances.' Or how about, 'Gee, Captain Morales, it must really suck for you to suddenly turn into horrid human bat shit that's compelled to suck blood.' Or how about, 'Gee, Captain Morales, we promise to abide by your original request. We're going to take you out to the back parking lot and put a bullet in your brain to put you out of your fucking misery.' In fact, I'm going to hold you boys to that promise you made to me when I first got here."

"We made you no such promise," the colonel said. "Just because you turned into a night crawler doesn't mean that you're going to turn into a murderer. I don't think you're going to turn out to be anything like Romero Lopes."

Captain Morales looked away in shame. After all, he was already a murderer. He was suddenly overwhelmed by a sense of guilt when he remembered that he had killed Stumpy Wheeler in the morgue after the young man was viciously bitten by Romero Lopes. At the time, Captain Morales tried to justify what he had done as a mercy killing sanctioned by the federal government.

"Look, Colonel, I don't deserve to be a member of this team," Morales confessed. "I'm not the man that you think I am. In fact, perhaps I'm no longer a man at all in any true sense of the word."

Morales reflected upon the fact that what he had done was a capital crime. What he had done was a mortal sin. What he had done was an unjustifiable act of pure evil, and it was as vile as any sin that Romero Lopes had ever committed.

"I'm not going to ask you what happened to Stumpy Wheeler during the massacre at the morgue. Frankly, I don't want to know what happened," Placard said. "I'm not even going to ask you why you barged into Miguel Pastore's hospital room brandishing a pistol. I asked you to go up to Santa Fe to simply protect that man, but it's clear to me now that you were planning on putting a bullet in his head."

"Guilty as charged."

"I'm certain that you're a good officer and that what you did was *not* on your own accord. Somebody must have been directing you to carry out very specific missions. Is my supposition correct?"

Morales remained mute.

"Just tell me one thing," Placard said to Captain Morales. "What agency was giving you the orders?"

"It was the NSA," the captain replied.

"Goddammit!" Placard exclaimed.

"Colonel?" Shiftless asked, hoping for clarity.

"Typical government bullshit where the right hand doesn't know what the left hand is doing. Look, Morales, your sins can only be absolved if you join my team. If future sins are to occur, I'll commit them on your behalf. I promise you that. The first thing that you have to do is to resign from your position with the National Guard and become a civilian. I promise you, we'll offer you a *very* generous financial contract."

"Why in hell would you want me to resign from my commission as a captain?" Morales asked.

"For one reason only," Placard answered. "It happens to be the very same reason that Joe Cephas Smoot will not be allowed to officially enroll in the military, although he's asked to enlist on multiple occasions."

"Pray tell," Morales requested.

"Uncle Sam is one tight-ass, penny-pinching son of a bitch," Placard replied. "We have no idea how long a human vampire might actually live. The federal government doesn't want to get into a situation where it pays benefits or offers service-connected medical care through the VA system to an individual who is a night crawler. If Uncle Sam takes a long hike down that rocky road, the government may find itself in a situation where it will have to pay benefits to such an individual in perpetuity."

"You can't be serious," Morales said.

"I'm dead serious," Placard replied. "To be frank, our beloved uncle is hoping that the members of the bioweapons division will simply do their patriotic duty and die in combat while in service to their country in a timely fashion. Make no mistake about it: everybody in this room is considered to be expendable."

"Speak for yourself," Dr. Shiftless said.

"Think about it," Placard said. "Since the US Congress has essentially transformed itself into a self-serving House of Lords, this useless legislative branch of our federal government seems to make sure that it takes care of itself, only itself, and nobody else. That's why our veterans get shit upon. Up one side and down the other. Just ask any Vietnam War vet. You should know. After all, you were in the bush at the same time that Shiftless and I were out there sniping at the 'Cong."

"Yes, sir," Morales answered. "Sadly, I was also in the 'Nam, as you know."

"If our bioweapon team is successful, we should go up to DC and kill every member of Congress." Placard sneered. "Sorry, don't repeat that, Morales. That was more of a hyperbolic editorial comment than a real threat."

"Nice to know where I fit in between the shit and the Shinola, Colonel Placard," Captain Morales said.

"Let's go to the clinic so I can do a new baseline blood profile on you," Dr. Ron Shiftless said. "After that, it'll be time to start your accelerated physical training program."

"Not so fast," Morales said. "Before we get started, somebody better go down to the blood bank and grab me a couple of units of blood to pound down. I think I'll need a snack before I hit the gym."

Romero Lopes was now a torpedo for the Calle Vampiro drug cartel. On behalf of these vicious drug dealers, Lopes managed to brutally murder and consume no fewer than four individuals in Juárez. He needed to feed again soon, however, as it had been three full days since he enjoyed his last meal back in Juárez when he was out and about, eliminating members of the competing Routa gang. When he developed an unrelenting pounding headache, the vampiro knew that he had to ingest nourishment, and he had to do it immediately.

The cartel had promised Lopes that a toady named Carlos would meet him south of Ciudad Juárez in Villa Ahumada with two units of human blood for his personal enjoyment and per his nutritional requirement. Despite the fact that he hadn't fully completed his assigned mission in Juárez, Lopes was at least able to considerably loosen the strong grip that the Routa gang had on the drug trade in Ciudad Juárez.

The Calle Vampiro cartel had given Lopes the explicit order to hunt down and kill the man named Flaco who was the titular head of the competing Routa gang. Try as he might, Lopes was unable to find Flaco. It seemed that the members of the Routa gang who knew where Flaco may have been hiding weren't talking. If that were indeed the case, Romero Lopes made sure that the stubborn Routa members whom he had encountered in the border town would never talk again.

In no time at all, Romero Lopes had established a fierce reputation. The dark underbelly of Juárez now had a mysterious new gran brujo to contend with known only as "El Mago."

Despite his ultimate failure to exterminate Flaco, the vampiro's employers were pleased with his efforts, and they rewarded their new hit man with some well-deserved time off before his next mission. Romero's business arrangement with the Calle Vampiro was as straightforward as it was lucrative. For his services as an enforcer, Romero Lopes would be handsomely compensated monetarily. In addition, he would be afforded safe passage throughout the whole of Mexico without fear of any reprisal from the pesky Federales. As icing on the cake, he was promised all the human blood that he could possibly ever desire.

While he was in Ciudad Juárez, he managed to kill and consume three members of the Routa gang: El Primo, El Gato, and El Segundo. He would have spared the life of the toothless old prostitute after he had his second interrogation of her in as many days if she had only revealed where her boss, Flaco, was hiding out. Because the old whore refused to spill her guts about what she knew, Romero Lopes had to spill her guts on his own accord.

In any event, his energy was now starting to wane at the time Mexican Highway 45 intersected Highway 19 at Villa Ahumada. It was high time to pull off the road, find the cartel's courier named Carlos, and then get a bite to eat. Romero's handler told him that Carlos would be driving a yellow microbus. A prearranged meeting was to take place at the Pemex petrol station on the outskirts of town at sundown.

By 8:00 p.m., there was still no sign of any courier named Carlos, no sign of a yellow microbus, and no evidence that the cartel had even remembered the prior arrangement to appear for the clandestine meeting with the vampiro at the Pemex gas station. Villa

Ahumada was a very small village with dining options that appeared to be quite limited. The famished ghoul felt that he had waited long enough for somebody from the cartel to show up at the scene. It was now time for him to forage for a blood meal. It was clear that the only person Romero Lopes could rely on was himself.

Lopes thought it best to avoid the arousal of any suspicion among the few scattered impoverished citizens of Villa Ahumada, so he chose the safer option of partaking of a domesticated pig blood feast at a farm immediately adjacent to the gas station.

At this point in his career as a human vampire, Romero Lopes was becoming more sophisticated in his feeding techniques, and his table manners were certainly becoming a bit more genteel. When he entered the adjacent farm, two large sows came close enough to experience Romero's pheromones, and as if under a spell, the domesticated porkers became rather docile as they willingly exposed their necks to the looming parasite. Romero spoke softly to the first sow as he reached down and stroked her with what could only be described as apparent affection.

Once the barnyard animal appeared to be completely relaxed, Lopes slowly buried his teeth into her neck and subsequently ingested approximately a pint of blood. The pig, for its part, appeared to be totally cooperative during the therapeutic phlebotomy procedure. Well, at least it was a therapeutic procedure for the vampiro, if not for the pig per se. Before he withdrew from the stockyard, Lopes approached the second sow for an additional feeding. Once he had consumed his fill, he patted both the animals on the rump and sent them on their way.

This was the first time that Romero Lopes had taken a blood meal from living subjects where he allowed the hosts to survive the ordeal. Although he still felt a rageful compulsion to slaughter both the pigs, somehow he mustered the self-restraint to allow his blood donors to live and see another day.

Romero Lopes began to cast a rather harsh verbal assault upon his very own moonlit reflection, which he saw in a shallow puddle of standing pig urine. "What in hell is the matter with you?! Are you not un gran brujo? Are you not El Mago?"

The vampiro was afraid that he was starting to get soft around the edges. Un gran brujo could not afford to get soft around the edges. El Mago could not afford to show any mercy. A fearsome vampiro could never be allowed the luxury of feeling *anything*. Time would soon tell if Romero's self-doubts were warranted and his fears would someday come to pass.

As Romero Lopes slowly strolled away from the farm and walked back to his car, which was still parked at the Pemex station, he realized a yellow microbus was parked directly beside his vehicle. There was a young man holding a small ice chest and standing between the two vehicles. He was obviously patiently waiting for Lopes to return to the designated meeting spot set up by the handler whom the cartel had assigned to manage their new assassin.

"You must be Mago. Your reputation precedes you. My name is Carlos, but the members of the Calle Vampiro cartel call me El Sapo. I have a present for you." The courier handed Romero Lopes the ice chest. The vampiro opened the small cooler and saw two units of packed red blood cells of human origin in plastic transfusion bags sitting on a chunk of ice. Lopes set the ice chest on the front seat of his car and proceeded to scrutinize the courier, a slender effeminate man appearing to be in his early twenties who was about six feet tall with bronze skin and thick black hair.

"You're nearly three hours late," the vampiro said. "What kept you? I had already given up on you, so I went to the farm next door and got a bite to eat over there."

"*Lo siento,* señor. I got lost coming down here. As Romero's pheromones took control, the courier purred. "I'll do anything you ask to make it up to you."

"So I see," Lopes said as he leaned over and started to gently lick the young man's cheek.

El Sapo reached down and started to loosen the vampiro's belt. "I want to please you in every way that one *hombre malo* can please another."

"If that's the case," Romero said, "I'll tell you how you can make it up to me. Get into the back of your van and take your pants off. I want you to hump my face like a gay caballero riding a wild stallion!"

After making love, El Sapo asked, "Where are you going from here, Mago? I want to stay with you."

"I have business to attend to in the hamlet of Santa Sangre. There's una gran bruja down there named Lorena Pastore. I have to find her. She stole my sacred obsidian knife. I have no choice but to kill her and take it back. I also have a son named Nathan," Lopes said, intentionally lying about having sired offspring. "He's my only child, and she kidnapped him. I love that boy very much, I tell you. I'm desperately trying to find Nathan. So, you said you want to stay with me? Let me ask you something: are you willing to work for me and only me? If you offer a pledge of loyalty to me in blood, I'll personally petition the cartel and request that you be my understudy and assistant."

"Thank you, Mago, but I want to be more than that. I want to be your love slave," El Sapo replied.

"So be it," Romero Lopes said as he bit the neck of the amorous young toady. The vampiro proceeded to pass on his infection to the unwitting young man. "Your wish is my command!"

As Lopes rocked his incisors in and out of the toady's jugular vein in a slow and rhythmic fashion, El Sapo writhed about in the back of the microbus in painful sexual ecstasy, firmly clutching the atrophic penis and withered testicles of the vampiro. Romero Lopes's new love slave continued to squirm and quiver, much like any postorgasmic man would writhe about in painful sensory overload if his sexual consort continued to blissfully rake away at his reproductive member with her front teeth.

Romero Lopes pulled off the black eye patch that covered his now empty left eye socket. It was now quite apparent to the evil ghoul that a new left eyeball would never grow into the painful permanent cavity in his skull. He exposed the gaping chasm in his face to his new concubine. "I want you to take the tip of your cock and jam it into my empty eye socket. I want you to skull-fuck me like a wild man until you fill the hole in my head with the thick wad of tasty tartar sauce that's going to blast right out of your loins! I'll flutter my eyelids against the crown of your cock until you blow your load."

"*¿En tu calaca?*" El Sapo asked. "Are you sure?"

"Don't hold out on me, *tramposo*. Do as I ask!"

"If you ever become afraid of anything, *te aye watchto,*" Carlos assured Romero Lopes as he nestled in the crook of the older vampiro's shoulder.

As he gently stroked his new sexual consort, Romero Lopes replied, "That's very sweet of you to say. I promise that I'll do everything I can to protect you too. In fact, *I'll always keep an eye out for you!*"

"¿'Queen' es más malo?" El Sapo asked with a smile.

"Yo soy más malo, pendejo. Don't you ever forget it, either."

4

TORPEDO

Right after Miguel Pastore and John Stewart left the pheresis laboratory at the CDC, John stopped abruptly in his tracks in the hallway. With a stunned look upon his face, Stewart reached out and grabbed Miguel's elbow, attempting to digest what the vampiro had just said to him. "What in hell do you mean that you told Lorena that you never wanted to see her again?" John asked. "She's you're sister! You told me that she's the only sibling you have. Man oh man, I'm sure as shit glad right now that you're not *my* brother."

"Stop right there," Miguel Pastore said. "You don't understand. You weren't there. The last time I saw Lorena, I felt as if I might attack her and kill her."

"Well, you don't feel that way now, do you?"

"No. It's strange," Miguel answered, "as time goes on, it has become quite a bit easier to control the feelings of rage in my mind."

"That's good," John Stewart said. "Otherwise, I wouldn't want to be sitting this close to your sorry ass, whether I am personally immune to human vampirism or not."

"Don't worry, dude. I'd never dream of biting you," Miguel said. "After all, you're a damned gringo redneck, and I'm quite certain that your blood would taste like shit on a shingle."

"Nice! I have an idea," Stewart said. "When we get out of here, let's go down to Mexico and find your sister. I know that the minute she meets me, she'll want to please me in every way that a woman could possibly please a man. Does she like it rough?"

"I want to make one thing perfectly clear to you, John," Miguel said.

"There's nothing else for you to say, Miguel. I promise you that when Lorena decides to shack up with me, we'll name our first child after you."

"¡Señor Stewart, eres un cerdo! This is *exactly* why I don't want my sister to date a gringo like you."

"Thanks, Miguel," John Stewart said with a wry smile. "I hope I resemble that remark!"

"All kidding aside, I do have some serious concerns about this CDC vaccination program we're tied into. I feel like you and I are like, well—" Miguel Pastore hesitated to speak the obvious.

"Like, well—what?"

"Prisoners," Pastore answered. "Tell me something. We've been at this now for weeks. Thus far, I've been injected with multiple unsuccessful vaccination formulations based upon your serum immunoglobulins, and it doesn't seem like we're making any progress. Frankly, I'm worried about what might happen to us if they pull the plug on this program. It seems to me that you know more than what you're saying. Spill the beans. What aren't you telling me?"

"I'm discouraged, amigo," John Stewart answered. "Nobody tells me diddly-squat around this place, but I overheard Dr. Blanks practicing for a presentation that he's going to give during an upcoming scientific seminar. He didn't know that I was listening in on his practice session, but I heard him say that the virus that causes this disease is undergoing something called 'rapid genetic drift.' Now, I don't know what that is precisely, but it would seem to me that Dr. Blanks personally believes that it will actually be quite impossible to *ever* make a successful vaccine for the disease that you're infected with."

"We have the right to know," Miguel said as he cradled his forehead in the palm of his hands. "Look, I'm not a doctor, but as I was a mortuary diener in my former life, I do indeed have a strong background in science. An example of genetic drift is what occurs in the common flu virus. That's why the flu vaccine needs to be reformulated every year. As a case in point, sometimes the flu vaccine doesn't even work because of the fact that the pathogen is a moving target!"

"Oh no!" John exclaimed. "That would suck for you."

"Wake up, pendejo!" Miguel said. "That would also suck for you."

"How so?"

"Think about it." Miguel explained, "If this mysterious virus that causes human vampirism is going through genetic drift, you might not still be immune to this disease process by this time next year. Hell's bells, amigo! You might not still be immune to this disease process by this time next week!"

"Where do we go from here?"

"Dr. Blanks needs to come clean," Miguel said. "If this is a dead-end project that's gonna get shitcanned, you and I need to get the hell out of here before that fellow named Colonel Placard and his goons from San Antonio show up and haul us off somewhere to turn us into some kind of bioweapon."

"I don't want any part of that."

"Me neither," Miguel said. "Who knows? Captain Morales from the National Guard might show back up someday and try to finish off the both of us. After all, it appeared that he planned to kill me once before at the university hospital in Santa Fe. He's a man whom I thought was my friend. I'm not going to stick around here to see if that's going to happen again."

"Morales is a guy who scares the hell out of me," Stewart said. "I never told you that after Romero Lopes wiped out the staff at El Chopo Restaurant in New Mexico, Dr. Morales showed up with the National Guard. I'm absolutely certain that the son of a bitch was planning on killing me in the restroom. He would have done it if Dr. Blanks hadn't shown up."

"Well, there you have it."

"I'm sorry, buddy boy," Stewart remarked. "Our crappy existence on this planet has certainly taken a shit-storm turn for the worse."

"Indeed. Indeed it has," Miguel said. "Sorry to say, but you and I need to sit down and hammer out some kind of exit strategy."

Blake Barker hit the streets of El Paso looking for clues of what might have happened to his son, Nathan. In order to find the missing child, Blake would have to first hunt down the woman who had kidnapped the boy. Blake was propelled by powerful paternal instincts, fear, rage, and one other important driving primary biological force: hunger.

At the hospital in Santa Fe, Miguel Pastore claimed that his sister, Lorena, was deep in Mexico, hiding out in the town of Santa Sangre. Given that Blake trusted no one, he didn't believe Miguel's story for one minute. However, all that Blake Barker had to go on was a bogus note that Lorena had left on his refrigerator at the farmhouse in Mesilla. His first inclination was to visit an old friend from high school named Don Blanco.

Blake long had an affinity for the kindhearted giant who played center on the high school football team. Blanco was a power blocker who had a knack for making a gaping hole like an exploding torpedo in the defensive line once the ball was snapped into the hands of the quarterback. Blake was the running back on the team who would breeze through the line for frequent gains of ten yards or more by simply drafting through the chasm that Blanco would leave in his wake.

Don and Blake were an unstoppable force throughout high school. Because Blanco could read the defensive schemes better than the quarterback, the high school football coach gave the massive center the responsibility of making audible play changes at the line of scrimmage.

Given that Blanco was a gifted athlete and scholar, nobody was surprised that his physical prowess and intellect led him to a scholarship to study at West Texas College in El Paso. When a ruptured Achilles tendon he sustained during his senior year in college ensured that he would be sadly overlooked in the NFL draft, the gentle giant resigned himself to the fact that his days of playing football were over.

After joining the El Paso Police Department (EPPD), Blanco quickly rose in the hierarchy and was soon promoted to the rank of lieutenant. He kept his attention focused sharply on the ugly world of illicit drugs and narcotic trafficking. He was the detective who was eventually appointed to be the official director of the Criminal Gang Task Force.

Blake Barker had lost contact with his old teammate over the years, so Blanco was quite surprised to see his high school chum walking into the office at the Westside Substation. "Well, look what the possum dragged in here!" the police lieutenant exclaimed. "You were never a particularly good-looking fellow to begin with, but Blake, I swear to God Almighty, you look like warmed-over shit. Come over here, you rascal. Let me take a look at you."

"I think I liked you better when you wore a blue police uniform," Blake said. "Now that you're all gussied up in a coat and tie, you look like a used-car salesman on steroids."

"You don't even have to say it; I can tell something's wrong, Blake," Blanco said as he scrutinized his old friend. "All kidding aside, I can tell that you've come down with some type of illness. You best get in here and tell me what's going on. Close the door behind you."

The time for jokes and brotherly banter was now over. Don Blanco was visibly shaken when Blake Barker told him that his wife had been murdered by a vicious vampiro and that his son was now missing. After all, the police officer had served as a groomsman at Blake and Lynne's wedding several years before.

"Despite the proximity of New Mexico's Rio Grande Valley," Blanco explained, "we've not had any verified reports of human vampirism in El Paso, at least not yet, for whatever reason. All of that might be soon changing, however. We just heard about some really weird and evil shit that went down in the ciudad on the other side of the Bravo."

"As in Juárez?"

"Yep," Blanco answered as he cautiously started to back away from his old friend, who was sitting across the desk from him.

"Blake, there's a six-hundred-pound Sasquatch sitting in this room that we have to talk about."

"Let me save you the trouble," Blake said. "You're a smart guy. I know that you are looking at my huge incisors as if you were Little Red Riding Hood having a chat with the Big Bad Wolf in Grandma's boudoir. I'm infected. There—I said it. Happy now? Yo soy un vampiro. I'm a night crawler. I'm a goddamned bloodsucking human *murciélago*. Get over it. I haven't killed anybody, at least not yet. I sustain myself on animal blood and organs."

"Keep it that way," Blanco said. "If you're having any thoughts right about now of the prospects of coming across this desk and trying to bite me, rest assured that I'll blow your head off. I mean it. I don't give a shit if you were my best friend at one time. No hard feelings if that happens."

"Understood."

"In the meantime," the police lieutenant said, "I'll help you as best I can. You'll be happy to know that I have complete access to the police information database. Give me the correct spelling of the last name of this woman called Lorena who allegedly absconded with your son, Nathan."

"I can do better than that," Blake said. "She was my former domestic, so I also have her date of birth and social security number, if that would be helpful."

"Nicely done. Come with me, Blake. It's time for us to go out and beat the bushes."

Within a matter of hours Don Blanco and Blake Barker were knocking on the door of an old adobe farmhouse, in search of Lorena's cousin Alfredo Pastore. Their visit would be brief because Alfredo was not home. However, a girl about ten years old answered the door. She told the two men that Lorena had indeed been there with a young boy named Nathan.

"Lorena was here," the young girl said, "but she left last week. Her car broke down, and we're keeping it here. It's still parked in

Daddy's garage. Daddy told Lorena that he would try to get the car fixed for her and that she could come back for it at any time."

"Thank you, sweetie," Blanco said. "What's your name?"

"I'm Alicia, but Mommy and Daddy call me La Rana Pequeña because I like to sing at night when it's time for me to go to bed!" Alicia pointed at Blake Barker and said with a big smile, "You look very handsome to me. May I give you a hug?"

Blake Barker shrugged his shoulders and said, "Sure, why not?"

Don Blanco was astounded by the little girl's behavior because, if the truth be told, Blake Barker was now a man who was anything but handsome. In fact, Don Blanco found his old friend to be completely repulsive to look at.

"I can't help it," Barker said as he looked over toward Don Blanco. "I don't understand it myself, but I have the same effect on small animals and even livestock. What do I know? Go figure."

"Tell me something, Alicia," Barker asked. "What did Lorena have to say about the little boy who was with her?"

"Nathan? Lorena said that he was her nephew. He's really cute!"

"That's nice," Don Blanco said. "Alicia, can you tell us what happened to Nathan? Maybe you know where Lorena has taken him."

"Sure," Alicia answered. "Lorena and Nathan took a taxicab across the Fabens-Caseta Bridge into Mexico. She told Daddy that she didn't know if she would ever be back."

With the lights atop the police prowler flashing, the two men sped back to El Paso. Fortunately the interstate was empty, which made for fast passage back to town. "Look, Blake, this thing is starting to spiral out of control, and it's clearly out of my jurisdiction," Blanco said. "This has now escalated from a missing person investigation to a cross-border kidnapping. I can tell you right now that the FBI is going to swoop in and shit in your cat box. I'm taking you in for questioning right now." Don Blanco sent a radio communiqué to the police substation that he was bringing in a "person of interest" for a thorough interrogation in the matter of an apparent kidnapping.

Blake realized that Don Blanco was generally not the type of man to cut corners. The police detective was duty-bound to turn this case over to the federal gumshoes. Blake became agitated because he was running out of both patience and time. "You simply can't do this," he said. "By the time the feds ramp up an investigation, the trail won't just be cold, it will be frozen in a solid block of ice. Help me out here, buddy."

Also problematic was the fact that Blake was starting to feel the pangs of hunger. It would appear that the answer to both his problems would soon be found in Juárez, Mexico.

"You just don't know what you are asking me to do," Don Blanco said.

"What'll happen to me if the feds get involved?" Blake Barker asked. "I'm probably already under a microscope. If the truth be told, I've only roughed up a few people from time to time, but Uncle Sam won't see it that way. Once they get their hands on me, it's unlikely that I'll see the light of day ever again!"

"Hold your water, Blake," Blanco said. "I think you're jumping off into the deep blue, and frankly, you're sounding more than just a bit paranoid to me."

"I understand your obligations to report this to the FBI, but you have to let me go," Barker pleaded. I'm running out of time. Look at me, Don; I'm sick as a dog. I'm not sure what's going on, but my skin is so yellow that I almost glow in the dark. My piss looks like root beer, and the only thing I can get down into my stomach without vomiting is animal blood or raw flesh. Listen to me: I have to get across the border to Juárez! I have to get there tonight."

After Don Blanco hit an early exit ramp before downtown El Paso, he pulled into an empty parking lot, threw the cruiser's transmission into park, and killed the car's ignition switch.

"What are you doing?" Blake said as he contemplated making a mad dash through the cruiser's passenger door to escape the new perilous predicament in which he was ensnared.

"I'm going to help you out of a jam, I guess. To be honest, it's against my better judgment. I have a dilemma, however: I can't simply let you walk away from this. I already notified the station that I was bringing you in. If you were to disappear now, it would look very suspicious to my colleagues," Blanco explained. "You're going to have to help me out."

"What do you want me to do?"

"Don't worry. I have plan. Before you leave this squad car, however, I have to give you some very specific information as to what you might be up against. Listen carefully," Blanco said. "Do you remember a nasty little dive in Juárez called Tequila Town?"

"How could I forget? There's about a hundred places in old Mexico that claim the fame for inventing the margarita, and Tequila Town is wedged onto that ledger somewhere."

"Maybe so, but it is not exactly the kind of place that you'd like to take your girlfriend for a nice, quiet date," Blanco said.

"On one occasion I got so bombed at that place that I was afraid I'd go blind in my left eye."

"Now that's the place I'm talking about all right," the police lieutenant said. "Look, I understand your plight. What I'm going to tell you is off the record. Your best bet for finding out what may have happened to Lorena Pastore and your son, Nathan, is to go to that particular bar. I told you earlier that some evil shit went down in Juárez."

"What happened?"

"There's been some talk about a new hit man who has been trawling the streets of old Juárez. This guy must be one filthy, sadistic bastard. He's been credited with killing no fewer than three banditos—maybe more—of the local Routa gang."

"Well, who are the Routas?"

"These are some bad hombres with a lot of muscle," Blanco said. "They're affiliated with the Chihuahua cartel. In addition to the three Routa gang members who got greased, there was an old prostitute who was brutally murdered at about the same time. As it turns out, she was a paid informant for the Routa banditos."

"Bad things happen at the border all the time," Blake said. "How is this any different?"

"Check this out: the bodies were completely drained of their blood. Now, don't get me wrong, these cartel members are notorious for using torture techniques. It's right out of the drug cartel playbook. In fact, it's the cornerstone of their standard operating procedures. To be honest, they prefer to leave a bloody signature, which is intended to simply intimidate the competition. However, these four murders were different. In fact, they were *way* different."

"In what way?"

"The bodies were mutilated beyond recognition," Blanco proceeded to explain. "Three of the victims were male, and their genitalia were removed. The fourth victim, the old female prostitute I told you about, was *disemboweled*. In addition there was evidence that her internal organs were subjected to predation while she was very much still alive."

"Wow! That sounds like the work of a vampiro," Blake said.

"Precisely," the detective said. "It's quite unusual for the Mexican Federales to call in a forensic team from El Paso or to consult with the EPPD. They even brought me on board to run it past the task force. Unlike the typical cartel murders, these were *very* different. The crime scenes were immaculately clean. There was not a fucking drop of blood anywhere. No signature splatters. No pools of body fluid to be found at all. The wounds on the victims were clean and dry."

"Pretty strange," Blake said.

"Hang on," the lieutenant said, "because this is where things get weird. As soon as the Mexican Federales called us in on the case for technical support, the investigation was immediately shut down cold. Now, we know that the Federales are, by and large, in the pocket of the Calle Vampiro cartel. We suspect that these murders were sanctioned assassinations ordered by the Calle Vampiros in an attempt to eliminate the Routas, as their parent organization happens to be the Chihuahua cartel. The Chihuahuans and the Calle Vampiros are sworn mortal enemies. The Calle cartel is likely the only organization that has the cojones to shut down such an important criminal investigation."

"How are these crimes in any way associated with my particular problems?" Blake Barker asked.

"Hear me out. I think everything in the universe is connected somehow," Blanco said. "As I said, the male victims in the Juárez murders lost their external plumbing. Now, the coroner didn't find the genitals in the mouth of any of the victims. Personally, I would have guessed that the genitals would have been shoved up into the rectum of one or more of the murdered individuals, but this was also not the case."

"Don't tell me," Blake said. "Let me guess—"

"I think you already have it all figured out. Their dicks were simply gone! The coroner found bite marks all over the bodies of the victims. For the love of Jesus, Blake, the coroner thinks that these poor bastards had their peckers bitten off at the hub, and the murder victims were likely still alive when it happened."

"To be honest," Blake Barker said, "I actually know of one individual who is fully capable of doing something like this."

"I thought you might," Blanco said. "Word on the street is that it was done by somebody with the handle 'El Mago.' Mean anything to you? Looks like the Calle Vampiro cartel is now armed with a deadly new torpedo!"

"Good God!" Blake exclaimed. "It has to be same person."

"Tell me, what do you know of the name El Mago?" Don Blanco asked.

"The vampiro responsible for the crime spree in the Rio Grande Valley is a shit bat named Romero Lopes. He calls himself El Mago. The direct translation of this name in English is 'the Magician.'"

"Well, there you have it. I can't lie to you, Blake. You have your work cut out for you. I know that you probably think that you're invincible, as if you're some kind of superman on a sacred mission of retribution. Be careful out there. When you enter the bar, ask to talk to a man named Flaco. When you meet him, tell him that you're friends with Officer Blanco. Most of the cartel subsidiaries are usually involved in some way, shape, or form with the kidnappings that occur along La Frontera. If your son, Nathan, or your housekeeper Lorena has been kidnapped, then Flaco will certainly know about it."

"Why would this cocksucker be willing to tell me anything at all?"

"He owes me, bro! He owes me big-time. Try not to piss him off. Flaco is actually a bloodthirsty nasty bastard in his own right with a very short fuse. If the pin gets pulled on that grenade, mark my words, you won't be able to get a word in edgewise. Nonetheless, he'll be your contact because he has eyes and ears at the fifty-kilometer mark south of the border at the Mexican interior inspection stations. He'll be able to tell you if Lorena and Nathan have left La Frontera. I'm sorry, but this is the best that I can do for you, stud. Before you go, you have to do something for me. I have to be absolved of the sin that I'm committing for allowing you to walk."

"What do you want me to do?" Blake asked.

The detective unholstered his revolver and strategically placed the barrel directly against the anterior aspect of his own thigh, making certain that the femur of his lower extremity would be medial to the bullet's trajectory and out of the blast zone. "Listen, Blake, take the gun and hold it steady. Put your finger on the trigger. I'll give you exactly ten minutes to get across the border before I send out an emergency radio request for an ambulance to pick me up and haul me off to the hospital. Are you ready, amigo?"

Blake nodded without saying a word.

"Okay," Don Blanco said. "Do you remember what you used to say to me when we played football together and you wanted me to create a rent in the defensive line? Well, bro, it's now my turn to ask the same of you: *make a hole!*"

Because the windows of the squad car were rolled up, the sound of the gunshot from the detective's service revolver was stifled. Blake dropped the pistol on the floorboard of the car as he made his exit. The smell of Don Blanco's blood that gushed forth from the wound in his leg only heightened Blake's senses and whetted his appetite even further. It was hard for the vampiro to walk away from a fresh blood meal, but Blake Barker mustered his resolve, turned quickly away from the squad car, and headed straight toward the Mexican border.

Blake entered the pedestrian walkway that would lead him across the border and into a foreign country. He reached into his pocket to grab some coins in order to pay for the crossing toll when he saw the "white hands" protruding through a slot in the dark glass window of the tollbooth to collect the fare. The white hands no doubt belonged to the woman who was an immigration agent who worked on the United States side of the Santa Fe Bridge. Always wearing white gloves, this individual collected the tolls, made change, and activated the turnstile that led directly to no-man's-land, which was the section of the bridge between the United States of America and Los Estados Unidos de México.

No-man's-land was usually congested with women and children who were huddled together on the ground with the palms of their soiled hands pointing toward the sky in a petition for either manna from heaven or perhaps a simple handout of spare pocket change. Blake wondered what dreadful circumstances had brought these unfortunate souls to such a dismal realm of marginal existence.

When he was in high school, Blake used to pay the toll to cross into Mexico with a dollar bill. He would then take the change that he received in return and carefully dole out the coins to the individuals on the bridge who appeared to be the most physically or spiritually desperate. When he was young and naïve, he took great delight in this noble act of charity. He felt as if he was going to somehow make the world a better place. Blake prayed that perhaps God would bestow grace and heavenly blessings upon him for his adherence to the greatest of all the commandments.

Now bursting at the seams with cynicism, he could only recall the words of a certain itinerant rabbi from Nazareth: "The poor will *always* be with you."

In light of this grim perpetual truth about the wretched existence that cursed most human beings who walked about on the face of the planet Earth, Blake Barker was thoroughly devoid of any residual attributes of compassion or altruism. He hung his head in shame, as his only identifiable residual emotion was the heavy burden of regret that cast an ever-darkening shadow over what little humanity he had left.

Miguel Pastore rapped his knuckles on the laminated desktop as he confronted Dr. Blanks in the director's office at the CDC. "I've seen my laboratory parameters, Doc. I'm not an idiot. I have a master's degree in biology. I know what's going on. I can tell that I'm continuing to hemolyze my own red blood cells like a wild man."

"Well, Miguel, that's indeed true. I believe it would be fair to say that we've had a few setbacks in the development of an effective vaccine," Dr. Blanks replied. "Nonetheless, I truly believe we're on the threshold of a major breakthrough. You just need to be patient a bit longer.

"You promised me weeks ago that you'd always be square with me," Miguel countered.

"I'm not lying to you," Dr. Blanks said.

"Why didn't you tell John Stewart and me about the problem that your team has encountered with genetic drift?" Miguel asked.

"Who told you about that issue?" Dr. Blanks asked in astonishment.

"The jig's up, Dr. Blanks! You can't perfect a vaccine against a moving target, now, can you? Were you ever planning on telling me this fact?"

"There's nothing out there for you, Miguel," Dr. Blanks petitioned. "If you ever leave this facility, you'll be hunted down and either exterminated or taken prisoner and hauled off to San Antonio against your will to be turned into some kind of bioweapon."

"As if I'm not a prisoner now?" Miguel asked. "You've known me long enough to realize that I'm not a threat to any other human being."

"I know that, but I'd like to try to see you explain something like that to a man like Captain Morales," Dr. Blanks said. "Stay here and work with us. I can protect you here."

Just then, John Stewart burst into the room. "I think you might be overestimating your ability to protect any of us, Dr. Blanks. Colonel Placard and that bastard Morales are coming down the hallway. In addition, the two other goons from the bioweapons division whom we met in Santa Fe are coming along for the ride. It seems to me that they mean business. If you want to see the end of this day, Miguel, you'd better come with me!"

EN LA TIERRA DE LOS CIEGOS
EL QUE TIENE UN OJO ES REY

5

ROAD TRIP

Miguel Pastore and John Stewart flew through the hallway and vacated the CDC, going down a stairwell that led to the main parking lot. "How are we going to get out of here?" Miguel asked.

"Take a deep breath," John Stewart replied. "I stole Doc's car keys! I think this would be a fine day for us to go on a road trip to Mexico, don't you think? I want to find Lorena. How about you, amigo? I'll drive."

"Okay, but don't think for a minute that I would ever let you date my sister," Miguel said.

"As I told you once before, I don't want to *date* her, Miguel," Stewart said. "I just want to *do* her! She's so hot, I'd even be her 'bottom boy'!"

"¡Señor Stewart, eres un zorillo! This is *exactly* why I don't want my sister to date a gringo like you."

"Thanks, Miguel," John Stewart said with a wry smile. "I hope I'll always resemble that remark!"

Dr. Blanks retreated behind his desk. It was imperative for him to portray a calm and collected façade upon the arrival of Dr. Placard and his team from the bioweapons division.

Upon finding Dr. Blanks, Colonel Placard and his team members simply invaded the physician's small office without so much as even abiding by the social norm of exchanging superficial pleasantries. Placard and Ron Shiftless were flanked by Morales and Joe Cephas Smoot, who stood on either side of Dr. Blank's desk as if they had him penned up in a corral.

"Well, I'm disappointed to hear that your efforts to find an effective vaccine have been unsuccessful to date," Ron Shiftless said as he rudely leaned back in an office chair and glared at Dr. Blanks. "I must say that I'm rather annoyed that you didn't even bother to keep us in the loop. Rumor has it that your vaccine program ran into a brick wall. Tell me, Blanks; what was it—genetic drift?"

"What?!" Blanks replied. "Where in hell did you get that idea?"

"As I'm the appointed scientific director of the bioweapons team in San Antonio, I'd like to think that I'm a fairly competent experimentalist with extensive in-the-field experience. After all," Ron said as he turned his head toward Augustus Placard for validation, "am I not still a really smart guy?"

"You have your moments," Placard casually answered as he dug into the small gap behind his upper left incisor with a toothpick that he had pulled out of his shirt pocket.

"Well, there you have it," Shiftless proudly stated. "Perhaps I could have offered some much-needed advice to your research team along the way before you boys got bogged down in a quagmire of futility. As it stands, you've been dicking around with this vaccine study for the better part of half a year with absolutely nothing to show for your herculean efforts."

Dr. Blanks scoffed at the overtly duplicitous offer of assistance from Dr. Shiftless. "You make me sick. The only thing that you wanted to do from the get-go was to spy on our work here at the CDC so you could swoop in and snatch away our valuable biological assets the very first minute that we encountered an unforeseen benchwork delay or otherwise experienced some type of clinical setback here or there!"

"True, but would that not be far better than allowing the CDC to release infected subjects into society at large after the very next occasion when Uncle Sam decides to yet again pull the plug on your project? The funding allocated for your vaccine research dried up once before, after the last outbreak of this clinical oddity back in 1979, did it not?" Ron asked. "Perhaps if you were a simply a better scientist, you would have gotten to the finish line by now!"

"This is precisely where I tell you to kiss my ass," Blanks said.

"That's a bit juvenile, don't you think?" Shiftless asked.

"Pot calling the kettle black as far as I can tell," Dr. Blanks replied.

"Be that as it may, I thought we had an understanding with each other, did we not?!" Ron Shiftless asked harshly, clearly irritated by the rebuke from Dr. Blanks. "After all, we're supposedly on the same team here."

"Are we now?"

Ron Shiftless stretched out his legs, propped them up on the corner of the desk, and crossed them at the ankles. "Tell me, Blanks, when were you planning on giving us an update on your vaccine project?"

Dr. Blanks failed to answer while he carefully scrutinized Joe Cephas Smoot and Morales, who silently flanked either side of his desk.

"That's a rather pertinent question," Colonel Placard interjected. "Answer the man, Dr. Blanks, unless of course you're purposefully trying to keep the military in the dark about what's been going on around here at the CDC."

Without a single word, Dr. Blanks swiveled in his desk chair and faced the countertop on his back office wall, where he had a small, terminally ill potted ivy plant. On the counter beside the houseplant was a plastic spray bottle filled with water that was used to hydrate the plant and keep the leaves free of dust. If this particular disciplinary technique was good enough for the nurse to employ on John Stewart, then it would be a good enough for Dr. Blanks to utilize in a similar fashion against his adversary, Ron Shiftless. Dr. Blanks set the spray bottle nozzle on stream and proceeded to blast away at Dr. Shiftless until he dropped his feet to the floor.

"Don't look at me that way!" Dr. Shiftless said. "You can take your condescending load of arrogant CDC crapola right now and shove it as far as I'm concerned! You've always looked down upon me for the work that I've chosen to do, and I resent that. What I'm doing in San Antonio is just as important as what you're trying to accomplish here at the CDC. I just wish for once that you treated me like a colleague. I just wish for once that you treated me like a peer. We're both trying to save the world, are we not? We're just approaching this same objective from opposite directions."

Dr. Blanks was not about to miss this golden opportunity to further torment the scientific director of the bioweapons division. "Did little Ronnie get his ego bruised? I'm so sorry. Would you feel better if Mommy kissed your boo-boo to make your pain go away?"

"As for our bioweapon team, we've completed our initial objectives, smart-ass!" Shiftless said. "It's plain to see that your vaccine program has taken a torpedo below the waterline. You're going to have to start over from scratch from what I've heard. Ha! Too bad, so sad. Piss on you, buddy boy."

"None of our work is published. I was going to present our data at the Night Crawler Symposium that's coming up in DC," Dr. Blanks said as he stared at Augustus Placard. "How in hell are you boys privy to any of our results? Don't tell me that you've got a spy embedded here at the CDC. I won't stand for that—not for one minute!"

For his part, Colonel Placard maintained a poker face and said nothing.

"Why are you boys cluttering up my office?" Blanks asked. "You didn't come all the way out here from Texas just to torment me, now, did you?"

"We've come for Miguel Pastore and John Stewart," Placard said.

"They both booked out of here when you showed up," Dr. Blanks answered.

"What?!" Placard replied. "Where did they go?"

"Beats the hell out of me. If I would have to make a guess, I would venture they went on a road trip to Mexico. Good luck on trying to find them down there. I suppose Mexico is not exactly within your jurisdiction," Blanks said with a chuckle.

"You're wrong about that, Blanks," Placard said. "The entire *planet* is our jurisdiction!"

Dr. Blanks turned once again toward Morales and Joe Cephas Smoot who had remained completely silent the entire time since they had arrived at the CDC facility. "I'd like to make you gentlemen a very generous offer. Hear me out. It's clear to me that you men are far too old to still be out there playing G.I. Joe."

"You're not authorized to speak to my men," Placard cautioned Dr. Blanks.

"What?" Dr. Blanks asked. "Did somebody revoke the First Amendment to the Constitution while I was out taking a whiz or something? Why don't you guys stay here at the CDC with me? Yes, I'll be the first to admit that we've had a few setbacks in developing a vaccine for the disease that has infected you both, but realistically we offer you the best chance for successful treatment and perhaps even a cure than any other place in the world. I'll make it worth your while."

This generous new offer from the CDC suddenly made Dr. Shiftless and Colonel Placard visibly alarmed, as Morales and Joe Cephas simultaneously furrowed their brows and looked at each other intently. Clearly, Dr. Blanks was trying to sow seeds of doubt and discontent among the members of the bioweapon team.

"We've taken up too much of your valuable time already, Dr. Blanks," Ron Shiftless said as he stood up. He took Morales and Joe Cephas each by the arm and then guided them out into the hallway.

"I agree," the colonel said. "Promise me this, Dr. Blanks: do a better job in the future of letting us know what's going on around here. As for now, we have places to go, people to do, and things to see. I bid you a good day, kind sir."

Upon the departure of the bioweapon team, Dr. Blanks ran out to the parking lot, but there was neither hide nor hair of Miguel Pastore or John Stewart. He noticed something odd: his car was gone! He reached into the pocket of his lab coat and found his house keys and office keys, but his car keys had mysteriously vanished from his key ring. Dr. Blanks extended his palms, looked up to the heavens, and shouted out a bevy of curses to his now departed experimental subjects. "John Stewart, you're lucky I removed the termination clause from your employment contract!"

Blake had to eat. Strangely, his first thought of a place where he could find nourishment was a place called Frederico's Sandwich Shop. This was an old high school haunt, frequented after illicit nights of underage beer consumption by rowdy teenagers. A fresh-toasted *bolillo* with a smashed avocado, *frijoles refrito,* pickled jalapeños, asadero cheese, and spicy carrots sounded delicious. The vampiro wandered down Avenida Benito Juárez and took a right turn to amble along the side streets, finally finding Frederico's. Blake ordered a torta and a strawberry Fanta in an effort to try to recapture some of his lost youth, but unfortunately any attempts at ingesting the food made him nauseous. After violently regurgitating the contents of his stomach, he stumbled back onto the street that intersected Avenida Juárez.

Maslow's proverbial five-tiered hierarchy of human motivation had devolved into a new paradigm, namely, the hierarchy of human misery. It revealed itself in full force, and in all its ignominy, for Blake to personally experience as he hungered to the point of desperation.

The famished vampiro followed the scent of fresh blood in the air to another eatery he remembered well. The old Parilla Tejas was a mecca for grilled meat in Juárez. One could order *queso fundido* and fresh, handmade corn tortillas. The molten cheese with crispy brown edges would be served on a clay platter from a cast-iron hibachi, sizzling from red-hot charcoal. There was also a public hibachi available for patrons to grill their own raw meat. This side grill afforded diners the opportunity to braise their personal selections to their own satisfaction. Blake took a seat and ordered raw *ligado, arrachera, puntas,* and *corazón de cerdo*. He also placed an order for crunchy *criadillas* for dessert. When his last order of food was brought to the table, the noisy arthropods were still very much alive, although they each appeared to be afflicted with a lethargic sensorium, if such a thing could actually be said about a humble cricket.

Blake never bothered to put any of the raw meat on the grill at all. He voraciously assaulted the flesh, ingesting large slabs of the bloody organ tissue without even chewing. He saved the criadillas for last, grabbing them by the handful and jamming them into his mouth as if he were stuffing his face with popcorn at a movie theater. It was exhilarating for Blake to feel the tiny creatures kicking and jumping about in his mouth, trying to escape their ultimate fate, as he masticated their exoskeletons to a pulp. It was late in the afternoon, so the establishment was nearly empty. Nobody noticed the vampiro's feeding frenzy except for the grill attendant, and he was too horrified to render any editorial comments about what he had just witnessed.

Once satiated, Blake acknowledged that it was time to resume his quest to find out what had happened to Lorena and his son, Nathan. He realized that although he had only been out in the sunshine for a few hours, his skin was already starting to blister on his forehead, nose, exposed arms, and ears. He developed photophobia, as his eyes also suffered from a burning sensation. His next stop would have to be the Pharmacia del Norte. Avenida Benito Juárez is lined with souvenir shops, bars, eateries, and also pharmacies. Blake knew that, surprisingly, most of the pharmacies in Juárez were staffed by quite knowledgeable and well-trained pharmacists who were eager to help diagnose and treat a variety of maladies. Ergo, the pharmacists of the community served as the poor man's primary care clinicians.

As a case in point, Blake remembered in high school when his brother, Cletus, managed to contract a nasty case of urethritis that was caused by a petulant sexually transmitted bacterium scientifically recognized as *Neisseria gonorrhoeae*. The infection sadly occurred after Cletus had been serviced at a notorious establishment in Juárez known as Paloma de la Noche. Fortunately, Cletus received a curative dose of doxycycline at the Pharmacia del Norte. Thanks to the friendly pharmacist, no members of the

Barker family would ever be privy to that most embarrassing and uncomfortable happenstance.

As Blake stepped through the open door of the pharmacy, he was immediately approached by a well-groomed middle-aged gentleman wearing a light blue guayabera. In flawless English, the proprietor of the establishment made a few inquiries about Blake's troublesome symptoms. The pharmacist prescribed aloe gel and a steroid cream for the sunburn, and he also suggested a topical high-SPF sunblock, sunglasses, and a broad-brimmed hat if Blake was ever out and about in the future on bright sunny days.

On a piece of paper, the pharmacist had written in large block letters PORPHYRIA CUTANEA TARDA and then handed the paper to Blake Barker. "By the way, I am the pharmacist at this establishment and my name is Roberto Guzman. Do you plan on returning to the United States after your visit with me today?"

"No," Blake replied, "my son is missing and I might be going as far south as Jalisco."

"I wish you the best of luck with all of that," the pharmacist replied, "but if you are going as far as Jalisco and you get sick while you are down there, I want you to find my sister who is a hematologist named Roberta Guzman. She is a professor of medicine and the director of the bone marrow transplant service at the San Agustin College of Medicine in the Southwest corner of Guadalajara. You show her this piece of paper that I just gave you, and we'll see what she thinks about your situation. Pardon me for being so bold, but it would seem to me that you're afflicted with a blood disorder called porphyria."

"Is that so?"

"I don't know if it is true or not, but I have been told that there have been occasional severe outbreaks of something like porphyria happening every ten or twenty years or so north of El Paso, up in the Rio Grande Valley of Nuevo Mexico," the pharmacists explained. Obviously, the pharmacist didn't know about human vampirism.

"Well, you might be on to something," Blake said.

"I've heard that people who come down with the unusual cyclical form of this blood disorder can become quite violent. And they might even viciously attack other people," the pharmacist added. "Are you aware of anything like that?"

"Lo siento, but I wouldn't know anything about that particular problem," Blake said as he cast his eyes down to the floor.

Blake found out how prescient the pharmacist actually was. While acting in his unofficial capacity as an amateur diagnostician, the pharmacist suspected Blake had a rare but well-recognized blood disorder. Porphyria is an inherited disorder of hemoglobin metabolism, and it certainly can present with the hemolytic features and cutaneous solar sensitivity similar to human vampirism. Of course the pharmacist was unaware that his client was afflicted with something a hell of a lot worse than porphyria.

"Gracias, señor," Blake said as he shook the pharmacist's hand. "I have a very busy schedule today. I must be on my way."

Time was running out. While Blake had gotten burned up from the sun, he had, in turn, burned up an entire afternoon. By the time he found the Tequila Town establishment, the sun was already starting to set. The hot pavement of Avenida Juárez was starting to cool as dusk gently rolled into the city. By the time Blake walked to the bar, he had already smeared the aloe gel on his face. The cooling sensation was a welcome respite. He found that the evening stroll to the tequila bar was actually quite invigorating. The vampiro felt quite a bit better as the blisters on his skin had already begun to spontaneously regress by the time he entered the nightclub.

As Blake entered the barroom, he sensed a disturbing odor that put him on a high level of alert. He was able to quickly discern the reason for his sudden onset of agitation; there was a faint residual older from a vampiro that was imprinted within the confines of the tequila joint. Could it have been the odor of his hated nemesis, Romero Lopes?

Blake passed the barroom and went straightaway to the bathroom in the back of the establishment. Several inconspicuous glances gave him a quick layout of the premises and allowed him to discern the locations of the patrons who were scattered about the joint. A booth on the left side of the bar that was near the exit hosted a group of three men and one unkempt woman who appeared to be slightly dazed prey being lubricated for an upcoming contact sport tag-team match. The long bar to Blake's right was staffed by a huge and imposing bartender along with a tall but slender underage boy who was employed as a bottle washer and table waiter.

There were two men sitting at the bar who appeared to be middle-aged businessmen who were arguing over esoteric statistics from the popular sport of professional *fútbol.* There were six other tables in the nightclub; however, only one of them was occupied. Two morbidly obese tourists, gazing into each other's eyes with lust, were apparently patiently awaiting simultaneous sudden-death coronary thrombotic events while drinking margaritas and chain-smoking unfiltered cigarettes.

Once Blake Barker had reached the bathroom, he found an elderly blind attendant standing militantly erect as if he were a Swiss guardsman at the Vatican. His specific job was to keep the urinal packed with ice in an effort to minimize the foul odor of the nitrogenous liquid waste expelled forcefully by the firm urinary bladder contractions of a multitude of inebriated male patrons. His other official duty was to pass out fresh hand towels and to offer the patrons a spritz of cologne, if so desired. The misfortunate blind old codger worked for tips alone. There was a sign on the wall that was stenciled above the row of urinals that read: EN LA TIERRA DE LOS CIEGOS, EL QUE TIENE UN OJO ES REY!

Blake read the sign and began to laugh. Although the elderly restroom attendant spoke only Spanish, Blake addressed him directly in English as if the blind man could understand every word the vampiro said. "I don't know if having an eye in the land of the blind would indeed make one a king, but I think it would dramatically improve the likelihood that the man with one eye would likely be able to piss in the pot and not on his own shoes!"

Although the toilet attendant had no idea what Blake said, he began to laugh. After all, the inflection in a person's voice who is telling a joke is the same throughout the world irrespective of ethnicity, gender, language, or culture.

Blake stepped up to the urinal and tried to void, but only a few drops of brown urine were painfully expressed from his bladder. He began to reminisce about how much he enjoyed melting the urinal ice with a forceful stream of his own hot piss back in the days when he was in high school.

Back in the main barroom there was a tiled trough with a floor drain directly in front of the long wooden bar where patrons sipped mescal. The trough was eight inches wide and fifteen feet long, and it ran the entire length of the ornate mahogany bar. There was a perpetual trickle of water sloshing through the trough. The device was ostensibly a modern version of a bar spittoon. The plumbed and tiled in-floor lavatory device was decidedly *not* to be used as a urinal. Nonetheless, Blake's brother, Cletus, and his buddies from high school used to piss in it in a clandestine manner while they were seated in the tall chairs in front of the long, carved wooden bar. If the boys were caught, the bouncer would show up, grab the miscreants by the scruffs of their necks, and deservedly cast them out into the street.

As for Blake, he always preferred to try to melt the ice that was packed high in the restroom urinal. By the time he graduated from high school, on the occasions at least when he was not too inebriated, he could actually create small ice sculptures in the urinal with well-aimed streams of his hot, steaming urine. His old high school football teammate Don Blanco was at one time amazed by Blake's artistic talents as demonstrated in the restroom at the Tequila Town bar. For the remainder of his days, Blake would never forget what he once told his friend Don after one particular exhibition of his lavatory ice sculptures: "An artist is only as good as his tool, and I, Blake Barker, Esquire, am endowed with a really good tool!" Blake could now only shake his head in bewilderment as he wondered how his life had jumped so far off the rails.

After Blake zipped his fly and washed his hands, the restroom attendant immediately handed him a fresh towel. In addition, Blake was offered a shot of peppermint-flavored mouthwash and a variety of men's colognes, which he respectfully declined. In the Spanish language, Blake proceeded to ask the restroom attendant some very dangerous questions. "I will give you a tip of ten American dollars if you will tell me something."

"For ten American dollars, I'll tell you anything that you want to know, señor."

"What can you tell me about the leader of the Routa gang? I'm looking for un hombre named Flaco. I need to meet him."

"*Mijo*, you're just looking for trouble. The Routas are at war with the Aztecas, who are controlled by the Calle Vampiro cartel. If you go around asking questions, you'll get your throat slit—or worse."

"Look, I'm *not* looking for trouble," Blake explained. "I'm not looking for *drogas*. Neither am I'm looking for *mujeres*. My son was kidnapped. A woman took him and came across the border from New Mexico. I have to find my son, and I understand the gangs around here know what's going on when it comes to the trafficking of human beings. Please help me."

"Okay, señor," the old man said, "I'll help you, but you need to tell me something also. To my nose, you don't smell, well—*normal*. Are you un vampiro?"

Blake was amazed by the olfactory acuity of the blind old man. "How could you tell?"

"A vampiro came in here over a week ago and caused a lot of trouble. Two of Flaco's men were killed in this very bar. Down the street, this vampiro killed an old prostitute who worked for Flaco. Her bodyguard, El Segundo, was also viciously murdered and partially consumed. Are you here to kill any more of the Routa gang members? If so, I'm not going to help you. You see, El Segundo was my nephew."

"Was the vampiro a man called Mago?"

"A friend of yours?" the old man asked.

"I should say not," Blake replied. "This *otro* vampiro killed my wife. I want to find him and rip his heart out. If he killed your nephew, maybe you can help me. Do you know where Mago is right now? Is he still in Juárez?"

"*No se*, joven," the old man said as he led Blake Barker back to the bar. "When Flaco gets here, why don't you offer him a shot of mescal? It's what the Routa gang members drink when there's business to attend to. Personally, I think mescal tastes like shit. It doesn't have a refined taste like aged tequila."

"Well, I would certainly agree," Blake Barker said. "Why would anybody want to drink mescal, anyhow? I'd rather drink lighter fluid or turpentine. Don't tell me it's because there's a stupid pickled worm sloshing around at the bottom of the bottle."

"No, señor," the restroom attendant explained. "It's actually not a worm. It happens to be an insect larva of the taxonomically recognized *Hyopta agavus* moth. Technically, the insect at the bottom of a bottle of mescal is therefore a caterpillar, not a worm. In my humble opinion, the caterpillar is quite tasty. I happen to like the *gusano rojo* variety the best. It has more meat than the more common *amarillo gusano de maguey*."

"Wow! I'm impressed, señor."

"Well, I might be and old and blind, but I'm not stupid," the restroom attendant proudly reported before he turned to his guard post at the urinal in the men's room. The elderly man added, "By the way, my name is Diego del Mar. It was a pleasure for me to meet you. I certainly hope you have a chance to hunt down and exterminate the vampiro that murdered my nephew. I'd like to visit with you again someday, but as for now, *buena suerte,* señor."

While the bartender poured Blake Barker a shot of Siete Leguas, the vampiro was acutely aware that a beefy nightclub attendant was discreetly going about the entire barroom and asking all the patrons to vacate the premises. It was apparent that the disheveled woman and her three suitors fully comprehended the gravity of the situation; they were the first to flee in haste. The other customers quickly followed suit, all except for the beached cetaceans, who were clearly recalcitrant to abide by the order to depart from the establishment. As they held their ground, they continued to puff away on unfiltered cigarettes, while the two of them batted their eyes at each other.

One of the Routa gang members approached the bar and deliberately sat beside Blake Barker. The stranger nodded to the bartender and said, "Amigo, let me have a mescal *y un barril grande*."

"Do you want me to put it on your house tab?" the bartender asked.

"*Chinga no!* Put it on this ugly gringo's tab." The menacing stranger scoffed as he wagged his middle finger toward Blake Barker. "*Hombre amarillo,* I don't like your face. Who are you, and why you here?"

"Officer Don Blanco from El Paso informed me that I might be able to find a man named Flaco at this bar. I see that you're drinking mescal. You wouldn't by any chance happen to be Flaco, now, would you?"

"A-mar-ee-cone, I theenk you need to get back to your side of the border. You must be some *pinche gringo salado policía*! *Va chinga un gato, gringo, mientras que la miedra tu abuela.*"

Blake Barker remained very calm and simply stared at his own reflection in the mirror behind the bar. He could only wryly smile. After the stranger threatened to rape Blake's grandmother, the vampiro replied, "I'd be careful if I were you, amigo. If you ever try to fuck my grandmother, she'll make you eat own pecker after she hacks off your damned plumbing with a dull butter knife."

"¡Chingow!" the stranger exclaimed yet again. "When Flaco gets here, you're going to be sorry, *ese*. *¡Puta madre!* We're going to have some fun with you, *guedo*."

The bartender became annoyed when he looked up to see that the two giant ocean-faring mammals were still sitting at a table, totally oblivious to the violent melee that was about to erupt.

"Hey! Listen to me, you fat fucks," the bartender said as he pulled out a sawed-off pistol-grip side-by-side twelve-gauge from behind the bar and placed it upon the counter. "Get out of here. Now!"

The two wide-bodies finally realized they were in harm's way. The couple jumped up and motored to the front door as fast as their corpulent extremities could possibly propel them. Perhaps the woman was lactose intolerant, or maybe she was hyperflatulent because of a myriad of other morbid medical maladies. In any event, short, loud bursts of noxious fumes blasted out of her ass with each step that she took toward the exit. It was as if she had ramjet auxiliary power to help her achieve the breakneck escape velocity of a garden slug.

"Damn, she stinks worse than you do, gringo. Look at the size of *las nalgas* on that porker!" the hostile stranger at the bar exclaimed.

The bartender laughed and hurled another insult at the mortified monster who was trying to scurry away. "Her ass is the size of Tejas and smells even worse. *¡Más jamón por este par de juevos!*"

The terrorized pachyderm began to openly howl in anguish when the nightclub attendant who had held the front door open for her ended up slamming *la puerta* on her posterior just as she waddled past the threshold. "*Que huele*; what in hell are you?" the attendant inquired. "*¿La reina de los elefantes?* I bow down to you, Your Royal Highness."

The traumatized patron was in high gear, dashing along at the astonishing speed of perhaps one, or maybe two, kilometers per hour as she fled the vicinity. Once she made it out of the tequila bar, her boyfriend was nowhere to be seen. The object of her unbridled passion had booked out of there as fast as he could, and it was rather obvious that he wasn't stopping for shit (either hers or, apparently, anybody else's).

The nightclub attendant locked the front door and placed a sign on the glass that said ¡CERRADO! to make certain nobody else would be coming into the bar that night, except for perhaps Flaco and more Routa soldiers.

While several members of the Routa gang circled about Blake in a menacing fashion, the vampiro simply savored the Siete Leguas tequila. Blake fully realized that as he was now a vampire, the act of drinking a shot of hard liquor would likely cause considerable abdominal cramping and nausea. Nonetheless, he was honored to have been offered such an excellent tequila that was actually *from* the township of Tequila in Estado de Jalisco. As this spirit was rarely found north of the border, Blake Barker was also sadly aware that he might not ever have another opportunity to partake of such a mellow exotic tequila ever again, regardless of the dyspepsia that it would probably engender once consumed.

What Blake found was even more impressive than the rare tequila was the rare shotgun that was perched on top of the bar. As an aficionado of firearms, he was impressed by the old relic with exposed hammers. He looked the weapon over from a distance and was stunned to see that the scattergun was an old L. C. Smith creation. He was angered to see that such a finely crafted weapon had been bastardized into a sawed-off bar sweeper. To his advantage, Blake was also quick to note that when the bartender grabbed the weapon from behind the counter, he failed to cock the hammers ...

When Flaco arrived, the nightclub attendant unlocked the door and let him in, along with an entourage of six tattooed thugs wearing khakis and heavily starched white shirts that were untucked but nonetheless buttoned at the top. Flaco sat down on the other side of Blake, and the rest of the crew filled in behind the two men. Blake could readily see all of them reflected in the mirror on the back bar wall.

"Tell me, gringo," Flaco said, "why should I give you the time of day?"

Blake Barker calmly explained his situation and also provided the details of his relationship to Officer Don Blanco. Flaco seemed to be at least superficially sympathetic to Blake's plight, as Don Blanco had helped Flaco's mother walk away from a prostitution sting that was set up by the EPPD when Flaco was only a ten-year-old gang member on the streets of the barrio de Chihuahuita in El Paso.

"Let me tell you what I know," Flaco said. "I'm aware that a woman from New Mexico with a small gringo passed the fifty-kilometer mark interior inspection station going to Jalisco. She said that she was on her way to visit her *tio* in Santa Sangre."

"I was told she was headed to Santa Sangre once before," Blake said, "but originally, I was too stubborn to believe the news that was told to me. Well, I want to thank you for your generous hospitality. I guess I should be on my way. It looks like I'll be making a road trip to Santa Sangre after all. May I buy you a premium shot of mescal, if such a thing actually exists, for your time and trouble?"

"*Un momento, por favor.* Before you leave, let me take a better look at you. Something—well, something just doesn't seem right with you. In fact, you don't look so healthy to me, gringo. Why is your skin yellow? You look very similar to un hombre who came into this bar last week and caused a lot of trouble," Flaco said as he scrutinized Blake Barker's jaundiced hue and icteric sclerae. "Open your mouth, amigo. I want you to show me your teeth."

6

AN AXE TO GRIND

When Flaco asked Blake Barker to bare his teeth, the vampiro thought nothing of it and readily complied. Once Flaco and the other Routa gang members witnessed Blake's generous incisors, the gang boss jumped off his barstool and recoiled in terror. Blake's meeting with the Routa gang had gone south in a hurry. Weapons were drawn when Flaco said, "You're un vampiro! Tell me something, do you know un vampiro named Mago?"

If Blake had been thinking clearly, perhaps he would have told Flaco that he was actively hunting down Mago and planned to kill him. If Blake had been thinking clearly, perhaps he would have explained that Mago had killed his wife and he was seeking vengeance. If Blake had been thinking clearly, perhaps he would have offered his services to the Routa banditos, as he would have been happy to assist the gang in tracking down Mago and exterminating him like the vermin that he truly turned out to be. Unfortunately, Blake was not thinking clearly at that particular moment.

"Yes, I do know a vampiro named Mago. It's funny that you should ask. As you see—" Blake's explanation was rudely interrupted.

"I've done something nice for you out of respect for Don Blanco, and this is what you tell me? You make me sick. *¡Pendejo, no cages donde comes!* So, if you know this motherfucker, you must be working with the Calle Vampiro cartel and the Aztecas!"

"Now wait just a moment," Blake interjected.

"Orale, cabron–that son of a bitch Mago killed Primo and two more of my men! He even killed the toothless old whore, and he ate her innards. Do you know who the toothless old whore was?" Flaco peeled up his left shirtsleeve to reveal the new tattoo on his forearm that said LA MADRE. Now you're telling me that you're working with that parásito?!"

"Now, wait just one damned second here," Blake said as he tried to push Flaco away. "There's been a big misunderstanding! I'm sure as hell not working with Mago or the Aztecas, or the Calle Vampiros who pull their strings. I'm not working for the police, Deputy Dog, Santa Claus, or even the goddamned tooth fairy! I do *not* want any kind of trouble with you boys. I suggest you let me go about my business, and you'll never see me again."

Flaco grabbed the shotgun and pointed it at Blake Barker. Because El Primo had previously died at the hands of El Mago, Flaco had recently promoted one of his other henchmen, El Grifo, to be *capitán.* While holding the sawed-off shotgun firmly by the pistol grip in his right hand, Flaco extended his left index finger and drew an imaginary line across the anterior aspect of Blake Barker's neck. "Grifo, *¡llevar a este vampiro y decapitarlo! ¡Ahora!*"

"Oh, how nice," Blake said. "So, it's going to come down to this now, is it?"

Flaco had just ordered his thugs to cut Blake's head off! The hapless vampiro who had come down to Mexico to find his missing son was certainly not looking for a fight, but nonetheless, through no fault of his own, it would seem that a fight had found him.

"I don't think it's a good idea for you to go all the way down to Mexico to look for a woman who rejected you once before. Please reconsider what you're doing. Trust me on this. With age comes wisdom, and I want to impart some of mine to you. I'm afraid that you'll only find heartache. Well, heartache and *danger*," Señora Naranjo said as Dr. Cloud loaded the trunk of his car with two black leather bags.

"I can't explain why I'm doing this," Cloud said. "Everything in my heart tells me to go and find Lorena, but everything in my head tells me that I'm making the biggest mistake of my life. All I know is that I can't live my life haunted by any more regrets than I already have. I'm tormented with guilt about things I've done in the past and also for things that I have left undone."

"What are you talking about, Dr. Cloud?" Mrs. Naranja asked. "You're one of the most decent people I've ever known."

"I'm talking about the times I've turned a blind eye to the alcohol abuse and abject poverty of my very own tribe," Cloud explained. "I should have done more for my people. Once I completed my medical school education, I never even had the courage to go back to visit the reservation. I'm embarrassed to tell you this, but I originally received a scholarship from the tribe to go to medical school, and all I ended up doing was abandoning the very people who loved me and supported my higher education."

"Then stay here and make amends if it will make you feel better."

"I've lost my very identity. Perhaps I've lost my very soul," Cloud explained. "I look back now on how I've lived a very self-absorbed, self-centered life and I feel nothing but shame."

"We *all* do at times, mijo!"

"That's right, Mrs. Naranjo," the lovesick doctor said. "We *all* do at times. However, if a man tries to follow a righteous path, the guilt of his past sins of commission, and also his sins of omission for that matter, might be mitigated."

"Is this your quest?" Mrs. Naranja asked. "Redemption is through grace, not deeds."

"I'm not so sure about that. When I'm an old man, I don't want to think back on this time and realize that the one last chance I had left to win the heart of this woman whom I love dearly had forever disappeared into the smoke and haze of timidity and indecision."

"And what of the little boy you spoke of? He's not your child. He's the flesh and blood of another man," the old woman said. "Stay here, mijo. You shouldn't concern yourself with this matter."

"You're wrong, Mrs. Naranjo. You and I usually disagree about everything, and it looks like this time won't be any different. Once and for all, I'm going to do the right thing," Cloud said as he bent down and softly kissed the elderly woman on the cheek.

"Before you go, there's something I must give you," the woman said. "My *tia* was a curandera. She told me that there are very few natural materials that can harm un vampiro. I don't know why, but the volcanic glass known as obsidian appears to be deadly to the bloodsuckers. Any part of their body that gets injured by obsidian will never heal. Another element that is dangerous to los vampiros is silver, of all things."

"Are you certain about all of this?"

"About obsidian? Dr. Cloud, I'm as certain about this fact as I am about anything in my life," Señora Naranja said.

"Okay, fine. Well, what about silver?" Cloud asked.

"No. Frankly that's just bullshit," Señora Naranjo said with a sly grin. "Silver is harmless to los vampiros, but they don't know it! Most vampiros are idiots, and they're just walking around out there believing in that silly myth! What a joke! Next thing you know, we'll be able to convince those stupid vampiros that they're being hunted by a pack of werewolves. They'll shit their *chones*!"

"You crack me up, Mrs. Naranjo," Dr. Cloud said with a laugh. "You should do stand-up!"

"I'm sorry that I don't have an obsidian knife for you to ward off any evil vampiros, but I do have something for you nonetheless." Señora Naranjo handed over to Dr. Cloud a sterling silver letter opener that had been honed to a very sharp blade. "Seven years ago when the last vampiro attack happened in the valley, I was able to ward off a vampiro with this silver letter opener."

"You can't be serious."

"Have you ever played poker, Dr. Cloud?" the elderly curandera asked.

"Strip poker when I was in college," Dr. Cloud said. "I lost, which, I guess, means that I technically won. It afforded me the opportunity to *finally* get butt naked with a sweaty chunky-monkey coed named Mary Ellen Fokkengruber and her catastrophically obese twin sister, Bertha."

"Que horrible."

"No, it was beautiful. I told the sisters the bald-faced lie that I was afflicted with low blood sugar that adversely affected my vastly enormous, pulsating, turgid *intellectual* prowess. The girls decided it was their duty to resurrect me from the dead, so they tied me to the bedpost in their dorm room and forced me to eat jelly doughnuts until I slipped into a hyperglycemic coma. It remains one of my fondest memories!"

"Well, there you have it. There's a strategy often employed in poker that's called the bluff. It also works during the warfare one might encounter in the art of tag-team lovemaking with sweat-drenched twins who are little more than hunky, horny hippos armed with delicious jelly doughnuts!"

"And now?"

"It also works well in the warfare one might encounter with a band of vampiros," Mrs. Naranja explained. "Not only does silver work, but so does a variety of other harmless things, including garlic, holy water, and even a crucifix."

"You've been a great neighbor to me, Mrs. Naranjo," Dr. Cloud said. "I'm going to miss you. I want you to feed Saber Stripe while I'm gone. He's an excellent mouse hunter, and he'll keep the varmints out of your house. He doesn't need a cat box, as he's smart enough to poop outside like a dog."

"Are you absolutely certain that I can't change your mind?"

"Adios, Mrs. Naranjo," Dr. Cloud said. "You're looking at a man who's going on a mission. You're looking at a man who's going on a road trip!"

When Grifo lunged at Blake Barker, the vampiro deftly stepped aside. He grabbed the shotgun by the barrels and clocked the bartender with the butt end. Blake was actually amused by his own speed, strength, and agility. Suddenly, another bandito raised a nine-millimeter Uzi and pressed it against Blake's cheekbone, right underneath his left eye.

"Back off, amigo!" Blake ordered as he grabbed the assailant by his wrist and then pointed the automatic weapon into the air. "Give me that damned thing!"

The ceiling of the establishment was peppered with an angry burst of automatic weapon fire. With a backhanded elbow, Blake broke the gunman's jaw. The Uzi-toting Routa bandito dropped to the floor, falling face-first into the tiled spittoon drain on the floor running directly parallel to the ornate mahogany bar.

Blake Barker grabbed Flaco by the arm and twisted it behind his back. Blake placed Flaco into what would be the incoming line of fire, directly facing the other Routa gang members. To make absolutely certain that his adversaries knew that the vampiro in their midst meant business, Barker snapped Flaco's forearm, causing a midshaft compound fracture of both the man's radius and ulnar bones. As if he were merely peeling away the outer skin of a ripe plantain fruit, Blake stripped away the sinew of Flaco's fractured arm to reveal the remnant shards of his arm bones.

"Did that hurt?" the vampiro asked as he tempered his overwhelming desire to suck out Flaco's fatty yellow bone marrow while the gang leader screamed in agony and ordered his Routa crew to back down from the violent confrontation.

The altercation happened so fast that Blake felt as if his assailants were moving in slow motion. The vampiro firmly held the muzzle of the twin-tubed weapon against Flaco's temple and barked an explicit order to the Routa henchmen in no uncertain terms: "Back, you fuckers! Back, back, back, I'm telling you. Do it now!"

When the Federales arrived in force, a battering ram was utilized to break down the front door of the nightclub. Wisely, Blake Barker dropped the sawed-off scattergun on the floor the moment the front door was breached. The national police steamrolled into the joint like a tsunami, and then they started busting heads.

If ever raided by the cops, the Routa gang would actually look forward to a visit from *la policía local de* Juárez, as several of the regional law enforcement officers were already on the take. The same, however, could not be said of the Federales, who were zipped up into the pockets of the Aztecas and their Calle Vampiro cartel overlords. As it turned out, the Routa gang had absolutely no influence over judicial interdiction from the national police.

"If we're being arrested, I must insist and that you take my crew down to the local police department," Flaco said as he winced in pain. "We've done nothing at all that would warrant a trip to a federal booking station." Apparently, the Federales didn't see it that way. When a burly officer jammed his nightstick into Flaco's groin, the gang leader fell to his knees.

Flaco, the broken-jawed unconscious gunman, and the bartender with a handful of broken teeth were all promptly escorted to the hospital under armed guard for medical care. Blake Barker and the rest of the members of the Routa gang were taken by the Federales to a holding cell downtown to be shared with a menagerie of other hostile guests. A few of the cellmates locked up with Blake Barker and the Routa gang were merely tourists who were incarcerated for the infamous Mexican Shakedown.

After paying a generous "fine" in cash, these tourists would soon be released, but not before they were afforded the opportunity to also "buy back" their confiscated automobile license plates for the minor traffic infractions that had been committed. What choice did they have? These tourists were previously warned about La Mordita (the Bite), a reference to the corruption and graft that was so prevalent as a way of life south of the border. However, with the tourists now sharing a jail cell with a living, breathing vampiro, perhaps La Mordita had suddenly taken on an entirely different and dire meaning.

While in jail, Blake Barker had a front row seat to the usual customary hospitality the predatory denizens of the penal system offered the other, unwitting incarcerated visitors.

Buey and Gilberto were two local hooligans who were accustomed to spending a great deal of time behind bars. Although Buey was a large balding man who sported menacing matted tufts of springy hair that encased each earlobe, the narrow-set beady eyes of Gilberto made this lesser of the two banditos an even more frightening adversary. The two thugs tried to entice the tourists into parting company with their meager trinkets.

"Listen, bitch," Gilberto said, "give me your ring. Do it now, or I'll break your fingers." The frightened woman glanced over to her husband but he was unable to render any aid as Buey was busy pulling a watch off the man's wrist.

Blake Barker became annoyed at the dramatic spectacle that was unfolding before his very eyes. "Okay, children, you've had enough fun. Playtime's over. Why don't you juvenile delinquents go sit in the corner, suck your thumbs, and take a nap? For shit's sake, leave these people alone."

The two miscreants stopped in their tracks and quickly wheeled around to face the bold gringo. "Gilberto, if I'm not mistaken, this *ratón* just implied that we're nothing more than children. I'm thinking that maybe *we* should give this pendejo something to suck on," Buey said.

"I'm shocked!" Gilberto replied with a grin. "Shocked and offended, I tell you!"

"This can't be! Even un *ratón blanco* wouldn't be stupid enough to say something like that," Buey replied to his partner in crime. "It's your call, amigo!"

"Un momento, Buey. This ratón is not blanco. He's amarillo! He must be *un Chino*. Por favor, señor, *¿es Chino o Japonés?*"

"Back off, dickheads," Blake said to the two hoodlums who now encircled him. "I'm not Chinese. I'm not Japanese, either. Right now, I'm just a pissed-off gringo with a burr up my ass. Now, if either of you boys know what's good for you, you'll shut the hell up right about now and get out of my face."

After the bloody mayhem at the tequila bar, the members of the Routa gang wanted no part of this pending altercation. They huddled together in one corner of the cell, as far as feasibly possible from the vampiro.

When Gilberto stuck his index finger into Blake's ear, a very short and very fast-burning fuse had suddenly been lit with a match. Blake made one final, futile attempt to avoid a violent altercation with the two thugs who were molesting him.

"Hey, officers!" Blake called out to the Federales who were standing outside the holding cell. "I don't want to get into a fight. Why don't you move these boys out of here and stick them in a separate jail cell?" His emphatic pleas apparently fell upon unsympathetic ears, as the Federales only laughed derisively.

As a consequence of the direct enthusiastic encouragement from the Federales, the resolve of the two thugs was bolstered. Gilberto and Buey methodically pressed forward with the intent to violently disassemble Blake Barker. Money appeared and bets were being placed among the Federales as to how long the gringo would last before he was cut to pieces.

One Federale officer whispered to another, younger colleague, "Go get our friends from the Azteca gang. They have an axe to grind with these Routa scum. Hurry up and do it now! Give them a few pig stickers and put them in the cage. It's time for us to say goodbye to the Routa gang once and for all!"

"Aren't you worried about the physical safety of the two tourists also locked up in there?" the younger Federale asked.

"They're gringos," the older officer answered. "I don't give a shit about them, and you shouldn't either!"

Blake Barker backed into the concrete corner of the cell that was opposite where the Routa gang and the tourists had huddled. "This is exactly why Mexico should build a barrier wall along the riverbanks of the Bravo," Blake said with a wry grin.

"Why?" Buey asked as he circled closer to the vampiro.

"There is something dangerous out there that might try to slip across the border," Blake answered.

"Dangerous?" Gilberto asked. "Like what?"

"Like me!" At least Blake Barker had tried to give his two assailants a fair warning.

As he waited for the inevitable assault, Blake must have appeared to be easy prey for the two hooligans, but nothing could have been further from the truth. By the time the two assailants finally rushed at Blake in tandem, it was too late; the vampiro finally gave into his simmering rage.

For Blake, it all turned out to be child's play. He thrust his extended fingers into Gilberto's anterior neck, right above the man's sternum. He ripped out the man's trachea and made a second pass to sever the carotid arteries before he pulled back and dropped the mortally wounded thug to the ground. Gilberto clenched his throat and made gurgling sounds as blood gushed forth from the gaping neck wound. This was the first time that Blake Barker had ever killed another person, and it felt—well, it felt *good*!

It was now Buey's turn to take the big dirt nap. Buey outweighed Blake Barker by at least fifty pounds, yet the vampiro lifted him up against the wall with only his left hand.

The Federales, quickly realizing that things weren't going as planned, apparently decided it was now time to open the jail door and send in the armed Azteca gang members to specifically kill everybody in the holding cell. After the jail cell was successfully swept clean of all forms of life, human or otherwise, the Federales would expect the Aztecas to simply dispose of the dead bodies in the desert, as if the lifeless corpses were little more than the *basura* one might find in an alleyway dumpster.

Buey reached into a pocket and managed to retrieve an old pearl-handled straight razor that he had kept hidden from the Federales when he was jailed. The big man tried to frantically break loose by kicking away at the vampiro, but it was all to no avail. Buey was finally able to flick open the blade of the deadly razor and slash away at Blake, but the big man only managed to unwittingly provide the vampiro with a new instrument of horror. "Gracias, señor. I'll take that if you don't mind," Blake said to Buey, quickly wresting the sharp blade from the hand of his adversary.

Blake Barker's face was soon doused with a pyroclastic blast of hot blood from Buey's headless torso. As if playing a freestyle game of hacky sack, Barker juggled the head of the big man as his body fell away to the floor. The vampiro deftly kicked the bloody head against the bars of the holding cell and boldly asked, "Next?"

Game on! Once the jail door had been opened by the Federales, the Azteca members poured into the cell to take down Blake Barker and the unarmed Routa crew. Blake moved effortlessly through the crowd of violent men who flew toward him. With the arrival of his new party guests, Blake slashed away and quickly traded one new dance partner for another with remarkable grace and speed.

Intimately dispatching one Azteca gang member after another, Blake made a quick flick of the wrist to sever an ear of one assailant and a quick gouge with his thumb to blind another. A slice across the face with the gushing of blood, a rupture of the abdomen with the spilling of intestines, and a hack at an upper extremity with the amputation of a hand surely made for a delightful scene that rivaled any choreographed Broadway musical.

Blake targeted the face and neck of his Azteca prey, regaling in the violent spurts of blood liberated from severed arteries. Decapitated heads rolled about the floor of the jail, and scores of fileted limbs swayed from butchered torsos by mere remnants of sinew.

While the Federales were mesmerized by the carnage, El Grifo realized that the door to the jail was still very much wide open. When Blake went into a feeding frenzy, El Grifo flicked his index finger toward the door, and the Routa crew sprang into action. A bull rush at the jail door ensured that the Federales were quickly overtaken by their Routa guests. Once liberated of their firearms, the Mexican federal police were rounded up and taken into the men's room, where they were summarily executed by the Routa banditos.

Sadly for the Routa gang members, one Federale escaped and made it to a patrol car to call for backup on the police radio. The officer also paid mandatory respect to the Calle Vampiro cartel by informing them that their affiliated Azteca gang had been exterminated to the very last man by a violent vampiro whom the police had incarcerated earlier. When asked the name of the ghoul who had perpetrated such a grisly deed, the officer informed the cartel that it was the handiwork of a vampiro named Blake Barker.

The two tourists who had been locked up in the holding cell successfully crawled on their hands and knees to escape the jail. They quickly disappeared into the darkness. Later they were able to inconspicuously slip across the border and make it back into Los Estados Unidos de America. With a solemn vow made to each other, the tourists were determined never to return to old Mexico under any circumstances.

When it was all over, Blake Barker stacked up the dead bodies of the Azteca gang members like cordwood, relishing the quivering flesh and eviscerated bodies. The holding cell was awash with blood. Blake enjoyed every bit of the carnage. This was the very first time that he had ever tasted human blood, and the sensation was exhilarating. It was nothing like the blood of beast or fowl, which was previously his only form of nutrition since he'd been infected by the contaminated egg. He delicately licked the blade of the straight razor clean and folded it back into the handle, having elected to keep the deadly weapon as a prized souvenir. Who could know? A straight razor might come in handy in the future.

The vampiro went straightaway to the restroom, where he had to step over the dead bodies of the Mexican federal police. He stripped off his bloody rags and bathed at the sink. Once he had cleaned up, he donned the green uniform of one of the dead officers. His haute couture ensemble was made complete with accessory handcuffs, a hat, sunglasses, and a truncheon.

Once outfitted in his new disguise, Blake Barker walked to the office of the Federale commandant, where he placed a long-distance phone call to his brother, Cletus, in Houston. As per usual, Cletus refused to answer the phone. Nonetheless, Blake left a message when the telephone recorder was electronically activated. "Answer the goddamned phone, Cletus! I hope you get this message. I can tell that you care for Lorena Pastore. I found out that she kidnapped Nathan and is hiding out in a little shithole of a town called Santa Sangre in Mexico. I'm on my way down there now to find my son. I promise you that I won't harm Lorena, but she's in danger nonetheless. The vampiro Romero Lopes is after her. If you give a shit about her, or if you give a shit about anything at all, you should just come down here." With that, Blake Barker hung up the telephone in disgust.

When El Grifo showed up in the hallway, he raised his hands in the air and slowly approached Blake Barker in the commandant's office. He said, "*Dios mío,* señor! You must be El Diablo himself. On behalf of the Routa gang, we would like to offer you our sincerest apologies regarding what happened to you. I thought you were only one of those horny *pinche* American *jotos*."

"Spare me your patronizing bullshit."

"On the other hand, Flaco was convinced that you were one of those bloodsucking Mayos in league with Mago."

"Well, if you boys would have only given me a chance to get a word in edgewise," Blake Barker said, "all of this shit could have been avoided!"

"You've done a great deed tonight," the captain of the Routa gang proclaimed, "because now you just completely wiped out most of the Azteca crew who worked for the Calle Vampiro cartel. These people were our mortal enemies. I need to get you out of here before more Federales show up. Rest assured, they will be here much sooner than later."

"How did you get the name El Grifo? Are you the mythical, magical griffin who's been reincarnated, or are you just a dope-smoking stoner?" Blake Barker asked.

"Come with me and I'll show you," the Routa captain answered.

Once El Grifo and Blake Barker left the police station, the other Routa gang members fled into the darkness before more federal police arrived to the crime scene. After walking several blocks, El Grifo led Blake Barker to a secured parking lot. "You asked me how I got the name El Grifo. Well, this is one of the reasons."

The Routa captain directed Blake toward the most beautiful automobile that the vampiro had ever seen. It was an extraordinarily rare 1966 Italian American hybrid Gran Turismo. Interestingly enough, the *corazón* of the car was a high-performance Corvette small-block 327-cid power plant that was mated to a five-speed tranny and a De Dion semi-independent transaxle rear suspension. The car was none other than an original Iso Grifo! The Iso was, without a doubt, Giorgetto Giugiaro's undisputed masterpiece of automotive design. When it was originally penned up on a drawing board back in 1963, the artist labored under Gruppo Bertone's flagship coachworks in Turin.

"You know," Blake Barker said as he looked at the vehicle with lust, "there are cars I've seen that I would not mind having sex *in*.

However, señor, I must tell you this is the first car I've ever seen that I want to have sex *with*."

After the two men climbed into the high-performance vehicle, they sped off into the night. El Grifo fired up a blunt and passed it over to Blake Barker. "Here you go, vampiro; this is the second reason the Routa gang gave me my special name, El Grifo. *Te gusta mota?*"

"No thanks. I need to stay on top of my game," Blake said as he waved off the generous offer of marijuana.

"As you wish, but this is some serious shit from Michoacán, ese. I'll only take you as far as the location of the fifty-kilometer-mark interior inspection station, but from there on out, you'll be on your own to get to Santa Sangre. I wish you the best of luck, señor."

"I certainly appreciate everything that you've done for me," Blake Barker said, "but I hope you'll understand when I tell you that I never want to see you or any of your henchmen ever again."

Just before the rumbling Gran Turismo reached the interior inspection station, El Grifo pulled to the side of the road and let Blake Barker jump out of the Iso Grifo while it was slowing but decidedly still moving. The vampiro didn't bother to look back when the Routa captain executed a fast U-turn in the middle of the highway and quickly headed back toward Ciudad Juárez. Blake had to be careful now, as word about the jail massacre had already reached the Calle Vampiro cartel. From this point forward, the cartel and the Federales would be on the hunt for this mysterious deadly gringo vampiro named Blake Barker.

"Cletus, I can't believe that you're resigning your position," the secretary said. "After all, you just got a promotion. Don't tell me that the Squat and Poot engineering firm finally got their meat hooks into you."

"No, it is nothing like that, Mrs. Barbera," Cletus Barker said. "There's a woman down in Mexico whom I care for deeply. I just learned that she got into a jam, and I'm going down there to try to help her out as best I can. I don't know how long I'll be gone or even if I'll ever be back."

"Are you absolutely certain that I can't change your mind?"

"Adios, Señora Barbera," Cletus said. "You're looking at a man who's going on a mission. You're looking at a man who's going on a road trip!"

7

EL TIEMPO

"This is it!" Colonel Placard said as he entered the conference room at the bioweapons division in San Antonio. "Our team has been officially activated, and we've been assigned our very first mission."

"Well, don't leave us flapping out here in the breeze," Ron Shiftless said. "What does Uncle 'Spam' want us to do?"

"The Mexican Federales have asked our government for help, and the DEA has volunteered our team to throw our collective hats into the ring," Placard explained. "Apparently a subsidiary gang of the Chihuahua cartel slaughtered all of the national police at the substation in Juárez. I saw the pictures. The scene was rather nasty, if I may say so. The group we're after is called the Routa gang."

"Is this a surveillance and infiltration mission or perhaps something a bit more, well, spicy?" Morales asked.

"Straight up, boys," Placard answered, "it's a search-and-destroy mission!"

"What happens if we get shit on south of the border?" Joe Cephas Smoot asked. "Is the State Department going to bail us out?"

"No such luck, son," Placard answered with a shrug. "If we get killed or captured by the cartel, the State Department will disavow knowledge of our very existence."

"Nice," the three men of Placard's team said in unison.

When Lorena and Nathan arrived at the outskirts of Santa Sangre, they came into the village largely unnoticed by the local *gente.* Lorena, along with her young ward, managed to settle quietly into the rural tranquility of El Rancho Feliz on the edge of town. Pepe Umbo was the current proprietor of the establishment. As events would soon to unfold would reveal, however, the elderly patriarch would sadly be the last jefe ever to serve in such a capacity at the ranch.

Lorena and Nathan's integration into a new life of domestic servitude was a rather seamless endeavor. Lorena Pastore quickly learned not only the layout of her new residence at the sprawling ranch but also about the complex turmoil that had roiled the hacienda in the past.

The house was a massive whitewashed adobe structure built in the territorial tradition. It was a U-shaped complex with a shaded portico that ran the complete circumference of the edifice. The courtyard was immense with several large deciduous trees and two massive twenty-five-foot-tall columnar saguaro cacti. With extended arms, the saguaro anthropomorphically appeared to beckon wayfarers to come inside for a neighborly visit and to take a refreshing sip of *agua fría* from a ceramic ladle that was tied by a leather lanyard to a wooden stake adjacent to the courtyard's hand-pump water well.

Extensive previous university-sponsored biological surveys of the flora and fauna of Mexico essentially confirmed that the natural latitudinal southern extent of the saguaro range begins to disappear in the Sonoran Desert geographically around the coastal fishing village of Guaymas. However, don't bother trying to explain any of that to the people who lived at Rancho Feliz, which was located much farther south in Estado de Jalisco. After all, Jalisco is deeply wedged within the Tropic of Cancer. As a case in point, if one were to jump into a boat and motor westward across the Pacific, the next body of land that one would encounter would be the Big Island of Hawaii, of all places. That being said, a desert cactus like the saguaro should theoretically not be able to thrive in such a humid and wet environment.

Although the two giant saguaros growing in the hacienda courtyard were originally transplanted ages ago to their current ostentatious and prominent location on the spread, El Rancho Feliz could proudly boast that no other saguaro cacti had ever been identified to be growing anywhere south of that particular isolated and remote area in Mexico.

Much farther north in the Sonoran Desert, it is generally believed that most saguaros will not grow any arms until the cacti are about sixty to eighty years old. The arms normally protrude horizontally from the vertical central column of the prickly plant until the colossal cacti are at quite mature. Therefore, the saguaro cacti in question found at El Rancho Feliz must have indeed been ancient specimens.

Before the current proprietor of the ranch, Pepe Umbo, was even born, his grandfather immigrated to Mexico in 1864. In an effort to avoid the US Civil War, which was raging north of the Rio Bravo at the time, Pepe's grandfather Kurt von Humboldt, who was originally from Germany, cast his aspirations upon the ostensibly safer political climes of old Mexico. With a burning desire to start a new life in the Western Hemisphere, Kurt originally left Europe on a twin-mast auxiliary steam-powered sailing ship to stake a claim in the potentially lucrative wilderness of North America. Kurt elected to start his new life in a territory that was originally wrested away from the local native tribes by the Spanish conquistadors over 350 years before Kurt's arrival as a new European settler.

A man of letters who was politically astute, Kurt was soon appointed to be a regional emissary for Mexico's flaccid ruler known as Maximillian. This designated puppet emperor of Mexico, assigned to be nothing more than a dull, blunt tool in a figurehead-only position, served at the bidding and the whim of his much more powerful French puppet masters.

Inevitably, as the French government became literally exhausted by financing a largely pointless military intervention in Latin America, the Mexican liberal opposition to the presence of Maximillian, a perceived European interloper, became considerably stronger over time. Napoleon III and his allies were finally cast out of Mexico in 1875, but not before Kurt von Humboldt had been granted a large estate for his political gamesmanship.

Lacking true hierarchical convictions about any man's caste or particular lot in life except for his own, Kurt von Humboldt was far from being a stringent ideologue about such matters. If truth be told, Kurt was little more than a self-serving opportunist who would wear the hat and wave the banner of whatever "Juanito-come-lately" political movement would best serve his personal and financial interests.

Despite being an outsider, Kurt von Humboldt was rather smitten by the beauty of the tropical but largely unpopulated landscape. Maestro von Humboldt had come to embrace the warmth of the weather and local culture. Often compelled to seek refuge and solace among mestizo women, Von Humboldt eventually took one as a bride to start a new family.

Over time the family name was gentrified, and the surname devolved into simply "Umbo." In the domain of Pepe's grandfather, the founding patriarch was reverently referred to as "El Umbo Rojo," in recognition of his prominence and larger-than-life image. The redheaded German immigrant became a successful rancher and offered extensive gainful employment to the relatively impoverished indigenous people of the area. By all accounts, Kurt and his lovely wife, Paloma, made a most happy couple and spawned a total of three children including a son, Rocio, and his two sisters.

The family became an integral part of the Santa Sangre village, and they were recognized as benevolent employers and landowners, decidedly unlike many of the other surrounding ranches where barons would treat the peasant population little better than slaves. During the following years of the Mexican Revolution, Paloma became a stalwart community leader in her own right. She was a gracious and kind woman who helped to bring peace, safety, and prosperity to her native people in the region.

Before Pepe was born, two small saguaros were transplanted by his father, Rocio, to the courtyard on his wedding day to symbolize the commitment to the longevity of his marriage. At that time, the house was modest in size, but it would expand room by room over the next fifty years as Rocio became more prosperous. Rocio took Thelma, a local girl, as his bride, and they had one child. Thelma was left barren after almost dying during labor and was never able to conceive again. Their son, Jose, who became known as Pepe, had a wonderful childhood surrounded by his grandparents and extended family members. Over time, the house expanded into its familiar U-shape to accommodate the three generations.

Rancho Feliz, as the name implies, was a place of contentment as Pepe fondly recalled, but it's implicit in the second physical law of thermodynamics that entropy and constant change (usually *not* for the better) is inevitable. This immutable law of the universe also applied to the multigenerational ancestral enterprise, which had undergone considerable changes with the advent of the early twentieth century.

It was 1920 when Pepe's parents passed. As one of the last of the aristocratic landowning families in Jalisco, they successfully managed a ranch that encompassed a few hundred square kilometers inland. As Pepe grew older and developed a deeper appreciation for contemporary Mexican politics, the family ranch actually became for him a source of political irritation and embarrassment. Over time, his family had kept most of their holdings even as the land and assets around them were nationalized and redistributed among the peasant population.

As it often occurs, the younger generation takes on a contrarian view to their parents' way of life. Perhaps it should not have been surprising that Pepe conjured opposing political viewpoints to the ones that his parents had held. Pepe rejected the elitist landowner social hierarchy in favor of what he simply believed to be was a morally superior course of action embodied by the agrarian movement with its objective to reallocate land and other valuable tangible assets. After all, the misguided ideology of the left has *always* embraced wealth redistribution, as if that would ever change anything in the world we live in. Unbeknownst to Pepe at that time, socialism and communism would ultimately fail *every single time* that these flawed economic constructs would ever be employed as part of a sanctimonious, quasi-religious social experiment.

Be that as it may, Pepe became wrapped up in the politics of the Zapatistas and joined the Mexican Revolution in 1910 at the tender age of twenty-four. By the time that Pepe became a political firebrand, it had been over five years since he had seen his parents. When Pepe fled south and eventually returned to Estado de Jalisco to escape General "Black Jack" Pershing and his angry *soldados americanos,* both of his parents had become weakened from the ravages of tuberculosis. Pepe and a few of his compadres were involved in the March 8, 1916, Camp Furlong raid in Columbus, New Mexico. This was the first foreign invasion of US soil since the War of 1812, and General Pershing was bound and determined to annihilate the Mexican leader known as General Francisco "Pancho" Villa and his Division del Norte.

For Pepe, a new social order and modernity were as eminent as the arrival of General Pershing's caravan of black Model T Fords brimming with US soldiers rolling across the border and into his beloved sovereign nation of Mexico. Perhaps if there was only one thing that the titular head of the bloody Mexican Revolution, Pancho Villa, had failed to learn prior to the Battle of Camp Furlong, it was that it was *never* a good idea to piss off los americanos!

Pepe's last words to his mother before he took exile in the rocky hills of the wilderness during the revolution expressed his contempt and disdain for the old traditions. He was furious when he learned that his mother had performed the Maya *huevo limpia* cleansing ceremony with a bright yellow chicken egg that had been passed over his body as he slept during the last night that he ever saw his parents alive. When Pepe awoke in the morning, he could smell the *albahaca* from the clay bowl and the charcoal and ash at his feet. He discovered that an egg had been placed beneath his bed to draw out the vicious evil that was apparently dwelling within his mother Thelma's only child.

Pepe charged into the kitchen and demanded an explanation from his mother. "Don't ever try this witchcraft on me ever again! I can hear you and Father coughing up wads of blood all night long. If the huevo limpia ceremony can't cure you and Father from the galloping consumption that's now killing you, then you shouldn't still be performing these ridiculous superstitious ceremonies! You're nothing but a fool!"

While his mother, Thelma, began to cry, Pepe went into a rant about the ridiculous beliefs of the old world. After all, if his parents were allegedly Christians, then superstitious ceremonies such as the huevo limpia ritual should have had no place at Rancho Feliz. When aroused from his slumber by the shouting he heard coming from the kitchen, Rocio intervened by gently removing the egg from Pepe's hand.

In an effort to placate his concerned wife, Rocio cracked the egg into a glass of water. Thelma took one look at the egg and immediately became hysterical! Sadly, the white of the fresh egg had assumed a cloudy gray color, and the yolk was floating on top of the water with a distinct bloody red spot that was about three millimeters in diameter.

"Mijo," she cried, "you are under the influence of El Diablo! The cleansing ceremony was not complete. Please let me finish what I've started." Tragically, Pepe's very last encounter with his ailing parents was the defiant act of an arrogant young man. He grabbed the glass and, in a single gulp, consumed its entire contents. That was the very *last* day that he saw his parents alive, and it was also the very *first* day that Pepe became infected with an evil force that his mother so dreaded.

Miguel Pastore and John Stewart had absolutely no difficulty in driving the automobile that had been stolen from Dr. Blanks across the border into Mexico. It was apparent that the border officials didn't care, weren't paying attention, or perhaps both. When the two men pulled into a gas station in the heart of Durango on Mexico's Highway 40, Miguel was absolutely shocked when he realized that the car fueling up at the pump directly in front of him belonged to his friend and former attending physician, Dr. Cloud.

"It would seem to me that everything in the universe is connected somehow," Miguel said with a broad grim as he approached his old friend.

"What in hell are you doing here?" Dr. Cloud asked, apparently less than pleased to be reacquainted with the vampire. Cloud was also clearly reluctant to meet Miguel's yet to be identified new colleague John Stewart. "Why aren't you at the CDC? I was informed by Dr. Blanks that his team up in Atlanta was working diligently on a new specific vaccine for your particular problem."

"Sadly, that's ancient history now. The vaccine study turned out to be a bust," John Stewart interjected. "Miguel and I 'borrowed' a car and booked it down here to Mexico. Truth be told, we're on the lam from Colonel Placard's bioweapons laboratory in San Antonio."

"Who in hell are you?" Cloud asked as he scrutinized John Stewart.

"I'm John Stewart. By the way, who in hell are you? I've just met you for the first time, and I can already discern that you're one rude son of a bitch, aren't you?"

"John, I would like to introduce to you an old friend named Dr. Cloud," Miguel answered in a soothing tone to try to defuse what was turning out to be a surprisingly tense situation right off the bat. "Cloud and my sister, Lorena, used to be, well, an 'item,' I'd have to say."

"Well, well, well! The world seems to be a very small place after all," John Stewart said.

Why in hell did you guys come down here?" Cloud asked. "Are you boys trying to find Lorena? Tell me the truth right here and right now: is Lorena going to be in any danger from either of you?"

"I had overwhelming homicidal ideations toward my sister at one time," Miguel admitted, "but I certainly don't feel that way anymore. I must be developing some kind of symbiotic relationship with this virus that has infected me. I no longer feel the rage that I once had."

"A small comfort, no doubt," Dr. Cloud said.

"I've never killed anybody, nor have I ever attacked anybody as a prey item either. I'm totally able to sustain myself on animal blood and raw animal organ tissue," Miguel said. "It's not perfect, but I'm just trying to make the best of a bad situation."

"Swell." The doctor turned to carefully scrutinize Miguel's traveling companion from head to toe. "What's in it for you, paleface?"

"I'm headed south for a long-overdue scheduled appointment to get a truckload of hugs and kisses, Tonto!" Stewart responded, somewhat bemused at the invective that Dr. Cloud had hurled in his direction. "You might try it out sometime, as it just might improve what would appear to be the rather foul disposition that's troubling you. Do you always go out of your way to insult complete strangers?"

"When necessary," Cloud answered.

"Straight up, red man," Stewart said, "that's a good way to get a boot swiftly shoved up your ass."

"You don't fool me. I know what you're up to," Cloud responded. "You're *way* out of your league, amigo. Just to show you that I'm looking out for your best interests, you should know that I met a toothless blue-haired hag at a service station back in El Paso. A woman like that should be right up your alley. Here, let me draw you a map so you can get back there pronto."

"You got it all wrong," Stewart said. "My only suggestion to you is that *you* should consider looking for love north of the border, Cochise—in fact, *far* north of the border, right about now ..."

Dr. Cloud obviously realized that John Stewart was a new suitor who had assuredly wandered across the Bravo to seek the affection of Lorena Pastore. At that juncture, Cloud was certainly in no mood for potential competition over the object of his romantic desires, especially if that competition would be coming from some bumpkin Anglo interloper.

"Are you the baggage boy whom Miguel brought along to tote the luggage?" Cloud asked. "When I get back to New Mexico, I'm planning on holding a seminar on Indian culture. I'll be personally offering a class called Wagon Burning 101. I'll also present a popular lecture called 'Everything You Wanted to Know about Scalping but Were Afraid to Ask; Is It Front to Back or Back to Front?' Get it? I would be honored if you'd volunteer to be a living model for this educational series."

"You need to back off right about now, Geronimo! Lorena is anxious to meet me. Deal with it, you savage!" John Stewart said with the overt intention of poking Dr. Cloud in his left eye with a sharp verbal saber directly from the archives of Custer's Seventh Cavalry.

"Oh, is that so? Lorena is anxious to meet you now, is she?" Cloud asked.

"Yes, indeed," Stewart answered. "She just doesn't know it yet!"

"Yeah, just as I thought. You make me laugh, white man!" Cloud crowed.

"Hold the fort out here, Dr. Cloud," Miguel said in an effort to quell the burgeoning brouhaha between his two friends. "I'm taking John inside the station to grab a cold beverage for him. Can I get you anything?"

"No, I'm okay. I'm in no mood for a snack," Cloud said. "While you're in there however, grab me a crowbar or any other heavy blunt instrument that you might find that I could readily use as a lethal weapon. I'm having overwhelming homicidal ideations myself right about now, come to think of it ..."

"Don't be that way," Miguel said with a nervous chuckle. "We should team up together, and the three of us should take Santa Sangre by force to find Lorena once and for all. We'll be like the Three Musketeers!"

"Swell," Dr. Cloud said yet again as he clandestinely eyed the tires of the car driven by Miguel Pastore and John Stewart.

When John Stewart and Miguel made their exit from the snack bar in the service station, they were somewhat surprised to see that Dr. Cloud had already vacated the area. "I guess he didn't want to hang around and wait for us," Miguel said. "We should be on our way. We still have a long drive ahead of us before we get to Estado de Jalisco."

After a few miles down the road, the chariot that John Stewart had originally stolen from Dr. Blanks simultaneously developed flats on both the front and rear tires on the right side of the car. "What's this?" Miguel asked. "You must have run over something. How could we otherwise drop two tires on the same side of the car at the same damned time?"

Once the car had been pulled over to the side of the road, Stewart jumped out of the vehicle to see what was awry, but he found no evidence of a nail or other puncture mark that could have accounted for two relatively new tires suddenly going flat. He unscrewed the caps from the valve stems and found that a small pebble had been put inside each of the caps to place direct pressure on the two valve stems to let air out of the tires after only a short time. Stewart handed the evidence to Miguel Pastore and said, "I would surmise that this Dr. Cloud fellow had concerns about what kind of man you really are. It would seem to me that he didn't want you to catch up with your sister after all."

"Don't be an idiot," Miguel said. "Look, I gave Dr. Cloud an honest update of my current circumstances, and I have no doubt that he believed me. That being the case, I would surmise that this Dr. Cloud fellow had concerns about what kind of man *you* really are. It would seem to me that he didn't want *you* to catch up with Lorena."

"Think so?" Stewart asked with feigned incredulity and a boyish façade of righteous indignation.

"*Chistoso!* To be honest, I don't blame him one bit!" Miguel said. "I don't know why I like you, John."

"Well, you better like me," John Stewart said with a wink. "After all, I'm your future brother-in-law! I've given this a lot of thought, and I've decided that I want to be a stay-at-home husband. I could watch old movies on the television and spend my days working on my golf swing. I've got a wicked slice that I just haven't been able to hammer out at the driving range. I have an excellent putter, though. I have no doubt that Lorena will *love* my putter, also! When it's all said and done, I'm sure that Lorena wouldn't mind being the breadwinner for the family so I can hang out in my boxer shorts all day long and eat doughnuts."

"¡Señor Stewart, eres un serpiente de pantalón! This is *exactly* why I don't want my sister to date a gringo like you."

"Thanks, Miguel," John Stewart said with a wry smile. "I hope I resemble that remark!"

In 1920, Pepe returned to Rancho Feliz to bury his parents next to his grandparents and aunts. When Pepe finally returned home, he was a different kind of man. During the revolution he became a cold-blooded, ruthless killer. He was a particularly skilled soldier, and he had earned a reputation for his speed, endurance, strength, and tactical savvy. He was part of a guerrilla band known for nocturnal ambush raids and counterinsurgence operations. This was the favored tactic of the famous revolutionary General Pancho Villa. It just so happened that guerrilla raids were also the most effective methodology that suited the needs of a hungry, angry vampiro.

Pepe was wounded time and again, only to quickly return to battle within a few days of his injuries possessing even more vigor and rage. His legend only grew after riding with the famed Los Dorados unit.

Pancho Villa had a peculiar habit of consuming whatever his men were preparing for themselves, often taking food directly from a shared plate. When Pancho dined, Pepe was usually at his side, and the vampiro *always* ate first. Although Pepe had a difficult time eating meals prepared by Villa's chefs because the food gave him nausea and heartburn, Pancho nonetheless relied on Pepe's uncanny ability to recover from poisons that may have been surreptitiously added to the food intended for the general. As Pancho grew fond of Pepe, he granted the young vampiro many indulgences.

Thus, as the revolution afforded Pepe the luxuriant opportunity to exploit his unique biological attributes, the violent conflict also readily provided Pepe with a direct outlet for his own rage and frustration over not only his family's *malinchismo* gravitational pull toward archaic ideology but also in alignment with what historians now refer to as the "conservative" Mexican political movement.

Interestingly, Pepe was left-handed. His close yet mysterious relationship with Pancho Villa was regaled in Mexican lore and also in a popular folk song that erroneously implied that "Lefty" was a traitor who willingly sold out the general to the Federales. How else could Pancho have succumbed to an ambush killing? If the truth be told, this was a total fabrication and bastardization of actual events. Historical documents suggest that after the death of Venustiano Carranza in 1920, Pancho actually "retired" to a place called Parral.

Pepe joined Pancho and many of the Dorados briefly in what could now only be described as a military internment camp. After a few weeks, Pepe had grown weary of the government's hospitality and had slipped away to El Rancho Feliz in Santa Sangre (not to the state of Ohio north of the Bravo, as the folk tune proclaims). When Pancho Villa was finally assassinated a few years later, the shocking news was eventually relayed by way of a telegraph communiqué that was sent directly to Pepe from Villa's widow, Luz.

The Umbo family holdings were much smaller after the revolution. Long before the arrival of Lorena and Nathan to Rancho Feliz, Pepe had been running only a few hundred head of cattle to satisfy his personal needs *para sangre caliente* and also to pay his rancheros and servants. Pepe also provided the local orphanage and church with occasional beef, surplus corn, beans, tomatoes, chilies, and cotton. If anybody in Jalisco was in need, Pepe was always there to help such a person through hard times by offering work on the ranch in exchange for food and shelter. For Lorena and young Nathan, it would be no different ...

When Pepe finally returned home to his family hacienda after the war, an apparent new benevolence filled his heart and soul. Who could know the reason? At times it appears that warfare can permanently harden and damage a man's spirit. Perhaps at other times, it has the unexpected contrary outcome. In any event, Pepe divided up the family land and gifted most of it to a few of the Dorados and other family friends in the village of Santa Sangre. The old warrior also voluntarily recognized the legitimacy of the natives' historical rights to the land that was illegitimately appropriated by the French emperor Napoleon III during the Maximilian regime. He was surrounded by many local villagers and benefactors who fiercely protected him just as he protected them. Although Pepe could not precisely recall exactly when the nickname "El Tiempo" was bestowed upon him by the villagers of Santa Sangre, it was nonetheless a nickname that he surely relished, as best as Lorena could tell.

Over time, El Tiempo Umbo began to investigate his very own peculiar medical affliction. Over the last century, as he accumulated a vast amount of knowledge about human vampirism, he established a network of curanderas, shamen, and brujas to gather information and monitor the periodic outbreaks of this disease process in Mexico and also in the Southwest along the Rio Grande Valley of New Mexico. Lorena's mother, Angelica, was only one curandera among this large group of faith and folk healers who collaborated with El Tiempo over the years.

Angelica had instructed Lorena long ago in the art of healing in the Mexican tradition, which was an admixture of ancient Spanish and native tribal lore. With this being the case, Lorena Pastore was no stranger to Pepe. She was previously introduced to El Tiempo by her mother when Lorena turned fifteen years of age at her *quinceañera*, just as Angelica was introduced to El Tiempo when she turned age fifteen at her own quinceañera by Lorena's grandmother. By these respectful customs, and by reverential adherence to oral traditions, knowledge of the vampiro was generationally passed among the curandera, shaman, and bruja.

Although Cletus Barker had already gassed up his car at a fuel station in the heart of Durango off Mexican Highway 40, he was compelled to open up a map to try to determine how much longer it would take him to reach the small village of Santa Sangre in Estado de Jalisco before he pulled away from the fuel pump. Time was fleeting, and it was imperative that he find Lorena Pastore and his nephew, Nathan, before the evil Romero Lopes could stumble upon their whereabouts. After folding the map and neatly placing it back into his glove box, Cletus inadvertently noticed that a very peculiar man with yellow skin was gassing up a microbus that was parked adjacent to the fuel pump directly in front of his vehicle.

When the odd-appearing individual failed to stifle a yawn, Cletus could not help but recognize the large incisors that the man displayed. Cletus immediately realized that the queer-looking individual had the very same malevolent features that characterized Blake when Cletus had last seen his younger brother in Mesilla, New Mexico. There was no mistake about it: Cletus was looking directly at a vampiro! What to do?

It is most assuredly illegal for tourists to take weapons across the border into Mexico. If one is caught doing so, a stiff monetary fine and mandatory jail time is rendered as punishment. Nonetheless, Cletus was clever enough to sneak a pistol across the border that was hidden underneath the jack stand within the trunk of his car.

Cletus made a discreet exit from the front seat of his vehicle and retreated to the trunk, where he quickly recovered his .357 Magnum. He slowly lowered the lid of the trunk in an effort to avoid drawing any unnecessary attention, but it was already too late. The vampiro was now standing directly at the rear fender of his car and smiling at him with a toothsome grin.

"Well, hello there, Cletus Barker," the vampiro said. "Although we've never been formally introduced, I certainly know who you are already! As a matter of fact, I've had unbridled lust for you for quite some time now. I've always wondered what it would be like to taste your blood if ever I had the opportunity to rip your throat out. Before I do, I was wondering if you would be so kind as to tell me what might have become of the of the obsidian knife that was found among the burned-out rubble of my ranch house in Mesilla?"

"Romero Lopes, I presume?" Cletus politely asked as he pulled back the hammer on the large-caliber weapon.

"At your service," Lopes replied. "I hope you won't mind me draining you right now. After all, we're standing here at a filling station, so I might as well fill up on you at the same time as I'm filling my car. I promise you, if you don't struggle, I'll make it easy on you. In fact, you might very well find the experience to be most pleasurable. Certainly, others have. Now, where in hell is my goddamned obsidian knife? Give it to me now."

"I'll give it to you!" Cletus answered. As Romero Lopes lunged at Cletus, the frightened man buried the barrel of his revolver into the epigastric region of the vampiro's abdomen. Cletus pulled the trigger until the gun cylinder was exhausted. Although still very much alive, Romero Lopes was now writhing about on the ground, verbalizing hostile invectives in Spanish while uttering guttural moans of excruciating pain.

Cletus realized that he had a singular golden opportunity to finish off the vicious parasite once and for all. All he had to do was to reload his pistol and discharge a single round into the brain of the bloodsucking tick, but alas, it was not to be.

Unbeknownst to Cletus Barker, the concubine and toady of Romero Lopes, El Sapo, was blissfully nestled in the back of the microbus taking a nap after his love master had tucked him under a soft blue blankie for the arduous journey south from Villa Ahumada to Santa Sangre. Awakened by the unmistakable sound of gunfire, the loyal and betrothed assistant to Romero Lopes jumped out of the van and ran toward the back of the car owned by Cletus to investigate what was happening.

Upon seeing Romero Lopes bleeding on the asphalt, the inexperienced younger vampiro was frozen in his tracks with indecision. He didn't know whether the best course of action would be to immediately attend to his fallen master or to attack and annihilate the still armed and looming mysterious assailant who had apparently shot his lover without any obvious provocation.

This brief moment of hesitation was all the time that Cletus Barker needed. He took the butt end of his pistol and cracked it against the temple of his new adversary. When El Sapo fell to his knees, Cletus Barker pulled the fuel nozzle out from the filler neck of his vehicle and doused both the ghouls with a generous splash of gasoline before igniting them with a lit match. As Romero Lopes and El Sapo emitted high-pitched screams of agony, Cletus pulled out a large Churchill cigar from his front shirt pocket and cautiously approached El Sapo, who was now crawling on his hands and knees to lovingly spoon his master within the confines of one big vampiro bonfire.

"Stay still, goddamn you! I'm trying to light up my stogie, and I'm fresh out of matches. It looks like I used my last one to start this campfire!"

After the cigar was alit from the petroleum inferno, which instantaneously immolated Romero Lopes and his loyal consort, Cletus elected to vacate the premises before the Federales and local police could arrive to ask a bevy of time-consuming and annoying questions.

A sturdy cowgirl called Ranchera escorted Lorena and Nathan to an inner chamber that served as a study located deep within the confines of the hacienda. The room, filled with books from floor to ceiling, was dimly lit by a handful of candles. Pepe was waiting for his guests to arrive as he eagerly anticipated hosting a stimulating formal conversation with them.

Although the locals reverently referred to Pepe Umbo as El Tiempo, Lorena addressed him as "Tio." Nathan was young, but nonetheless he was able to discern that there was something very different about this ancient individual whom Tia Lorena treated with such deference. Pepe Umbo looked to be very old, much like a pile of old leaves emanating the distinct odor of organic decay. Nonetheless, the ancient one moved with alacrity and purpose.

"You have become a beautiful young woman since I saw you last. I see that you've also brought your son," Pepe said.

"No, Tio," Lorena replied, "this is Nathan Barker. He is part of the reason that I've come to see you." Lorena turned to her young ward and said, "Nathan, go take a look at the collection of salt dishes that Tio Pepe has on the bookshelf."

"You may take them out of the display case as long as you are careful and put them back when you're finished looking at them, mijo" the old vampiro instructed the child.

Once Nathan moved out of earshot, Lorena quietly continued. “His father is actually involved in this most recent cycle that you had previously warned the multitude of healers north of El Paso about. I must say, this has been a big surprise to the community of curanderas with which I’m now affiliated. The last cycle was in 1979. We weren’t expecting another outbreak until the millennium, as oral tradition led us to believe that these dangerous cycles only occur at twenty-year intervals or so.”

“Well, as the gringos say, one tree does not a forest make. As for me, I’m not sure what to think of this most current cycle that appeared so prematurely. I’ve honestly never witnessed a cycle become active after only a seven-year hiatus. Very strange indeed,” the old vampiro declared. “Maybe this will be a self-limited event, and perhaps the scheduled outbreaks the ancients like me are so accustomed to seeing will eventually revert to their customary twenty-year cycles. Maybe, just maybe however, Mother Earth is becoming angry and is growing weary of the abuse she is subjected to at the hands of human beings. I just don’t know. In any event, I’ve never been a particularly good weatherman. Despite my advanced age and the alleged wisdom that is supposed to naturally accompany my years of life, I still have a hard time even now of predicting when a violent storm is just over the horizon.”

“Years ago, my mother instructed me that if I ever saw a resurgence of this infection, I should alert you in person as soon as possible,” Lorena explained. “I brought Nathan with me in an effort to protect him from any potential harm from his father and also from an evil neighbor. They have both become infected. I’ve cared for Nathan since he was an infant. He recently lost his mother to a vicious vampiro attack by this neighbor named Lopes, whom I’ve just told you about. He’s a cruel and vicious animal. Nathan is unaware of the danger he presents.”

“You and Nathan should both be quite safe here at El Rancho Feliz.”

“Romero Lopes is also searching for his obsidian blade I stole from him. I’m now in possession of actually two of these weapons. Can you imagine such a thing? The other blade belonged to Blake

Barker. I stole that knife from him after he had eaten un huevo limpia and became infected," Lorena said, reaching into her handbag and extracting both of the razor-sharp implements.

"Oh no!" Tio Pepe said with a laugh. "I must tell you, that's exactly how I became infected when I was once a petulant and immature young soldado, ready to fight in the Mexican Revolution. You see, man is destined to repeat the sins of the past if man does not know history, *verdad*? Well, in any event, I know a thing or two about history. I also know a thing or two about these knives. Señorita Pastore, por favor," Pepe said, reaching out his hand.

"This first obsidian knife in my possession is the one that belonged to the evil vampiro Romero Lopes." Lorena explained.

Tio Pepe carefully examined the blade for many minutes before he finally spoke. "I've never seen obsidian as black as a tiger's eye. It has certainly been fashioned in the classic ancient design originally adopted by the Maya. However, I've never seen obsidian this opaque before. I'm considering the possibility that this may be Sangre de Indio, but as I hold it up to a bright light, I don't detect the prism effect that I would otherwise expect. It must be a very powerful tool indeed," Tio Pepe said. "I have no idea if a blade crafted from this peculiar type of obsidian could be harmful to un vampiro, as up until now I've had no knowledge of its very existence."

"It clearly is a dangerous weapon to un vampiro!" Lorena said. "After all, I stabbed Romero Lopes in the leg with this very knife, and I know for a fact that he still walks with a limp!"

8

EL ESTRAGO

As he gently handed the blade back to Lorena, Tio Pepe furrowed his brow and said, "This knife is most fascinating to me. If that is indeed the case, you should guard this artifact with your life. Whether this is merely Sangre de Indio covered with a thick layer of soot or oxidation, or whether it is perhaps some other type of obsidian that I have never seen before, anything that can cause a permanent injury to a vampiro is worth its weight in gold."

"Tell me about obsidian and how it might permanently injure or kill a vampiro."

"Un momento," Tio Pepe replied. "Before I do, I would like to examine the obsidian blade that you took from Nathan's father."

Lorena explained the story as best she understood it, telling Pepe the history of the obsidian knife that had previously been in the possession of Blake Barker. As she handed the blade to Tio Pepe, she said, "This is something Mr. Barker found while hunting in the Portrillos in New Mexico. He's looking for us right now, and I know damned well that he's already figured out that I've stolen his obsidian knife."

"Let me take a look. It may have some significance to what you're up against."

Tio Pepe took the blade, wiped it clean with his handkerchief, and placed it near a candle for closer inspection. As he moved close to the light, Lorena gasped in shock at the old vampiro's putrefied appearance. He was a pale aggregation of open oozing skin wounds and excoriated scaly red plaques. "Don't be afraid, mija." He chuckled. "I was born in 1886, and my age is catching up to me. I turned one hundred years old this past February. Did you know it's estimated that only one in ten thousand people live to be one hundred years old? I'm not certain if my longevity is actually a blessing or a curse, however."

Lorena composed herself and asked, "Tio, what can you tell me about the history of obsidian?"

"The Aztecs and Mayas enjoyed wealth and prosperity thanks to obsidian," the old vampire explained. "It provided a basis for trade, and the material ended up all over the Americas for use in tools. It was the mineral of choice for arrowheads and knives because of the relative ease in crafting this volcanic glass into a sharp edge. To this day, obsidian remains one of the sharpest materials man has ever discovered. In Mesoamerica, obsidian was so valuable that it was considered by the Mayas to be a gift from their pagan gods."

Tio held the shard of volcanic glass up to the light and was actually able to peer through the edge of the bladed weapon. "Lorena, this obsidian is of a very specific type. Except for perhaps the obsidian blade that you utilized to injure Romero Lopes, there have been only two kinds of obsidian that are known to cause harm to los vampiros, at least up until now."

"Well, what is this type that you are now holding?" Lorena asked.

"This one comes from San Isidro Mazatepec," Pepe replied. "When I was growing up, my mother, who was a curandera, told me of a sacred place that was mined by a mysterious lost culture. Obsidian from Guadalajara, here in Jalisco, is easily exploited from open pits. However, this obsidian mine of which I have just spoken is quite unique. To this very day, *mineros* avoid the caves in which this type of obsidian is hidden because it is very difficult and dangerous to enter such places."

"Danger from cave-ins?" Lorena asked.

"No, mija," Tio Pepe replied. "The cave of this type is specifically avoided by the locals because it is full of the murciélago vampiro. No, I'm not referring to creatures like me; I'm talking about real bloodsucking flying vampire bats! In my humble opinion, these creatures are little more than flying rats that drink blood and carry rabies. Believe it or not, they scare the shit out of me! The blade in my hand is a rare piece of obsidian known throughout South America as vampire glass! Keep it close and safe; it's definitely valued and feared by los vampiros. They know the harm that it can cause, and it's the weapon of choice that can give one vampiro the edge over another of its kind during a fight to the death."

"I don't understand, Tio," Lorena interrupted. "Are fights between los vampiros a common occurrence?"

"All too common, mija," Tio Pepe replied. "You see, it's actually quite difficult for one vampiro to be in the presence of another. The odor of one vampiro is clearly offensive to another vampiro. It puts us in a fighting mood!"

"It sounds like that would be quite a deterrent to reproductive activity," Lorena said half-jokingly.

"Whether male or female, a human vampiro or vampira is barren. When a vampiro finally dies, his or her bloodline also dies."

"I'm sorry."

"No, mija, that is indeed a good thing," Pepe replied. "Trust me."

"What else can you tell me, Tio?"

"The other, more common type of obsidian that is known to be effective against los vampiros is called Sangre de Indio. Others may refer to it by its more common name, rainbow obsidian. This black-tinged glass comes from the Yucatán area of Mexico," Pepe explained. "If you look through this type of obsidian with a bright light, you'll see it has bands of different colors. When I examined the mysterious piece of obsidian that you used to injure Romero Lopes, I failed to detect this characteristic prism effect. In any event, Sangre de Indio was indeed the preferred material for the Maya sacrificial knives. It was by pure chance that the Mayas discovered that these two types of obsidian had power over the vampiro and caused injury that was difficult, or even impossible, to heal."

"How could that be?"

"Well, I'm not completely certain, but I've heard a theory that the lack of crystalline structure in obsidian and the high iron content of both the vampire glass and Sangre de Indio may be responsible for causing nonhealing open wounds and nasty infections in los vampiros. An arrow or spear composed of these two types of obsidian reportedly cause deep and irreparable damage to un vampiro."

"I believe that this is the case. I've seen it with my own eyes!" Lorena said.

"Mija, are you familiar with a nasty little spider called the brown recluse? It has also been referred to as the fiddleback spider?" " Tio Pepe asked.

"Of course."

"Well, there you have it," Tio elaborated. "If an unfortunate individual is bit by this tiny brown spider, the poison will continue to spread throughout the adjacent tissues around the entry site until the flesh literally rots away. The deadly poison from a brown recluse spider bite can actually disintegrate the flesh all the way down to the bone! It's terrifying to witness. It would seem that this is no different from the type of injury that obsidian can apparently render upon un vampiro."

"Thank you, Tio," Lorena said. "That's certainly valuable information."

"Moctezuma II was killed an obsidian implement," Tio Pepe continued. "Did you know that his death is the primary source of the myth that a wooden stake to the heart can kill un vampiro?"

"I assume vampiros have been referred to as various different mythical creatures in the past, including werewolves, zombies, and ghouls!" Lorena speculated.

"You have no idea." Tio Pepe laughed out loud. "I remember a time when somebody thought I was a chupacabra!"

At that point, Nathan wandered over to interrupt the conversation. "What's so funny, Tio? Tell me the joke!" Nathan demanded. Lorena and Tio began to laugh, but Nathan's next question was met with awkward silence from the two adults. "Tio, why does your skin look so ugly?"

"You are a very curious young man," Pepe finally replied. "Do you know what a *chiste* is? A chiste is a funny joke. You just asked me what the funny joke was that Lorena and I were laughing about, so now I will tell you. You see, Nathan, God has played a joke on me for my wicked past. He has branded me with a cancer that is medically known as the 'red man syndrome.' The doctors at the Universidad Autonoma de Guadalajara treated me with PUVA light box therapy, but my sun sensitivity made it intolerable. They also said that this cancer is a type of leukemia. I should have died twenty years ago!"

"I'm sorry, Tio," Lorena said. "I had no idea."

"No, Lorena," Tio Pepe said. "You see, I *deserve* this and so much more! The T-cell leukemia is what is making my skin appear to be so angry. Don't be afraid. Every day I try to make amends for my past. I've been told these days that although I may be disagreeably *maloliente*, I am nonetheless still *un hombre simpático*! I suppose I wouldn't have it any other way!"

"Nor would I, Tio. Nor would I."

"I have spent the last decade of my long life learning as much as I can about these ailments that I'm now afflicted with," Pepe revealed. "I'm learning new languages, and I have extensively studied Mesoamerican history. In my seclusion, I have dedicated myself to becoming a man of knowledge! My parents, God rest their souls, advised me to attend college when I was a young man. Sadly, I summarily rejected this sage advice. If the truth be told, I now hunger for knowledge as much as I once hungered for blood when I was a young vampiro filled with unquenchable rage!"

"I'm not afraid of you, Tio," Lorena said. "Not at all."

"Nor should you be," Pepe replied. "I've noticed something most curious about this disease called human vampirism. Quite some time after I became infected, all of that hatred, anger, and rage simply disappeared. I have no idea if there is a similar regression of such hostility among other vampiros that may occur long after they've been infected, but I would assume so."

"I would hope that is indeed the case," Lorena said. "Maybe someday I could be reunited with my brother, Miguel. He also got infected. His disease happened to be caused from an encounter with Romero Lopes."

"It sounds to me as if Romero Lopes is irredeemable," Tio said. "This creature needs to be destroyed."

"The sooner, the better," Lorena added.

"Sit down with an old man, mijo," Tio Pepe said to Nathan. "I was just going to tell Lorena a story about the cowboys and Indians. Have you heard of the Olmec?" Before the *abuelito* began his story, he motioned to his ever-present *mayordomo*, Señor Bosque, with his right hand. Until Bosque stepped forward from the corner of the room, Lorena hadn't even known that Tio's personal assistant was present in the darkened study. However, El Tiempo's trusted manservant must have been there the entire time.

Señor Bosque disappeared momentarily, only to return with the young ranchera who had originally presented Lorena and Nathan to the ancient vampiro. She set a small table with *caldo de res*, four cold bottles of Topo Chico, and quesadillas made of fresh corn tortillas, *queso menonita*, and *huitlachoche*. "Por favor!" Tio Pepe exclaimed. "It's getting late. The two of you must be getting hungry by now."

It had been a long day for Nathan. He quickly gorged himself. A few moments later his head settled on the tabletop and he drifted off to sleep. Once Lorena was finished eating, Tio Pepe motioned to Señor Bosque and La Ranchera to enjoy the remnants of the refreshments, which the domestics gladly consumed.

Lorena covered Nathan with a blue blanket. His mother had brought him home from the hospital wrapped up in that same rectangle of soft fabric. Although it was now worn ragged, Nathan would habitually rub it against his cheek while he sucked his thumb. Lorena's previous attempts to break Nathan of this infantile habit of thumb-sucking, and also to successfully cleave the child from the blue rag before the dreadful time when his mother was viciously butchered, were largely futile endeavors. In light of what Nathan had been through, however, his psychological dependence upon the blue blanket for stability and tranquility rendered Lorena's unsuccessful interventions rather inconsequential given the larger scope of life's mercurial events.

Tio shared the story of how he became one of the damned many years ago when he was a petulant young man. After he elaborated about his life's journey, he provided Lorena with a historical account of the rise and fall of the infectious cycle and how it tied in to the rise and fall of several civilizations in Latin America. "My mother told me this disease was a curse of the wicked. When men became evil, El Estrago emerges. It has been said that it was delivered from heaven by birds."

"That appears to be the case." Lorena laughed. "I certainly know about the huevos amarillos."

"Modern science and even Christianity have ignored or misunderstood what has been known by the native people here in Mexico for centuries. There are two gods represented in the Olmec, Maya, and Aztec religions. One is Quetzalcoatl, or the feathered serpent. It's no coincidence that feathers and fangs are a representation of this god. He was a vampiro, originally infected by eating the contaminated egg of a bird. The second god is none other than the supernatural being known as Tezcatlipoca. He is a mischievous antagonist who happens to be the god of sorcery. His name in the Nahuatl tongue translates literally into 'smoking mirror.' Incidentally, 'smoking mirror' is also what the Nahuatl call obsidian."

"Maybe everything in the universe is connected somehow," Lorena said.

"So it would seem," Tio agreed. "Mirrors were commonly shaped from obsidian in ancient times. Images of Tezcatlipoca usually depict the god without a right foot, and in its place is often an image of an obsidian mirror. Nahuatl legend says that Tezcatlipoca's foot was lost in battle."

"I'm not sure I understand," Lorena said.

"Don't you see where this is going? Tezcatlipoca was a vampiro who lost a foot in a vicious battle. His foot didn't regenerate because it was hacked off with a Sangre de Indio obsidian knife!"

"Oh my God!" Lorena said.

"God? Frankly, God must have been taking a siesta when all of this shit was going on! Science and Christianity blatantly ignored what was right in front of them as a direct consequence of their Eurocentric belief systems. In the specific case concerning the Aztec and Mayas, extensive historical manuscripts were all destroyed by the church as heretical mythology. The documented existence of human vampirism was merely edited out of historical records well over 450 years ago. The Maya calendar and a few Latin translations of Aztec history are all the evidence that is left to document the cycles of El Estrago."

"What does this all mean to us in modern times?" Lorena asked.

"Good question," Tio Pepe replied. "Current Mesoamerican linguistic scholars have all made a gross error. The two ancient mythical gods that I spoke of are *not* the benevolent cocreators of the universe. Rather, I believe that they are the *cause* of these cyclic occurrences of human vampirism!"

"If that is indeed the case, these ancient people had a much better understanding of these outbreaks than we could possibly fathom," Lorena said.

"The Olmec developed their calendar based upon the sun to predict the seasons and weather patterns for legitimate agricultural purposes. This is known as the Xiuhpōhualli, and it is based upon the 365-day calendar. There is a second component to the calendar that was utilized by the high priests to mark ceremonial rituals based upon a 260-day year system. Oddly enough, if you do the math, this 260-day year system was comprised of 13 months, with each month allotted only a total of 20 days. The third component was a 52-year life cycle. Every 52 years, the gods would destroy everything if human beings had become too wicked."

"Destroy everything?" Lorena asked. "How?"

"By any number of means, I suppose," Pepe said. "In the very center of the calendar was the face of the sun god Tonatiuh. His tongue is an obsidian blade that signifies his appetite for human blood and hearts! The Olmec people were the ones who originally devised the calendar, but it was eventually adopted by the Mayas and the Aztecs. You see, it was not just an agricultural or religious tool; it was also used to document the past and to predict the resurgence of natural disasters such as famine, flood, drought, fire, storms, and—" Tio Pepe paused for just a moment before he emphatically added, "El Estrago!"

"Fifty-two years? I don't understand. The curandera told me that these outbreaks show up every twenty years or so," Lorena said. "How can you possibly account for such discrepancies in the theories, Tio Pepe?"

"Look, Lorena," Tio Pepe explained, "you previously mentioned that the most current outbreak occurred after only a seven-year hiatus. Is it not possible that over millennia the cycles are naturally appearing at much more frequent intervals? It's possible ..."

"I pray that's simply not the case, Tio."

"I do too," Pepe said. "In any event, the Olmec, the Mayas, and the Aztecs all suffered from the cyclic ravages of natural disasters and from outbreaks of El Estrago. It is well-documented that these cultures fell from prominence on recurrent cyclical occasions. It's interesting to note that each of these cultures also avidly embraced the practice of human sacrifice. They considered human blood to be *agua preciosa*, and the turmoil of El Estrago created a monarchy of bloodthirsty rulers engaged in tribal warfare and human sacrifice. Nonetheless, over the centuries, these societies were often able to rebound from these episodic cycles of vampirism and the mass slaughter of human beings to which the epidemics were inexorably linked."

"I was taught in school that the primary decline of the Mesoamerican societies was a direct consequence of the invading conquistadors," Lorena added.

"Maybe," Pepe said, "but there's more to history than meets the eye. The last-known mass outbreak of vampirism appears to coincide with the end of the reign of the ruler Ahuitzotl. He was a skillful leader and the grandson of Moctezuma. Under his rule, the Aztecs grew their empire into the largest organized city-state on earth."

"Greater than Rome?"

"By far," Pepe answered. "Ahuitzotl organized mining, standardized tooling, established trade routes, solidified communication relays, built pyramids, constructed roads, and created a vast highway system. I must say, what he accomplished was quite remarkable for a primitive native running around butt naked in the jungle, as he would eventually be uncharitably characterized by the Eurocentric invaders who showed up in the early 1500s. Under his rule, the Aztecs flourished and enjoyed wealth, sports, arts, and education."

"Well, what happened?" Lorena asked.

"As Ahuitzotl's health began to decline and impede his abilities to rule, Moctezuma II assumed the reign over the Aztec empire," Pepe explained. "Although the Aztecs and the Spaniards both had a way to record history in a written format, the actual truth is quite vague about what precisely caused the Aztec demise. When the conquistadors arrived, they destroyed almost all the written history of the Mayas and the Aztecs. There are many theories about their downfall, such as the brutality of the Spaniards, that our current history books seemingly gloss over, or perhaps it was the spread of previously unknown diseases introduced to the New World from Europe. There is no doubt that Hernán Cortés brought smallpox, gonorrhea, and a host of other Old World infectious diseases."

"There must be more to it than that," Lorena suggested.

"Well, a massive fire is also a competing theory that may have been a contributing factor to the decline of the Aztecs," Pepe said. "To this day, there's documentation of scorch marks all along the Avenida de los Muertos, which was the highway that connected the Pyramid of the Moon and the Pyramid of the Sun, ending at the Temple of Quetzalcoatl. The Spaniards who brought Christianity were appalled at what they interpreted to be a systemic wicked nature among the Aztecs. By the time that human sacrifice was first institutionalized by the Aztecs, there were existing Spanish accounts of twenty thousand sacrifices that occurred during the first few months of the conquistadors' arrival. Scholars think it was closer to eighty thousand victims. To be honest, these human sacrificial ceremonies performed by the Aztecs were not all that unusual in the annals of human depravity."

"How so?"

"As a case in point," Pepe said, "the Druids, in what is now England, were also involved with mass human sacrifice when the Romans invaded Britannia two millennia ago. It was done, no doubt, in an effort to appease the pagan gods and somehow magically thwart the foreign invaders. How was this any different from what the Aztecs did fifteen hundred years later? In fact, the way that the Druids engaged in human sacrifice was nearly identical to the brutal and bloodthirsty methodology employed by the Aztecs. Think about that for a moment."

"Human nature is human nature, I suppose," Lorena noted. "Good, bad, or otherwise."

"Precisely," Tio Pepe concurred. "In answer to your question, it was probably a combination of many things that contributed to the ultimate demise of the Aztecs. In my humble opinion, there is one inescapable fact not currently recognized by modern historians: human predation as the preferential dietary mandate of los vampiros. It likely eventually exhausted the Mesoamerican population. Once prey became scarce, the vampiros turned on each other. The Spanish, in their myopic quest to find gold, and also to convert the heathen population to Christianity, never willingly acknowledged the presence of los vampiros among their conquered subjects. The Spaniards merely sat back and watched the Aztec nation disappear in front of their very eyes. Did you know the Aztec warriors outnumbered the conquistadors one thousand to one?"

"How could the Aztec empire possibly lose with such overwhelming odds in their favor?" Lorena asked.

"Moctezuma was sadly manipulated by the woman now known as La Malinche, who had come from an opposing tribe with ulterior motives. If it had not been for this self-serving Spanish collaborator who became the interpreter and eventual wife of Cortés, the Aztecs would have easily overrun the Spanish invaders."

"Or so it would seem."

"The Spanish were eventually driven out by the Aztec warriors for only a brief moment, but the conquistadors returned in force just two years later, only to find a much smaller indigenous population. For the brief period when the Spaniards executed a strategic retreat, the surviving Mesoamericans figured out how to contain those infected with human vampirism. Several cultural traditions and methods of quarantine were rapidly developed. The mass graves and bones found in remote cenotes confirms that a most efficacious and ingenious protocol was formulated to isolate an infected person from the general population. If someone was suspected of being un vampiro, they were cast into a deep cenote, which, incidentally, was all but impossible to escape. The dead were oftentimes cast into these dark voids as well, as this was an effective prophylaxis to ensure that no postmortem transformations would occur. This would ensure that the dead would not return from the grave to bite the tribal members in the ass, if you catch my meaning. As it turned out, a cenote was an inescapable lethal trap."

"That sounds terrifying to me," Lorena said.

"In areas lacking cenotes, there came the invention of the shaft tomb," Tio Pepe added. "It worked on the same principle as an inescapable isolation pit. In fact, the shaft tomb became a traditional burial practice in western Mexico. The Colima dog is also an artifact of the vampiro isolation practice. It became common to place a dog in the pit with a deceased family member. If the corpse became reanimated as un vampiro, the dog would hopefully bark and alert the grave attendants. To this day, clay statues of dogs are placed in graves to facilitate the transition of the deceased to the other side of life, whatever that may be."

"Tio Pepe," Lorena petitioned, "would you mind if I asked you a few questions?"

"Fire away, Señorita Pastore. I'll answer your questions as best I can."

"Tell me something, Tio: what percentage of individuals who get bitten by un vampiro will actually turn into un vampiro? Is it 20 percent? Is it more?"

Pepe answered, "No se."

"You have to be able to tell me something. How about life expectancy? Do most vampiros live to be one hundred?"

"Look, Lorena," Pepe answered, "although yo soy un vampiro, and although I have personally lived with this disease for seven decades, there are just a lot of things that I don't know. I have no idea if other human vampires can live for 150 years or more, but I'm certain that my life is drawing to a conclusion. After all, now that I have cancer, I can actually look into a mirror and see myself disintegrating before my own eyes."

"It was wrong of me to pester you with these rather impertinent questions," Lorena said.

"Even for me, life's a mystery," Tio Pepe said. "It's become late, and the rantings of an old man have surely upset you *este noche.* I will have my servants prepare a room for you and the *jovencito.* You're safe here among the gente of Santa Sangre. Please feel free to stay here as my guest as long as you like."

"Gracias, Señor."

"I anticipate that you'll soon be having visitors, welcome or otherwise," Tio Pepe wryly added. "In the morning, I will begin to make arrangements for the arrival of these vampiro ghouls who are apparently trying to hunt you down. I promise that my staff and I will give them a glorious reception that they will likely never forget. In the morning, please provide Señor Bosque with as many details about these vampiros as you can remember. This will all be very helpful for our preparations."

"*Buenas noches,* Tio Pepe. Buenas noches, *mi amigo viejo.*"

Under a generous clandestine financial contract offered by the Federales, the hit squad assembled by Colonel Placard was about to make short work of the surviving members of the Routa gang at the Tequila Town bar. Perhaps Morales and Joe Cephas Smoot could have walked into the joint without brandishing any weapons at all and simply massacred the entire gang to the very last man using only their bare hands and bared fangs. Then again, perhaps not. In any event, Colonel Placard was not taking any chances, as both vampiros who entered the Routa gang's stronghold were bristling with an array of high-powered weapons provided by the generosity of American taxpayers.

Fully automatic long weapons chambering the deadly .308 round with a complement of a dozen magazines were at hand, complete with carbon-fiber-encased barrels, courtesy of Christensen Arms

Company. Each of the assault rifles that were brought to the party by Placard's bioweapon team were also optically accentuated with a Vortex HD 3–15×42 scope. As if these weapons of warfare had a mystical living volition of their own, they appeared to be ready and willing to hose down any adversary within the confines of the cantina with scorching-hot lead.

Morales selected a Kimber .45-caliber 1911-A sidearm that was parkerized, while his colleague Joe Cephas preferred even heavier artillery. Incarnated in the form of an enormous .460-caliber hogleg, this double-action hunting revolver was nothing less than a veritable hand cannon, complete with a 10.5-inch stainless steel barrel and topped off with a heavy-duty Vortex red dot. At the time, no holster on the planet could readily accommodate this handheld howitzer, so Joe Cephas encased the weapon in a simple sling that allowed easy retrieval in case the pending combat degraded into a cheek-to-cheek ballroom dance-a-thon.

Once Joe Cephas and Morales entered the tequila bar, it was all over in but a moment. The colonel and Ron Shiftless were stationed behind a parapet across the street, and as it turned out, they had a front row seat not only to the carnage but also to the ensuing high-pitched screams of agony emanating from the Routa gang members who were being violently disassembled.

Although Flaco's left arm was encumbered by a heavy plaster cast that was suspended at the wrist by a loop of gauze that encircled el jefe's neck, he was nonetheless able to flee in terror before either of the two vampiros had a chance to devour him. Sadly for the gang leader, a projectile expelled from the barrel of a bolt-action M40A3 sniper rifle, personally aimed and fired by Colonel Placard, ensured that Flaco did not get very far away from the scene of the slaughter.

"Round up the men and equipment, Shiftless, and let's get the hell out of here," Placard ordered. "We've had a good night. Let's get back to Los Estados straightaway. I want to get up to DC by Monday and attend the inaugural Night Crawler Symposium to hear what Dr. Blanks has to say about the state of the art of human vampirism and the management thereof. Did you hear that I'm an invited speaker at the wingding?"

"No kidding?" Shiftless responded. "Are you going to show the audience some of your slides of Mary Ellen Fokkengruber and her twin sister, Bertha? I love that snap you took of them eating jelly doughnuts."

"Silence, knave," Placard said. "I'm going to give a closed presentation about the history of biological warfare and its potential modern applications as exemplified by our bioweapon team. Only members of Congress will be allowed into the auditorium when I present my slide show. After they witness my dog and pony pitch, I'm certain that they'll allocate a ton more black-op pesos for our clandestine project."

"Oh yeah?"

"Of course, anything we did here tonight will remain top secret, but I can at least give a hint of our capabilities," Placard said. "You know me, amigo; I can charm the fangs out of a rattlesnake if push comes to shove ..."

"Very cool, Colonel!" Shiftless exclaimed. "So, am I to understand that Dr. Blanks will be the moderator for this symposium?"

"Sadly, yes."

"I hate that guy. If that's the case, I'm going to back him up into a corner just so I can personally shit all over him. I *really* hate that guy," Dr. Shiftless proclaimed as he peered at the carnage through a pair of binoculars. "Wait just one moment, Colonel," Shiftless said in alarm as he scanned the nightclub's exit door. "Something's wrong at the tequila bar!"

"Spill it," Placard demanded.

"Our boys look okay, but Joe Cephas is bringing out some crippled old bastard from the cantina. It looks like Morales also has a Routa gang member in tow, and that dude is a monster and a half."

"What do you mean?"

"He's covered with tats. He's got extensive scars. It's as if his face caught on fire sometime in the remote past and somebody put out the flames with an ice pick," Shiftless said, still looking through the binoculars.

"Nice," Placard said as he shouldered his sniper rifle and looked through the scope. "I have a bead on him now. You have a broader field of vision with your binoculars. What else do you see?"

"Wait a minute," Dr. Shiftless said excitedly. "Wait, wait, wait! Oh, shit, Colonel, I can't make this up; the old coot that Joe Cephas took outside as a prisoner looks like he's *blind*!"

"How do you know?" Placard asked.

"He's wearing sunglasses. He's got a long white cane. He's tapping on the ground that's directly in front of him. If that old bastard isn't blind, then he must be beating on the sidewalk to kill *las cucaraches*. After all, this nasty shithole of a Third World country is Mexico, is it not?"

"Shut up, Shiftless," Placard ordered. "Did I ever tell you that you were a juvenile delinquent?"

"On a daily basis."

"I told those boys to take no prisoners," Placard lamented, "and look what they've done. Let's get over there. Move!"

Placard and Shiftless brought down their sniper rifles from the top of the parapet they were hiding behind and ran into the street to meet Morales and Joe Cephas.

"What in hell is going on here? You purposefully disobeyed my direct order!" Placard exclaimed. "What were you boys thinking? I made no contingency arrangements for this type of situation."

"Hang on, Colonel Placard," Joe Cephas pleaded. "I just couldn't put this guy down. Look at him; he's just some blind old coot. He happens to be the attendant in the men's room. His name is Diego del Mar. I assure you, he doesn't know shit about shit. His only job is to dump ice cubes into the urinal and pass out hand towels while he slaps a little cologne on you. Here, Colonel, I want you to smell the stink water Diego put on my neck. It's called El Toro Grande. He said it would make me virile!"

"Oh, for shit's sake," Placard said. "What's your excuse, Morales? Who's this big rascal you brought out from the bar?"

"It's a Routa captain," Morales said. "They call him El Grifo. I thought he would be able to give us some valuable intel, but now he refuses to talk."

"We don't have time for this," Placard said as he turned to Joe Cephas Smoot. "Okay, I have a job for you, Joe. Go bring up the van while Doc secures the weapons. Morales and I will quickly interrogate these men to see if they know anything at all. Hustle up, gentlemen; this won't take long. Wheels up in three. Come with me, Morales. We've work to do."

As soon as Joe Cephas and Ron Shiftless trotted off to complete their appointed tasks, Morales grabbed the elderly blind bathroom attendant and El Grifo, both of whom were now in zip tie handcuffs, and pushed them back into the tequila bar that was splattered with blood and the dismembered remnants of the Routa crew.

Colonel Placard pulled out his sidearm, waved it in front of Morales, and said, "You have the honors. Finish them off." Realizing that his very life was in peril, the old man began to pray in his melodic Spanish tongue. El Grifo, however, looked upon his two captors with utter defiance and disdain.

"Don't ask me to do this, Colonel. I've killed in cold blood before, and it left a stain on me. It's a stain that will never go—"

The colonel reeled back the weapon and pulled the trigger before Morales could finish his sentence. As El Grifo fell to the floor, Placard chirped, "One down, one to go. So, there, I did it. It's on my head, Morales, not on yours. Happy now?" the colonel asked.

As a fountain of blood boiled out of the occipital aspect of El Grifo's shattered skull, Morales rationalized that it would be wrong to let such a readily available meal go to waste, so he affixed his mouth over the bullet hole in the head of the dead Routa captain and began to vigorously suck away.

Before Morales finished his snack, Placard turned to Diego del Mar and barked, "Okay, old man, I'm going to let you live, but you now work for me. Your act doesn't fool me for one minute. I'm certain you know quite a bit about what goes on in La Frontera concerning the drug trade. In the future, when we need information, we're going to come and find you, and I expect you to sing like a canary. Am I clear?"

"I'll tell you anything you want to know," the old man agreed. "I'll be your eyes and ears on the ground. Well, perhaps I'll just be your ears," he said with a forced grin.

"Good," Placard said as he cut the old man's zip tie handcuffs. "Now get your ass back into the men's room and play dumb when the police get here. I suspect the authorities are already on their way."

Once Colonel Placard and Morales rejoined the other two members of the bioweapon hit team, the four men sped away from the scene of the crime in an unmarked white van. Joe Cephas was the first to speak. "What about the old man? Please don't tell me you greased him."

"Relax, son. He works for us now," Placard said. "I'm quite certain that old Diego del Mar will be Johnny-on-the-spot for us in the future."

"Okay, but what about El Grifo?" Shiftless asked.

"I'm reasonably sure that when we left him, he didn't have a single thought in his head about anything important," the colonel replied.

"Perhaps you should have brought El Grifo along with us," Ron Shiftless noted. "I hope you didn't leave an important intel asset back there that might come back later to bite us in the ass."

Dr. Shiftless and Joe Cephas Smoot looked at each other with a considerable amount of apprehension when Dr. Placard proffered a cryptic response. "No. This El Grifo character would have just turned out to be nothing more than dead weight if we had brought him along with us. As for now, we have to get back across the border, ladies. Pronto!"

WHAT DO WE KNOW ABOUT HUMAN VAMPIRISM?
.RV-1986 Viral Infection
.Question: Is a worldwide pandemic infection possible?

9

STATE OF THE ART

The ambulance attendant arrived at the service station in Durango only to find that the two victims were immolated beyond recognition. After the Federales photographed the carnage and took multiple statements from no fewer than three direct eyewitnesses to the unspeakable horror, the police finally released the bodies of Romero Lopes and El Sapo to the state morgue. It was mandatory that the charred remains receive a thorough forensic postmortem examination.

"*¿Que onda, Carnal?*" Officer Sergio asked.

"Madre de Jesús, Sergio! How do you possibly expect me to get these remains hauled to the morgue?" the ambulance driver asked the police officer in charge. "These bodies are fused to the asphalt. I'm sure as hell not going to put these corpses in my ambulance. I'll never get the stench of burned flesh out of my vehicle. I own this ambulance, I'll have you know. It doesn't belong to the state. It belongs to me and me alone!"

"Relax, amigo," Sergio answered. "Marco is getting a poop shovel to scrape this shit up, and then you boys can load these bodies into the back of my pickup. Before Marco gets here, set a tarp down in the back of the bed. You owe me *una pista fría* when this is all over, Chico. No, on second thought, you'll owe me two beers!"

"Chilongo, you're a lightweight. Two beers and you'll be *un crudo pinche guey*," the ambulance attendant answered.

"Seguin went to the fire station to get the power washer. He should get back here in about *cinco minutos, más o menos*," Officer Sergio explained. "After you load the bodies into the back of my pickup truck, I want you and Seguin to hose the rest of the physical remains into the street. We'll just let the wild dogs that are roaming around in this neighborhood have a little bedtime snack to feast upon."

"That's disgusting! What do I look like to you, a janitor? Maybe you think that I'm just some peasant farmhand who shovels shit all day."

"If you give me any more grief," Officer Sergio said, "you'll owe me three beers, Chico!"

"Fine, but what're you going to be doing while Seguin and I are cleaning up this mess?" Chico asked.

"I have to set up a roadblock on the east and west end of Highway 40. We have to catch this evil gringo who set these two men on fire. We still don't know yet who these two dead men are. Maybe the pathologist can help sort it all out. I have no idea where this American might be hiding out, but we have to find his ass and bring him to justice. I swear to God, Mexico had better build a big barrier on the riverbanks of the Bravo someday to keep these bad hombres out of our country! If I were El Presidente, I would even make those *pinche* americanos pay for the wall!"

"Lorena," Nathan said, "it's still dark outside. Why do we have to wake up now? I want to stay in bed a bit longer. I'm warm like a piece of toast."

"I'm sorry, mijo," Lorena replied, "but it's time to get up! I'm afraid some people might be coming to pay us a visit, and these people are not very nice."

"What do these people want?"

"I don't want you to be afraid, Nathan," Lorena said, "but these are bad people who might want to hurt you and me."

"I'm not afraid," Nathan said. "When Mommy died, my daddy told me to be brave."

"Are you brave, Nathan?"

"Very!" the small boy answered. Nathan threw the covers off, jumped out of bed, and ran to Lorena's bedroom. In but a moment, he returned with a small Kachina. He handed the totem to the curandera and said, "Here, Lorena, I found the little worry doll that you keep hidden in your bedroom. Hold this doll like it's a little baby, and it will make you brave like me!"

Lorena feigned surprise when she said, "You know, mijo, I believe this item has special healing powers. Now, how in the world did you find the special place where I keep this Kachina hidden? You're not supposed to play with this."

"Not only am I brave, but also I'm smart!"

"I agree," Lorena said with a smile as she took the Kachina from Nathan and clutched it tight. "When you grow up, maybe you'll become un gran brujo!"

"I have something else to show you," Nathan reported. "Last night, one of my baby teeth fell out. I put it under my pillow, but the tooth fairy never came."

"The tooth fairy is not allowed to cross border into Mexico," Lorena explained.

"Why not?"

"The tooth fairy doesn't have *los papeles correctos* to enter the country," Lorena said with a laugh. "Don't worry, Nathan. Put the tooth under your pillow tonight, and a magical rodent named Ratoncito Pérez will pay you a visit instead. He'll put a peso under your pillow, and then he'll take your tooth."

"A peso? That's terrible! A peso isn't worth anything," Nathan lamented. "I can't even buy a Chiclet with a peso."

"True," Lorena admitted, visibly annoyed at what was otherwise a rather innocent remark from a small child. "Don't forget, Nathan, this *is* Mexico. It's time you started acting like it."

"Lorena," Nathan asked, "will you give me a hug?"

"No, you're a big boy now," Lorena said. "Big boys don't need hugs."

"You're wrong," Nathan said. "Everybody needs hugs!" This was the first time that Lorena had ever refused to relinquish to the small boy the universal and emblematic act of human affection. Nathan was not particularly pleased about the change in Lorena's demeanor.

"Well," Lorena added, "perhaps I don't think I need hugs anymore."

Once Chico and Seguin arrived at the morgue in Sergio's pickup, they jumped out of the cab to retrieve the two incinerated bodies from the pickup bed. Their plan was to lug the two dead men into the morgue, heave the burned stiffs onto the very first gurney they could find, and then beat a hasty retreat after filling out a legal form or two. There was only one problem: the two bodies were gone without a trace!

"I told you that you were driving too fast," Seguin said with a frown. "You probably hit a bump in the road back on Highway 40 and the two corpses flew over the truck's tailgate."

"*Orale cabrōn*, Seguin!" Chico said to rebuke his colleague. "I never drove faster than sixty kilometers per hour. I sure as hell did *not* hit a bump in the road. I have an idea: those dead bodies came back to life and jumped out of the back of the truck of their own accord!"

"You're an idiot, Chico."

The two colleagues were mortified when they suddenly heard the pickup truck doors open wide. As they stepped out from behind the open tailgate, Chico and Seguin were astonished to witness the two reanimated burnt corpses enter the cab and assume comfortable positions on the bench seat.

"Madre de Jesús!" Chico exclaimed as he and Seguin repeatedly made the sign of the cross.

"I'm afraid that the mother of Jesus has very little to do with what's going on right about now," the vampiro who was once known to be a man called Romero Lopes cheerfully replied. The ghoul then stuck his head out of the driver's-side window to politely make a request. “Now, why don’t you be a good fellow and walk up here? Hand me the keys to this truck, and we’ll be on our way. Somewhere down the road is a gringo I need to catch up with so I can rip his throat out.”

“Don’t give him the keys!” Seguin said to Chico. “I’ll run inside the morgue and call Officer Sergio to come with help.”

As Seguin turned and ran inside the morgue, Chico said, “I can’t believe that you guys are still alive. I saw your dead bodies at the service station. You men were burned to a cinder. Maybe I should take you boys to the hospital right now.”

“I appreciate the offer, but my friend and I will be just fine,” El Sapo answered. The younger vampiro then turned to his lover and asked, “Say, are you hungry, Master Lopes?”

“Famished,” Lopes replied. “Do you mind if I eat his liver?”

“I’ll defer to your personal preferences, Master Lopes,” El Sapo answered.

“Wait,” Chico said. “What are you boys talking about?” Sadly for Chico, his life was over in but a moment.

From the morgue’s front desk, Seguin placed a telephone call to the police station and explained to Officer Sergio what was going on. By the time Seguin went back outside to the morgue’s front parking lot to wait for the Federales to arrive, he discovered that Sergio’s pickup truck, the two reanimated burned corpses, and his colleague Chico had all simply disappeared.

When there was a break in the dissertations at the scientific seminar reviewing the current fund of knowledge regarding human vampirism, the colleague of Dr. Blanks from the CDC was mad enough to spit nails. Although standing in a crowded hallway, Dr. Hoefferle made no effort to mask his ire toward the elected federal representative from California. “Frankly, Congresswoman Rivers, I’m quite surprised that now you’re showing *any* concern at all over the fact that representatives from the pharmaceutical industry were not permitted to attend this state-of-the-art Night Crawler Symposium.

As a case in point, you were on the committee that established the federal guidelines that only opened the doors of this symposium to scientists, health insurance executives, select members of Congress, military personnel, and various representatives and cabinet members working on behalf of the executive branch. Your turnabout on this issue is, well, shocking."

"Pardon my faulty memory, Dr. Hoefferle, but I don't recall all the specific details about the organizational meeting for this symposium," Manteen Rivers said with a shrug.

"Well, perhaps you might not remember, but *I* certainly do," Dr. Hoefferle answered while baring his teeth. "I specifically remember that it was *you* who adamantly refused to allow any representatives from the pharmaceutical industry to attend this meeting. The whole purpose of this educational seminar was to bring the scientific community, government officials, and industry leaders together to share what is currently known about the outbreak of an illness that might become an epidemic. To my way of thinking, pharmaceutical executives are the very definition of industry leaders."

"Is that so? As it turns out, I'm just wasting my time here today. All of this intellectual mumbo-jumbo actually means very little to me. The *only* thing I care about is making sure that I'm able to personally benefit from each and every calamity or misfortune that happens in this country. After all, a politician should never let a disaster go to waste."

"Rather cynical of you, but somehow not surprising."

"Open your eyes," Manteen Rivers said. "*Every* congressperson becomes filthy rich by the time that he or she eventually retires from being a 'public servant.' My objective is to become so deeply buried in the deep state that I'll score a big fat job as a paid lobbyist someday. Don't be naïve, boy. Other than stuffing my garter belt with greenbacks, I just don't care."

"Well, you should care," Holbert Hoefferle said. "I thought it was your job. You're right about one thing: I am indeed naïve. What an idiot I must appear to you! At the time when the groundwork for this symposium was being laid, I specifically informed you that your narrow-minded initial decision about who could or could not attend this seminar was indeed a profound mistake."

"I concede that point."

"I was stunned when you made a hideous comment about the, and I quote, 'purile motives' of the very companies that toil away in an attempt to develop efficacious therapeutic modalities to treat emerging new diseases such as human vampirism."

"What's your point?" Rivers asked. "What's in it for me?"

"You collectively referred to the entire drug research and development industry as 'evil Big Pharma,' did you not?" Dr. Hoefferle asked. "Shame on you. Your constituents must be hoodwinked."

"*All* constituents are hoodwinked. How else could I possibly explain that I'm standing here and having this existential chat with you about life, liberty, and the pursuit of the all-elusive 'American dream'? I've been inside the beltway far too long not to recognize a sanctimonious load of crap when I hear it. So, you want to know why I originally closed the door on allowing Big Pharma to attend this seminar?"

"I most certainly do."

"I thought it was best to queer the deal with Big Pharma once I found out that *you* already had secret meetings with the German pharmaceutical firm Leben Kur AG," Manteen Rivers explained. "My sources told me that the director of developmental therapeutics from Leben Kur AG already paid you a friendly visit in San Antonio. You managed to try to cut yourself in on a side deal with those Eurotrash Nazi Huns, did you not?" Manteen Rivers asked as she rolled her eyes in contempt.

"I have no comment to make about your salacious allegation. Tell me something: what made you change your mind?" The research scientist from San Antonio asked this new question in an obvious attempt to deflect any personal criticism. "I wonder why you're now making this specific demand to allow pharmaceutical reps to attend the Night Crawler Symposium? Madam, you're a hypocrite!"

"Simmer down, Dr. Hoefferle. Your tone is not appreciated. After I had the opportunity to finally meet with a certain representative from Leben Kur AG, I suddenly realized how profoundly important a biotechnology firm might prove to be in this particular scenario I now find myself in," the congresswoman smugly answered.

Dr. Hoefferle didn't back down for a moment. "What a load of unmitigated crap. It would seem to me that you just learned how important a biotechnology firm may very well be to your own personal bank account, or maybe your reelection campaign slush fund. You disgust me."

"I have a compact in my purse," Manteen said. "Let me pull it out so you can look at yourself in a mirror."

"Congress has become nothing more than a self-ordained, self-serving North American version of the House of Lords," Hoefferle proclaimed. "My irrefutable supposition is self-evident to anybody with a pair of eyeballs in their head!"

"Is it you who just called me a hypocrite? Spare me! The irony that I'm a black woman has not escaped me, but what's going on here is simply a pot calling the kettle black, is it not?"

"I'm on the straight and narrow, lady."

"You're out of your league, junior. If you haven't figured it out by now, the only job that Congress has is to take care of the other members of Congress," Rivers said.

"Are you above the law?"

"The rules we establish to control you peons don't apply to congresspeople," Rivers smugly replied. "There's a two-tiered justice system in this country."

"Obviously!"

"If I don't get to line my pockets with a few shekels, nobody else will either. Now, if you'll just be a good boy and keep your mouth shut regarding what's about to unfold, maybe I'll let you take a sip of the slop that's sloshing about in the pig trough while I enjoy a gourmet meal. I'm warning you now: play your cards right, you strange little man. It goes without saying that you'd better start treating me with the deference and respect that I deserve," Manteen Rivers said. "Oh, by the way, you're not recording this conversation with me, are you?"

After Hoefferle rendered a hostile stare at the Congress member for several tense moments, Manteen Rivers simply picked up her briefcase and defiantly walked back into the auditorium to attend the pending question and answer session featuring the CDC physician Dr. Blanks as the moderator.

"Before I make my summary remarks, I would again like to thank everybody in the audience today for attending this inaugural symposium. It has been an honor for me to be selected as the moderator for this first-ever Night Crawler Symposium." Dr. Blanks proudly beamed.

"In a moment, I'll turn the podium back over to Dr. Holbert Hoefferle from San Antonio. He's been assigned to present a presentation about the most pressing questions that still need to be answered about this mysterious disease process. However, before I hand over the reins, I need to remind those in attendance today that it's strictly forbidden to take any photographs of the slide presentations that you see on the projector screen," Blanks cautioned. "As all of you have just now sadly witnessed, Congresswoman Shiva Jacklyn Grant from Texas was unceremoniously removed from this auditorium because she brought in a small video camera and tried to make a clandestine recording of these proceedings. Ladies and gentlemen, that will *not* be tolerated."

"Fine, Dr. Blanks, but we weren't even granted the luxury of a simple handout for any of these lectures," a member of the audience shouted out to the moderator without first being called upon.

"During the refreshment break, I received vociferous complaints that there were no handouts or even an outline provided for any of these presentations. Ladies and gentlemen, that was assuredly not my call. If anybody has an issue with these peculiar seminar regulations, I suggest that you take it up with Uncle Sam. Are there any other questions before I present an overview of the state of the art?"

Dr. Blanks glanced over the audience and was well aware that many of the attendees were less than pleased with what was an intellectually stifling environment. When he saw there were no further questions, Dr. Blanks proceeded with his summary statement.

"Okay, everybody, this next slide is a bullet-point highlight of what we know. First, we are dealing with a peculiar RNA retrovirus that our colleagues at the WHO have tentatively labeled as RV-1986. It has features similar to the well-recognized feline leukemia virus," Dr. Blanks explained. "It is *not* Homo sapiens–specific, as its natural reservoir has been found to be domesticated birds such as chickens and ducks. Oddly, fowl are apparently just carriers of this virus, as birds do not appear to be affected symptomatically. On an interesting note, it appears that the virus may lie dormant for decades before it reappears among humans. For unclear reasons, it would seem that the nidus for this infection is around the Rio Grande Valley in New Mexico. At the CDC, we failed to induce an active infection with any other mammals, including murine subjects, canines, and even higher primates. Despite the fact that RV-1986 is similar to the feline leukemia virus, the common domesticated house cat also appears to be impervious to this infection. Much like hepatitis B, the nasty virus that causes human vampirism can be transmitted through oral ingestion and also through transcutaneous blood or serum exposure. Human vampirism clearly can mimic the features of porphyria, as solar sensitivity is now a well-recognized complication of this disease."

Dr. Blanks pressed the advance button on the slide carousel, but the bulb in the projector suddenly blew out. "While we're waiting for the audiovisual technician to come down and get the projector working, let's move on to bullet point number two. Through some of the work that was previously done in Santa Fe and by our own meticulous follow-up studies at the CDC, we've confirmed that RV-1986 is a marrow, gut mucosa, and renal tropic virus."

The audiovisual technician quickly appeared and was able to expeditiously return Dr. Blanks's slide projector to an operational status. Dr. Blanks continued with his summary.

"After the kidneys are infected by this entity, a renal gradient occurs that allows serum iron to be wasted through the nephrons. This is one of the main differences between human vampirism and the tiny vampire bat that that lives down in Latin America. The vampire bat does *not* waste iron in this fashion. In regards to the bone marrow, the virus appears to have an affinity for infecting erythroblasts and early marrow progenitor stem cells. When an erythroblast becomes infected, the virus is passed on to red cell reticulocytes, which eventually cause the red cells to rupture. This event reduces the red cell life span to a matter of a few days at most, as the red cells will quickly succumb to hemolysis, which showers the bloodstream with additional free viral particles that presumably wash downstream in the vascular system and then infect other organ sites. Once the bone marrow gets infected, the body develops marked difficulty in constructing hemoglobin. That is why a person afflicted with human vampirism needs to consume either a blood meal or iron-rich viscera to survive."

"Excuse my interruption," an attendee interjected, "but I'm a gastrointestinal physiologist from Baylor. I don't understand what happens to the lining of the gut from a pathological standpoint that would allow for the direct absorption of hemoglobin that has been consumed and also allow the oxygen-carrying molecule to directly transit the gut lining without being first degraded by the digestive process."

"Good question," Dr. Blanks replied. "Just like there's a renal gradient that allows iron to be wasted by the nephrons, there's a gut mucosal gradient that occurs that allows hemoglobin to be absorbed directly across the small bowel mucosa entirely intact. There is no other biological model that has ever been recognized that demonstrates this peculiar and extraordinary phenomenon. Red blood cells labeled with radio tracers have confirmed this observation. Are there any other questions?"

A thin man in the front row raised his hand, and Blanks acknowledged him. "It was reported earlier this morning that patients who are infected with RV-1986 have extraordinary rapid tissue healing if an injury occurs. Could you be so kind as to elaborate on any theories you might have on how that might occur?"

"I ought to hire you to be my setup man," Dr. Blanks said with a smile. "Your question brings me directly to bullet point number three. As I previously mentioned, the bone marrow stem cells can get infected by this virus. We discovered that something amazing occurs when this is the case. It would appear that a unique process of histone deacetylation drives these marrow stem cells to actually dedifferentiate into embryonic-like pluripotent cells that enter circulation. If a tissue injury occurs, these pluripotent cells are recruited to the site of tissue injury by inflammatory mitogenic cytokines."

"What are these cellular signals that recruit the pluripotent stem cells to exit the circulatory system and migrate toward damaged organs with the explicit purpose of engaging in tissue repair?" one of the scientists asked. "Could it be intrinsic alpha interferon released by the immune system?"

"As of yet, we don't have a handle on what these pluripotent recruitment cytokines might be," Blanks answered. "In any event, when these pluripotent stem cells move into their new neighborhood, these embryonic-like entities are able to rapidly undergo cellular differentiation to take on the characteristics of the immediately adjacent surrounding tissues. This occurs whether we are talking about an endodermal, a mesodermal, or an ectodermal tissue subtype. The pluripotent stem cell will actually morph into the tissue type that it finds itself among. As it stands, one of the other intercellular 'telegrams' that we have failed to isolate is the chemical signal or signals that initiate cellular differentiation at that point. Nevertheless, as you can readily appreciate, this process initiates rapid tissue repair and results in an astonishing recovery and repair of the damaged tissues from even very serious injuries."

Dr. Blanks looked at his watch before he added, "Because of time constraints, I'll only be able to tackle one more question from the field before we have to move on to the other items in this symposium. I promise to avail myself to the members of this august body of scholars and elected government officials during the next refreshment break if anybody would like to discuss some of these fascinating discoveries in greater detail." Dr. Blanks pointed to the audience and said, "Okay, you in the back row, one last question."

A scientist stood up and said, "I'm sorry, Dr. Blanks, but somebody needs to ask about the six-hundred-pound Sasquatch that's sitting smack-dab in the middle of this symposium. Rumors have been floating about that your RV-1986 vaccine project is caught deep in the briar patch and might not ever see the light of day. Would you care to elaborate on the state of the art of your vaccine research?"

The symposium moderator instinctively looked down to the floor in shame as he stammered, "Well, uh, you see—"

Dr. Blanks had to quickly come up with a plausible answer to the question from the floor, even if his reply would turn out be fallacious. When he replied with overt deceit and obfuscation of the truth, the elected government officials who were present at the Night Crawler Symposium became quite suspicious. After all, who could possibly be more adept at recognizing a lie than an elected congressperson already well versed in the practice of constituent deception?

"I'm sorry," Dr. Blanks concluded, "but there's nothing that I can divulge to you at this time. Our active research in this endeavor is currently classified ..."

Cletus Barker was driving west on Mexican Highway 40 when the line of traffic directly in front of him came to a dead stop. He pulled his car to the shoulder, turned off the ignition, exited his vehicle, and then walked down the highway to see if he could ascertain the reason for the traffic jam.

What Cletus witnessed made the hair stand up on the back of his neck. There was a roadblock set up by the Federales, and the policía were carefully evaluating every vehicle and every traveler who wanted to pass the makeshift security checkpoint. Clearly, the Federales were looking for somebody. Clearly, the Federales were looking for Cletus Barker!

Cletus had recently doused two people with gasoline at a service station in Durango and then intentionally set them on fire. Regardless of the fact that the two individuals he had torched were actually vampiros, there were several eyewitnesses present who had watched in horror. If Cletus were to be apprehended by the authorities, there would be hell to pay. Whatever tactical advantages he once had over Romero Lopes or El Sapo were now long gone. His only recourse now was to return to his vehicle and quietly slip away before his presence was discovered by the authorities.

Cletus fired up his vehicle, put the car in reverse, and slowly backed down the shoulder of the highway. The drivers in the long line of vehicles that were stopped on the highway could only offer Cletus a hostile stare and a middle-finger salute as he passed them in reverse. The driver of one of the vehicles that was stalled in the traffic jam rolled down his window and actually proffered a hostile editorial assessment of Cletus Barker's presumed biological lineage. Nonetheless, Cletus was able to successfully negotiate his automobile in reverse all the way back to a perpendicular dirt road intersection.

As best as Cletus could tell, the rough-hewn road was little more than a rarely utilized truck path that meandered toward the horizon and disappeared into a hazy arid wilderness. Although his decision was little more than a last-ditch act of desperation, Cletus wisely decided to turn down the primitive off-road trail and trek into the gloomy badlands in an effort to disappear for a while.

At that juncture in time, and also at the junction in the byway, Cletus couldn't render a guess as to when Mexico Highway 40 would again be safe for him to travel. Hopefully, this detour that he was about to take would only be an inconvenience of short duration. However, as his ill-equipped sedan jostled about violently on the rutted path that led deep into sparsely populated rural squalor, he valiantly attempted to suppress his intrusive and unwelcome doubts that he would perhaps never see his beloved Lorena ever again.

"Here, Sapo, I bought something from the pharmacy that will make us feel better until our skin completely rejuvenates within a day or so," Romero Lopes said as he passed a large blue jar of a topical emollient to his lover through the pickup truck's open window.

"How do you know so much about taking care of burn injuries?" El Sapo asked.

"Sadly, this is the second time that I've been burned to death. The first occasion was when I was caught in a recent house fire. Take this cream, Sapo, and apply it to your remaining open wounds. The pharmacist suggested that we use a silver-impregnated antibiotic cream, but I rejected his recommendation. I decided to get this lubrication cream instead."

"If the pharmacist thought that the silver-based antibiotic cream would be better, why did you decline the offer, master? After all, in my experience, pharmacists are actually quite knowledgeable about such matters. Please tell me you didn't eat him."

"Don't be silly, sweet cheeks! A while back, some fat gringo gouged out my left eye with a silver ballpoint pen," Lopes explained. "I'm not certain, but I'm suspicious that the element silver might actually be harmful to creatures like you and me. After all, why didn't my left eyeball grow back after it was carved out of the socket?"

"I've given that some consideration," El Sapo thoughtfully replied. "Perhaps the ability of a vampiro to recover from an injury is predicated upon whether or not there's any tissue left behind to repair."

"What do you mean?"

"Even when you and I got burned up, we still had little patches of skin left behind that our bodies used as a model to build upon," Sapo explained.

"How does this apply to my empty eye socket?"

"When you lost your left eyeball, there was no template left behind," Sapo said. "There was no blueprint to be found in the empty eye socket to initiate cellular repair."

"You're a genius, Sapo," Lopes said. "Let me lick you. I want to lick you for hours!"

"Wait a moment, master. Were you able to place a call to our handler at the cartel?" Sapo asked.

"We have a new mission," Lopes explained. "An old enemy of mine named Blake Barker has been spotted down in the town of Santa Sangre. Blake is a night crawler like us. The Calle Vampiro received a report that this ghoul wiped out our affiliate gang in Juárez. A four-man hit squad from the cartel will be sent down to meet us in Santa Sangre, and our orders are to take Blake Barker back to our headquarters in Guadalajara. The cartel wants him alive!"

"You told me that the man who burned us alive back at the gas station was named Cletus Barker. Are Cletus and Blake—"

"*Exactamente,* mi amigo. They're brothers!" Lopes interrupted. "Everything in the universe is connected somehow."

"What do you mean, master?"

"When we get to Santa Sangre," Lopes explained, "we'll find Lorena Pastore and I'll be able to get my obsidian knife back. We'll capture Blake Barker for the Calle Vampiro cartel, and if we're lucky, we'll extract a pound of flesh from his brother, Cletus, if we happen to run into him down there. There's only one hurdle we have to get over before we meet up with the cartel's hit squad that's waiting for us down in Santa Sangre."

"Is there a problem, master?"

"The pharmacist said there's a roadblock checkpoint a few kilometers down the highway," Lopes cautioned.

"Maybe we should get to the town of Santa Sangre by taking a different route," El Sapo suggested.

"We'll be fine, lover boy," Lopes said with an air of confidence as he fired up the engine of the stolen pickup truck. "You know me, amigo; I can charm the fangs out of a rattlesnake if push comes to shove. Those Federales are a load of pendejos. They won't know what hit them until it's too late!"

All that Blake Barker knew was that Lorena Pastore and his son, Nathan, were hiding out somewhere in the township of Santa Sangre. He had no idea that his brother, Cletus, was only a two-day drive away. Nonetheless, going from door to door was turning out to be quite an arduous task for the vampire, who was still dressed up in the outfit of the dead Mexican federal policeman who was killed in the Routa prison riot in Ciudad Juárez.

Few residents of Santa Sangre, if any, would open their doors to Blake. Those who reluctantly answered the knock upon their door were reticent to say anything at all. While canvassing an east side neighborhood, Blake was startled when he heard somebody from across the street call out his name.

"Well, Blake, you just never know when the wind might blow a tumbleweed down a dusty street," Miguel Pastore called out.

Blake made a quick pivot and realized that Lorena's brother, Miguel, and the former line cook from the old El Chopo Restaurant, John Stewart, were a mere thirty feet away. "You boys stay right there. Don't move an inch, I tell you. I'm not looking for any trouble. I'm just trying to find my son, Nathan."

"Suppose I told you where Lorena and Nathan were hiding out? Then what?" Miguel asked.

"When I first became a vampiro, I was filled with anger and hatred," Blake Barker said with a sigh. "For some reason, those negative vibes have completely subsided. I have absolutely no residual hostile feelings toward Lorena, and I assure you that I could never hurt her *or* my son. I fully understand now what Lorena did, and I actually want to thank her for keeping my son safe. She might have very well saved his life back there in Mesilla. So, what do you say, Miguel? Can you throw me a bone?"

"Wish I could," Miguel Pastore answered. "Somewhere down here in Santa Sangre is an old family friend they call El Tiempo. Unfortunately, I never met the man. Lorena came down here when she was fifteen years old to be initiated as a curandera. At that time, I was a rebellious seventeen-year-old, and I foolishly rejected the invitation to partake in the fiesta. As for now, John Stewart and I are planning on going from door to door to try to find Lorena. It looks like you had the same idea."

"Maybe we can form our own pop trio and rock this town! I'll bet our gig will warrant a standing ovation when we take a bow at the curtain call," Blake suggested.

"Agreed," Miguel answered. "However, I need to ask of you a big favor on behalf of the citizens of Santa Sangre, Señor Barker."

"What might that be?"

"Promise me that you won't eat anybody," Miguel requested.

"Fine," Blake Barker said, "but I need you to make the same promise to me."

Blake and Miguel each ran their index fingers and thumbs symbolically across their respective lips as if they were zipping their own mouths tightly shut to avert any potentially violent gustatory mishap.

"We should take a look at my map. The three of us should be able to make short work of this manhunt," Miguel concluded. "After all, Santa Sangre is a pretty small town. Blake, why don't you tackle the rest of this east side neighborhood? I'll take the midtown section out to the river. John Stewart can zip through the neighborhoods from the riverbank all the way to the western boundary. Somebody in this town is going to eventually break down and spill the beans. The three of us can then reconvene at the midtown bridge at about noon and compare notes."

"Sounds like a plan, but what's in it for you, John Stewart?" Blake asked.

"What do you mean?"

"Well, you don't strike me as a man cut from the same bolt of linen as Dudley Do-Right, that's all." Blake eyed the younger man with considerable suspicion before asking, "Are you planning on opening up a restaurant down here? If not, maybe it was just the right time for you to crawl out of your mother's basement and strike out on your own. Good for you!"

"Bite me, asshole!" John Stewart exclaimed. However, after a moment of careful reflection, John tugged at his left earlobe while he issued a swift retraction of the insult he had just uttered. "Right about now, I believe wisdom would dictate that I should make a full and unconditional apology to you, Mr. Barker. Mea culpa!"

"Forget it, junior," Blake said. "My original query still stands, however: why are you now south of the Bravo with Miguel Pastore?"

"We're friends. I want to see this through with him to the very end," Stewart replied.

"And?"

"Lorena's madly in love with me." Stewart beamed.

"Is that so?" Blake asked as he squinted at Miguel's younger companion. "I employed Lorena for a long time, and I never heard her even mention your name. Not to me, and not to anybody else for that matter. Not once."

"Well," John Stewart added, "she loves me, but she just doesn't know it yet. Once she meets me, she'll be filled with unbridled passion. I won't even try to stop her from ripping my clothes off and having her way with me right there on the spot!"

As Blake Barker broke out into laughter, he pinched the bridge of his nose, closed his eyes, and shook his head in utter disbelief. For his part, Miguel Pastore did not appear to be particularly amused by the proceedings.

"¡Señor Stewart, eres un cerdo! This is *exactly* why I don't want my sister to date a gringo like you."

"Thanks, Miguel," John Stewart said with a wry smile. "I hope I resemble that remark!"

"Before you go, John, put this chain around your neck," Miguel said as he handed John Stewart a silver chain with a small gold ring. "You'll need this just in case you find Lorena and Nathan."

"What's this?"

"It's Lorena's class ring. She gave it to me as a memento. Seeing as she's never met you before, you'll need this as a calling card," Miguel explained. "Don't lose it!"

"Let's wrap up the loose ends with the most pressing questions that remain about human vampirism," Dr. Hoefferle said as he leaned toward the podium and pulled the microphone closer. "Although this infection is clearly spread through blood and serum exposure, we have absolutely no idea if mosquitoes, ticks, or other bloodsucking parasites can spread it from one individual to another.

We also don't know at this time if RV-1986 may affect the temporal lobes of the brain. During the prior outbreak that occurred in 1979 in New Mexico, we certainly noted hostile behavior in individuals who were newly infected. However, on an interesting note, it appeared that these personality changes were by and large only short-lived events."

"How can you possibly account for that?" a member of the audience asked.

"Other than a symbiotic peace treaty between the infectious entity and the host," Dr. Hoefferle sarcastically answered, "I haven't a clue. "During the last refreshment break, other attendees asked some very pertinent questions that were actually under my radar. We can't account for the reason why individuals who are infected with RV-1986 typically grow impressive one-inch incisor fangs."

"How can you find out?" one of the scientists asked, pestering the speaker.

"Simple," Dr. Hoefferle replied. "If my team in San Antonio can get our hands on a fresh cadaver previously infected with this virus, we should be able to ascertain if the temporal lobes of the brain or the maxillary tooth sockets are also sites of active RV-1986 infection. We suspect as much, but as for now, it's just a theory. I'll be the very first to admit that we're on the left side of the bell curve related to our fund of knowledge regarding human vampirism at this state-of-the-art symposium."

"How long can one live if infected?" an attendee asked.

"Please don't ask me about the projected life expectancy of infected individuals, or if most or all of those infected will be destined to eventually die from some horrible hematological or solid tumor malignant process," Hoefferle answered.

"Surely you could at least speculate."

"Intuitively, we currently believe that infected individuals will indeed have a prolonged life span, but these unfortunate individuals will also face an increased risk of dying from a myriad of malignant illnesses," Dr. Hoefferle replied. "At this time, however, this is truly pure speculation on our part."

As Dr. Hoefferle gathered his notes from the podium, he said, "I have time for one more question before Colonel Placard steps up to the plate." The scientist from San Antonio looked around the auditorium before he elected to field a question from a man in the third row. "Go ahead, sir, fire away."

"From my own personal communiqué with the CDC, I've been informed that individuals infected with RV-1986 appear to display amazing powers of persuasion. I've also been told that individuals of all ages, and also a variety of nonhuman animals, are strongly attracted to human vampires," the attendee noted. "Any theories?"

"Yes! Bingo! Finally I've been asked a question that I have an answer for. There's a young man we have under contract at the bioweapons division in San Antonio. He's infected with RV-1986. We did a mass spec analysis on a sample of his sweat, and we isolated a specific chemical that seems to be responsible for causing these peculiar phenomena that you've asked about. The chemical appears to be a powerful pan-mammalian pheromone! I must admit, I've personally found the odor of this chemical in a concentrated quantity to be absolutely irresistible!" After a brief pause, he said, "The allotted time for my presentation is now up. I would like to thank you all for your undivided attention. It was an honor for me to speak to you today."

"Thank you, Dr. Hoefferle," Dr. Blanks stated as he stepped back up to the podium. "There are obviously a lot of unanswered questions about the RV-1986 virus that is responsible for human vampirism. I was asked a question at the last break regarding what kind of risk the disease of human vampirism poses to the population at large. The answer to that question is uncertain as we don't have a good explanation of why the disease only pops up from time to time. Nor do we have an idea why there has not been an explosion of this disease process into a true pandemic event that could alter human life on this planet as we know it."

"You must be able to at least make an educated guess," a person in the audience called out.

"For unclear reasons, the disease appears to have a tendency to burn itself out and go into a dormant state before it reappears mysteriously later on. I've heard an unsubstantiated rumor that the Latina folk healers in the lower New Mexican Rio Grande Valley have dealt with human vampires in a brutal fashion," Dr. Blanks said. "Stories abound that the curanderas have actually dispatched with human vampires by cutting out their hearts, starving them to death, or viciously beheading them using ceremonial knives fashioned out of the volcanic glass called obsidian. Well, whether that's true or not, nobody within New Mexico's secretive curandera coven is willing to talk about it."

"That's preposterous," the attendee from the audience stated.

"Look, I'm not telling you that this is a confirmed fact," Blanks said. "I'm just telling you about what I've heard. Do you have a better explanation? If not, the next presentation is going to be a closed meeting. The only conference attendees who will be permitted to sit in on the presentation by Colonel Augustus Placard are the members of Congress in attendance today. There will be no exceptions to this rule. Before the members of Congress learn about the potential military applications of human vampirism, there's time for one more question."

Dr. Ron Shiftless from San Antonio was in the audience. Despite the fact that he was sitting in the very front row and was waving both arms about frantically in an effort to ask a question, Dr. Blanks went out of his way to make sure that the bioweaponeer from Texas was purposefully snubbed.

"There's an individual I see in the center of the auditorium. Please stand and state your question, sir," Dr. Blanks instructed one of the scientists, a rather robust blond Teutonic-appearing attendee in the middle of the vast crowd.

"Dr. Blanks, you've done an excellent job as moderator for this intellectually challenging seminar," the conference attendee stated in a rather heavy Germanic accent. "I have a simple question: have you given consideration to any of the obvious future lucrative commercial applications of the RV-1986 virus?"

"I don't follow you," Dr. Blanks replied as he scratched his chin.

"You're clearly missing the big picture. Perhaps the virus can be attenuated in such a way that it only infects the marrow stem cells.

In that way, a venerable human factory could be created that would allow an aggressive pharmaceutical firm to exploit such infected individuals for the purpose of harvesting pluripotent stem cells that could then be utilized for tissue regenerative purposes or perhaps even to extend the human life span. Any company that could get a patent on this biotechnology would become filthy rich."

"Is that so?"

"If viral attenuation were actually successful," the attendee elaborated, "the new strain could be safely injected into human subjects while avoiding the infection of other critical tissues of the human body such as that gut, kidneys, and erythroblasts. As best as I can tell, it's the infection of these other tissues and organ systems, outside the realm of the infected pluripotent stem cells, that's strictly responsible for the clinical manifestations of human vampirism."

"So, let me try to wrap my head around your suggestion," Dr. Blanks summarized. "You want to take perfectly healthy normal human beings, infect them with an attenuated version of RV-1986, and then commercially exploit them? Are you serious?"

"Dead serious! It's a field of gold ready to be strip-mined."

"Your proposal, sir," Dr. Blanks replied in anger, "is quite unethical. Maybe the fascists would have tried something so reprehensible forty-five or so years ago, but certainly no human subject review board that's affiliated with any modern pharmaceutical firm would ever authorize that such experimental studies be undertaken in this highly enlightened and morally cognizant era."

"You're wrong about that, Dr. Blanks," the attendee said. "I guess you've not been paying attention to current human events. Surely even an optimist like you should be able to recognize the relentless encroachment of evil upon a fallen world."

"That's outside the scope of this seminar," Blanks said.

"No, it's not," the attendee said. "Embrace my suggestion, as this is not a far-fetched idea. After all, we currently employ BCG bacterial bladder washings to successfully treat superficial lower urinary tract transitional cell carcinomas, do we not? In remote times, active cowpox inoculations were utilized to vaccinate at-risk patients against the more dangerous smallpox virus. Ever since the middle of our own twentieth century, we've routinely utilized attenuated living virus inoculations. Vaccines are now a trusted therapeutic weapon in our armamentarium that we confidently employ against a host of infectious diseases!"

"Perhaps, but it's quite apparent that the risk for malignant transformation of these infected marrow cells that dedifferentiate into a pluripotent stem cell that you speak of is theoretically extraordinarily high. Can't you see? There's no 'free lunch' here. In the animal studies that were done in Santa Fe utilizing immunologically nude mice, teratocarcinomas developed among the test subjects. Also, in the case of one unfortunate human being who became infected with RV-1986, I'm personally aware that a preleukemic state was recently discovered in a—"

Dr. Blanks stopped dead in his tracks. Something was wrong! The symposium moderator took a moment to actually scrutinize the individual in the audience who was addressing him.

"Wait!" Dr. Blanks barked out to the projector attendant. "Turn off the slide show. Do it now! It would appear that we have an uninvited guest in our midst." At that moment, the man in the auditorium who'd asked the question about the potential commercial value of RV-1986 was quickly retreating to the exit door at the rear of the auditorium.

"Doctor, I don't remember your name, but I met you at an industry display booth at last year's AACR conference," Dr. Blanks exclaimed. "You're the research director from the Leben Kur AG pharmaceutical firm, are you not? How did you get in here in the first place?"

According to explicit federal regulations, Big Pharma was strictly forbidden to attend the Night Crawler Symposium. This edict especially applied to a specific disreputable foreign firm that had previously collaborated directly with the Nazis during World War II.

"Security! Security!" Dr. Blanks pleaded. "Stop that man. Look, he has a tape recorder. He's not credentialed to attend any segment of this private conference!"

By then it was too late. Just before the Leben Kur AG pharmaceutical company's chief scientist in charge of new product development could be apprehended and stripped of his illicit recording machine, the interloper fled the auditorium and quickly evaporated among the busy denizens and inner beltway influence peddlers who were bustling about on the congested avenues of Washington, DC.

10

SANGRE IMPÍA EN SANTA SANGRE

"I apologize for my rather callous misidentification of your gender, but with your voluminous Leonese coif and your nappy sequined pantsuit outfit that's no doubt mercifully shielding the public from the visual horror of your furry stovepipe lower extremities, I erroneously assumed that I was talking to none other than the legendary soul singer named James Brown," Augustus Placard rudely remarked to the woman standing directly in front of him.

"I didn't know that I looked like James Brown," the woman said, obviously failing to recognize the hostile sarcasm that had been levied directly at her. "Nobody ever told me that before. Do you really think that I look like James Brown?"

"You do, indeed," the colonel noted. "For just a moment I was quite certain that you were going to break out into a profuse gummy sweat and belt out a heartfelt rendition of 'Try Me.' Momentarily, I was convinced that the James Brown backup vocal group the Famous Flames were about to run out and throw a towel on you! To be frank, I'd pay good money to see somebody throw *something* on you," Colonel Placard said with a sneer.

"Oh my! How charming you are. Allow me to be so bold as to introduce myself. I'm the one and only Congresswoman Manteen Rivers. I represent the downtrodden and humble people of color in Los Angeles. May I call you Augustus? That's your first name, is it not?"

"No! My first name is Colonel, and my last name is Placard. Therefore, I would appreciate it if you addressed me as 'Colonel Placard,' if it's all the same to you, madam. By the way, didn't several Democratic Party power brokers get accused recently of trying to illegally gerrymander your congressional district?"

"Those were just nasty rumors," the congresswoman said. "That particular accusation is just another example of the white racism."

"Whatever," Placard said in disgust. "What can I do for you?"

"Frankly, Colonel, you should be asking the question of what I can do a lot of for you. You're getting close to the end of your military career, and I'm certain that you'd like to grab onto a golden parachute and gently float down into a comfortable retirement. I have generous friends in the pharmaceutical industry who would like to get their hands on a living specimen who's infected with the human vampire virus, RV-1986. If you make that happen, I can assure you that you'll be generously compensated."

"I read a public report about you that was published by the conservative watchdog group known as the Americans for a Responsible and Ethical Government," Placard said defiantly.

"Plain and simple, that was a smear campaign."

"You must be very proud that the AREG organization recently issued the report that you're the most corrupt member of Congress that America has seen since the post–Civil War Reconstruction era."

"Wait just a moment," the congresswoman protested.

"No!" Placard exclaimed. "I know that you're a member of the House Financial Services Committee, and as I recall, you pushed through a bill to bail out a failed savings and loan company located in Los Angeles."

"What if I did?"

"I remember that the outfit was called United People's Union of Regional Assets," Placard said.

"It was a respectable financial institution that specifically catered to minority citizens."

"If I'm not mistaken, the acronym for that particular failed savings and loan organization has been referred to by the political pundits as UP UR ASS. That's quite appropriate, if you ask me," Placard said.

"You sound like one of those racist conservatives."

"Hardly," Placard said. "As it turned out, your husband was the *only* stockholder of that disreputable financial firm. As it's quite rare for any 'downtrodden and humble' military personnel to actually have an opportunity to meet somebody of your microscopic stature, perhaps I should ask you for your autograph."

"Now, Colonel, I'm not going to stand here and let you pummel me with inconsequential stories that are little more than despicable and desperate political innuendoes," Rivers replied. "Do I make myself clear?"

"Crystal."

"Don't be naïve! Take the money that'll be soon offered to you. That's how we do things inside the beltway," the congresswoman pleaded. "You're truly a fool if you think otherwise."

"No, you're wrong. However, that's how they seemingly do things within the confines of this filthy, stagnant, corrupt, primordial shit box from which you've apparently emerged. Look, I happen to be personal friends with members of the Army Corps of Engineers. Maybe I should give those boys a call someday soon and have them show up here in DC so they can drain the swamp."

Manteen Rivers simply stared at Colonel Placard in stunned silence. Never before had she been spoken to in such an inflammatory manner.

"If you would excuse me, I'm about to give the follow-up Night Crawler Symposium lecture that's scheduled to start within the next two minutes. As it now stands, there's nothing that I can do to keep you from attending my presentation. Nonetheless, I assure you that our business here is finished," Placard said in his own defense. "Do I make myself clear?"

"Crystal."

"Good," Placard said with a menacing grin. "If you ever try to bribe me again, I won't even bother to turn you over to the Congressional Ethics Committee, if such an effete and hypocritical aggregation of corrupt legislators so named actually exists. I won't have to. I have no fewer than two human vampires on my hit-squad team. I'll just bring them up here to your precious DC beltway and let them eat you. As I previously said, I'd pay good money to see somebody throw *something* on you—dirt, to be precise."

"Well, I never!" the congresswoman howled.

"Keep it up," the colonel said, "and I can guarantee that what I just told you will soon be your ignominious fate. Rest assured, I would be honored to render a stirring eulogy about your wondrous attributes (or perhaps lack thereof) at your glorious bon voyage into the celestial hereafter, which would most assuredly be a 'closed casket' event. Do you catch my meaning?"

"That's a threat!"

"Why, it most certainly is! As for now, I'm due at the podium. Therefore, madam, I must bid you a fond adieu, and I trust that you'll enjoy the rest of the Night Crawler Symposium."

Romero Lopes realized that at any moment, the Federales were going to poke their big, fat noses into the cab of the stolen truck and start asking a lot of damning questions. "Okay, Sapo, we're up to bat."

"What do you want me to do, master?"

"Simple: lean back against the headrest and pretend that you are asleep," Romero Lopes instructed. "Let me do all the talking."

Within a matter of just a few moments, a Mexican federal policeman cautiously approached the vampiro duo as they pulled up to the roadblock. Another federal officer stood directly in front of the truck with his arms folded. "Who are you people, and where are you going? Let me see your identification papers, please," the most proximal officer instructed.

"I'm terribly sorry about this situation, Officer," Romero explained, "but my friend and I lost all of our identification papers, including our wallets. We were recently set on fire by a gringo at a gasoline station in Durango, and that's why we don't have any clothing. I truly apologize for driving about naked like this, but it does provide for a few distinct advantages. When I become sexually aroused, my lover, El Sapo, just has to lean over and give me a blow job while I'm driving the truck. It actually works out quite well."

The federal officer looked into the truck and scrutinized the perineal region of Romero Lopes before he spoke with a glazed look upon his pale face. "As best I can tell, you don't have a pecker anymore."

"Oh, it's there are all right," Lopes answered. "I just have a teeny-weeny 'peeny,' that's all. I'm not particularly proud of my current circumstances, but I try to get by as best I can."

"You're also missing your left eye!" the officer noted.

"It has often been said," Romero Lopes answered, "that *en la tierra de los ciegos, el hombre con un ojo es el rey*."

The officer nodded his head in agreement and said, "You know, I once saw those very words written on the bathroom wall of the Tequila Town bar in Ciudad Juárez, years ago. At that time, I was not sure what the graffito meant."

"Well, now you do," Lopes said. "As a case in point, to confirm that I am now indeed the king, I want you and your colleague who's standing at the front of the truck to give me a blow job before El Sapo and I pull through your checkpoint."

"We'd be happy to accommodate you."

"Good! Are you boys looking for the gringo who set my friend and me on fire?" Romero asked.

"Why, we most certainly are," the Federale replied. "Tell me something: if you and your friend were set on fire in Durango, how did you survive?"

"Well, funny you should ask," Romero Lopes replied. "My friend who's taking a nap beside me is a vampiro. As a matter of fact, I am too. We're both hit men for the Calle cartel. As you probably know, the Calle Vampiro cartel *owns* the Mexican Federales. Alas, you boys technically now work for me, and I command that you do everything I tell you to do!"

"You won't get any argument from me," the federal officer replied. "Say, doesn't this truck belong to Officer Sergio?"

"I have no idea. I stole this truck. You don't have a problem with that, now, do you?" Romero asked.

"Not a bit. What would you like my colleague and I to do for you right now?" the police officer politely offered.

"First, I want you to break down this roadblock. After all, there's a long line of cars behind me, and I don't want to be rude to the other motorists who have been patiently waiting at this checkpoint," Romero thoughtfully replied. "After that, I want you and your friend to follow El Sapo and me into the brush just about a hundred meters or so. After you give us oral pleasure, we're going to eat you and then steal your clothing."

"Sounds like a solid plan. Hey, Gilberto," the officer called out to his colleague, who was still standing at the front of the truck, "it's time for us to end this roadblock. When we're finished here, we're going to follow these two vampiros out into the wilderness, and then we're going to let them have their way with us." The officer who was named Gilberto smiled at his colleague's instructions with apparent unbridled enthusiasm.

"Hey, Sapo!" Romero Lopes exclaimed. "It is time for you to wake up and have a midday snack."

From the roof of his disabled vehicle perched upon the embankment of a rise in the wilderness north of Mexican Highway 40, Cletus Barker watched in horror through the lenses of his binoculars as a ghastly scene unfolded. Much in the same fashion that the oil pan of his sedan's engine was violently eviscerated by a sharp boulder that was embedded in the exodermal layer of a rutted dirt road, the two Federales Cletus witnessed were being violently eviscerated during a vampiro feeding frenzy. There was absolutely nothing that he could do to interrupt the murder and consumption of two fellow human beings.

Cletus was completely baffled as to why the two victims appeared to be completely complicit in their own horrific demise.

After all, the two police officers didn't appear to put up any kind of resistance whatsoever when they were gutted and eaten.

Cletus tried to avert his eyes from the massacre, but he was compelled to watch the entire crime. Once the two vampiros had finished their meal, the older Barker brother watched the ghouls don the attire of the two dead Federales, climb into the cab of a pickup truck, and then simply speed away. The vampiro sitting in the passenger seat of the truck stuck his head out of the window and yelled, "*¡Adelante, Comandante!*"

If there was any good news, it was that at least Cletus wouldn't have to contend with the police checkpoint. If the roadblock had remained intact, it would have led directly to the apprehension of Cletus and his subsequent incarceration. His car, however, was irreparably damaged. Unless he could get his hands on another vehicle, he would simply be stuck out in the wilderness. If that turned out to be the case, then he would painfully have to accept the consequence that his two vicious vampiro adversaries would eventually find Lorena and Nathan hiding out in the town of Santa Sangre sooner rather than later.

Fortunately for Cletus, the answer to his prayer for an alternative motorized conveyance was actually right in front of his face. The cars on Highway 40 were speeding past a recently abandoned police cruiser on the shoulder of the road. The patrol car, no doubt, had previously been assigned to the pair of police officers whose earthly remains were now entrapped within the confines of the upper gastrointestinal tracts of Romero Lopes and his partner in crime, El Sapo.

After retrieving the contents from the trunk of his sedan, which included the weapons that he had smuggled across the border, Cletus cautiously approached the dormant police cruiser. He was pleasantly surprised to find that the keys to the highway prowler were still in the ignition. As a bonus, a twelve-gauge pump and a box of shells were readily apparent in the back seat. Avoiding the passing traffic, Cletus was able to quickly enter the vehicle on the driver's side, turn over the ignition, and resume his road trip that, to date, had been anything but an enjoyable excursion.

The personal bodyguard of El Tiempo jammed the barrel of his shotgun firmly against the back of the head of Dr. Cloud. "Don't shoot!" the physician pleaded. "I'm a good friend of Lorena Pastore. I've come all the way down here from New Mexico to find her and also to locate Blake Barker's son, Nathan. Listen to me: I'm not here to cause trouble. I'm actually here to help."

"Is that so? How did you find our ranch?" the bodyguard asked. "The villagers of Santa Sangre know very well that trouble is coming this way. I would have expected them to keep quiet, especially when a stranger showed up in town."

"I told a waitress who worked at the midtown café that I was Lorena Pastore's long-lost fiancé. Fortunately, once the waitress took pity upon me, she was more than happy to tell me the location of Rancho Feliz," Cloud answered. "Otherwise, I would've never found this place."

"Well, we'll just have to see about that," the bodyguard said. "I'm giving you fair warning: if Lorena doesn't recognize you, I'm going to blow your head off, and then La Ranchera and I are going to dice you up and bury you underneath the two big saguaro cacti near the entryway. I suspect that you're so full of shit that what's left of your body would become an excellent fertilizer."

Roused by the commotion at the front door, Lorena poked her head out into the portal to see what was awry. "Oso, don't!" she said to the bodyguard. "I know this man. He's a friend of mine."

As Lorena gently pulled the barrel away from the back of Dr. Cloud's head, the bodyguard said, "He told me that he was your fiancé. Is this true?"

"Well," Lorena said, "maybe at one time. Forgive my manners. Cloud, I would like you to meet Oso Negro."

"We've met!" Dr. Cloud said with a scowl as he rubbed the back of his head.

"Oso provides security here at the ranch," Lorena explained. "Everybody has been a bit on edge because we've been certain that trouble is coming for Nathan and me."

Oso Negro looked at Dr. Cloud with suspicion and asked, "*¿Eres Indio nativo, verdad?*"

"Navajo," Cloud said. "Deal with it!"

"Oso," Lorena said, "why don't you take a short break? Go into *la cocina* and enjoy *una cerveza fría*." Lorena embraced Cloud and kissed him on the cheek. "I'm going to take Cloud to meet Nathan, and then I'm going to introduce the good doctor to none other than El Tiempo. After all, it would seem that there's a lot of catching up that we need to do."

Romero Lopes was crestfallen to see that the hit squad that the cartel had sent to Santa Sangre was only comprised of a few foot soldiers. Nonetheless, manners dictated that the vampiro offer a polite and cordial introduction to his soon-to-be new colleagues. "My name is Romero Lopes. I'm certain that some of you already know my understudy El Sapo, as he's been a member of the cartel a lot longer than I've been associated with the organization. For hierarchical clarity, I suppose that you gentlemen may consider me to be a 'tactical consultant.' Who's the leader of your group?"

"El Mago! Your reputation precedes you," a member of the hit squad said as he and his three colleagues strolled onto the midtown causeway. "It's an honor for me to meet you. I'm in charge of this squad. My men know me as Tiburon, but my friends call me Tibby." When the leader of the hit team smiled, he revealed a mouth of full of mangled, decayed and misshapen teeth. "I apologize for my ugly smile, but I think my dentist was huffing on his own laughing gas when he last worked on my grille!"

"There are only four of you?" Lopes asked. "Frankly, I expected a larger contingency of foot soldiers to participate in this operation. Who are the three men under your command?"

"The big man standing directly behind me is known as El Gusano," Tiburon replied. "The other two men are brothers from Monterrey. The one on your left is one nasty cheap-ass son of a bitch called El Codo. Don't even think about ever letting this guy borrow even one measly peso from you, as you'll never get it back. The striking individual behind me on your right is Codo's greasy brother Pirata."

Lopes nodded toward Pirata's left arm. There was a steel hook where a hand should have been attached. "Born that way?"

"Oh, hell no," Tiburon replied. "Last year, Pirata was caught in the act of licking *la mujer* of another cartel member. He was punished for this transgression by having his left hand cut off with a broken beer bottle."

"That's terrible! Who would do such a thing to such a bronzed and virile masculine specimen?" El Sapo asked as a twinge of throbbing passion stirred in his loins while he gazed upon the handsome man. El Sapo slinked toward Pirata and arched his back like a cat that pined to be scratched. With the dorsum of his index and middle finger, Sapo gently brushed Pirata's ear. He then clicked his tongue sympathetically as he took a good look at the metallic hook affixed to Pirata's left arm stump. "*Cara de temptacion, querpo de repentamiento,*" El Sapo sadly said as he slowly retreated from Pirata's shadow to rejoin his master.

"Well, his brother, El Codo, enforced the act of contrition," Tibby said. "After all, la mujer in question belonged to El Codo! It seems to me that the only things worth fighting for in this world anymore are drogas y mujeres. Isn't that right, El Codo?"

Codo answered this pertinent question with a grin. El Codo was obviously blind in his left eye from what appeared to be a posttraumatic cataract. El Sapo wondered about the sibling dynamics to account for such a situation, and he suspected that somewhere along the way Pirata was the likely suspect responsible for El Codo's permanent left eye injury.

"I hope you run this crew pretty tight," Lopes said. "If you include El Sapo and me, that will only make us a six-man hit squad. In my opinion, an assignment of this magnitude should warrant a dozen men or more. Doesn't the cartel realize that we're going up against another vampiro? If Blake Barker is at Rancho Feliz, he'll be a dangerous adversary, especially if the cartel expects us to bring him back to Guadalajara while he's still alive."

"I'm sorry, but these are all the resources the cartel can currently allocate to this specific mission," Tibby said. "After all, the cartel is facing considerable logistical constraints at this particular time."

"Why would that be the case?" Lopes asked. "I thought that Blake Barker would be a much higher priority to the cartel, especially after he wiped out the members of our affiliate Azteca gang at the federal prison in Ciudad Juárez."

"That's precisely the problem that we're facing," Tibby explained. "The Azteca gang has to be virtually reconstituted with new members from the bottom up in order to reestablish successful commerce with our business associates north of the Bravo. Until we can recruit new members, the cash flow for the Calle Vampiro cartel will be pretty slim. However, we're going to have a hard time recruiting new members while it's widely known that Blake Barker is still very much alive and a potential threat to our business, regardless how lucrative it might turn out to be."

"Well, if that's indeed the case," Lopes said, "we have our work cut out for us."

"All we know at this time is that Blake Barker is headed for some place called Rancho Feliz, but we don't know exactly where this ranch is located. We'll have to get somebody in this community to open up and spill their guts about it."

"Don't worry about that," Lopes said with a malevolent grin. "I have a personal score to settle with a woman named Lorena Pastore to begin with. Capturing Blake Barker will simply be icing on the cake."

"So, you have a history with Lorena Pastore. Would it be romantic in nature?" Tibby asked.

"Perish the thought," Lopes answered. "She stole an obsidian knife from me, and I want it back. In any event, I believe it would be fair to say that my manservant El Sapo and I are no doubt well-endowed with a particularly effective skill set that will readily enable us to get somebody in Santa Sangre to open up and spill their guts. *A la ver, gatos y ratones.*"

"In summary, biological warfare is certainly not a new concept," Augustus Placard elaborated to the members of Congress. After the colonel pulled the microphone from the podium stem to which it had been firmly anchored, he began to walk back and forth across the stage at the front of the auditorium as if he were a caged predator. "I would like the slide projector technician to go back to the last slide, as it would appear that my control button is currently malfunctioning."

In no time, the technician resurrected the final slide. "All set, Colonel."

"Thanks!" Returning his gaze to the audience, Placard continued. "Ladies and gentlemen, we shouldn't become too sanctimonious about the horrific acts of savagery committed by the Unit 731 biological warfare team from World War II. After all, European settlers of the North American continent gladly gave away blankets contaminated with smallpox to the native populations they encountered. That was clearly a shameful act of biological warfare pure and simple, was it not? I for one am not particularly proud of that fact, as I'm obviously a descendant from a long line of European settlers to this continent."

"Not one of us should be guilty of the sins of our forefathers!" a congressional member called out from the audience.

"I suppose you're right," Placard answered, "but that doesn't mean we should sweep our history under a rug. That wouldn't make any more sense than tearing down the Confederate monuments that were erected after the end of the American Civil War, now, would it?"

"That's subject to debate!" Manteen Rivers vociferously responded.

"Be that as it may, in or around AD 1346, the Tartar horde that laid siege to the fortified city of Caffa was devastated by an epidemic outbreak of the plague. Dead bodies that were infected with the bubonic plague were systematically loaded upon catapults by the Tartar warriors and then heaved over the walls of Caffa to purposefully infect the city defenders. This is another example of biological warfare, ladies and gentlemen. Incidentally, the city of Caffa was completely and irrevocably wiped out, down to the last man, woman, and child. If you don't believe me, take a look at a modern map of the Soviet Union. You simply won't find any evidence that Caffa ever existed!"

"What does this historical vignette have to do with today's seminar?" a congressional member asked.

"In light of what we've learned about human vampirism at this inaugural Night Crawler Symposium," Placard explained, "one must give pause to wonder if all of the bodies that were heaved over the fortified walls of Caffa were actually dead, if you catch my meaning. Are there any questions?"

A Congress member in the audience raised his hand and asked, "Is there any evidence that biological warfare contributed to the demise of the pre-Columbian cultures in Mexico and Central America?"

"Recent historical findings suggest that this may indeed be the case," Placard reported. "In Seville, an ancient document believed to have been written by Cortés himself was discovered this past October. The document indicates that human vampire hit squads were employed to exact revenge upon neighboring villages for any insult, real or perceived. It was not uncommon for a hit team comprised of four uninfected foot soldiers and two vampiros to simply show up in a village to rain down terror on the adversaries and engage in extortion, kidnapping, and the like. At this time, we're not certain of the historical significance of the bladed weapons crafted from the volcanic glass known as obsidian. One of my associates from San Antonio, Dr. Hoefferle, has a theory that the noncrystalline structure of obsidian is highly toxic to any unfortunate individual infected with RV-1986, but as of yet, this theory has not been substantiated."

"One last question if you don't mind, Colonel Placard," somebody else from the audience called out. "At this time, no members of the House or Senate are privy to the contents of the secret Night Crawler Protocol, and frankly, I find that appalling. Are you able to confirm or deny the rumor that the NSA has a contingency plan to utilize low-yield tactical kiloton-range atomic weapons directly upon American citizens within the confines of the continental United States if a truly massive epidemic of human vampirism were to actually occur? Now, of course, I'm not talking about the few isolated and self-limited cases that we now must currently contend with from time to time. What I'm talking about is a true epidemic, just like the bubonic plague we spoke of. What I'm talking about is a true extinction-level pandemic event. Any comments?"

"I'm not at liberty to discuss these matters at this particular venue," Placard answered as he gathered his papers and quickly fled the auditorium. The collective members of Congress were, as usual, slow on the uptake. Nonetheless, once they started to grasp the gravity of Placard's nebulous answer, a din of dissent began to simmer among them at the seminar's conclusion.

"Lorena Pastore must have a lot of romantic suitors," the waitress from the midtown café told John Stewart with a chuckle.

"What do you mean?"

"Well, earlier today, a young doctor named Cloud came in here and wanted to know the directions to Rancho Feliz. Just like you, he said that he was from New Mexico. Just like you, he said that he was the fiancé of Lorena Pastore. I wonder how many *muchachos* are out there walking around on the streets of Santa Sangre who want to marry this woman named Lorena Pastore."

"I know this fellow called Dr. Cloud," Stewart said. "I met him at a gas station in Durango. Although I dislike him intensely, I'm not particularly concerned about him. Cloud presents no real competition when it comes to winning over the affection of Lorena Pastore, as far as I'm concerned."

"Oh yeah?" the waitress asked. "Well, he might not offer you much competition, but I can't say the same about the six bad-looking hombres who came through here about a minute before your arrival. They, too, were not only looking for Lorena Pastore but also asking questions about somebody named Blake Barker. If there's somebody in this town named Blake Barker, he has, as of yet, not come through my café."

"Good God in heaven!" Stewart exclaimed. "What on earth did you tell these six men?"

"I told them nothing," the waitress said. "Four of the men became angry and actually threatened me, but there were also these two odd-looking hombres with yellow skin, yellow eyes, and big teeth. They took charge of the situation and ordered the other four men to go outside and look elsewhere."

"Were the men with yellow skin Asian?"

"No!" the woman exclaimed. "They were Latinos. One of the yellow fellows was very polite. In fact, he was quite charming. I'll have you know that I'm a chaste woman, but I would've gladly let him have his way with me right then and there. As a matter of fact, my heart is still pounding away in the middle of my chest after meeting him. I would've let that bad boy eat me alive, if you know what I mean!"

"I know exactly what you're saying! Thanks for your help." As John Stewart left the café, he faced a conundrum that had serious implications. Should he go back and find Blake Barker and Miguel Pastore in an effort to gather reinforcements to confront the dangerous men who just showed up in town, or should he press on to Rancho Feliz and warn Lorena and Nathan that trouble was coming? Stewart painfully realized that no matter what course of action he would be forced to take, it would ultimately be the wrong decision.

Although very young, Nathan realized that something had fundamentally changed with Lorena. Ever since Lorena and Nathan's arrival at Rancho Feliz, Lorena was slowly becoming aloof. The more she was around El Tiempo, the more she was becoming withdrawn from Nathan.

"What's wrong, Lorena?" Nathan asked. "You're not happy anymore. Don't you like the ranch?"

"I shouldn't be here anymore." Lorena scowled. "I'm being pulled away. I have to leave this place."

"Where will we go?"

"You're not going anywhere," Lorena said. "You'll stay here, but I have to go south. I have to get out of here."

"What will happen to me?"

"You'll grow up," Lorena answered. "Hopefully you'll have a good life, but that is up to you."

"Don't leave me!" Nathan pleaded. "I need a hug."

"Well, I don't."

"Don't say that!" Nathan exclaimed. "Everybody needs hugs. I love you, Lorena."

"I know you do."

As he flipped a dollar bill to the coffee shop waitress to settle his tab, the research scientist nervously glanced at his watch to make certain that he wouldn't miss his flight from Dulles International Airport to San Antonio. "Look, I don't have a lot of time," Dr. Shiftless explained to the director of new product development from the Leben Kur AG pharmaceutical firm. "Now that the seminar is over, I'll be returning to San Antonio with Colonel Placard and Dr. Hoefferle. I must say, it was really stupid of you to open your mouth at the symposium and express your ideas to Dr. Blanks about the commercial possibilities of pluripotent stem cells. I thought for certain that when the security team chased you out of the auditorium, you were going to get nailed to the wall!"

"Not one of my finer moments," the research scientist admitted. "I had no idea that Dr. Blanks was such a zealot. Before you depart, I want to know if you've given any further thought to my request to allow Leben Kur AG to get its hands upon an individual infected with the RV-1986 virus. If you go through with this, you will be rich beyond your wildest dreams."

"I've given it a lot of thought, and I've formulated some ideas. Let's talk soon. For our mutual safety, I insist that our future communications be through public pay phones only," the doctor said.

"Agreed."

Meanwhile, on the walkway between concourse A and concourse B at Dulles International Airport, another member of Placard's bioweapon team nervously glanced at his watch to make certain that he wouldn't miss his flight back to San Antonio. "Look, I don't have a lot of time," Dr. Hoefferle explained to the scientist from the Sangre Impía Perfume Company who was in charge of new product development. "Now that the seminar is over, I'll be returning to San Antonio with Colonel Placard and Dr. Shiftless. I must say, it never occurred to me that the odd pan-mammalian pheromones found in the sweat of individuals infected with RV-1986 would have any commercial value."

"Truly one of my finer moments," the research biochemist boasted. "Before you depart, I want to know if you've given any further thought to my request to allow the Sangre Impía Perfume Company to get its hands upon an individual infected with the RV-1986 virus. If you go through with this, you will be rich beyond your wildest dreams."

"I've given it a lot of thought, and I've formulated some ideas. Let's talk soon. For our mutual safety, I insist that our future communications be through public pay phones only," the doctor said.

"Agreed."

At the Pentagon, the military director of the top-secret bioweapons division nervously glanced at his watch to make certain that he wouldn't miss his flight back to San Antonio.

"Look, I don't have a lot of time," Colonel Placard explained to the deputy director of the NSA. "Now that the seminar is over, I'll be returning to San Antonio with Dr. Ron Shiftless and Dr. Hoefferle. I must say, it never occurred to me that the Mexican Federales would use my team like a rented mule to do their own dirty work. I was an idiot. What a bunch of chumps those goddamned Federales must think we are."

"Not one of my finer moments," the deputy director said. "It's my fault, Colonel, not yours. We should have known the Federales were in bed with the Calle Vampiro drug cartel all along. All that you and your team managed to do when you boys went down to Ciudad Juárez was to wipe out the competition for the Federales and the Calle Vampiro cartel, I'm ashamed to say. As soon as the cartel is able to reconstitute its subsidiary Azteca gang to fully operational status in Juárez, our intelligence community predicts that there will be a fourfold increase in the amount of drugs, crime, and illicit sex-slave traffic flowing over into the United States from the border."

"America should build a security wall on our side of the Bravo to keep these bad hombres out."

"I'm sorry, Colonel, but you and I both know that with the corrupt Congress the public is sadly saddled with, the very security of the American people is the furthest thing from the minds of these useless politicians. It would seem that the only thing they're interested in is finding new constituents who will vote them into power in perpetuity."

"Sad, but no doubt true."

"Before you depart, I want to know if you've given any further thought to taking your team back down to Los Estados Unidos de México and running an unsanctioned mission to exact a pound of flesh from the Calle Vampiro cartel and maybe even the Federales. If you elect to do this mission, it will certainly be without an invitation from the Federales this time around. If you're killed or captured on this mission, the State Department will disavow any knowledge of your actions, much less acknowledge your very existence."

"I've given it a lot of thought, and I've formulated some ideas. Let's talk soon. For our mutual safety, I insist that our future communications be through public pay phones only," the colonel said.

"Agreed."

"Put down the damned gun!" John Stewart pleaded as the personal bodyguard of El Tiempo jammed the barrel of the shotgun firmly against the back of his head. Stewart was regarded as little more than a potentially dangerous unexpected visitor who had suddenly appeared at the front door of the hacienda at Rancho Feliz. "Don't shoot. I'm a good friend of Lorena's brother, Miguel Pastore. I've come all the way down here from New Mexico to find Lorena and also to locate Blake Barker's son, Nathan. I'm not here to cause trouble. I'm actually here to help."

"Is that so? How did you find our ranch?" the bodyguard asked.

"A waitress who works at the midtown café told me how to get here."

"Well, we'll just have to see about that," the bodyguard said. "I'm giving you fair warning: if Lorena doesn't recognize you, I'm going to blow your head off, and then La Ranchera and I are going to turn you into fertilizer!"

"Listen, take this silver chain and gold ring that I am wearing around my neck. It's a ring that belongs to Lorena. Show it to her, and explain to her that her brother, Miguel, and also Blake Barker are in town looking for her and the young boy, Nathan. Tell her that six bad hombres are coming this way and that they're looking to cause trouble.

When the old vampiro El Tiempo was aroused by the commotion at the front door, he poked his head out into the portal to see what was awry. "Oso, don't!" El Tiempo said to the bodyguard. "I don't know this man, but if he's a friend of Lorena Pastore's brother, he's a friend of mine. Put the gun down, you *maldito torpe*."

As Oso slowly retracted the barrel, moving it away from the back of John Stewart's head, the newly arrived visitor exhaled a deep sigh of relief. "My name is John Stewart. Six dangerous men are coming this way. I'm quite certain that they'll be here shortly. They're looking for Lorena and also for Blake Barker. Lorena used to work for Blake. The young boy, Nathan, is Blake's son. Blake doesn't want to cause any harm to Lorena. He just wants to get his boy back. Listen to me, you people have to get ready! Two of the six men who are coming this way are vampires."

"*¿Dos* vampiros?" the old patriarch asked "¡Dios mío!"

"No shit, daddy-o!" Stewart exclaimed. "You must be the old codger they call El Tiempo. Miguel Pastore told me that you were a badass vampiro when you were in your prime."

"Maybe at one time," El Tiempo said. "Forgive my manners. John Stewart, I would like you to meet Oso Negro."

"We've met!" Stewart said with a scowl as he rubbed the back of his head.

"Oso provides security here at the ranch," El Tiempo explained. "Everybody has been a bit on edge, as we've been certain that trouble is indeed coming for Nathan and Lorena."

Oso Negro looked at John Stewart with suspicion and asked, "*¿Eres Tejano, verdad?*"

"I was born in Texas," Stewart said. "Deal with it!"

"Oso," El Tiempo said, about to make a specific request, "I need you to take this silver chain and gold ring and show it to Lorena. If these items do indeed belong to her, you'll need to take Lorena, Dr. Cloud, and Nathan away from the hacienda and hide them in the feed bin. When you're finished, find La Ranchera and bring her here with you when you return. Please hurry, Oso, as time is of the essence. In the meantime, Mr. Stewart, I would like you to give me more details about these troublemakers who will be paying my ranch an unwelcome visit today. By the way, amigo, do you know how to use a shotgun?"

"Why, certainly."

"Great!" El Tiempo said. "That means three of us will be armed, including you, Oso Negro, and a very angry and aggressive young woman you've not met as of yet named La Ranchera. Don't forget to count me in, *chema*. Although I'm not a young man anymore, I'm still essentially a biological weapon!"

"Wait," John Stewart said. "I don't have a good feeling about this. Maybe we should batten down that hatch until Blake Barker and Miguel Pastore get here. After all, they should already be on their way."

"There's no *tiempo*," El Tiempo replied.

"Why don't you have more armed men under your employment, especially at a time like this?" Stewart asked.

"I run a tight ship here," El Tiempo answered. "As the old saying goes, *entre menos burros, más elotes*."

After leaving the midtown café, the Calle Vampiro hit squad split up and began to go house to house through the east side neighborhood to see if anybody would be willing to reveal the location of Rancho Feliz. Romero Lopes got lucky and was able to charm an elderly widow who invited the vampiro inside her home to have a bite to eat. Without offering any resistance, she told him everything he wanted to know. After Lopes slaughtered the elderly woman, he stuck his head out the front door and yelled loudly for El Sapo to come down the alleyway and join him in the festivities.

"Did I get here too late?" El Sapo asked as Romero Lopes gently handed his junior assistant the old woman's cirrhotic liver.

"No, not at all," Lopes answered. "This old hag said that the place we're looking for is just beyond the eastern boundary of Santa Sangre. I was very gentle with her when I drained her dry and took out her heart and liver. She must have consumed a lot of mescal in her life, because her liver seems to be as tough as an old boot. I am sorry about that, Sapo. I should have saved you her heart instead."

"I really don't mind, master," El Sapo replied. "Not one bit."

"Did Tibby and his crew bring up the truck?"

"It's right outside," Sapo answered. "We're ready to roll!"

La Ranchera ran into the courtyard and said, "Pepe, we're out of time! A truck is a thousand meters out with dos hombres in the cab and four in the bed. The enemy is upon us."

"Ranchera, this is John Stewart. He's a new friend of ours. Do you have a weapon for him?" the old vampiro asked.

The ranch hand approached Stewart and handed him a Remington 870 twelve-gauge pump with a box of double-aught shells. A rough-hewn woman lacking even the most modest of feminine attributes, La Ranchera grabbed John Stewart by the collar and pulled him close. After she gave him a passionate kiss, she said, "You'd better survive this battle, gringo. When this is over, I'm going to take you behind the barn and have my way with you!"

"Now, wait," Stewart said with a quiver in his voice, "Lorena is my fiancée, and she might not be happy with either of us right about now."

"Don't make me laugh, gringo!" Ranchera said. "I spoke to Lorena before I came over here, and she said she's never even met you before. Lorena doesn't care about you. In fact, since she's been here at the ranch, she doesn't seem to care about anything anymore except her own hide."

"What about the little boy?"

"Nathan?" Ranchera asked. "As far as I am concerned, she doesn't seem to give a flying fart about that child, either."

"Be that as it may, Lorena's in love with me," Stewart replied. "She just doesn't know it yet."

"Is that so? If I may be so bold, I believe I've already changed your disposition. Tell me something, gringo; is that a *pito* in your pocket or your *quete*?

When Oso Negro arrived, playtime was over. "Ranchera, meet me at the courtyard entry. I'm going to set up El Tiempo and Señor Stewart behind the big saguaros to ambush anybody who makes it this close to the hacienda. I think we're as ready as we'll ever be. Let the fiesta begin."

"*Que padre!*" La Ranchera said enthusiastically. "I'm ready to dance!" She turned to John Stewart and added, "Like the old song goes, gringo, save the last dance for me. After we take care of these pendejos, I'll take a bath and get all gussied up for you."

"Now, wait just a minute!" Stewart protested.

"I'll take a pocketknife and scrape out the dried-up cow shit that's lodged underneath my fingernails," La Ranchera said as she ran her tongue across her upper lip. "After that, I'll steal some of Oso Negro's aftershave and splash some on *la pequeña gato hembra*. I promise you, I'll make it worth your while."

Tiburon carefully drove the truck to the outer limits of the compound, but he found that a tall security wall served as the perimeter's enclosure. As was often customary in upscale Mexican haciendas built in the remote past, broken shards of glass were cemented into the top of the security wall to discourage anybody from trying to scale the barrier.

"We've got no choice," Tiburon said, "but to charge through the courtyard in a frontal assault. I hope they're not waiting for us. We'll enter the courtyard in a standard two-by-two box formation. I'll have Pirata y Codo carry the Mac-10 machine pistols and take point. The dos vampiros will be the heavy armor bringing up the rear. El Gusano and I will be in the midpack, toting long arms. Once inside, fan out and kill anybody you encounter, but remember, Blake Barker is possibly here already. As the cartel wants us to take him alive, leave this dangerous gringo for El Sapo and Romero Lopes to neutralize. Well, I guess there's nothing else for me to say. Let's do it."

Codo and his brother, Pirata, were walking abreast as they slowly entered the courtyard. Because Codo was blind in his left eye, he was totally unaware that the twelve-gauge shotgun barrel wielded by La Ranchera was a mere six inches away from his left temple when the trigger was pulled. The percussion of the blast showered Pirata with the bloody intracranial contents of Codo's exploded skull.

Before La Ranchera could eject the spent shell casing, Pirata was able to pivot and hose her down with an entire magazine of nine-millimeter lead from his automatic weapon. Sadly for the drug cartel hit man, Pirata failed to realize that Oso Negro was hiding directly behind the right entry pillar, armed with another shotgun.

The life of Pirata came to a violent conclusion. The point-blank twelve-gauge blast from Oso's weapon was airmailed directly into the hit man's dorsal thorax. Unable to utter an intelligible word, Pirata was nevertheless able to render a low-pitched, albeit brief, gurgling gasp of agony as he witnessed with his own eyes the shredded remnants of his ruptured heart escape the confines of his rib cage, which had completely disintegrated at the costal-sternal junction.

Thinking his odds were better with an automatic weapon, Oso reached down to try to retrieve one of the MAC-10 machine pistols. Although the corpse of the hit man Codo was missing essentially all of its anatomic accoutrements north of the Adam's apple, the lifeless body was still clutching a fully loaded automatic gun that hadn't yet been fired in the course of the violent melee. Oso was able to grab the machine pistol, but a hail of bullets from Tiburon and El Gusano dropped the big man where he stood.

Although he only had one eye and was slowed from the previous leg injury rendered by Lorena Pastore and the obsidian knife, Romero Lopes pushed past Tiburon and Gusano. El Sapo was in tow. The two vampiros quickly decimated the defenders inside the hacienda after they breached a shuttered window on the side of the house.

The faithful mayordomo, Señor Bosque, ran out onto the portal and called out to El Tiempo and John Stewart, who were entrenched in a safe spot behind the two big saguaro cacti in the courtyard. El Tiempo was trying to keep his head down while Stewart exchanged gunfire with El Gusano and Tiburon. "El Tiempo!" Bosque cried out. "Dos vampiros have breached the inner sanctum of the hacienda. Rancho Feliz has fallen!"

"It hasn't fallen yet!" El Tiempo defiantly replied. "Get to the feed bin. Put Lorena, Cloud, and the boy into the old Jeep, and get them out of here. Give them the map for how to find my old friend El Mayo down in the Yucatán. Hurry, Señor Bosque, before we run out of time." Bosque circled around to the side of the hacienda and went straight to the back shed to specifically order Lorena, Dr. Cloud, and young Nathan to abandon ship.

"No!" Lorena said as she held Nathan at arm's length. "This child will only slow me down."

"This child has a name," Señor Bosque said to rebuke the curandera. "His name is Nathan, and God forbid that you'll ever forget what brought you to Rancho Feliz in the first place. What's going on here is all because of you!"

"Please take me with you," Nathan pleaded. "I'm afraid! Don't you love me anymore?"

Lorena covered her ears as if she was annoyed by the gunfire, but this afforded her the opportunity to ignore Nathan's most pertinent question.

"I love you, Lorena."

"I know you do."

When John Stewart briefly held his fire to reload, a ranch hand who had taken cover behind a pillar on the portico swiftly attacked El Gusano with a wood ax. When the hit man dodged the ax blade, El Gusano deftly planted the blade of a machete that he held in his left hand deep into the skull of his adversary.

Once this was done, Tiburon and Gusano erroneously believed that Stewart had depleted his supply of ammunition. If that was indeed the case, it was time to finish the task at hand and violently neutralize John Stewart and El Tiempo.

Unfortunately for the hit squad, nothing could have been further from the truth. When the two cartel members were within mere yards of the giant saguaros, John Stewart barrel-rolled out from behind his hiding place and fired away, blowing off Gusano's right foot just above the ankle. In the meantime, El Tiempo lunged at Tiburon. Within seconds, the cartel team leader was eviscerated.

Gusano took off his belt and tried to fashion a tourniquet around his right lower extremity, all the while cursing at John Stewart and El Tiempo. John Stewart loomed over Gusano and was about to finish him off with another blast from his twelve-gauge shotgun when El Tiempo said, "I haven't fed in a while. Let me drain him."

Just before El Tiempo began to vigorously suck away at the arterial blood that was gushing out of the Gusano's amputated and macerated right lower extremity, the old vampire said, "Reload your gun, John, and get to the feed bin. Make sure Lorena and the others got out of here safely. Once I've finished feeding, you and I will need to hunt down the two vampiros and finish them off. I'm certain they're still somewhere here within the confines of this compound."

Stewart ran toward the feed bin while El Tiempo took in much-needed nourishment. "Are you comfortable, my son?" El Tiempo asked Gusano as he vigorously massaged the cartel member's posterior thigh in an effort to promote the flow of blood from the dying man's severed extremity.

"I'm quite comfortable," Gusano replied with a smile. "Thanks for asking."

"I'm indeed glad to hear that," El Tiempo said. "Just relax. This will be over soon." Sadly, by the time the old vampiro caught the scent of the younger, stronger El Sapo, who had crept toward the rear of El Tiempo's rather impromptu feeding session, it was already far too late for the patriarch to defend himself.

In the shed, Bosque was able to give the hand-drawn map to Dr. Cloud, who was already behind the wheel of the vehicle and fumbling with the ignition key. Lorena climbed into the passenger seat of the Jeep while Nathan crawled into the back seat.

"Where to?" Lorena asked Bosque.

"The map provides precise information on how to find refuge in the Yucatán jungle with a vampiro known as El Mayo. Get out of here!"

After Bosque turned away to rejoin the battle, he found Romero Lopes entering the enclosure. The mayordomo bravely threw himself at the vampiro in an attempt to afford the trio an opportunity to escape unscathed.

Cloud frantically tried to fire up the Jeep to ferry Lorena and Nathan out of the shed and on to safety as soon as he possibly could. However, there was something wrong with the vehicle. Every time he turned over the ignition, the engine would immediately fire up as expected, but a recurrent problem occurred when Dr. Cloud put the transmission into drive. The motor would suddenly sputter and die, and then the whole frustrating process would have to be repeated.

"We must have a clogged fuel filter," Lorena explained. "Let's leave Nathan here. You and I will have a better chance to escape if we don't take that boy with us."

"That's not an option! That boy is now our responsibility. He has a name. It is Nathan. We have to take care of him no matter what!"

"Fine, have it your way. Crank the starter again. The next time the engine turns over, rev up the motor hard before you engage the transmission. Hurry!"

Although the mayordomo fought ferociously, a vicious blow to the crown of his head dropped him to the ground. "Take a nap, old man," Lopes instructed. "Today's your lucky day! Somebody must remain alive to bear witness to my handiwork. Through my benevolence, I've selected you to be the one to spread the legend of my terror far and wide. El Gran Brujo has spoken!" Because he sustained a concussion that rendered him unconscious, Señor Bosque was no longer in any position to render aid to help Lorena out of her perilous situation.

Suddenly, the passenger-side window of the Jeep exploded as Romero Lopes reached into the passenger compartment to grab Lorena. "You filthy whore!" Lopes exclaimed. "I want my knife back."

"I'll give it to you, all right!" Lorena slashed away at Romero's face with the black obsidian knife that previously belonged to him. Lopes, humiliated, recoiled in pain. After all, this was the second time that a woman whom he believed to be a powerful gran bruja had inflicted another serious injury upon him.

Cloud turned over the Jeep's ignition yet again and revved the engine hard. The din of the motor muffled Nathan's exit as he jumped out the rear window to check on the welfare of his beloved uncle Romero.

"Throw it in drive, Cloud," Lorena ordered. "Do it now, damn you! Get us out of here!" The Jeep crashed through the door of the shed and escaped amid a thick wall of dust kicked up by the four-wheel-drive vehicle.

Nathan ran to Lopes, who was on his hands knees. "Did Lorena hurt you, Tio?" he asked.

"My son!" Lopes exclaimed. "I'm afraid I'm badly hurt. Help me up to my feet so we can get out of this shed." Nathan held Romero's hand tightly as the vampiro staggered out of the shed. Before Lopes realized what happened, his midabdominal torso exploded as a consequence of a shotgun blast from John Stewart. Lopes again collapsed to his hands and knees. Nathan screamed in horror and disbelief.

Stewart scooped up the young boy, who was kicking and screaming. "Settle down, Nathan. I don't have time to explain everything to you, but I'm a friend of your father," Stewart said. "Calm down. I promise to get you out a here!"

John Stewart was baffled when Nathan grabbed Lopes by the back leg and howled loudly in protest. "No! Go away! Don't hurt Uncle Romero anymore!"

Stewart learned a painful lesson that no good deed goes unpunished when the pan of a shovel hurled by El Sapo struck him in the back of the head. Before Stewart lost consciousness, he briefly saw stars and heard the unmistakable sound of a low-volume, high-pitched whine as he fell forward upon his face.

"Who's this pendejo, master?" Sapo asked.

"His name is John Stewart. He used to be a cook at a restaurant in New Mexico," Lopes said with a moan. "To be frank, I'm surprised to see him. I bit him in the neck a while back. I can't explain why he hasn't transformed into a creature like one of us. In any event, what happened to the old vampiro in the front courtyard?"

"The one known as El Tiempo?" Sapo asked. "I was able to slip up on him and take him out while he was dining on the remains of El Gusano. In any event, I subjected him to what the cartel refers to as 'the extreme punishment.' For now, the old bastard is still hanging around—well, at least for a while. Later today, he'll meet the *zopelotes*."

"Good. I order you to convey the very same hospitality to John Stewart," Lopes said. "Do it now, before he wakes up."

"You're badly hurt, master. I should stay here and take care of you," Sapo said.

"My belly will heal, but my face will be permanently injured, just as my soul is. I'll take Nathan to Guadalajara with me in the truck. The cartel is holding an emergency room doctor at our headquarters as a prisoner of war. He's called 'Russian Bear.' Hopefully, he'll be able to patch me up."

"What should I do, master?"

"I want you to track that Jeep down. Follow it to the ends of the earth if you must, but find the occupants. Recover my obsidian knife."

"Before I go, let's feast upon the wounded," Sapo said.

"No," Lopes said. "Our adversaries were honorable people. Let them rest in peace."

"That doesn't sound like you, master. Are you feeling okay?"

"I most assuredly am *not* okay," Lopes answered. "I'm injured. I'm tired. I'm disgusted."

"Disgusted with what?"

"With myself," Lopes replied as he surveyed the bloody carnage he had wrought.

"Be of good cheer!" Sapo crowed. "This was a great victory for you, master. The cartel will forever remember you as a great warrior."

"Really?" Lopes asked. "So, tell me, Sapo, what's the difference between a great warrior and a mass murderer?"

"I don't know, but I love you, master," El Sapo said. "Your wish will *always* be my command. *Hasta la vista,* jefe. Rest assured, before I see you again, Lorena Pastore will have surrendered the blade."

As planned, Blake Barker and Miguel Pastore met at the midtown causeway and patiently waited for John Stewart to show up, as the river bridge was the predetermined point for the three men to rally at noon. The sudden unmistakable report of automatic gunfire coming from the eastern horizon was readily recognized by the two men. Danger was afoot, and the cacophony was a call to arms!

The two men sprinted toward the sound of fury, and within minutes they found themselves at the gates of Rancho Feliz. "Good God," Blake said. "It's all over!"

As the two vampiros cautiously entered the courtyard, Miguel was the first to witness the horrific methodology employed: the cartel's brand of discipline known as "the extreme punishment." "Blake! Blake! I need you!" Miguel gasped as he averted his eyes. "Blake! Blake! I need you!"

Barker followed Miguel's voice, which was coming from the direction of the two giant saguaro cacti. When his eyes focused on the terror that had been first recognized by Miguel, Barker dropped to his knees and began to pray. Before him, John Stewart and El Tiempo had been crucified to the giant columnar cacti!

Not only had the old vampire been crucified, but also he was decapitated. By the amount of blood poured upon the ground at the base of the giant cactus, it was clear that when the old patriarch was crucified to the saguaro, he was likely still very much alive before being beheaded. It was quite curious to note that Tiempo's missing head was nowhere to be found.

John Stewart was still alive, although his bowels dangled from his abdominal cavity as if they were pink and red streamers gently swaying in the breeze at a ghoulish birthday party. He appeared to be oblivious to the gravity of his abdominal injury that had been inflicted upon him by the two vampiros. "Cut me down from here, boys. I need to get back into the fight."

"The fight's over, John. Is Lopes still here?" Blake asked. "Where's my son?"

"Romero Lopes was seriously injured," John Stewart explained, "but he managed to grab Nathan and abscond with him to Guadalajara from what I heard."

"What's in Guadalajara?" Barker asked.

"The Calle Vampiro cartel headquarters, as best as I can tell," Stewart answered with a faltering voice.

"Well, what about Lorena?" Miguel asked as he used his own bare hands to pull out the long framing nails that had been utilized to affix Stewart's wrists and feet to the giant saguaro.

"Lorena and Dr. Cloud flew out of here in an old Jeep. They blew through the side gate like a bat out of hell," Stewart answered as Miguel gently lowered his dying friend to the ground.

"Are they safe?" Miguel asked.

"No," Stewart sputtered. "Another vampiro was in hot pursuit."

Miguel cradled John's head to offer what little comfort he could. "Oh God! Are those my innards?" John asked as Blake gently tried to repack the critically injured man's eviscerated gastrointestinal tract back into his empty body cavity. At best, it was only a cosmetic gesture and not a therapeutic intervention in any way, shape, or form. "I'm dying, boys, and I never even had a chance to meet Lorena face-to-face. For that, I'm truly sorry. Even if she had only said hello to me and I had a chance to give her a hug and a kiss, it would have perhaps made my life complete."

"God bless you, John," Barker said as he turned away and started to breathe with a heavy and rapid pant, as if he were an overheated canine on a sultry, muggy day. Barker just couldn't bear to look upon another person who had been killed by Romero Lopes or his evil associates.

"You're a good man, amigo," Miguel said as he began to weep. "I'm going to miss you dearly. I know that there will a beautiful place in heaven waiting just for you."

"You think so?"

"¡Señor Stewart, *eres un gran héroe*! This is *exactly* why I wanted my sister to date a gringo like you."

"Thanks, Miguel," John Stewart said with a wry smile. "I hope I resemble that remark!" Sadly, those were John Stewart's last words.

The Jeep continued to cough and sputter until it finally meandered to the shoulder of the road and puked under the throes of an undignified automotive cardiac arrest on Mexico Highway 15-D, just east of Magdalena. "Give me your pocketknife, Cloud," Lorena requested. "I'm going to clear this clogged fuel line once and for all."

In a jiffy, Lorena cut away the contaminated fuel filter cylinder, which was a nonstock replacement part about the size of a small lime. Obviously, the filter was previously jury-rigged into the fuel line during a remote makeshift repair attempt. When Lorena put her lips against the intake nipple of the filter and blew hard with all her might, a near-complete obstruction was confirmed. Lorena tossed the clogged filter to the roadside and deftly reattached the fuel line directly to the carb's intake. The Jeep was now ready to roll.

"Pump the accelerator pedal twice and fire it up, Cloud," Lorena instructed. Cloud followed Lorena's orders. When the engine turned over, the six-cylinder vehicle melodiously purred as if it were a mechanical brass ensemble proudly performing at a snobby chamber music festival in Santa Fe.

"Swap out," Lorena demanded when she returned to the cab of the Jeep. "It's my turn to drive." Cloud climbed out of the Jeep and circled around the front of the vehicle to allow Lorena to take over at the wheel. Before he jumped into the passenger seat, he pulled back the blanket in the rear seat where he had erroneously believed

Nathan was napping. "Lorena! Nathan's gone! He must have jumped out of the vehicle when we were still back at the ranch."

"Good riddance. I'm tired of wiping that little brat's ass. I don't know why that kid is so drawn to Romero Lopes. To be frank, I'm literally sick of his temper tantrums," Lorena said, showing little, if any, concern for the child's welfare.

"What in hell are you saying? He's just a child! Turn around, Lorena! Turn around now! We've got to find him," Cloud pleaded.

"No!" Lorena replied as she planted her foot on the accelerator and continued to drive east on Highway 15-D. "We're not going back for him. Am I clear? If Nathan is in the clutches of a vampiro, it's all over anyhow. He can't be saved. If you want to stay with me, you'll have to abide by my decisions whether you like it or not. Deal with it, Cloud."

11

THE CARTEL

Fredalicious Wilkins realized that she was about to face the ire of two other Congress members, so she pulled her black and pink sequined cowboy hat tight over her springy afro hairdo in an obvious act of defiance when she showed up late at the coffee shop. As she approached the table where Manteen Rivers and Shiva Jaclyn Grant were sitting, it was quite obvious that her two colleagues, who'd been impatiently waiting for her, were annoyed. Thinking that the best defense is often a better offense, Fredalicious wasted no time in hurling aspersions at the two other women.

"Good morning, ladies!" Fredalicious said. "It looks like one of the most *corrupt* members of Congress and also one of the most *idiotic* members of Congress are already waiting for me. Did somebody order me a jelly doughnut? I like doughnuts. They're near and dear to my heart."

"You're late, Fred. Has anyone ever told you that those sequined cowboy hats that you wear make you look like a gay stripper at a bachelorette party?" Manteen Rivers asked.

"I'll take that as a compliment," Fredalicious Wilkins replied.

"Right about now, I would like to yank it off your nappy head," Congresswoman Rivers said. "It wouldn't do any good though, as I know you own more than one of those stupid hats. By the way, how many of those ridiculous things do you have in your personal wardrobe?"

"I own *all* of them!" Fredalicious answered. Wilkins then turned toward Congresswoman Grant and said, "Hello, Shiva. I heard you got chased out of the Night Crawler Symposium for trying to film the proceedings in secrecy. Girl, are you going to spend your entire life on the short bus?"

"Where's the short bus?" Shiva asked, not realizing that she had just been insulted.

"You've got those braids wrapped so tight around your head that you're not letting any oxygen get to your brain," Wilkins said as she sat down at the table. "You need to afro up. It might make you a whole lot smarter. Okay, ladies, enough of these superficial pleasantries. You called this meeting, so let me hear what's on your mind."

"Shiva and I have been trying to foster personal relationships with various cosmetic and pharmaceutical firms for the potential patents that might be forthcoming from the ongoing human vampirism research," Manteen Rivers explained. "As for now, it looks like we're going to get cut out of any potential deals. It's quite obvious that the military and scientific personnel who have access to a human vampire can't be corrupted or are otherwise likely going to negotiate with the cosmetic and pharmaceutical companies directly without using either Shiva or me as a proverbial middleman, or middlewoman as the case may be. If that happens, that means the members of Congress who usually broker these secret side deals are going to be kicked to the curb."

"It happens," Wilkins said. "Deal with it. You can't have your hand in every cookie jar, now, can you?"

"Not on my watch," Rivers replied. "If Shiva and I don't get to line our pockets with a few bus tokens, nobody will!"

"What do you propose?" Wilkins asked.

"Aren't you friends with a lobbyist who can influence the Armed Forces Committee?" Shiva asked.

"Well, we're not exactly friends per se," Wilkins explained, "but the DNC *owns* that boy. Although he's *allegedly* cozy with the Republicans, he does whatever we tell him to do. We control him, ladies-lock, stock, and barrel, I'll have you know. What do you have in mind?"

"If a medical or cosmetic patent doesn't pan out for us from a financial standpoint, I want you to tell the lobbyist to pressure Senator Lumpy McStain to pull the plug on the army's United States Army Department of Biological Warfare. After all, Lumpy is the chief cook and bottle washer on the A.F.C.," Rivers answered. "I'm now bound and determined to make sure Colonel Placard and his team gets caught with their pants down around their ankles someday."

"Might that not be directly injurious to our nation?" Wilkins asked.

"As if I give a shit," Rivers huffed.

"Frankly, I don't either," Fredalicious Wilkins added. "My only objective in all of this is to make sure that the Reagan administration ends up looking bad. I don't want to say too much right now, but there's some back-burner bullshit battle brewing that just might break out into a fabricated national scandal. It could possibly get our president impeached down the road!"

"Ain't *my* president," Shiva Grant said. "What's the angle here?"

"With some much-needed help from our corrupt friends in the news media, the deep state is already working on a story line that Reagan has been colluding with the Russians on national security matters!"

"Is that so?" Shiva Grant asked.

"Well, there's more to it than that," Wilkins answered. "The DNC recently gave a lot of money to a now discredited British spy."

"The purpose being?" Grant asked.

"Well, this slimy limey was consigned with the enviable task of coming up with a dossier about the women with whom Reagan may have been involved with while he was out there in Hollywood during the time between his two marriages," Fred said.

"Any truth to it?" Grant asked.

"Of course not!" Fred answered. "When does the truth have to do with anything a politician has to think, do, or say?!"

"Sounds like you've got a bad case of 'Reagan derangement syndrome'!" Rivers proclaimed.

"Be that as it may, I'll see what I can do to help y'all out, but you bitches are going to owe me big-time after this is all said and done," Fred said. "Next time you sisters are lined up to get a big boost in your offshore bank accounts, I want in on the action. Clear?"

"Crystal," Rivers conceded.

"If our business is now concluded, we'd better get out of here. After all, if John Q. White Man sees three angry black women from Congress sitting around a table in a DC coffee shop, it might be perceived that we're engaged in some kind of unethical conspiracy," Fredalicious Wilkins said with a chuckle.

"Wait—" Shiva Jaclyn Grant exclaimed with an obvious look of confusion upon her face. "I thought that we were *always* engaged in an unethical conspiracy of one type or another."

When the white unmarked delivery van pulled up and parked across the street from the Tequila Town bar, Colonel Augustus Placard turned his head to address the hit team that was assembled in the back of the vehicle. "Nobody, and I do mean nobody, will ever play us for fools again. It makes me sick to my stomach that we did the dirty work for the Federales."

"It's all our own doing," Ron Shiftless said. "We've got nobody to blame but ourselves for how all of this turned out." Shiftless remembered the old saying that no good deed goes unpunished, and he also remembered the rule of unintended consequences. "Well, here we are, boys. The shame is on us, and we've got to set this right." The Calle Vampiro cartel was taking over the drug trade in Ciudad Juárez, and it was directly one of the unintended consequences of the prior interdiction of Placard's hit squad.

"Agreed," the colonel said. "Morales, you come with me and help translate what our spy in the men's room has to tell us. I want the rest of you boys to hold the fort. If any Federales come around here and try to stick their noses into our business, drag their asses into the van and kill 'em. Try not to bloody up their green uniforms. We can use those if we need to. We'll be back shortly."

Placard and Morales casually walked across the street to enter the recently refurbished Tequila Town bar. Placard sat at the bar and ordered a club soda with a wedge of lime. Morales went straightaway to the men's room to hold a private conversation with the elderly blind urinal attendant, Señor Diego del Mar.

"Hola, señor," Morales said. "I hope that you remember me. Your old friend Colonel Placard sent me in here to ask you a few questions. Where might we find the remnants of the local banditos affiliated with the Calle Vampiro cartel?"

"Please don't hurt me!" Diego del Mar pleaded. "I recognize your voice—and your smell. You're one of the Americans. I remember exactly who you are. ¿No eres el vampiro Morales? No quiero más problemas. ¡Por favor!"

"My name is Morales, but nobody's here to hurt you, señor," Morales explained. "We just need some information about the Azteca gang. Are there any members around?"

"The Azteca are not hard to find," Diego del Mar explained, "but if you want to have a meeting with them, friendly or otherwise, you will find them in a bar playing *toques*. The way that they play, it's a very dangerous game, this—this toques. Tell me something: are your men brave enough to take the toques challenge?"

"Are you here to help me bury the dead, or are you just going to stand there like an idiot and stare at me?" Miguel Pastore asked the stranger who had just arrived at Rancho Feliz in a stolen highway police cruiser. As Miguel took the shovel back from Señor Bosque, he wiped the sweat from his brow upon his trousers. Then he stepped back to take an overview of the fresh graves that he and Bosque had just prepared for John Stewart and El Tiempo.

"My, what big teeth you have, Grandma," Cletus Barker said to Miguel as the vampiro dug another shovelful of dirt from the grave site designated for El Tiempo.

"Is this how you usually greet a total stranger?" Miguel asked. "You must be lost. Maybe Señor Bosque and I can help direct you back to the main highway."

"The familial resemblance that I recognize between you and a woman I know named Lorena Pastore is rather uncanny. I have no doubt that you're her brother. You must be Miguel. My name is Cletus Barker. What in hell happened here?"

"The Calle Vampiro cartel sent a six-man hit team to raid the ranch. They were specifically looking for a man named Blake Barker, whom I presume is your brother. Blake and I weren't here when all of this evil shit went down. Blake left the ranch just a little while ago. He's a man on a mission."

"Who's the old man digging the graves with you?" Cletus asked.

"Forgive my manners," Miguel said. "This happens to be Señor Bosque. He's the mayordomo at this hacienda. A vampiro named Romero Lopes trussed him up, stuffed him into a burlap sack, and left him in the barn. I discovered his whereabouts just a few moments before your arrival."

"Unfortunately, I know Romero Lopes," Cletus said. "He's a top-shelf bastard if I've ever seen one. If I ever meet him again, I'll personally cut his heart out and hand it to him."

"Well, fancy that. You'll have to take a number and stand in line," Miguel said. "Spill it to me; what's your story?"

"I am indeed Blake's older brother," Cletus said.

"That would have been my guess," Miguel said. "I don't exactly know all of the details as to why the cartel was looking for your brother, but when they found out that he wasn't here, they kidnapped his son instead. They also went after my sister. I assume you've come across the Bravo to find your brother."

"Your assumption would be wrong," Cletus said. "For quite some time I've had the distinct impression that my brother would have absolutely no qualms about killing me. Like you, he's become a vampire. As for you, I want to let you know that I'm heavily armed. I have enough weapons to launch a full-scale assault upon the slopes of Mount Suribachi if duty should call. If you come any closer, I'll drop you like a stone, and then I'll cut off your head. You better not have any aspirations about making a meal out of me."

"Keep your shirt on," Miguel said. "Just for the record, I'm not a cannibal. I can testify that your brother, Blake, is actually a decent person, if there is such a thing anymore in this evil world that we live in. He may have had homicidal tendencies in the past, but he has them no longer as best as I can tell."

"Fine and dandy," Cletus said, "but be that as it may, I'm not looking for him. I am actually looking for your sister, Lorena. She's in love with me."

"Is that so?"

"She just doesn't know it yet," Cletus said. "Please tell me that she survived this carnage."

"You just missed her. She left here about an hour ago. From what I was told, she fled to the Yucatán to take refuge with a man down there known as El Mayo," Miguel explained. "Señor Bosque has the map that shows where she's headed. I was told by my best friend John before he died that a vampiro was in pursuit of Lorena."

"Do tell," Cletus said. "If that's the case, why in hell are you sticking around here trying to bury the dead? The dead can wait. After all, they aren't exactly going anywhere, if you catch my drift. If you give a shit about your sister, you should have gone after her, especially if a vampire is chasing her."

"She'll be fine," Miguel said. "After all, she's not alone. My friend Dr. Cloud is with her, and he should be able to protect her. In fact, I would entrust Dr. Cloud with my own life. After your nephew, Nathan, was captured by the cartel, he was taken to Guadalajara. Blake is on his way there to surrender himself. He's going to try to do a straight-up trade; he'll give up his life in order for his son to be freed."

"Oh, for shit's sake," Cletus said. "Do you think that'll really work?"

"Not for a minute.'

"I'll wager that if Blake turns himself in to the cartel, then his fate and the fate of my nephew, Nathan, will be forever sealed."

"I agree," Miguel answered. "Get a shovel from the shed behind the house and help me bury the rest of the dead. Now, four of these dead bodies are cartel members. I don't know how you might feel about it, but I won't lift a finger to bury any of these nasty assholes. I suggest that we let them decompose back into the filth from which they came."

"Fine by me," Cletus concurred, "but when we're done, somebody is going to have to go after Blake, and somebody is going to have to go after Lorena. How are we going to decide which one of us goes in what direction?"

"Easy peasy," Miguel said. "We'll settle it like men."

"A fight to the death?"

"Damnation, Cletus! Must you be such a melodramatic dumbass?" Miguel asked. "A simple game of paper, rock, and scissors should readily suffice. In the meantime, I'll have Señor Bosque help you haul the bodies of the dead gangsters outside the walls of the compound to feed the buzzards!"

The mayordomo looked at Miguel Pastore with disdain. "I've heard an expression you americanos say when you're displeased with an edict. I believe the expression is 'no dice'! I don't care if the four cartel members were our enemies. I insist that they receive a proper burial."

"Oh, for the love of Jesus, Señor Bosque," Cletus complained. "Please don't tell me you have any compassion for these people who decimated your ranch."

"I don't!" Bosque answered. "You people are just visitors. As for me, I happen to live here. I just don't want any of these dead fish stinking up the joint."

When Romero Lopes arrived at the cartel headquarters in Guadalajara, he was treated like royalty. "I don't mean to bother you, Mago," the cartel's henchman said to the vampiro, "but El Tor wants to reward you for the excellent job you did at El Rancho Feliz in Santa Sangre the other day. Even though you didn't capture Blake

Barker, you kidnapped his son, Nathan. The boss is convinced it will be only a matter of time before Blake Barker shows up here and surrenders. Therefore, El Tor has sent me over here to see you and give you a well-deserved present for all you have done for the cartel."

"A monetary reward, I presume?" Lopes asked.

"No, not exactly, Mago," the henchman answered. "I have your present right here in this basket. Please accept this tasty meal with complements from El Tor." With that, the henchman passed a small bassinette to Romero Lopes. When Lopes took the basket, he peeled back a blanket to reveal a small infant who must have been only a few days old. The tiny baby was resting in blissful slumber.

"What in the blue fuck am I looking at over here?" Lopes cried out.

"It's a baby! It was spawned by one of our whores. El Tor wants you to eat it. All of the inner-circle members of the Calle Vampiro dine on suckling infants when the opportunity arises, as it does from time to time. It's just one of the glorious traditions we've established here in Guadalajara. We keep the whores as breeding stock just for this purpose."

Lopes recoiled when he realized his employers were far more disgusting than he could have ever possibly imagined. "Tell me right now," Lopes said, "where's this baby's mother?"

"Why, she's over in the whorehouse," the henchman answered. "I can tell that you're upset about something. Tell me what's wrong, Mago, and I'll make it right. Now that El Sapo is chasing the gran bruja down to the Yucatán, I've been assigned to become your new valet. My name is El Punto. Would you like to suck my blood?"

"Maybe later," Lopes said. "For now, I have job for you, Punto. I want you to go to the whorehouse and bring me the mother of this baby. Do it now."

"Yes!" Punto exclaimed with unbridled excitement. "I can tell that tonight you want a main course *y un desierto delicioso. ¡Qué magnífico!* If I may be so bold, I would like to ask for your permission to stand by and watch you while you dine this evening. I promise that I will remain completely silent. I only ask for the opportunity to dip a piece of pan dulce into the baby's blood so that I may have a small taste of such a delectable treat."

"No. I prefer to dine alone. Now, I've given you an important assignment. Be quick about it. Bring this baby's mother to me right now!" Lopes grabbed his new valet and forcefully pushed him out the door and into the hallway of the cartel's dormitory complex.

After a short while, Punto returned from the whorehouse with a young woman whose hands were tied behind her back. Although the unfortunate sex slave had a thick piece of duct tape plastered across her mouth, her fear was palpable to the vampiro.

Something must have fundamentally changed in Romero Lopes during the slaughter at Rancho Feliz. Amid previous feeding opportunities, demonstrable fear among his victims would have launched the ghoul into an immediate feeding frenzy. On this occasion, however, Lopes experienced an emotion that he was not accustomed to feeling. For lack of a better word, Lopes suddenly felt *compassion*, or at least something akin to it.

After bringing the young woman to the quarters of El Mago, Punto quietly slipped into the room. He tried to hide in the entryway closet in an attempt to witness what was about to take place. The vampiro, however, was already wise to the voyeuristic disposition of his new valet. He subsequently caught Punto red-handed.

"I told you that I dine alone!" Romero said as he dragged Punto out the closet and slammed him against the wall. "Get out of here before I tear you to pieces." After tossing Punto into the hallway, Lopes stood guard for a few moments at his portal to make certain there would be no further interruptions.

Once he was absolutely convinced that he was not under any kind of surveillance, electronic or otherwise, Lopes returned to his quarters and quickly approached his presumed victim. Without a single word, he untied the woman and pulled the piece of tape from her mouth. He went to his top dresser drawer and found two hundred dollars in cash, which he quickly stuffed underneath the blanket covering the baby in the bassinette.

Lopes opened his window. Motioning the young woman to exit, he handed her the basket that cradled the tiny infant. As a reward for his uncharacteristic humanitarian efforts, Romero Lopes received a quick kiss on the cheek from the young woman before she escaped into the night with her newborn baby in tow. At that point, the only thing left for Romero Lopes to do was to hope that the young woman would try to find a new and honorable life worth living, far from the deadly grasp of the Calle Vampiro cartel.

"Well, if this is where the Azteca gang hangs out, it's certainly a cut above the Tequila Town bar," Joe Cephas Smoot opined as Placard's hit squad entered El Submarino Amarillo Bar and Grill. Decorated in a maritime motif, El Submarino actually employed genuine ship portals that were salvaged from an ocean liner that had crashed upon a barrier reef back in the 1950s. The small, round thick glass windows provided only a limited and somewhat distorted view of the outside seedy world of Ciudad Juárez.

"Okay, Morales; what did the barkeep have to say?" Placard asked.

"I told him we were interested in making arrangements for a shipment of recreational material to come across the border into Texas, and he said we have to first go downstairs and play a parlor game that he referred to as toques. We have to prove that we're worthy enough to meet with the Azteca gang members."

"Swell," Colonel Placard replied sarcastically. "What in hell is this parlor game all about?"

"I was afraid to ask," Morales answered as the four men circled down a winding staircase that led to a lower level. Upon reaching the dimly lit basement, they were met by a thin, balding individual who wore a pair of wire-frame spectacles that were of obvious marginal efficacy as a consequence of the extensive small cracks and scratches on the thick glass lenses. There was a thin-walled partition in the back third of the basement. Placard and his crew suspected they were being scrutinized, as there were whispers and low-pitched mumbles that could be heard from behind the partition

"Hello, gentlemen," the thin man said. "My name is Voltios. I've been told that you're quite interested in the import–export business and that you have a desire to make direct contact with the Azteca gang. There's only one way that this can be permissible. One chosen member of your group must be able to defeat an Azteca gang member at the parlor game called toques. It's now time for you to select your champion. Whomever you pick will be competing against the Azteca gang member known as Chispas."

"I'm up to bat," Smoot said.

"You don't know what you're doing," Dr. Ron Shiftless said. "Why don't you wait a moment until we sort this out? To me, at least, you're a valuable commodity. I want to keep you in one piece, at least for the time being."

"I'm just not feelin' love here, Doc!" Smoot replied. "Why haven't you ever tucked me in at night or read me a bedtime story before now? I, for one, am *not* a commodity. For your information, I just happen to be a God-fearing Christian man of righteous convictions!"

"I'm serious, Joe!" Shiftless cautioned. "You'll need to know what this game is all about before you volunteer."

"That's the difference between you and me, Ron," Joe Cephas said with a grin. "You're a chickenshit."

The bioweapon jerked his head toward the man called Voltios and said, "Whatever it is, bring it on, amigo!"

At that moment a hirsute ogre emerged from the darkness. It was quite obvious that his eyes were glazed over by thick cataracts. "What happened to this man?" Morales asked.

An alarm was registered among Placard's men when Voltios replied, "This man is called Chispas. He's been hit with the juice so many times that his eyes are now all frosted over like an electric eel in the Amazon River!"

When Voltios handed a pair of polished stainless steel electrodes to each of the contestants to hold firmly in each of their hands, it became quite apparent what the game called toques was all about. An electrical cord was affixed to the bottom end of each of the stainless steel cylinders, which made each electrode apparatus appear much like the flagellated tail of a spermatozoic gamete freshly liberated from its prior confines within a still pulsating, yet depleted, seminal vesicle.

Each electrical cord was plugged into a black box that had a simple on–off toggle switch. The most prominent features of the black sheet-metal box were the two rheostats that were located directly on the front face of the electronic device, presumably to control the voltage and amperage. The black box was plugged into a wall socket with an electrical cord that appeared to be rather frayed, as if an impertinent rodent frequently used the power cord as a strip of dental floss to maintain its personal oral hygiene.

"Oh shit. Oh dear," Joe Cephas Smoot said with a sly grin. "It looks like I'm about to get electrocuted!"

"You don't have to do this, Joe!" Morales warned.

"Yes, I do," Smoot answered. "After all, I simply have to prove to Dr. Shiftless that I'm a lot more than just a 'commodity.' Frankly, by now I'm sick and tired of him pissin' in my corn flakes. I'll gladly accept an apology from you anytime, Ron."

"Won't get one from me, bumpkin," Shiftless said defiantly. "It's your funeral, hayseed."

"I won't go above 240 volts at 50 amps. It probably won't kill you, but it will definitely burn your skin off," Voltios explained. "The person who holds onto the electrodes the longest wins the game. If you win this round of toques, gringo, you and your colleagues will be granted an audience with Los Aztecas. If you lose to Señor Chispas, you and your friends will be executed. Your hearts will be cut out of your chests while you are all still very much alive, and then you'll get beheaded. Afterward, your lifeless torsos will be dragged through the streets. Los Aztecas will subsequently present your rotting corpses to the Calle Vampiro cartel, and then what's left of your bodies will be staked upon fence posts for all to see from here to Guadalajara."

"Is that so?" Colonel Placard scoffed. "You and what army is going to do that to us, little man?"

"*This* army," Chispas said, speaking for the first time. From behind the walled partition emerged a dozen foot soldiers bearing automatic weapons of one caliber or another.

"Oh," Joe Cephas Smoot said smugly, "*that* army. Let the games begin, asshole!"

"Okay," Voltios said, "here we go. Try not to scream, gringo, as doing so would be a sign that you're *sin fuerte*." Voltios set the amperage rheostat at fifty and then started to slowly turn up the voltage dial. Much to the dismay of the Azteca gang members, Joe Cephas Smoot clutched the electrodes placidly.

Despite the odor of singed flesh, Smoot started to sing a popular song from the era that was originally recorded by the English artist named Peter Gabriel. Perhaps it was quite appropriate that the song he selected to sing was called "Shock the Monkey." No sooner did Joe Cephas roll through a strained and slightly off-key voluminous falsetto vocalization of the chorus, Señor Chispas experienced a grand mal seizure from the application of the high-voltage electrical current. The big man fell to the floor with agonizing tonic-clonic muscle spasms. He sadly bit off the tip of his own tongue during the neural electrical storm that occurred among the microcircuitry within the confines of his brain.

"We won," Placard said. He reached over to the black box and turned the toggle switch to the off position. Chispas continued to writhe about on the ground as if he were a live fish in a hot skillet. "If I'm not mistaken, it's time for us to have that promised powwow with Los Aztecas."

"I don't think so. Unfortunately, I must breach our original contract. I'm sorry about that. After all, it wouldn't be in our best interests to talk to four gringos, especially if two of them are vampiros." Voltios raised his right arm as he said to the other gang members, "Take them out, muchachos!"

In a flash of light, Joe Cephas Smoot extracted his .460 hogleg hand cannon from its pouch sling and proceeded to separate the head of Voltios from the rest of his body. Smoot immediately drew down on the other armed combatants and graciously extended the same courtesy to several other gang members. As Colonel Placard and Dr. Shiftless hit the deck, Morales pulled out his .45 and deftly put a bullet in the left eye of each of the remaining Azteca members who had initially escaped Joe's wrath. Morales and Smoot exhausted their hardware with deadly accuracy before any of the gang members could even discharge one spent cartridge from their automatic weapons. It was over in a heartbeat.

"Well, so much for having a powwow with Los Aztecas," Colonel Placard said with a grin. He approached Señor Chispas, who was still prostrate on the floor and moaning ever so softly. It appeared that the big man was just beginning to recover from the grand mal seizure induced by the high-voltage game of toques.

"My head is killing me!" Chispas proceeded to mumble. "On behalf of the Azteca gang, I've never lost a game of toques before."

"Speak up, asshole," Placard said. "Tell me where your distribution warehouse and headquarters are located, and maybe I'll let you live." The big man was handed a pen and paper, and he quickly wrote down the requested addresses that Placard had demanded.

"Here's everything I know," Chispas said with a painful groan as he wiped away a thick layer of frothy drool from his chin. "The main distribution warehouse is in Durango, and the cartel's headquarters is located at this address in Guadalajara. If you let me live, I can become a spy for you. I can be your eyes and ears on the ground here in Ciudad Juárez. Well, perhaps not your eyes, as my vision is not very good after playing the game of toques all these years, but I can certainly become your ears."

Without uttering a single word, Colonel Placard pulled the .460 hogleg hand cannon out of Joe's hand. After reloading the weapon, the colonel leveled the enormous barrel of the gun against the temple of Señor Chispas and pulled the trigger. "No, but thanks anyhow."

"Colonel?!" Joe asked in shock.

"We already have an old blind spy working for me in the men's room at Tequila Town. I don't need another one." Turning to his crew, Placard said, "Okay, boys, as soon as Morales and Joe Cephas have a quick snack, we'll need to gather up all these weapons and then get the hell out of here. Our next stop will be the cartel's cocaine storage warehouse in Durango."

"New orders when we get there?" Shiftless asked as his colleagues Morales and Smoot were busy lapping up as much blood as possible.

"Simple. We're going to kill everybody, and then we're going to burn the goddamned place to the ground."

As Placard's hit squad fled the scene, an uninjured Azteca member who'd been playing possum arose from the floor. He had overheard enough of the conversation between Colonel Placard and Señor Chispas to realize that the warehouse in Durango was going to be the very next target of the mysterious hit squad of gringos.

It was imperative for the surviving gang member to find a telephone and tell the cartel headquarters in Guadalajara what had just gone down. He also needed to warn them about Placard's plans. Once warned, the Calle Vampiro cartel would make certain that there would be a welcoming party to greet Colonel Placard and his team upon their arrival in Durango.

Blake Barker found it quite curious that there was no obvious recognizable security at the entryway of the Calle Vampiro compound in Guadalajara. There was not so much as even a chain-link fence surrounding the perimeter. "Of course you bastards wouldn't need a security fence," Blake shouted aloud into the empty guard station that he found at the front of a long driveway that meandered into the compound. Blake unzipped the fly of his trousers to relieve himself as he continued his vociferous rant. "You're getting protection from the Federales! Well, this is what I think of your entire goddamned corrupt country."

Blake proceeded to urinate on the wall of the empty guardhouse. Just then a stray porker wandered out of the brush and sidled up to him. As the feral pig began to emit gentle grunts, it rubbed its flank directly against Blake's pant leg. "Well, hello there, porky! You must be the head of the welcoming committee," Blake said with a smile as he zipped up his fly. "Your timing is impeccable."

After consuming the blood and viscera of the unwitting porcine emissary, Blake hiked up the long driveway to see if he could get anybody's attention. After loping along the driveway for approximately one hundred meters, he was suddenly surrounded by a half dozen men who were armed with automatic weapons. Obviously it was a security detail, but the cartel guards had appeared seemingly out of nowhere. The security team members had simply jumped out of the brush from either side of the long driveway and proceeded to escort Blake to the compound.

"I'm glad you fellows finally showed up," Blake said sarcastically. "I was starting to get lonely out here. My name is Blake Barker. I have a suspicion that you boys have been waiting for me. Well, here I am."

"We know exactly who you are, Señor Barker. My name is Hipopótamo. My friends call me Hipo, but I must insist that you call me Señor Hipopótamo. It will be necessary for you to treat me with the deference and respect that I deserve, as I am the head of security around here. El Tor has been quite anxious to meet you," the rather rotund and malodorous henchman said. "I'm certain that he'll be hosting a fiesta in your honor. Consider this to be a formal invitation. I can assure you, it will be a good time."

"Whenever you say, you fat stinky bastard."

El Hipo wheeled around and sharply struck Blake on the temporal aspect of the left side of his skull with the butt end of an AK-47 assault rifle. Blake saw stars before he lost consciousness and collapsed upon the ground.

A splash of ice water in the face revived Blake Barker from his concussion. Upon getting his bearings, Blake realized that he was handcuffed to the armrests of a heavy chair in front of a desk in what appeared to be a finely appointed wood-paneled business office. Sitting across the desk from Blake was a rather handsome-looking Hispanic male who appeared to be in his late thirties or perhaps early forties. Clean-shaven, the man had thick black hair that was brushed back neatly into a double jelly roll that perhaps would have been a more appropriate coif in the late 1950s.

"Señor Barker, I've been waiting to meet you for a long time. Allow me to introduce myself. I'm El Tor. I would like to personally welcome you to the Calle Vampiro headquarters. I think it's kind of ironic that the name of our organization is Calle Vampiro. We've been operational now for more than a decade, and it's taken us this long to actually get un vampiro to finally work with us. I truly thought it would never happen, but now we have a friend of yours, Romero Lopes, under our employment. I'm certain you'd like to have a visit from him. It'll give you an opportunity to get caught up on current events. I'll see if I can make the arrangements for a little chitchat."

"Don't bother," Blake said. "Romero Lopes is no friend of mine. I turned myself in to your organization for the express purpose of getting my son, Nathan, released from this place. Please let him go. Now that you have me, he's of no further use to you."

"I will assure you that at least for the time being, your son is alive and well," El Tor explained. "However, from where I'm sitting, you're certainly not in any position to negotiate a damned thing. I own you now. Since Romero Lopes has been working with us, my organization has learned a lot about the nature of human vampirism. There are certainly gaps in our fund of knowledge, however, in regards to the innate healing ability that un vampiro may possess. This is where you are going to help us out. At intermittent intervals we'll amputate various and sundry extremities to assess your ability to heal."

With that statement, El Hipo produced a pair of tin shears and proceeded to amputate the pinky finger of Blake Barker's left hand right across the most proximal interphalangeal joint. As Blake screamed out in pain, El Hipo took a cigarette lighter from his top shirt pocket and proceeded to burn the end of Blake's bloody finger stump to arrest the bleeding.

With a broken spirit, Blake looked up to his tormentor in anguish and said, "Señor Hipopótamo, I thought you said that this fiesta held in my honor would be a good time. Rest assured, as of yet I have not found any of this to be a particularly pleasant experience."

"With the formal invitation I extended to you to attend this fiesta, it should have been implicit that I was going to have a good time, not you!"

"Take another look at the map," Cloud instructed Lorena Pastore. "Are we still on Highway 184?"

"Well, so it would seem," Lorena replied. "The highway made a sharp turn at Peto, but as best as I can tell, we're still on the same path."

"Are you confident about that?"

"Reasonably so, although I'll be the first to admit that we've not seen one damned street sign on this jungle road since we left the last town. I told you we should've bought gas for this Jeep before we got this far out into the sticks."

"I couldn't stop back there," Cloud explained. "The goddamned skinny vampiro showed up yet again, and this time he was right behind us!"

"Look, Cloud, I'm from the desert. I've never seen jungle like this before in all my life," Lorena complained. "I'm so scared right now that I'm shaking in my boots."

"I hope we're not on a wild-ass goose chase."

"Wait, Cloud. Stop, stop, stop!" Lorena ordered. "There's a white cross on the right side of the road with writing on it. The letters are faded, but I think this is the place where we're supposed to make a right turn and then go south."

"Why don't you jump out and see what's written on the cross? We have to be absolutely sure that this is where we make our turn," Cloud said. "Please hurry. I know for certain that the skinny vampiro is still on our tail. What in hell does he want with us?"

"He wants the black obsidian knife that I took from Romero Lopes."

"Then why don't you just give it back to him?" Cloud asked.

"Absolutely not!" Lorena said. "That knife may very well protect us from a vampiro attack."

"I hope you're right," Cloud said. "No matter where we go, that little jaundiced fucker is always right behind us! We need to find refuge with this El Mayo character before nightfall."

Lorena popped out of the Jeep and jogged up to the white cross at the side of the road. When she saw the faded writing that said "¡Jesús salva!" she knew it was the right junction. She returned to the vehicle and told Dr. Cloud, "Hang a ralph right here. This is it."

As the Jeep ambled down a rough dirt road, Lorena and Cloud encountered a barefoot teenage girl who was walking in the opposite direction. Lorena rolled down the passenger-side window of the Jeep and yelled out to the traveler: "Excuse me, but we're looking for a man around here with the name El Mayo. We've been told that he lives at the end of this road. Can you tell me how much farther we have to go down this path in order to find him? We only have about a quarter of a tank of gas at this point."

"El Mayo?" the teenaged girl asked in astonishment. "He died from a cancer of the blood over two years ago."

"Well, that's just perfect," Lorena replied in disgust. "Can you tell me what's at the end of this road?"

"You'll find the sacred cenote. It's really deep. I'll bet it drops down to the center of the earth. That's where the ancients used to kill los vampiros and then dispose of their bodies down by throwing them into the big hole in the ground," the girl explained.

"Are you serious?" Cloud asked.

"You can't miss it," the girl explained. "It's right beside the old Maya pyramid. It's covered with vines, but you can still easily find it."

"There's a pyramid out there?" Lorena asked.

"The forest is full of pyramids that have been overgrown by the jungle, and they remain hidden to this very day. Most of them have not been rediscovered by archaeologists as of yet. The one at the end of this trail is such a structure."

"Who are you, and where do you live?" Cloud asked.

"My name is Lucia. I'm a descendent of the Maya. I live with my people here in our forest."

"I didn't know that there were any Maya left," Cloud said. "I happen to be a Navajo from New Mexico. Like you, my people lost our homeland to European settlers many centuries ago."

"I don't know anything about the Navajo people, but I'm quite confident that our great nation will yet again rise from the ashes," Lucia said. "All we need is a great leader to resurrect the Maya to our rightful place of prominence in this world."

"Tell me something," Lorena said. "Who could possibly elevate your tribe to any degree of importance at this point in modern history? After all, the time for your people has come and gone."

"The elders have spoken of una gran bruja who will soon be coming to lead us out of the darkness that has entrapped us for centuries. Mark my words: I'm certain that this will happen within my lifetime."

As the teenage girl walked away, Lorena turned to Cloud and asked, "What do we do now?"

"Maybe the vampiro doesn't know we came down this trail," Cloud said. "We'll set up camp near the pyramid that the girl told us about, and then in the morning we'll drive on to Tulum. We should have enough gasoline to get there. After that, we'll press on to Cancun, abandon the Jeep at the airport, and catch a flight back to the safety of the United States."

"I'm sorry I dragged you into all of this," Lorena said.

"I'm not," Cloud said. "I gave up everything to find you. I love you, Lorena."

"I know you do," Lorena answered. Although having no real affection for her traveling companion, or anybody else for that matter, Lorena was nonetheless certain deep down inside that Cloud would be willing to die for her. Because of that noble attribute alone, she should have at least been somewhat grateful.

"Something's not right with this picture," Placard said as he peered through his binoculars at the entryway of the warehouse in Durango where the Calle Vampiro cartel had their distribution hub.

"What gives?" Shiftless asked.

"Where in hell is everybody?" Placard asked. "The place looks abandoned."

"Well, I think it's highly unlikely that Chispas lied to us back in Juárez. Before you blew that dude's brains out, he was scared shitless. I'm quite certain that he would have sold out his mother to save his own sorry ass," Morales said.

"Maybe this is a trap," Placard suggested.

"How could it be?" Smoot asked. "Nobody knew we were coming here. Dead men tell no tales. We killed everybody in the basement at the Submarino Amarillo Bar and Grill, so there's no way in hell that the cartel could have been tipped off."

"Are we sure about that?" Placard asked.

"I'm dead sure, Colonel. Let's do this," Morales said. "It's simple. We'll roll in hot, kill everybody, burn the place to the ground, and then go home and pound down a cold beer. Well, maybe you and Shiftless can enjoy a cold beer while Joe Cephas and I suck down a Bloody Mary. A real bloody Mary, if you catch my meaning."

"Okay, so be it," the colonel said, acquiescing to the pressure from his crew. "Here's the setup: Shiftless will hang back here behind this berm and man the Barrett .50. The rest of us will mount a frontal assault right through the front door of the warehouse. I hope we're not making a mistake. Good luck, gentlemen."

As Ron Shiftless munched away on a chicken salad sandwich, he peered through the nightscope mounted atop the new Barrett sniper rifle. He observed his three associates running abreast toward the stash house. Initially all appeared to be going as planned. However, as soon as his three colleagues breached the front door of the warehouse, all hell broke loose. Although Ron was over forty meters from the warehouse entry, the unmistakable report of dozens of automatic weapons being fired all at once was nearly deafening to him.

Ron witnessed Joe Cephas back out of the warehouse door while firing his hogleg hand cannon as fast as he could. Once it was empty, he cast the now useless weapon upon the ground. The first cartel member who pursued Smoot through the warehouse door was toting a Sieg gun, but fortunately Ron was able to clip the assailant with a single shot. Ron's well-placed round now afforded

Joe Cephas a fully automatic Sieg long arm with a loaded twenty-round magazine.

Every time another cartel member left the safety of the warehouse, a gaping wound in the head or chest would suddenly appear, which ensured that the combatant was effectively neutralized. Smoot was able to make a strategic retreat toward the berm where Ron was hiding. With a quick dash under a hail of bullets, Smoot cleared the top of the berm and collapsed beside Ron Shiftless.

"Are you hit?"

"No!" Smoot answered. "I'm clean."

"What in God's name happened in there?" Shiftless asked.

"I assure you that God had nothing to do with any of this," Smoot answered. "We got ambushed! The cartel must have been tipped off somehow. The warehouse was completely empty except for the assassins who were waiting in there for us."

"Where's Placard?!"

"I saw the colonel go down!" Joe exclaimed. "He took a round."

"Well, I saw him strap on his body armor before he led the assault on the warehouse. Do you think that he's still alive?"

"Can't rightly say," Joe answered.

"What about Morales?"

"Oh shit!" Joe Cephas said as he pointed over the top of the berm. "There he is!"

Ron Shiftless and Smoot watched in horror as Morales was brought out through a side door in the warehouse and then loaded into the back of a van. It was clear to see that their colleague had a heavy fishing net cast over him as he was whisked away into the darkness.

"I'm out," Joe Cephas said as he dropped the Sieg gun. "How about you?"

"Empty. Let's get back to the van and get the hell out of here before they find us and finish us off," Ron said. "Back at the van, we've got a lot more toys in the playpen that I'd love to share with these cartel shitbirds. Move, Joe! We'd better get a bead on that vehicle that took Morales out of here, and we'd better do it pronto before our buddy disappears forever!"

Barker eyed the thin and chronically ill-appearing woman with dishwater gray hair rather suspiciously. "What's your story?" he asked the woman who was locked up in an adjacent sixty-square-foot steel-bar cage.

"Are you talking to me?" the haggard individual replied.

"Well, since the big bastard with the single eyebrow running across his forehead in the cage across the hall appears to be sound asleep, the answer is yes. I'm indeed talking to you."

Although the woman was in her early forties, Barker erroneously assumed she was approximately fifteen years older than that. "My name is Nancy Barber. I've been a prisoner here for the last nine years."

"What happened?" Blake asked.

"My husband, Frank, and I were on vacation in San Antonio, Texas, back in February 1977, when we were kidnapped by the Calle Vampiro drug cartel."

"Wrong place at the wrong time?"

"Precisely," Nancy answered. "I'd never been to San Antonio before. My husband took me there for vacation while he gave a lecture on health and hygiene at a community outreach center. Frank always tried to do good deeds. As you're aware, no good deed—"

"Yeah, yeah, I know the rest," Blake said.

"Don't be rude," the woman said. "You want to hear what I have to say or not?"

"My apologies," Blake said. "Please continue with your heartwarming cheerful tale."

"My husband was an emergency room physician from the Gulf Coast College of Medicine in Houston, Texas," she continued, "and it appeared that the cartel believed that he would be a valuable commodity to their organization."

"Where's your husband now?" Barker asked. "I presume he's locked up somewhere here in this dungeon."

"I haven't seen Frank since the day we were kidnapped," Nancy replied. "I was told that he escaped from the cartel back in the summer of 1981, but for certain reasons that may soon become obvious to you, they continue to hold me as a prisoner. I'm sure that back in Texas, nobody knows that I'm still alive."

"So, spell it out for me, lady," Barker requested. "I'm not a mind reader. Why is it that you're still locked up?"

"For a myriad of reasons, as you shall soon learn," Nancy answered. "If somebody is ever captured by the cartel, they'll *never* again see the light of day. I would guess that you're the man named Blake Barker that I've heard about. I know that the cartel captured your son. I don't want to be the bearer of bad news, but you'll never see your son again. And neither of you will ever get out of this goddamned prison. Have they tortured you yet?"

"Not so much," Blake answered. "Before El Hipo forcefully raped me, he cut off my pinky finger with a pair of tin snips. Other than that, I've had a rather delightful time!"

Their conversation was interrupted by none other than El Punto, who walked up to the cage housing the forlorn woman. Punto stuck a two-foot-long shank of steel rebar into the cage and rattled it around as if he were a man ringing a metal dinner triangle at a dude ranch.

"Take your clothes off, you whore," Punto instructed the woman. "El Tor is coming down here now, and his lust is running hot for you. I want you to reach over and grab your ankles and then just wait for him to come. This time, I get to watch!"

El Tor appeared from the end of the hallway and motioned to Punto to unlock the cage. Without a word, the head of the cartel violently sodomized Nancy Barber while Blake Barker tried in vain to avert his eyes. As the woman cried out in pain, the sleeping giant with one eyebrow who was caged across the hallway suddenly awakened.

"Be strong, Nancy!" the giant man called out. "Don't give in to that bastard! Listen to me, El Tor, I'm going to kill you someday!"

After the mounting head of pressure was suddenly released from the loins of El Tor, the cartel leader casually walked out of the woman's cage and filed a complaint with Punto. "I'm getting quite annoyed at the Russian. I don't care if he's a doctor or not."

"New orders?" Punto asked.

"Refresh my memory about something," El Tor requested. "Tell me, Punto—you were in a mariachi band years ago, were you not?"

"Trumpet! At one time I was skilled enough to be named first chair."

"Good," El Tor said. "I'm sending El Hipo down here. I want you men to take Russian Bear to the rack and administer a healthy dose of discipline. Am I clear? No mercy! While you play 'El Deguello' on the trumpet, I want Hipo to light him up with the propane torch."

When the giant man was hauled out of his cage and taken down to the rack to be tortured, Nancy Barber called out to Blake, who was still emotionally traumatized from what he had been forced to witness. "Well, you were the one who wanted to know specifically why I'm still being held as a prisoner down here in this dungeon. Hopefully, your question has now been sufficiently answered to satisfy your curiosity."

"I'm sorry I asked," Blake replied. "What can you tell me about the big bastard who just got hauled out of here to get put on the rack? He must have the balls of a brass monkey to give El Tor such a heavy rash of shit like he just did. As best as I can tell, what he said to those bastards was on your behalf."

"His real name is Ilya, but everybody knows him as Russian Bear," Nancy Barber explained. "After my husband escaped from the cartel a while back, these sons of bitches spent a long time looking for another doctor who was a trained emergency room physician whom they could use as a slave to patch up their foot soldiers and the men they use as mules to sneak drugs across the border into the United States. The cartel captured Russian Bear just a month ago or so in the town of Playa Caliente in Estado de Tamaulipas when he was doing missionary work with some sort of charity group."

"What in hell was he doing in Playa Caliente?" Blake asked. "This Bear fellow must be an absolute idiot. It was all over the news a while back that the Calle Vampiro cartel stormed Playa Caliente and killed every poor soul who was living in that wretched town. The entire community was virtually wiped off the map!"

"Bear told me he went to Playa Caliente because it was a spiritual calling."

"Whatever," Blake answered. "Somebody who was paying attention to the current events at that time should have talked the big son of a bitch out of what was essentially a suicide mission, not a spiritual calling. Who knows, perhaps they're one in the same."

"Slow down there, cowboy. You're not a cynic now, are you?"

"What gives you that idea?" Barker asked. "Look, lady, no good deed goes unpunished. There. I said it. You happy now? If you ever get to see your husband again in this lifetime, just tell him that. I'm quite certain that he would now concur with my viewpoint."

"I'm sure he would."

"Everybody gets shit upon in life as best as I can tell," Blake said. "It looks like this time it was just Russian Bear's turn to crawl into the barrel. I'll say this for the Russki: he might be an idiot, but at least he appears to be a brave man of righteous convictions. That's indeed a lot more than I can possibly say for myself right about now."

"As of yet, the cartel hasn't crushed Russian Bear's spirit, but they most assuredly will do so eventually. After all, they crushed mine. I feel as if I've been dead for a long time, and I'm just going through the motions of being alive."

"Join the club," Blake said. "I've felt that way ever since my first child died years ago in an accidental house fire. I've felt that way ever since my wife was murdered before my very eyes by an evil ghoul named Romero Lopes."

"Lopes? He's the new vampiro on the cartel's payroll, is he not?" Nancy asked. "You can't tell me that the taste of revenge would not be a beautiful thing. Do you have a weapon hidden in or on you?"

"Well, I did have a folded straight razor hidden up my ass. I originally picked it up when I was briefly incarcerated by the Federales in Ciudad Juárez before I came down here," Blake explained. "Unfortunately, El Hipo found it just about the time I was getting affectionately probed up the backside by his nasty one-eyed trouser snake."

"Been there, done that. It wouldn't be Christian, but by God, it would be sweet if one day I had a chance to kill El Tor! I'm truly sorry for the tragedies that you've experienced during your time on this planet." Nancy said. "Life's not fair, Blake."

"Oh, so true."

"I'm not telling you anything that you don't already know," Nancy said. "Perhaps life's nothing more than a series of hurdles that one must jump over until reaching the finish line."

"Philosophically, Mrs. Barber, you seem to be a kindred spirit."

"I only have one question: what's beyond the finish line in life?" Nancy asked.

"I would like to think redemption and perhaps even salvation."

"One may only pray for that to be the case," Nancy mused.

"Say, Nancy, tell me something," Blake Barker said.

"What's that?"

"It appears that your friend Russian Bear is tied up right now with some very important burning issues, or perhaps I should say some very important burning *tissues*. Therefore, I don't know if the Russki would be on board with any of this, as he's certainly not here at this time to cast a vote. Be that as it may, how would you feel about breaking out of this shithole and getting back home to Los Estados Unidos?"

12

REDENCIÓN Y SALVACIÓN

As he was a staunch Protestant from Texas, Cletus Barker had never previously attended a Catholic Mass, much less a funeral service presided over by a Catholic priest. He actually had suspicions that Roman Catholicism in some way, shape, or form was just on the fringe of true Christianity. He found it peculiar that Catholics were generally imbued with such a low level of self-esteem that they were often too timid to actually speak to God directly. It seemed that Catholics needed a litany of saints and the Virgin Mary to intercede on behalf of the whole planet Earth, of which the very surface was literally teeming with a multitude of unworthy sinners.

Be that as it may, Cletus was duly impressed that nearly the entire town of Santa Sangre had turned out to pay their final respects to El Tiempo and the others who had fallen in what would be forever known as the Battle of Rancho Feliz. The story would be etched into the annals of history of the local community, and it would be conveyed by way of oral tradition from generation to generation in perpetuity.

Passages from the scriptures were read aloud by the priest and laypeople alike, followed by a host of spiritual songs that were sung by all. Even a cynical vampiro named Miguel Pastore eagerly chimed in, albeit off-key. Countless bouquets of flowers were placed upon the graves. There was not a dry eye to be found in the courtyard of the grand hacienda.

Upon the conclusion of the funeral service, it was time to go to work. Cletus took a pistol and a box of shells from the arsenal in the trunk of the stolen police cruiser and handed them to Miguel. "If you go looking for Blake and Nathan in Guadalajara, I want you to be careful out there. After all, as best as I can tell thus far from my own somewhat limited personal experience, this country called Mexico is filled to the brim with badass Mexicans!"

"Try to be a good boy if you find Lorena and Dr. Cloud," Miguel countered. "Remember, Cloud is a decent guy. If I find out that you got into a tiff with him while vying for Lorena's affection, I'll hunt you down and kick your ass. For the life of me, I can't understand why Lorena is attracted to los gringos y los Indios."

"She has good taste."

"You make me want to gnaw on my own wrists. Mama always hoped that Lorena would settle down with a nice Latino boy. I have a theory that she got corrupted from hanging around you Anglos for far too long."

"Not *corrupted*, my friend—*enlightened*!"

"Spare me! She picked up a lot of bad habits while she was working for your brother. You gringo *salados* are loud and uncouth. In addition, your dietary preferences are truly appalling. Be honest with me; is it true that you really like to eat at Taco Hell?"

"Every day of the week and twice on Sunday," Cletus said with a laugh.

"Really, now?" Miguel said. "Frankly, you gringos scare the shit out of me. That certainly goes double for you fellows from Texas."

"I hope I resemble that remark," Cletus said with a sly chuckle.

"I wish you the best of luck, Cletus. I hope someday that I'll see you again, and in one piece at that. May I give you a hug before you leave?"

"Save it, Miguel," Cletus answered with a grin. "My feminine side was sent down to the dry cleaners to get starched and pressed."

Despite the torrential rain, Dr. Cloud valiantly clung to the back of El Sapo, firmly grasping the vampiro's belt with his left hand in an effort to retard his relentless climb up the steps of the steep-faced Maya pyramid. With his free right hand, the doctor valiantly flailed away with the sterling silver letter opener that had been given to him by Señora Naranjo. As a weapon, the letter opener was unfortunately too dull to render any serious injuries upon the vampiro. El Sapo, completely ignorant that silver was essentially a harmless element to vampires, was quite terrified. He believed it was only a matter of time before the silver blade of the letter opener wielded by his adversary would eventually find its mark.

"Keep climbing, Lorena," Cloud cried out. "This bastard's right behind you!"

Sapo crawled up the vine-covered thirty-foot-tall Maya relic in an attempt to retrieve the precious obsidian knife that was previously owned by his master, but the curandera was always just barely out of reach from the vampiro's grasp. Holding an obsidian knife in each hand, Lorena viciously slashed away at El Sapo's face, inflicting bloody lacerations with alternating blades until Sapo's face was shredded into ribbons of mangled flesh.

"Look, lady," Sapo pleaded, "just give me back the black knife and I promise I'll leave you alone. I honestly wanted to kill you people when I first chased you from the ranch, but I don't feel that way anymore. I just want to go home to be with my master!"

El Sapo's request was only met with cruel and derisive laughter.

"What in hell are you doing, Lorena? I don't know who you are anymore," Cloud cried out. "Just give him the goddamned knife! Let's be done with all of this."

"No!" Lorena exclaimed with a thunderous voice. As the curandera leaned forward and gouged out Sapo's left eye with the black obsidian knife, she made a proud proclamation that Dr. Cloud found quite chilling. "This knife is mine and mine alone!"

As Sapo screamed in agony, he reached out in a futile attempt to recover his enucleated eyeball that became immediately entangled within the thick, sticky vine that grew like a chlorophyll-impregnated DNA helix sprawling along the side of the ruin. Lorena wasted no time in finishing off the vampiro as she sharply thrust the black obsidian blade downward through the top of his right supraclavicular fossa. When Sapo's heart was cleaved, his grip upon the foliage growing along the pyramid wall began to slip.

If El Sapo was going to be pitched off the pyramid wall, it was clear that Dr. Cloud would also be swept away to his inevitable doom. Cloud reached out to Lorena with his right arm and exclaimed, "Lorena, grab my arm. Please! I can't hold on any longer!"

Lorena stood on an adjacent pyramid step with her arms thrust triumphantly skyward. She made no apparent effort to reach out to Cloud. The doctor was shocked to witness that no attempt was forthcoming to save him.

"I love you, Lorena!" Cloud proclaimed as he desperately clutched the back of the now dead vampiro who was soon to succumb to the force of gravity and crash down the side of the pyramid.

"I know you do."

Dr. Cloud and the corpse of El Sapo violently tumbled down the edifice and fell directly into the gaping maw of the cavernous cenote at the base of the Maya relic. To the very end, Dr. Cloud remained stoic and proud, as this was the long-recognized characteristic that precisely defined the members of his tribe. He uttered not a sound as he plunged into the darkness. Shortly, Lorena noted the report of a dull thud that echoed from the bottom of the huge chasm in the earth's crust. It was finished.

Now alone in a vast tropical jungle, Lorena Pastore proceeded to scramble to the top of the ancient Maya stone-block monument. "*¡Estoy aquí!*"

At that point, Lorena believed that she was no longer a humble curandera from the Rio Grande Valley in New Mexico. It was now time for her to make a grandiose declaration to anyone who was willing to listen. From the top of her lungs, she proclaimed an edict that was brazenly self-bestowed (or perhaps self-deluded). Her status had been elevated to Mesoamerican royalty. She anticipated that the entire world would stand up and take notice. Surely the indigent jungle denizens at large would at least pay homage and proffer the accolades that she believed she so rightly deserved.

Although she had no apparent subjects at the time to preside over, Lorena Pastore never once considered that perhaps the entire world was likely preoccupied with other, more pressing trials and tribulations of mundane daily living to take any notice of her existence. If the jungle failed to notice her bold ascendance to the newly claimed seat of Maya power, then so be it. Nevertheless, Lorena was undeterred when she proudly uttered another declaration from the top of the pyramid: "¡Yo soy una gran bruja!"

Morales strained hard at the leather straps that secured him to the stainless steel table that previously was reserved for veterinarian procedures such as the spaying of common household pets. Today, however, Morales was not about to be subjected to a vaginal hysterectomy, an orchiectomy, a nail trimming, a rabies vaccination, or even a diagnostic phlebotomy for the purposes of a routine laboratory assay to rule out a pesky, mosquito-borne canine heartworm infestation. El Tor actually had much bigger plans for the bioweapon who was captured in Durango: the cartel was about to turn Morales into home plate for the upcoming Calle Vampiro corporate family picnic and softball game! Allegedly, a good time would be had by all, present company of course excluded.

Romero Lopes entered the makeshift surgical suite with considerable trepidation. "You know, El Tor, I think it would be unwise to amputate this man's extremities. I actually know this fellow quite well, and I believe he can be turned. Why don't you assign him to my team? Let me work with him. If I can simply convince him to join us, the cartel would then have two vampiros under contract. Just think about how powerful our organization would be!"

El Tor pulled at his lower lip momentarily before making a decision about what Romero Lopes had just suggested. "No, but that was a very good idea nonetheless, Mago. I tell you what; I'll give you the honor of disarticulating this pendejo, but be sure you keep him alive!"

The cartel boss turned to one of the jailers who was present named Llaves and asked, "Has Russian Bear healed up from the burns on his back?"

"He still has several nasty open wounds from being punished on the rack," Llaves answered, "but he can still perform surgery in my opinion, if that's what you're concerned about."

"Well, bring the good doctor over here, Llaves," El Tor ordered. "Be quick about it. Somebody is going to have to attend to the injuries that Señor Morales will sustain when we hack off his arms and legs. Have a good day, gentlemen," El Tor said. He turned to leave the makeshift surgical suite. "I'll be in my office if anybody needs me. Remember, muchachos, I always have an open-door policy. Feel free to express your concerns to me about any problems you might encounter, no matter how big or how small they may seem!"

Upon El Tor's departure, Morales quipped, "Wow! What a guy! I wish I had a boss like El Tor." Morales then turned and glared at his nemesis. "So, what's it going to be, Lopes? Are you going to take me apart with a hacksaw, a machete, or perhaps a nail clipper? I don't have all day. After all, I've got a pretty tight schedule with a lot of shit on my plate. Just be done with it, you filthy animals. Don't forget that I'm a vampiro. Here's a fair warning: if you boys don't finish me off right now, my arms and legs will eventually grow back. Once they do, I'm going to come back here and kill every one of you motherfuckers!"

Señor Llaves returned with Russian Bear. The jailer instructed the doctor to scrub and get gloved up. "It's time for you to earn your bread and water, dancing bear. Every time we remove an extremity from the americano, you better be Johnny-on-the-spot and get his bleeding under control. If Señor Morales dies, then you die. Am I clear?"

Russian Bear reluctantly nodded.

El Punto walked up to the Mayo tray that was adjacent to the surgical table. He grabbed a machete, handed it to Romero Lopes, and said, "You have the honor, El Mago. Let the festivities begin!" It was a great surprise to all those present when Lopes pushed Punto aside and walked toward the exit.

Upon Lopes's unexpected departure, El Hipo picked up the machete and cursed the vampiro, who was already in the hallway. "You're a pussy, Mago! You don't deserve to be in our cartel!" With that comment, El Hipo went to work. As Lopes briskly walked away, the high-pitched screams that Morales emitted confirmed without a doubt that one of the United States Army's secret bioweapons was mercilessly being disassembled limb by limb.

Blake Barker had no doubt that something was terribly wrong. When Llaves returned Russian Bear to his cell in the dungeon, the big man was weeping inconsolably.

"Tell me what's wrong, big man," Blake said. "What happened when they took you down to the surgical suite?"

"You'll know soon enough," Russian Bear replied. "I can't do this anymore. I think I would be better off if I just killed myself right now!"

"Don't talk like that, Bear," Nancy Barber said. "You better man up. I mean it."

Punto and El Hipo seemed to be in extraordinarily good spirits when they arrived in the dungeon. Punto was pushing a gurney that carried the limbless torso of Señor Morales, who was still unconscious after being hacked into subcomponents. El Hipo, on the other hand, was pushing a shopping cart that had clearly been misappropriated from one of the many nearby Buena Comida grocery stores that one could easily find peppered about in the various barrios of Guadalajara. The shopping cart held three mysterious medium-size burlap sacks that appeared to be writhing about of their own volition.

Punto opened the door of Russian Bear's cage and proceeded to roll the critically mutilated victim off the gurney. When Morales bounced on the concrete floor of the cage, the impact caused a sound akin to a sexually aggressive wolf-whistler being slapped harshly in the face by an angry secretary scurrying past a high-rise building construction site on her way to work.

"You're supposed to be a goddamned doctor," Punto said to Russian Bear. "This Morales character is a vampiro, which means he may eventually be able to grow back his severed limbs. In the meantime, you'd better take care of him. I'll have Llaves bring you down a half gallon of fresh beef blood. You need to feed this vampiro as soon as he wakes up."

"What about me?" Blake asked. "It's been thirty-six hours since I've eaten anything. Are you bastards planning on starving me to death?"

"I'll feed you as soon as I have a chance to measure how much new growth you've had on your pinky finger since yesterday," El Hipo answered. "In the meantime, I have some company for you."

One by one, El Hipo grabbed each of the burlap sacks from the shopping cart and tossed them onto the floor of Blake Barker's cage. "I expect you to be a gracious host to your new guests," El Hipo said to Blake as he and Punto left the dungeon.

With great trepidation, Blake Barker opened the drawstrings on each of the three burlap sacks and carefully proceeded to remove the contents from each bag. Nancy Barber, who was in the adjacent cage, gasped when she realized that each burlap bag contained a living, breathing torso. It was quite apparent that the three limbless individuals had undergone the same surgical intervention that Señor Morales had just been brutally subjected to.

"Hello, gentlemen," Blake Barker said to his three new cellmates. "Welcome to my humble abode. My friends and I down here will try to accommodate you fellows to the very best of our ability and make you feel right at home. The lady who's in the cage to my immediate left is Nancy Barber. The big brute across the hallway is Russian Bear. The limbless fellow on the floor in Bear's cage is named Morales. Well, there you have it. While we're going through this round of formal introductions, it would be our honor to make your acquaintance. Who might you three gentlemen be?"

One of the limbless fellows who had a surprisingly well-trimmed goatee proceeded to barrel-roll across the floor until he stopped at Blake Barker's feet. "Hola. I'm First Base. The fat boy to my immediate right is Second Base. I'll bet a peso that you won't be able to figure out the name of my other friend who's directly behind me."

"Let me take a stab at it. Would his name happen to be, uh, Third Base?"

"Damn!" the sawed-off man with the goatee beard exclaimed with a laugh. "I guess I owe you a peso. How in hell did you figure that out?"

"Are you absolutely certain that El Hipo is going to attempt a coup?" El Tor asked as he pensively paced about his office.

"It will happen at the corporate softball game at the top of the third inning," Punto replied. "Think about it; you have a total of twenty captains in the cartel, and seventeen of them will be here this weekend with their families, all within the confines of a baseball diamond and bleachers. What better time to decapitate the entire organization?"

"If that's the case, I'll need to take care of this problem by the top of the second. Who's in on this?"

"Hipo and the five men in his security detail," Punto answered. "That makes a total of six traitors you'll have to deal with."

"And you know this how?"

"Hipo is convinced I'm in league with him. He believes that I'll become the seventh conspirator," Punto said with a grin. "He's convinced that I'm selling you out, El Tor."

"I'm deeply saddened," El Tor said. "Hipo and his boys have been with me from the very beginning. I've always treated the security detail like family. How could they do this to me?"

"Greed is a powerful motivator, señor," Punto answered.

"So it would seem," El Tor sadly agreed. "However, we have an equalizer. I'll have my twelve personal bodyguards hidden on the upper ridge above the third-base line on the athletic field. Before Hipo can initiate this ruthless coup attempt that he's planning, my men will exterminate not only Hipo but also his entire traitorous security detail. Besides, I'm not worried; El Mago is my secret weapon that I plan to unleash with all its fury!"

"Well, I'm not so sure about that," Punto declared. "Something has changed in El Mago. The other day, he refused to participate in the ambush you set up for the gringos at the warehouse distribution center in Durango. Just now, he turned down the honor of chopping off the arms and legs of Señor Morales in the surgical suite. I'm afraid he's getting soft."

"Is that so? I have an idea," El Tor said. "Let's subject El Mago to a little experiment. We need to find out if our vampiro can still function as a vampiro!"

"So, now that we know *what* you are," Blake said, "why don't you tell us *who* you are?"

"I'm Moritz the Mouse," the amputee with the goatee said. "My boys down here with me are El Jefe and Tuco. These two men happen to be brothers. We were once members of the Houston chapter of the Mexican Marauders motorcycle club, but we came down to Mexico in the spring of 1982 to settle a dispute that we had with the Calle Vampiro outpost in Matamoros. As you might gather, things did not work out so well for us. My friends and I have been kept alive for the last four years so the cartel members can use us as bases during the frequent softball games they play for tequila money. Looks like the unfortunate fellow across the hall will round us out as a foursome; we now have a home plate that will be joining us. How nice!" Moritz said.

"So, I must say for amputees, you fellows appear to be well-fed and in excellent hygienic condition," Blake noted.

"Naturally," Moritz the Mouse answered. "The Calle Vampiro members simply *love* softball, so it certainly behooves the cartel to take good care of their field equipment!"

“Well, today’s finally the big day. I hope you’re ready for the softball game, boss!” Llaves beamed. “Is there anything that I can do for you before the captains and their families arrive?”

“Yes,” El Tor answered, “as a matter of fact there is something I need you to do, Señor Llaves. Please come in and close the door.”

“Is there something wrong?” Llaves asked as he entered the office.

“I’m expecting a bit of trouble today during the softball game. There’s going to be an attempt on my life and the lives of my captains.”

“Señor, you should get the hell out of here!”

“Relax, Llaves. It’s nothing that I can’t handle. When the fireworks start, get down to the dungeon and put a bullet into the head of that gringo vampiro named Blake Barker.”

“It would be my pleasure,” the jailer answered. “Anything else?”

“After that, get the doctor out of his cage and sneak him out of the compound. Take him up to the safe house in Durango, and wait for my further orders.”

“No, El Tor!” Llaves protested. “Why don’t you let me kill that big Russian son of a bitch also? He has no respect for you.”

“Emergency room physicians are hard to come by,” the cartel boss answered. “I need to make sure that Russian Bear doesn’t get killed if things get out of control today. Just do as I say, and not a word about this matter to anybody else.”

“And what of Nancy Barber?” Llaves asked.

“Don’t worry about her,” El Tor answered. “She’ll be my consort at today’s festivities.”

“Tell me, Bear,” Blake called out from his prison cell, “how does Morales look today?”

“He looks mean,” Bear replied. “I’m afraid to get close to him. He might bite me.”

"Well, that's the spirit! From one vampiro to another," Blake said to Morales, "are you planning on causing any trouble today at the softball game?"

"I swear to God, Blake, you're such a dickhead," Morales said. "I should have killed you when I first met you in New Mexico last year. Everything is just a big joke to you, isn't it?"

"Hey! Do you talk to your mother like that with that filthy mouth of yours?" Blake asked. "Look, Morales, if we can't laugh at each other, what in hell can we laugh at? From now on, I'm going to call you Stumpy."

"Go to hell!" Morales said. "If I had a leg, I'd stick my boot up your ass."

"Say," Blake added, "if memory serves me correctly, I met a guy under your command named Stumpy Wheeler a while back. He seemed to be a good man. Tell me, Morales, whatever happened to old Stumpy Wheeler?"

At that point, it was suddenly clear to Morales that everything in the universe was connected somehow. After all, it was Morales who had prophylactically murdered Stumpy after the massacre in the morgue once Stumpy was viciously bitten by the vampire named Romero Lopes. Whether it was the universe, karma, or God in heaven, Morales realized that there was a penance to be made for the sins that he had committed in the past. The only thing that was left for him to do was to accept the painful dispensation of cosmic retribution that he so rightly deserved.

The ill-tempered insults that Morales and Blake had been hurling at each through the steel bars of their cages came to an abrupt end when the sound of footsteps and the unmistakable screech of a squeaky shopping cart wheel were heard in the hallway of the dungeon. Llaves had arrived with the shopping cart to take the bases and home plate up to the softball diamond.

"Okay, muchachos," the jailer said as he opened Bake's cage, "you know the drill. Get back into your gunnysacks. We've got to get you out on the field and dusted down with chalk powder to make you look nice and white like gringos before the game starts! You'll be happy to know that El Tor will not allow anybody to wear baseball spikes at the game today."

"That's good," the Mouse's friend Tuco noted. "I still have scars on my abdomen from the time some captain slid into me on a stolen base attempt this time last year!"

After loading up the three amputees and relocking Blake's cage, Llaves turned to face the cage on the opposite side of the dungeon hall. He unlocked the door of the Russian Bear's cell to retrieve Morales. "Now it's time for home plate. In deference to your recent surgical procedures, I'm not going to put you into a sack. You'd better not to try to bite me, though, or else there'll be hell to pay."

"Where's Hipo?" Bear asked. "That nasty fat bastard is usually the one who comes down here to do this kind of grunt work."

"I haven't seen him all morning," Llaves answered. "He's either jerking off somewhere or perhaps making final preparations for the fiesta." After loading Morales onto the shopping cart, Llaves disappeared down the hallway with the four amputees. He pushed the living, breathing bases and the new home plate toward the service elevator.

The dungeon dwellers were due for one additional visitor. The distinct sound of additional footsteps was readily detected soon after the departure of the jailer and his heavy-laden shopping cart. Blake had figured that it would only be a matter of time before Romero Lopes came to pay a visit down in the dungeon. That moment was now.

"Come here, you fucker!" Blake screamed as he lunged across the floor of his cage upon the arrival of Lopes. Sadly, Blake's efforts were futile. Lopes made certain to stand just out of Blake's reach.

"Relax, everybody," Morales said as he unlocked the cage of Nancy Barber. "I'm here to take this woman up to see El Tor in his private quarters."

"What does he want with me?" Nancy asked in terror.

"Today, my fair lady," Lopes replied, "you're going to be El Tor's personal escort to the corporate picnic and cartel softball game. He told me that he's going to personally bathe you very gently and then present you with a lovely summer dress to wear to the fiesta."

"Goddamn you, Lopes! What have you done with my son?" Blake asked. "Where in hell is Nathan?"

"I'm sorry, but I truly have no idea," Lopes replied. "I haven't seen him since I brought him here several days ago."

"I want to kill you!"

"And deservedly so," Lopes said with a profound look of melancholy upon his face. The vampiro then did something completely inexplicable. He tossed the key to the cell door onto the floor of Blake's cage and said, "Here's hoping you'll soon have the opportunity to do just that. After what I've put you through, the very least that I can do is to afford you the time and the place to even the score. When it happens, I won't even put up a fight. When this is all over, Blake, I pray that you may one day find solace."

"What are you doing, Romero?" Blake asked as he picked up the key and put it in his pocket. "What happened to you?"

"I'm just trying to make things right," Lopes said.

"It's too late for that."

"Maybe that's the case," Lopes said. "After all, a man is little more than a summation of his deeds, be they good, bad, or otherwise. Some sins are impossible to *live* with. It's now self-evident to me that some sins will be simply impossible to *die* with."

"I've heard about you," Russian Bear noted. "You're the one they call El Mago."

"It used to be a name I was proud of," Lopes explained, "but I see now that it has only brought me shame. I have a slash on my face that was rendered recently by the blade of an obsidian knife during the battle at Rancho Feliz. I contemplated coming down here and having you tend to my injury, but the more I thought about the matter, the more it became clear to me that I truly deserve this open wound on my face, and so much more."

"If you're in search of absolution, you won't find it here! Why don't you just leave us alone, you filthy animal," Russian Bear said.

"There's no prescription or act of penance I could perform that could ever offer me redemption or perhaps even salvation," Lopes added. "In any event, I hope you've enjoyed our hospitality at the Calle Vampiro cartel. I suggest that discretion will dictate when you gentlemen decide to depart. Just so you know, the current hotel management regulations mandate that your checkout time from our luxury resort must be no later than noon today."

Mago kept his personal promise to Nancy Barber. He refrained from binding her hands behind her back when she was led out of her holding cell in the dungeon. Nancy affirmed that she would cooperate and not cause any trouble when the vampiro took her from the basement and took her directly to the private quarters of El Tor. When Mago knocked upon the door of his employer, El Tor was auspiciously cordial and superficially gracious to his guests.

"Mrs. Barber," El Tor began, "I'm quite glad that you have the opportunity to accompany me today for the morning festivities."

"As if I had any choice," she replied.

"Oh, I rather like it when you get feisty with me," the cartel boss noted. "Why don't you go into the bathroom, disrobe, and draw a hot bath? I will be in directly to personally bathe you. I bought you a nice red cotton dress, and I demand that you wear it today. It has a pretty floral print of the Mexican bird-of-paradise flower on it. I can't wait to see you wear it. You will look *muy deliciosa*. In the meantime, I would like to have a private word or two with El Mago."

Upon Nancy's departure for the bathroom, El Tor asked, "Are you feeling well, Mago? I recently learned that you didn't participate in the Durango ambush. For some reason you also declined the opportunity to artistically remodel the torso of the americano vampiro named Morales."

"I don't know," Lopes replied. "I guess I just haven't been feeling like myself lately."

"You better not get soft on me," the cartel boss warned, "or else you and I may need to go our separate ways. Incidentally, nobody's ever allowed to part company with the cartel while they're still alive. Do I make myself clear?"

"Crystal."

"Good. I have a mission for you. Punto is waiting in your quarters with a specific job that you must accomplish before the softball game begins today. It's time for me to find out what you're exactly made of, because, frankly, I just don't know about you anymore. For your sake, I hope you pass the test."

With that, El Tor dismissed the vampiro. Upon the departure of Romero Lopes, the cartel boss went into the tub room to give Nancy Barber a gentle tongue bath, followed by a vigorous scrubbing with a loofah sponge.

When Lopes returned to his quarters, he found that Punto had come for a visit, and he had not come alone. Sitting on the bed was none other than Nathan Barker. Lopes had not seen the young boy since the bloody battle at Rancho Feliz.

"Uncle Romero!" Nathan squealed with delight. "I thought that I would never see you again!"

As the vampiro gave the boy an affectionate hug, El Punto said, "Well, how touching. I have direct orders from El Tor that you're supposed to eat this child, and I'm going to stand here and watch until the job is finished. Otherwise, Mago, there will be hell to pay."

"Don't eat me," Nathan pleaded to Lopes. "I promise you that I'll be a good boy!"

"Close your eyes now, Nathan," Lopes ordered. "I don't want you to see what's about to happen. This won't hurt. And I promise it will be over in a moment."

Nathan was trembling when he closed his eyes. He did not reopen them until he heard the sound of a scream followed by a loud thump on the bedroom floor. There was an eerie silence in the room when Nathan rubbed his eyes, opened them, and saw Punto's headless torso gushing out copious spurts of bright red blood from the stump where his head was previously affixed. Although he gasped for air, Nathan was far too frightened to make a sound.

"There are bad men in this place who want to kill you and me," Lopes explained. Once he had composed himself, Lopes briskly walked toward the hallway, grabbed Nathan by the hand, and exclaimed, "It's not safe here anymore, mijo. We have to go! We have to go now! *¿Estás listo?*"

Nathan held onto Lopes tightly. It was as if the vampiro was wearing the small child much like a man would wear a backpack on a camping trip in the woods. Lopes jumped out the window of his quarters and fled into the brush without being seen. If he and Nathan could only make it down the long driveway and disappear into the town of Guadalajara, safety would be at hand. Lopes and Nathan skirted the edge of the long paved drive, and the highway at the bottom of the hill was finally in plain sight. Freedom was only sixty meters away, when suddenly the vampiro was stopped dead in his tracks by the unmistakable sound of a gun being cocked.

"I don't know why I need this gun," Miguel Pastore mused as he walked out from the brush. "You're blind in one eye, and you also have a crippled leg, or so it seems by the way you hobble about. I've been looking forward to killing you ever since that fateful day when you murdered everybody in the morgue and turned me into a vampiro."

"I'm truly sorry for all of that," Lopes confessed.

"Too late for that," Miguel said, chuckling. "Maybe I'll cut you in half. This will be sweet! Before I kill you, tell me how I can find Blake Barker. If you let me know where he is, I'll end your life very quickly. If you feed me a line of bull—well, you're a smart boy. You can figure it out."

"You can't get to him even if you're a vampiro like me," Lopes explained. "He's locked up in a dungeon. I was planning on taking Nathan to safety, and then I was going to go back into the compound and help secure Blake's freedom. I've already secretly given him the key to his cell."

"Do you know where my daddy is?" Nathan asked.

"I do indeed," Lopes answered.

Nathan climbed down from Romero's back and ran to Miguel. "Please don't shoot Uncle Romero! He killed a bad man back there, and we're escaping from here. Listen to him! He said he's going to come back to help my daddy get away."

"Stay with Miguel," Lopes ordered the small boy. "Until your daddy is free, Miguel will be able to take care of you, but I can't."

"Uncle Miguel," Nathan pleaded, "take me back to Rancho Feliz with you. I miss seeing Señor Bosque."

"I will, Nathan," Miguel Pastore answered, "but I need to let you know that Lorena and her friend named Dr. Cloud are long gone, and I don't think they'll ever be coming back."

"That's okay," Nathan concluded. "Lorena seems to be mad all the time, and I know that she doesn't love me anymore."

In an unanticipated move, Lopes ripped open his shirt and exposed his chest to his armed adversary. "Here's your target, Miguel! Put a bullet right here." Lopes smiled broadly at the man he hoped would have the fortitude to end his life.

"Are you going to make it this easy for me now?" Miguel asked. "Nathan, I want you turn around. You don't need to see this."

Lopes reached out to carefully and gently adjust the barrel of Miguel's pistol so as to make certain that any projectile shot from the weapon would result in a lethal injury. After Lopes nudged the barrel of the gun to aim at the middle of his sternum, he tightly closed his eyes. The vampiro known as El Mago had been shot, stabbed, and even incinerated a time or two, but up until now, he had never received a fatal wound to his heart or brain. This time he hoped that the gunshot wound he was about to receive would result in a vastly different and conclusive outcome.

Lopes raised his arms outward from his sides as if he were a lone messianic figure about to be crucified. "I deserve this. Get it over with. What in hell are you waiting for? Put me down, damn it! Do you hear me? For God's sake, just do it!"

"What in hell is so damned funny, Shiftless?" Smoot asked as his colleague looked through a pair of binoculars. Ron Shiftless softly chuckled while he was busy surveying the compound for potential high-priority targets who were members of the Calle Vampiro cartel. From a safe location hidden in the deep brush at a distance of five hundred meters, Dr. Shiftless could readily see that the drug lords were about to begin a game of softball on a distant baseball diamond. What Shiftless found so funny were the six men he had inadvertently discovered hiding amid the trees on the opposite side of the athletic field. Without saying a word, Shiftless passed over the binoculars to his vampiro compatriot.

"Well, this scenario certainly explains why we didn't encounter a security detail when we slipped into this compound," Smoot said. "It seems peculiar to me that the security team would be all bunched together as they are. It just doesn't make sense."

"Well, it certainly does if we're about to witness a bloody coup," Ron answered, sporting a malicious smile. "You're missing the bigger picture, Smoot. Keep looking. Just think how Lady Luck must be smiling down upon us right about now. We've got deluxe balcony seats to what should be a glorious fireworks display!"

"A coup you say?" Smoot asked.

"Has to be," Ron said. "Scan the top of the hill." Just behind the armed men from the security detail were a dozen other fellows with automatic weapons drawing a bead on the soldados in front of them.

"You might be right. I think if that's the case, the jig's up. The cartel's ready for action. If it weren't for all the women and children in the bleachers, I'd say we should just let these nasty sons of bitches kill each other and be done with all of this."

"I don't give a shit about those women and children," Ron said. "They're cartel family members. They can all go straight to hell as far as I'm concerned."

"I don't know what happened to you, Ron," Smoot said as he continued to peer through the binoculars. "Somewhere along the way you lost your humanity and perhaps even your very soul. I'm worried about you. Perhaps I should say a prayer on your behalf."

"As if I need spiritual or moral guidance from a vampire," Shiftless countered. "I remember when you were first recruited to join our bioweapons program. Placard thought you were a Holy Joe.

Well, you're a Joe all right—a Joe Schmo, to be precise. The colonel thought you were a decent guy, but now with all of your sanctimony and Goody Two-shoes bullshit, I think otherwise."

"I'm truly honored that you hold me in such high regard."

"You're an idiot. The colonel's probably dead now, and he's not here to defend himself. Be that as it may, Augustus Placard never saw the big picture of how truly valuable a bioweapon such as you could be under the right circumstances. Nevertheless, your theological rants are going to diminish the value of the marketing campaign that I've launched on our behalf."

"What?!"

"You're just a country bumpkin, and you need to learn to keep your mouth shut. I don't want you to go around and tarnish recognition of our brand, which I am trying to establish in this nascent industry of modern biological warfare," Ron said. "Would it be asking too much from you to at least apply a thin veneer of agnosticism to your current résumé? Your adherence to classic Judeo-Christian principles may give potential customers pause to wonder just how truly committed you'd be to future locum tenens contract employment as a high-paid, ruthless, bloodthirsty mercenary."

"What in hell are you talking about?"

"I'll be your booking agent," Ron explained. "I'll ask for a 20 percent management fee, but I'll kick in major medical, dental, and also a long-term disability plan if you somehow manage to get wounded by an obsidian projectile weapon that renders some kind of permanent injury or otherwise causes the catastrophic dismemberment of one or more of your extremities."

"What?!"

"Of course," Ron added, "you'd be only a 1099 hired gun and not a classic W-2 employee, so you'd have to figure out on your own accord the FICA withholdings and the mandatory quarterly federal tax contributions you'd have to pony up for Uncle Sam."

"What in hell are you talking about?"

"Never mind," Ron added. "I hate Uncle Sam. Come to think of it, I fully understand and agree with your current objections to my suggested compensatory model. I don't blame you for being upset, and I know exactly what you're thinking."

"What?!"

"How about if we just farm you out as a hit man for cash under the table?" Ron proposed. "If that's not to your liking, we could also set up an offshore LLC in the Caribbean. I know at least one corrupt shithole country down there in the tropics that doesn't have a treaty to share banking deposit information or interest-generating data with our nosy uncle!"

"Listen, dipshit, I'm not a box of kitty litter or an aftershave lotion that's advertised in a low-budget television commercial during a *Star Trek* rerun midnight marathon. I'll have you know that I'm a man of righteous convictions," Smoot said.

"Do tell," Ron said. "Well, you can take your virtuous ideations and shove 'em where the sun won't shine, fang boy! I'm not buying into your pompous piety. We've got a job to do, so save your ethical dissertations for another time and another place. Our job is simple: we're going to find Morales and then get the hell out of here."

"I wonder what you taste like," Joe Cephas pondered as he licked his lower lip.

"Are you threatening me?" Shiftless asked. "That was a threat! Say that again and I'll unload a pocketful of grief on your sorry ass."

Clearly something horrid suddenly caught the attention of Joe Cephas Smoot as he continued to scan the baseball diamond through the field glasses. Before he could resume his rather hostile banter with Ron Shiftless, he violently vomited and continued to do so until he had dry heaves. Smoot threw down the pair of binoculars, rolled over on his back, and began to weep. His eyes were wide open with a look of abject fear on his face as he scanned the heavens. It was as if he were a man pleading for the intersession of Divine providence. He gasped for a breath of air before he simply and succinctly uttered the plaintive cry, "Oh God!"

"What's wrong?" Shiftless asked after witnessing that Smoot had acutely degraded into a state of terrified paralysis.

"I found Morales," Smoot said in a whisper.

"Well," Shiftless said, "spill the beans. Is he in the bleachers?"

"Home plate, man! Home plate ..."

Ron Shiftless picked up the binoculars and took a cursory glance at the athletic field. "The softball game hasn't even started yet," Ron noted. "There's nobody at home plate, and there's nobody waiting to take a pitch."

"He's not *at* home plate, you dumbass. He *is* home plate!"

"No, no, no!" Ron exclaimed as he surveyed the field through the binoculars. "I'll bet Romero Lopes is responsible for this atrocity. This certainly looks like his bloody handiwork. That son of a bitch must be around here somewhere. I'm going to find him, Smoot, and when I do, I'll unleash the pig gun on him."

"What else do you see, Ron?"

"It appears that the cartel members are using additional amputees for first, second, and third base also," Shiftless replied. "I can't stand it. It would be a tough shot at this angle, but maybe I should just put Morales and those other poor limbless bastards out of their misery. I should do it right now. Just what kind of sick fucks are we dealing with around here?"

"I don't know," Smoot sheepishly replied, his body still completely rigid with skeletal inertia. It appeared that the vampiro had lost the volition to move even a solitary muscle. "What are we going to do?"

"Well now, my bloodsucking friend," Ron replied, "the first thing you need to do is to pull your shit together and calm the hell down. Remember, Smoot, you're a superhuman bioweapon. Don't forget it. It looks like our unofficial mission in this godforsaken country has just been upgraded to a much higher priority that will demand immediate paramilitary interdiction."

Shiftless realized he was going need the heavy artillery, so he pulled back the bolt on the sniper rifle and ejected the cartridge that he'd previously chambered. He set the sniper rifle aside and motioned to Joe Cephas to pass over a green canvas gunnysack.

"It's time to take the pig out of the poke," Ron explained to his colleague as he liberated the M60 machine gun that the two men had brought along for the expedition. Shiftless extended the deadly weapon's bipod at the front end of the barrel and loaded it with a belt of ammunition.

Smoot slowly nodded his head in appreciation of the grisly and daunting task the two warriors were now facing. "New orders, Doc?"

"Simple. We're going to kill everybody, and then we're going to burn the goddamned place to the ground."

13

TONEL DE POLLO

As was the custom of the Calle Vampiro, the cartel captains were evenly divided into two teams for the softball game. The cartel members from the Gulf Coast region were called the Dinero squad, while the members of the home team from the western regions of Mexico were known as Las Drogas. At the bottom of the first inning, there was no score. It was time for the lead-off hitter for Las Drogas to step up to the plate. It was none other than the head of the entire cartel, who was also captain of the home team. El Tor took a couple of practice swings before he entered the batter's box and gently tapped the limbless torso of Morales, who was serving in the capacity of home plate, with the tip of his bat.

"Say, Morales," El Tor said to the limbless yet living, breathing home plate, "are you going to clap for me if I hit a home run?"

"Piss off, you nasty bastard."

After the first pitch resulted in a swinging strike at the plate, it was time for Shiftless and Joe Cephas to light the candles on the cake to get the party started. "From the dossier that Placard prepared for us, I recognize the man at the plate as none other than El Tor."

"The big cheese?"

"Looks like it. I'm annoyed by the fact that this man is still breathing. Let's see what we can do about that," Shiftless said as he gazed through the binoculars. "Now listen, Joe, I want you to work your way down toward the outfield fence. Once I see that you're in position, I'm going to unleash the pig gun on the dozen or so men on the opposite ridge and then work my way down. Take out as many men as you can on the field, and then I'll mop up the rest from up here."

"I'm on it," Smoot replied. "Be careful, Ron. If you put a hot smoking round up my ass by accident or otherwise, I am going to come back up here and stomp the holy dog shit out of you. Am I clear?"

"Crystal," Ron answered. "Don't worry, Smoot. You happen to be a valuable commodity. In fact, someday you're going to turn out to be a *very* valuable commodity. Now get going, fang boy. Keep your head down."

"The count is now three and two," the umpire reported.

"El Tor," Morales opined to the cartel boss, "I want to tell you that you look just like the ancient god Tezcatlipoca."

"Is that so?" El Tor asked as he commenced to overcut the next pitch with a vicious swing of the bat. When the ball weakly dribbled foul down the first-base line, the cartel boss inquired, "How, pray tell, did you come to this conclusion?"

"Well," Morales projected, "just like the pagan deity, you lost your right foot in a bloody battle."

"What are you talking about?" El Tor asked. "Both of my feet are still attached to my ankles."

"Not for long," Morales replied as he flopped over to his right side and buried his fangs into the distal shin of El Tor before the next pitch came over the plate. With jaws more powerful than those of a laughing hyena, Morales easily amputated El Tor's right foot in a lightning-quick ratchet-like fashion.

When El Tor fell back in agony, the dozen loyal men in his secret hit squad who were previously assigned to root out and ambush the traitors in Hipo's security detail bravely swung into action with their automatic weapons to neutralize the pending coup that now appeared to them to be fully under way. They never got off a shot. In less than twelve seconds, Ron Shiftless unleashed a burst of over a hundred rounds from the pig gun, and El Tor's vaunted bodyguards were unceremoniously cut into slabs of bloody sinew.

The din of distant machine-gun fire alarmed the jail keeper. Was it now time to execute Blake Barker? Perhaps it was also time for Russian Bear to be handcuffed and hauled away into protective custody at the safe house in Durango.

"I hear gunfire! What in hell is going on, Llaves?" Russian Bear asked. "You' better go topside and scope it out!"

"I'll be back," the jailer reported as he ran through the dungeon toward the service elevator with a twelve-gauge pump in hand.

That was all the time Blake needed. As soon as Llaves disappeared toward the lift, Blake unlocked his own cage and crossed the hallway to free Russian Bear with the stolen jail key.

"Hurry up, Blake," Bear pleaded. "Llaves will be back in no time. We only have a few minutes to escape from this hellhole!"

Russian Bear was wrong; the two desperate prisoners had less than a few seconds to escape. Just as Blake jammed the key into the lock on the door of Bear's cage, a blast from the trusty scattergun that Llaves faithfully toted ruptured the vampiro's right lateral chest wall. Blake never saw it coming. The vampiro collapsed upon the floor in agony. Before he lost consciousness, Blake weakly gasped, "I'm sorry, Bear!"

Maybe Llaves had come back to the basement jail prematurely to retrieve his sunglasses. Maybe Llaves forgot to grab his pack of smokes before he left the dungeon. Maybe Llaves had to take a leak. For whatever reason, after Llaves initially entered the freight elevator to auspiciously exit the basement, he immediately came back out of the lift with his riot gun blazing buckshot.

"*¡Qué desdichado!*" Llaves proclaimed as he spat a thick wad of snot upon the unresponsive Blake Barker, who was bleeding profusely. "¡Pendejo! I knew you gringos were up to something. As if you muchachos thought you could fool somebody like me. Didn't anybody tell you americanos that I'm the best jailer in the world? After all, El Tor told me so!"

Llaves produced a pair of handcuffs and tossed them onto the floor of Russian Bear's cage. "Put these on. No funny business, or else I'll make you bleed just like Blake. It's time for you and me to take a little vacation up to Durango. It's not safe here anymore, mijo. We have to go! We have to go now! ¿Estás listo?"

Unencumbered by El Tor's twelve-man team of bodyguards, who were all now dead in their rearguard position at the top of the tree line, Hipo and his five confederates from the security detail plowed through the brush and down the embankment on the ridge. The members of the traitorous coup were bound and determined to kill anything that was moving. They trained their automatic weapons upon the women and children in the bleachers and began to blast away without mercy.

As El Tor's personal consort, Nancy Barber was seated in a place of honor at the back of the bleachers. When the shooting started, she jumped out of her seat and pulled the dead body of a corpulent abuela over herself as protective cover from the fusillade of fire emitted from the automatic weapons wielded by Hipo's henchmen.

Despite repeated blows to the head from El Tor's baseball bat, Morales vigorously sucked away on the bloody stump of the cartel leader's right leg. From his position as first base, Moritz the Mouse was giving an enthusiastic play-by-play to the other amputees, El Jefe and Tuco. His friends were literally staked out at second and third base, respectively. Sadly, a rain of bullets from the ridgeline brought the lives of the Mouse and his colleagues to an abrupt end before they would ever have a chance to enjoy liberation from the cartel that had enslaved them.

In the chaos, Smoot cleared the outfield fence and was brutally dispensing with the remaining Dinero teammates on the athletic field before they could flee to safety. After Ron Shiftless successfully changed out the red-hot barrel of his M60 machine gun, he gleefully proceeded to pour hundreds more rounds into the Las Drogas squad's dugout along the third-base line. He continued to do so until all the high-pitched bloodcurdling screams that emanated from the enclosure finally and mercifully stopped.

Even then Shiftless snapped another belt of ammo into the receiver of the pig gun and went back to work. Several gravely injured cartel members on the baseball diamond had the audacity to crawl away from the bloody carnage in an attempt to find refuge from the terror, but alas, they too in the very end would be given no quarter.

Romero Lopes reluctantly opened his eyes at the distant sound of automatic weapon fire from the M60 only to discover that Miguel Pastore and Nathan Barker had vacated the premises without leaving so much as a trace. As Lopes was not originally privy to the coup attempt that was orchestrated by Hipo and his traitorous security detail, the vampiro had no idea what was going on.

By the time Lopes limped to the top of the hill, the gun battle was over. The vampiro decided to remain hidden in the tree line until he could ascertain what had transpired. He wasn't particularly surprised to see that Ron Shiftless and Joe Smoot were responsible for the bloodshed, as he remembered a rather unpleasant prior confrontation he had with these two individuals, among others, at the university hospital in Santa Fe.

This current situation appeared to bode rather well for Romero Lopes. Perhaps Shiftless or Smoot would be able to finish the job that Miguel Pastore apparently lacked the courage to carry out. Perhaps Shiftless or Smoot would be able to finish the job that Romero Lopes apparently lacked the courage to accomplish himself.

Lopes was quite pleased to see that El Tor was trussed up in the prone position with a crude tourniquet firmly applied to the proximal stump above an amputated right distal extremity. As El Tor was no doubt having a very bad day, the vampiro found the cartel leader's predicament to be most gratifying.

Sadly, Lopes soon realized that Joe Smoot was busy burying what remained of the body of Morales, who'd had his skull crushed in by a softball bat viciously employed by El Tor. At a distance of over one hundred feet away, Ron Shiftless was observed to be in the process of binding the hands and feet of Hipo and his five henchmen. Lopes bided his time and waited for the right opportunity to emerge from the tree line and surrender to the two angry men who had violently annihilated the Calle Vampiro cartel compound.

Once she was certain that the battle was over, Nancy Barber cast aside the dead body under which she had been hiding. It was Smoot who first realized that another living being had survived the slaughter, but Shiftless also heard the commotion. He meandered over to the woman to ascertain if she deserved a bullet in the back of her head.

"Hold it right there, lady," Smoot said. "Who in hell are you, and what are you doing here?"

"My name is Nancy Barber. I'm from Houston. My husband is an emergency room physician. We were captured by the cartel back in 1977. My husband escaped a while ago, but I'm certain he doesn't know that I'm still alive. I've been a prisoner here for the last nine years. I hope that you boys will be able to get me back home to Texas."

"We'd be honored to take you home, just as soon as we figure out what to do with these prisoners. We also have the kingpin tied up in a knot," Ron said as he gave the woman a triumphant grin.

"You boys captured El Tor?"

"He's right over there," Ron answered as he pointed to the bound and gagged cartel leader. "You have any suggestions?"

"Kill them!" Nancy answered. "Kill them all."

"Hold your horses, lady," Smoot cautioned. "That's not going to happen on my watch. Do you know if anybody else is inside the compound?"

"There's a doctor locked up in the basement. He's a prisoner we call Russian Bear. There's also a man down there named Blake Barker whom you need to free."

"Small world," Ron said.

"And indeed a very bad one," Smoot added.

"Smoot and I both know Barker quite well when we were all in Santa Fe a while ago," Ron explained. "How in hell did he get here? That man has some explaining to do. Anything else we need to know?"

"Yes, and this is very important," Nancy Barber said. "There's a whorehouse on the east side of the compound where they keep the sex slaves. The madam keeps women and even some teenage boys in chains. It's imperative that you liberate these people and bring the madam to me. I swear to Jesus, I will personally kill her."

"Now, why would you want to do something like that?" Smoot asked.

After a painful moment of silence, Shiftless slapped Smoot across the back of his head and asked, "Do you have to be a dumbass every single day of your life? I'm going to fire up the wireless and call in an extraction chopper. Check the basement for any prisoners, and then report back immediately."

Upon Smoot's departure, Nancy Barber remembered that El Hipo was a two-pack-a-day cigarette smoker. She went straightaway to the henchman to extract the butane cigarette lighter from his front shirt pocket that he always had on hand. She then marched over to El Tor to torment the cartel leader. With the cigarette lighter, she began to sear the stump of his right lower extremity. Although gagged, the cartel leader emitted audible screams of pain.

Meanwhile, Shiftless completed his call on the radio to ask for assistance from the bioweapons program administrator, named General Sibley, in San Antonio. After only a few moments, Shiftless threw the radio down upon the ground and began kicking it as if it were an empty soda can that a pedestrian might have found on the ground by the side of a roadway.

"Something wrong?" Nancy asked. "Is help coming or not?"

Before Shiftless could answer this pertinent question, Smoot appeared at the compound's main entrance. The vampiro shouted down a status report to his colleague. "I checked out the basement. There were several cages down there, but they were all empty. I saw a trail of blood on the hallway floor that led to the service elevator. I found no live bodies. I found no dead bodies either, for that matter. Do you have further orders?"

"Go over to the whorehouse and liberate the sex slaves over there," Ron ordered. "Be sure to bring back the madam who runs the joint. It sounds like we'll have the pleasure of witnessing a swift dispensation of ballpark justice. Be quick about it."

When Smoot trotted over to the eastern edge of the compound, Romero Lopes elected to finally emerge from the shadows. He hobbled over to Ron Shiftless, who was frankly startled to see such a dangerous creature appear from the tree line.

"I believe you're looking for me," Lopes said as he yet again held out his arms. "I deserve this. Get it over with. What in hell are you waiting for? Put me down, damn it! Do you hear me? For God's sake, just do it!"

Unlike Miguel Pastore, Ron Shiftless didn't hesitate. "See you in hell, dirtbag."

After Lopes was cut down, Ron Shiftless and Nancy Barber engaged in a near-orgasmic explosion of cold-blooded murder.

"Feed me! I'll man the trigger, and you guide the ammo belt," Ron instructed Nancy as they both rushed over to El Hipo and his five henchmen from the failed cartel coup attempt. "Let's see what you're made of, fat man!" Shiftless shoved the barrel of the pig gun into Hipo's mouth while the corpulent cartel member pleaded for mercy. It was to no avail. Ron held down the trigger until the fat man's head disintegrated. He then turned the machine gun on the other five terrified and defenseless prisoners. Shiftless made short work of them also.

Once that was done, Nancy Barber asked Ron for a minor indulgence. "Would you allow me the pleasure of dispensing with El Tor?"

"Madam," Ron replied, "it would be my honor."

Shiftless passed over the M60 to Nancy Barber, but she waved him off. "I have something else in mind."

Nancy trotted over to the bleachers on the athletic field where a toolshed was nestled beneath the stands. Ron Shiftless howled with unbridled enthusiasm when Nancy emerged from the toolshed atop a riding lawn mower. Although he wanted to give the execution of El Tor his utmost attention, Shiftless saw that Romero Lopes was still twitching just a bit. This warranted an immediate intervention.

While Smoot was at the whorehouse, the sound of machine-gun fire alerted him that something had gone awry. Fearful that Ron Shiftless had initiated the task of murdering the remaining prisoners of his own accord, Smoot hurried back to the athletic field with the angry madam from the whorehouse in tow. It was too late.

Smoot witnessed in horror as Nancy Barber slowly propelled the riding lawn mower over El Tor, starting at his lower extremities and working her way upward toward his torso in a methodical fashion. Occasionally the running lawn mower would unexpectedly stop with the sound of a loud thud as a thick shank of bone or viscera would stall out the spinning blade.

On these annoying occasions, Nancy Barber had no qualms about briefly tipping the mower platform over on its side to scrape out the body parts that periodically jammed up the mower deck. Once the befouled blade was liberated of sundry sinew, the lawn mower would invariably fire right back up, and Nancy would resume her grisly task. Soon, the head of El Tor was engulfed by the spinning blade bar. Nice!

While Nancy was thoroughly enjoying this rather macabre extracurricular activity, Smoot was apoplectic to see that Dr. Ron Shiftless was back on the athletic field and taking batting practice with the decapitated head of Romero Lopes. Ron repeatedly tossed the head of Lopes into the air, and then he'd take a swing at it with a baseball bat. Time and again, Ron wasn't strong enough to propel the decapitated head of the vampiro much farther than the pitcher's mound. Nonetheless, Shiftless finally raised his arms in the air and triumphantly called out a play-by-play to the dead bodies that were scattered about the diamond. "That was a solid Texas-leaguer, ladies and gents! With one down in the bottom of the ninth, Ron Shiftless is safe at first!"

Smoot turned to the madam he had taken prisoner from the cartel's whorehouse. As he unsheathed his Ka-Bar to liberate the woman from her zip tie bindings, he screamed, "Run! Run away, goddamn you! Get out of here before these monsters find you."

Once Shiftless and Nancy Barber collapsed with exhaustion, Joe Cephas approached the athletic field with considerable trepidation. "What's the matter with you, Ron? I just don't know who you are anymore."

"I'm the same man that I've always been," Shiftless answered. "I have no doubt, however, that you've been changed by this whole dreadful ordeal. You just haven't changed enough for the better as far as I'm concerned. It's time for you to grow up, bumpkin."

"Did you find the madam from the whorehouse?" Nancy Barber asked. "As for me, playtime's not over just yet."

"I found her, but she escaped," Smoot lied.

"Is that so?" Nancy asked with considerable skepticism.

"We've got far bigger fish to fry," Shiftless interjected. "Before I kicked the crap out of the radio, I was able to get a hold of San Antonio on the SW."

"Don't leave us guessing," Nancy said. "I could tell that there was a problem."

"Indeed," Ron confirmed. "I have bad news to report. Senator Lumpy McStain, who's the head of the Armed Forces Subcommittee, made sure that the plug got pulled on our bioweapons program."

"What's that mean for us?" Smoot asked.

"As far as the federal government is concerned, we no longer exist," Ron explained. "We're going to have to find a way back to Los Estados Unidos on our own accord."

"We're screwed!" Smoot exclaimed. "There's no way we can bail in the military van that got us here. We'll just be way too conspicuous."

"It looks like you guys have worn out your welcome here," Nancy said.

"Be of good cheer, boys and girls," Ron replied. "There's a shitload of dead bodies on this baseball diamond and a shitload of fancy cars on the compound's parking lot. I've got a job for you, Joe. Start digging through the pockets of these stiffs and find some keys that will match up with the most expensive car that we can get our hands on."

"I'm on it!" Joe said enthusiastically. "I'd be honored if you'd give me a hand, Mrs. Barber, as it would speed things up dramatically."

"I've always been partial to the fancy big Benz luxury cars," Nancy suggested. "I haven't ridden in a car now for nine years!"

"Done deal," Ron agreed. "Let's find a car and then get the hell out of Mexico as soon as we put a torch to this place."

"What about our van and all our weapons?" Smoot asked.

"Ditch it all here," Ron ordered. "We can't take any of that shit back. If we attempt to do so and get caught by the Federales, we'll all get hung out to dry."

The handwritten map that the mayordomo at El Rancho Feliz had given to Cletus Barker revealed precisely how he could find Lorena Pastore in the Yucatán. However, the map didn't give Cletus any clue as to what he would find once he got there.

No sooner had he arrived in the jungle than it was time for Lorena's coronation ceremony. There was no time for Cletus even to unpack his car before Lorena issued him a list of rather degrading yet nonetheless mandatory duties that he was to perform during the royal festivities. Cletus felt rather uncomfortable as soon as he saw the crowd of forest dwellers gathering at the base of the relic Maya pyramid. He was now deeply lost in a foreign land among people who looked upon him with considerable suspicion.

"I love you, Lorena."

"I know you do."

"Something—something's wrong. What's going on here, Lorena?" Cletus asked. "I just don't recognize you anymore. I feel as if our relationship has already gotten off on the wrong foot, and I just got here."

"Relationship? What could possibly make you think that you could still relate to me now that I'm royalty? I've evolved, Cletus," Lorena explained as she placed the elaborate crown of feathers upon her head and adjusted her formfitting white gown.

"I still want to be with you."

"If you want to be here with me," Lorena said, "I suggest that you accept who and what I am."

"What do you expect of me?"

"When I climb to the top of the pyramid to address my people, you must stand no more than two steps behind me at all times. I want you to hold the obsidian knives in the air and make sure that my subjects are able to see each knife over my shoulders."

"That's not what I meant," Cletus protested. "I'm not your servant."

"No," Lorena answered, "but you're only my consort. Don't ever think that you're my equal."

"If you've evolved," Cletus said as he followed Lorena up the steps of the pyramid, "just tell me if there is anything left of the person I fell in love with long ago."

"I shouldn't have to tell you that," Lorena vaguely answered. "Don't you know by now?"

"Spell it out for me, Lorena," Cletus pleaded. "Tell me the plain truth. You owe at least that much to me. By the way that you're behaving now, I truly don't know who or what you've become."

"Open your eyes, Cletus," Lorena answered. "Is it not obvious? ¡Yo soy una gran bruja!"

The incessant sound of nearby pig grunts aroused Blake Barker from the hiding place where he had taken refuge in the abandoned guard station at the entryway to the Calle Vampiro compound.

Surrounded by several porkers attracted by the pheromones emanating from the injured vampiro, Blake's unexpected feral guests would provide the sustenance he needed to help him recuperate. The shotgun blast inflicted by the jailer Llaves upon the vampiro's lateral chest wall was, after all, a very serious injury indeed. Something was wrong, however. It was not just an injury Blake received. He was now feeling quite ill. He started to run fevers and he would intermittently break out in sweats since he received the chest wound. What could be wrong? Did the injury that he had received somehow cause an exacerbation on his underlying viral infection that caused him to turn into a vampire?

After Blake had dined, the smell of smoke alerted him that the compound at the top of the hill was in flames. Blake hobbled up to the edge of the hacienda, where he witnessed a raging inferno. He could only hope that Nancy Barber and Russian Bear had escaped the conflagration while he took a quick survey of the compound's parking lot in an effort to find a vehicle that would allow him to escape the premises. As Blake crossed the softball diamond littered with dead bodies, he found the lifeless head of Romero Lopes near the pitcher's mound. "You're coming with me, amigo!" Blake cackled maniacally as he picked up the head of his vanquished foe and stuck it under his arm.

"I came to Mexico for a little fun in the sun, and all I've got to show for my trip down here is the pathetic dome of this nasty ghoul," Blake lamented. "Hell's Bells! I should've at least picked up a sombrero and a souvenir shot glass while I was down here."

Placard's hit team had previously abandoned their vehicle when they fled North, and their military van, bristling with sophisticated weaponry, had caught Blake's eye. The set of keys dangling from the van's ignition switch sealed the deal.

Before Blake climbed into the van, he jammed the skull of Romero Lopes securely upon the vehicle's hood ornament. "There! I'll bet nobody will fight me for a parking space when I'm behind the wheel of this bad-ass rig," Blake proudly proclaimed to the dead cartel members strewn about the field as little more than discarded refuse.

There were questions to be answered: should Blake retreat and regain his strength, or should he go to work straightaway to find his missing son, Nathan? There was also the matter of the deceitful curandera who was his former domestic employee. A promise was previously made to Miguel Pastore that no harm would come to his sister, Lorena, if Blake ever successfully hunted her down. After careful reflection upon his current circumstances, Blake Barker elected to unilaterally revoke the peace treaty that he had previously forged with Miguel. If Blake ever were to find Lorena in the future, there would be hell to pay.

Once Llaves pulled Russian Bear out from the driver's side of the vehicle, he escorted the hapless physician toward the entryway of a rather nondescript white masonry home that exuded an industrial ambiance. Isolated from other structures, the building was located on the outskirts of Durango. "This will be your new home, 'Dancing Bear.' I trust the accommodations will be to your liking."

Although handcuffed, Russian Bear decided to make a dash to attempt an escape after he gave Llaves a head butt that stunned the jailer and knocked him to the ground. Sadly, Russian Bear didn't get far. A shotgun blast over his head as he was in the midst of escaping was enough to get his undivided attention. "Do it again," Llaves pleaded as he regained control of the situation. "I've been looking for an excuse to put you down for a long time."

At gunpoint, Russian Bear was forced through the entryway of the domicile that had been purposefully constructed without any windows. There was another jailer inside the building, simply known as "The Cat Fucker", who quickly shackled Russian Bear's left leg to a U-bolt that was embedded in the concrete floor.

If there was any good news about the situation, it appeared at least that the doctor was going to have the opportunity to enjoy the company of another human being. Russian Bear immediately discovered that there was some other unfortunate soul incarcerated in the building against his free will. This man was shackled in a similar fashion, tethered to a chain affixed to the bare concrete floor.

"As it would seem that we're going to be spending some time together," Bear said, "please allow me to introduce myself. I'm an emergency room physician who was captured this past year by the Calle Vampiro cartel. My name is Ilya, but my friends call me Russian Bear!"

"As it would seem that we're going to be spending some time together," the other prisoner replied, "please allow me to introduce myself. I'm a military officer who was captured this past year by the Calle Vampiro cartel. My name is Augustus Placard, but my friends call me Colonel Placard!"

As he was in a rather foul disposition, Dr. Seth Blanks at the CDC was in absolutely no mood for any company. "Not now—I'm busy," he shouted out to the unexpected visitor in the hallway who was vigorously knocking on his office door. "Why don't you come back after lunch?"

Apparently this intrusive person wasn't about to take no for an answer. The associate directors of the Human Vampire Research Project, Dr. Kohl and Hoefferle, barged into Seth's office without an invitation and proceeded to take a seat in front of the desk.

"When were you going to tell the other members of the team that we just got the rug pulled out from under our feet?" Kohl asked.

Hoefferle was sneering at Dr. Blanks while he waived an office memo above his head in anger. "When Uncle Sam shut down the bioweapon team in San Antonio, I was told that I could continue my research here at the CDC. That's why I jumped ship and came over here. Well, I just got here, and it looks like the government is going to try and screw me again! It was a mistake for me to have moved here to Atlanta. I should have taken that job in private industry," Dr. Hoefferle regretfully concluded. "What in hell happened here, Seth?"

Kohl grabbed the memo out of the hand of his associate, crumpled it in obvious disgust, and then hurled it at the head of Dr. Blanks who was sitting on the other side of his desk. "Romero Lopes is dead. There's not been another confirmed new case of human vampirism since that nasty bastard named Romero Lopes got a really short hair cut down in Mexico."

"What do you want me to say?" Dr. Blanks asked. "Our funding has dried up, and the Night Crawler Protocol has drawn to a conclusion."

"Yet again, another research program is going into hibernation," Dr. Hoefferle said. "It's like I'm living in a bad dream."

"You boys better not bail on me," Blanks said.

"Whether you like it or not, I'm about ready to toss in the towel," Kohl said. "The exact same damned thing happened to us when the last outbreak of human vampirism burned itself out in a spontaneous fashion for whatever reason back in 1979. There's now an opening in the virology lab at Texas A&M. I think am going to jump ship, Seth."

"Relax," Dr. Blanks said. "We'll get a stay of execution as long as we can get our hands on another individual infected with the RV-1986 virus."

"Well," Hoefferle said, "how in hell do you propose to do that?"

"Cool your tool," Blanks answered sharply. "Why don't I let you guys in on a little secret? There's a 'Plan B' that you don't know about. I've always had a contingency blueprint on the back burner, and it's high time that I told you boys all about it."

Dr. Ben Fielder was a newly appointed associate professor in the Department of Family Practice at the Gulf Coast College of Medicine in Houston. The good doctor just completed a full physical examination on Nancy Barber. Despite nine years of brutal captivity, her only obvious medical issue was apparent stress-induced premature menopause. Nancy always believed it was a blessing that she had gone through ovarian failure in her midthirties, especially in light of the fact that she had been a sex slave for almost a decade.

"I can't believe that you found your way back to Texas after all these years, Nancy," Dr. Fielder said as he folded his arms and leaned against a desk in the exam room.

"Well," Nancy said, "here I am in the flesh."

"You and your husband, Frank, were kidnapped long before I started my medical training at this institution," the doctor said. Although Fielder had never previously met Nancy Barber, her mysterious disappearance was the subject of rumors at the medical school for many years. "Now that you've risen from the dead," Fielder added, "you're a bona fide legend!"

"I don't want to be a legend," Nancy said. "I just want to get on with my life."

"If that's the case," Dr. Fielder replied, "I'm actually quite surprised that you haven't made an effort to talk to your husband, Frank, as of yet."

"I'm afraid."

"What's to be afraid of?" Fielder asked. "From what I understand, Frank established a free clinic a few miles from here. He's now taking care of the homeless and indigent population of downtown Houston."

"So I've heard."

"Why don't you at least make a point of letting him know that you're still alive?" Fielder asked.

"I just don't know," Nancy replied, "but I think that something's seriously wrong with me. I'm filled with anger and hatred. All I think about is exacting revenge upon my captors. I know it's silly because most of them are already dead. Maybe you can help set me up to see a psychiatrist."

"I'll be happy to do that."

"Speaking of the psychiatry department," Nancy noted, "what's with all the yellow police tape that's been placed around the perimeter over there? I passed by that area when I came into the clinic for my appointment to see you today. Was there a break-in?"

"Funny you should ask," Fielder replied. "My office manager is my wife, Missy. When she unlocked the clinic early this morning before my arrival, she found a young woman who was dead and sitting in the lotus position in front of the entryway to the psychiatry department across the hall."

"What on earth happened?"

"When the crew from the emergency room arrived to address the situation," Fielder explained, "their preliminary finding was that the dead woman had been drained of all her blood!"

"Well, what do you think about that?"

"I've never seen anything like it," Fielder answered, "so I just don't know what to think."

Upon his return to the United States, Joe Cephas Smoot got his old job back at the poultry processing plant in Hope, Arkansas. One day he received a surprise phone call from his former colleague Dr. Ron Shiftless. "How're you doing, Joe?" Shiftless asked.

"I'm happy as a clam," Joe Cephas answered. "I get all of the chicken and turkey blood that I could ever want."

"Now that you're a civilian again," Shiftless began, "are you getting settled into some kind of a normal life?"

"Well, Sister Rawlene reluctantly let me move in with her, but she still leaves a light on in the bathroom when she goes to bed at night."

"So, are you still a pariah in your own community?" Ron asked.

"I talked to my preacher, Rectal Roberts. He's on television, I'll have you know. At a recent tent revival, he recanted his proclamations that I was in league with the Devil," Joe Cephas explained. "Now that all of those unfounded allegations are behind me, all is right with the world!"

"That's great, Joe," Shiftless said, biting his lower lip. "I'm going to be in Arkansas today on a business matter. Since I'll be in your neck of the woods, it would be great if I could meet you for some barbecue. I'll just tell the cook to leave your brisket platter raw! You'll know me when you see me. I'll be coming in a large white unmarked van."

"You're on, Doc! I'll meet you at Smokie Sam's at seven sharp!"

That evening, Joe waited patiently outside the barbecue joint. When a white van pulled up to the curb, the unsuspecting vampire naturally thought that Ron Shiftless had just arrived. Joe walked up to the van to greet his old colleague, but three burly strangers jumped out of the vehicle, tackled him, and secured his arms behind his back with handcuffs. Harshly thrown into the back of the vehicle, Joe Cephas Smoot quickly realized that he had just been shanghaied, and most likely for nefarious purposes.

True to form, his greatest concern, of course, was that he was about to miss what he thought was a legitimate meeting with Ron Shiftless. It never occurred to Smoot that his former colleague had actually sold him down the river for monetary gain! As his mysterious abductors were busy stuffing a gag in his mouth in the back of the speeding van, Smoot's other worrisome issue was that he, in all likelihood, would be late for work the following day. For Smoot, this was a most troublesome matter because he had a strong work ethic and he certainly didn't want his absence from the jobsite to place any kind of extra burden or hardship upon his supervisor or coworkers. Sadly, as it turned out, that would be the least of his concerns.

"Señor Bosque, I need your help."

"What is it, Nathan?"

"I have to take something to school tomorrow for show-and-tell. I asked Uncle Miguel what would be a good thing to present to my classmates, and he just started to laugh. He said that there were a lot of things here at Rancho Feliz that I can teach my friends about, but I just can't think of anything."

"Most of the children who live in Santa Sangre probably don't know *anything* about what goes on at a farm or a ranch," the mayordomo explained. "Why don't you go out to the barn and see if you can find something interesting to share with the other children?"

"You're the best, Señor Bosque," Nathan proclaimed. He gave the old man a hug and ran out the door.

Nathan went straightaway to the *tonel de pollo* where the poultry nested. He was once told by the old curandera who now lived at the ranch that los huevos amarillos were poisonous and should never be eaten. In addition, Nathan had been informed that under no circumstances should the bright yellow eggs be utilized for *any* other purpose except the special huevo limpia cleansing ritual. The temptation for young Nathan to take one of the special yellow eggs was, sadly, far too great.

"Shoo! Go away!" Nathan barked at one of the old hens that was bravely incubating a clutch. The chicken for its part was not about to move an inch. Undeterred, Nathan found a sheet of old paper on the floor of the chicken coop that miraculously was not befouled by bird droppings. The young boy aggressively waved the scrap of paper in front of the bird's face. A threat of that magnitude was just too much for Nathan's misfortunate domesticated avian adversary to tolerate! After the hen evacuated her lower cloacal aperture, she evacuated the premises. Nathan suddenly had a prime opportunity to exploit the circumstances.

"My, you're a lovely huevo amarillo," Nathan proclaimed as he gently picked up the only bright yellow egg that he had found in the entire coop. "I'll bet my classmates will be surprised to see something like this at show-and-tell!"

To Be Continued

COMPLETE GLOSSARY OF MEDICAL TERMS

VAMPIRO, VOLS. 1 AND 2

anterolateral: Referring to the position found in front of and to the side of a subject.

blast: An immature cell that is a precursor to a more mature subset.

choreiform gyrations: A writhing, snakelike motion.

cloacal aperture: The exit site of the combined rectal, vaginal, urinary tract repository found among lower vertebrate life-forms such as birds and reptiles.

Coomb's test: A clinical laboratory test to evaluate the presence of pathologic antibodies against circulating erythrocytes. A positive test by either direct or indirect methods confirms an immune hemolytic disease process.

coprophagic arthropod: An insect whose dietary requirements include (either partially or exclusively) the feces of other organisms. A nasty bug that eats shit.

creatinine: A nitrogenous waste product cleared by the kidneys. A rising creatinine level in the serum is consistent with renal dysfunction.

diener: A mortuary assistant.

ectoderm: One of the three primary embryonic tissue planes that constitute the outer layer of cells in embryonic development.

endoderm: One of the three primary embryonic tissue planes that constitute the inner layer of cells in embryonic development.

enteral: Referring to the gastrointestinal/digestive system.

erythroblast: An immature bone-marrow-dwelling precursor to a circulating red blood cell.

erythrocyte: A circulating red blood cell.

haptoglobin: An alpha-2 globulin in serum whose concentration is inversely proportional to the severity of active hemolysis.

hematocrit: A measurement in percentage of what proportion of the blood is actually made up of red blood cells.

hemithorax: One side of the chest cavity.

hemoglobin: The oxygen-carrying molecule found within red blood cells.

hemolysis: The clinical presentation of the pathological rupture of circulating red blood cells by either an immune or nonimmune process.

hemosiderin: A storage form of iron. An increase of this substance in the urine documented by clinical laboratory assay is found during episodes of active hemolysis.

heterozygous: The clinical state of having different genetic alleles within a chromosomal profile.

homozygous: The clinical state of having the same (matched) genetic alleles within a chromosomal profile.

hypoxia: A pathological clinical state where there is a low concentration of tissue oxygen.

icteric sclerae: A visible yellowish discoloration noted in the white part of the eyeball as a consequence of a rising serum bilirubin level.

inflammatory mitogenic cytokines: A biological or chemical substance that has the ability to induce cellular division, generally in reference to the induction of an immune response.

immunohistochemistry: Referring to a pathology service technique that selectively utilizes various immune markers to help ascertain the nature or characteristics of tissues that are being analyzed.

immunologically nude mice: A subset of rodents that lack an intact immune system.

indirect bilirubin: A by-product of hemoglobin degradation that is elevated in the serum in the setting of pathological hemolysis.

interphalangeal joint: A joint found between the digits of a finger or toe.

jaundice: A yellowish discoloration of the skin as a consequence of elevated serum bilirubin levels, often noted as a consequence of hepatic dysfunction or extraordinarily severe hemolysis.

LDH: Lactate dehydrogenase. A chemical marker that may be found elevated in the serum during a pathological hemolytic event.

Loop of Henle: A nephron component distal to the proximal convoluted tubule.

MCHC: Mean corpuscular hemoglobin concentration, which is an assay to determine the hemoglobin within the confines of circulating erythrocytes.

mediastinum: The center of the thorax where the heart and great vessels dwell.

mesoderm: One of the three primary embryonic tissue planes that constitute the middle layer of cells in embryonic development.

micturition: Urination.

Neisseria gonorrhoeae; A specific bacterium responsible for the infectious sexually transmitted disease known as gonorrhea.

nephron: One of many microscopic filtration units found in the kidney.

parenteral: Beyond the realm of the gastrointestinal tract, usually as a reference to nutritional support administered through an intravenous route.

phlebotomy: The therapeutic removal of a specified amount of circulating blood.

porphyria cutanea tarda: A metabolism disorder of a hemoglobin substructure.

priapism: A pathological unrelenting penile erection often seen as a complication of sickle cell disease.

protozoan parasite: A eukaryotic single-cell infectious organism.

pruritic vesicle: A skin blister with associated itching.

quadriplegia: A paralytic condition that involves both the upper and lower extremities.

reticulocyte: A new red blood cell that just entered circulation from the bone marrow.

sternocleidomastoid: A muscle in the anterolateral position on either side of the neck.

supraclavicular: The region of the body located above the thorax and collarbone.

trypanosome: A eukaryotic single-cell organism that is often parasitic.

COMPLETE GLOSSARY OF SPANISH WORDS AND MEXICAN SLANG EXPRESSIONS

VAMPIRO, VOLS. 1 AND 2

a la ver, gatos y ratones: Literal translation, "to see cats and rats." A clever play on words, as "a la verga," which translates into English as "into the cock (penis)."

abuelito: Little grandfather.

Adelante, Comandante: Later, commander. This is similar to the expression "See you later, alligator."

agua fría: Cold water.

agua preciosa: Precious water.

ahora: Now.

albahaca: Basil herb; often used in huevo limpia ceremonies.

amarillo gusano de maguey: Yellow maguey worm (caterpillar).

amarillo: Yellow.

americanos: Americans.

amigo: Friend.

arrachera: A reference to carne arrachera, which is a relatively inexpensive cut of beefsteak.

arroz, frijoles, y un delicioso pod de chile caliente en ocasiones: Rice, beans, and a delicious hot chile pod on occasion.

Avenida de los Muertos: Avenue of the Dead.

Azteca: Aztec.

bandito: Bandit.

barrio: Hispanic neighborhood.

bastardo: Bastard.

basura: Trash.

blanco: White.

bolillo: A bread roll.

Buena Comida: Good Food.

buena suerte, señor: Good luck, sir.

Buenas noches, Tio Pepe. Buenas noches, mi amigo viejo: Good night, Uncle Pepe. Good night, my old friend.

cojones: Boxes. Slang word for testicles.

caldo de res: Beef soup.

Calle Vampiro: Vampire Street; the name of a Mexican drug cartel.

capitán nuevo: New captain.

cara de temptacion, querpo de repentamiento: An old saying that translates as "the face of temptation, the body of repentance."

cerrado: Closed.

cerveza fría: Cold beer.

chema: Brother.

chilongo: A derogatory word for a resident of Mexico City.

chingar no: Fuck no.

Chino: Chinese.

chispas: Sparks.

chiste: Joke.

chistoso: Clown.

chones: Underwear.

chupacabra: A goat sucker; a mythical bloodsucking monstrous hairless canid, supposedly dwelling in Latin America, Texas, and other regions of the US Southwest.

cinco minutos, más o menos: Five minutes, more or less.

cochino: nasty

cocina: Kitchen.

comadreja: Weasle.

corazón: Heart.

criadillas: Crickets.

culo: ass

curandera: Folk healer.

dinero: Money.

Dios mío: My God.

drogas: Drugs (illicit).

El Codo: A frugal man. This is a derogatory slang word for a resident of Monterrey, Mexico.

El Diablo: The Devil.

El Gato: The Cat.

El Gran Brujo: The Grand Wizard.

El Grifo: The Gryphon.

El Mago: The Magician.

El Mayo: The Maya.

El Primero: The First (in command).

El Punto: The tip of a knife, or a point.

El Sapo: The Toad.

El Segundo: The Second (in command).

El Submarino Amarillo: The Yellow Submarine.

El Tor: A nickname for the leader of the Calle Vampiro drug cartel. El Tor is a deadly strain of bacteria that causes the infectious disease cholera.

El Toro Grande: The Big Bull.

en la tierra de los ciegos, el que tiene un ojo es rey: In the land of the blind, he who has one eye is king.

en tu calaca: In your skull.

entre menos burros, más elotes: An old saying that translates as "the fewer donkeys, the more corn for everyone else to share."

eres Indio nativo, verdad: You are a native Indian, true.

eres Tejano, verdad: You are a Texan, true.

eres un cerdo: You're a pig.

ese: A slang word that roughly translates as "dude."

Estado de Coahuila: The state of Coahuila. One of the thirty-one federated states in the country of Mexico.

Estado de Jalisco: The state of Jalisco. One of the thirty-one federated states in the country of Mexico.

¿estás listo?: Are you ready?

Estoy aquí: I am here.

estrago: Damage.

exactamente: Exactly.

fiesta: Party.

frijoles refritos: Refried beans.

fútbol: Soccer.

gato hembra: pussy cat

gente: People.

gracias, señor: Thank you, sir.

gringo: Slang word meaning a male Anglo individual.

guayabera: A stylish short-sleeved man's dress shirt.

guedo: A derogatory slang word for a male Anglo.

gusano rojo: Red worm (caterpillar).

hacienda: A grand estate.

hasta la vista, jefe: Until we see each other again, chief.

hipopótamo: Hippopotamus.

hola: Hello.

hombre: Man.

hombre simpático: A likable man.

huevo limpia: A chicken egg used in a spiritual cleansing ceremony.

Japonés: Japanese.

jefe: Chief.

Jesús salva: Jesus saves.

joto: A derogatory slang word for a gay male.

jovencito: A small male child.

La Frontera: The Frontier.

La Mordita: The Bite. This term reflects the deeply entrenched political corruption throughout Mexico.

La Ranchera: A female ranch hand.

ligado: Liver.

llaves: Keys.

llevar a este vampiro y decapitarlo: Take this vampire and decapitate him.

lo siento, señor: I am sorry, sir.

Los Dorados: Warriors who served with Pancho Villa during the Mexican Revolution.

Los Estados Unidos de America: The United States of America.

Los Estados Unidos de México: The United States of Mexico.

los huevos amarillos: The yellow eggs.

los papeles correctos: The correct papers.

madre: Mother.

maldito torpe: A clumsy oaf.

maloliente: Malodorous.

más jamón por este par de juevos: Too much ham for these eggs.

mayordomo: The manager of a hacienda.

Maya: A pre-Columbian Mesoamerican civilization that lived predominantly in the Yucatán region of Mexico.

Mexicanos: Mexicans.

mescal: A distilled alcoholic beverage made from any type of agave plant found in Mexico. Mescal is a spirit that is thought by many not to be as refined as tequila.

mija: Term of endearment. A conjugate word from "mi hija," meaning "my daughter."

mijo: Term of endearment. A conjugate word from "mi hijo," meaning "my son."

mineros: Miners.

mira: Look.

mojado: A derogatory term for any illegal alien.

muchachos: Boys.

mujeres: Women

murciélago: A flying mammal commonly known as a bat.

muy deliciosa: Very delicious.

nalgas: Buttocks; ass end.

no cages donde comes: Don't shit where you eat.

no se: I don't know.

noches: Night.

ojos amarillos: Yellow eyes.

orale cabrōn: Pay attention, you goat.

Oso Negro: Black Bear.

Paloma de la Noche: Dove of the Night.

pan dulce: Sweet bread.

para sangre caliente: For hot blood.

parásito: Parasite.

Parilla Tejas: Texas Grill.

pendejo, donde come no se caga: Dumbass, you don't eat where you shit.

Pequeña Rana: Little Frog.

Pharmacia del Norte: Pharmacy of the North.

pinche gringo salado policía: Damned salty Anglo policeman.

Pirata: Pirate.

pito: Gun.

policía local de Juárez: Local police of Juárez.

puerta: Door.

punto: The point of a knife.

puta: A derogatory slang word for a prostitute.

que huele: That stinks.

qué magnífico: How magnificent.

que onda, carnal: What's happening, bro.

que padre: The literal translation is "what father." This is a Mexican expletive similar to the American expression "cool, daddy-o."

quesadilla: An open-face grilled flour tortilla covered with cheese, among other food items.

queso fundido: Grilled cheese.

queso menonita: A white cheese originating from the Mennonite settlers in Chihuahua.

quete: A slang word for pistol.

quién es más malo: Who is the baddest.

quinceañera: a debutante party held in honor of a Latina who has reached her fifteenth birthday.

Rancho Feliz: Happy Ranch.

ratón: Rodent.

Ratoncito Pérez: Perez, the little rat. Hispanic version of the tooth fairy.

Redención y salvación: Redemption and salvation

regalo especial: Special gift.

Reina de los elefantes: Queen of the elephants.

Rio Bravo: Brave River; alternate name for the Rio Grande that separates Texas from Mexico.

routa: Route or pathway.

salados: Salty.

Sangre de Indios: Indian blood. This is a specific type of obsidian volcanic glass.

sangre impía: Unholy blood.

Santa Sangre: Sacred Blood.

Señor Stewart, eres un gran héroe: Mr. Stewart, you are a great hero.

serpiente de pantalón: Trouser snake.

Siete Leguas: A prized brand of tequila.

simpático: Agreeable or likable.

sin fuerte: Without strength.

soldados: Soldiers.

sopapilla: Fried bread.

te aye watchto: I'll be seeing you.

te gusta mota: Would you like some marijuana.

Tejanos: Texans.

Tejas: Texas.

tia: Aunt.

Tiburon: Shark.

tiempo: Time.

Tio Chico: A brand of carbonated water.

tio: Uncle.

tonel de pollo: Chicken coop.

toques: A parlor game where participants receive dangerous electrical shocks.

torta: A sandwich served on a bolillo bread roll with meat, vegetables, or avocado.

tú eres el vampiro con el nombre Morales: You are the vampire with the name Morales.

un corazón de cerdo: Pig heart.

un crudo pinche guey: A jerk with a hangover.

un momento, por favor: One moment, please.

una pista fría: Slang for a cold beer.

va chinga un gato, gringo, mientras que la miedra tu abuela: Go fuck a cat, white boy, while I'm fucking your grandmother.

vampiro: Vampire.

verdad: True.

voltios: Volts.

y: and.

y un barril grande: And a big barrel.

y un desierto delicioso: And a delicious dessert.

Yo soy más malo, pendejo: I am the baddest, you dumbass.

Yo soy una gran bruja: I am a great witch.

Zopelotes: Vultures.

zorillo: Skunk.

PRAISE FOR THE OBSIDIAN KNIFE

I was thrilled to see that Dr. Hill was able to resurrect many of the beloved characters that he first introduced to the public in his masterpiece *The DNR Trilogy*. This new work of fiction is a story that I wanted never to end. I'm grateful that Thomas Cavaretta pressed Dr. Hill to get on board with this project.

—**S. Carol Maple**, LPN. Casa Grande, Arizona

Stunning in its scope and depth, this is not like any work of fiction that I have ever read related to the subject of human vampirism. At times, I found that Dr. Hill's soaring command of written English to be no less than breathtaking.

—**Kelli Terrell**, Tucson, Arizona

Although certainly not a sequel to the triumphant *DNR Trilogy* in the truest sense of the word, this new work of fiction, *Vampiro*, certainly continues to espouse the mystical theme that everything in the universe is connected somehow.

—**Vicky Atkinson, RN**, Kona, Hawaii

This is not a novel that one can casually read, as it is an intense and disturbing work of fiction. It's all here: the evidence, the history, the legends, and the truth. ... At some point, you will invariably ask yourself, *"Am I really beginning to believe?"*

—**J. C. Sullivan**, Tucson, Arizona

Thomas Cavaretta's deep and reverential insight into the Hispanic culture of the American Southwest has bestowed upon this amazing work of fiction an undeniable patina of authenticity.

—**C. Darter**, Tucson, Arizona

Dr. Hill's scientific rationale for the possibility of human vampirism is certainly compelling. Just as important, the authors are able to successfully portray the perpetual human quest for salvation, even amid the darkest hour just before dawn.

—**Wynn Madden**, Tucson, Arizona

If one were to scrutinize the lore of human vampirism dating all the way back to the fifteenth century, one would find that it has generally consisted of little more than a ghastly folk tale about some desperate individual who rendered his immortal soul to the devil. Well, what if vampirism were actually a bona fide, horizontally transmissible illness? Hill and Cavaretta have certainly made a strong argument that such an infectious disease process is not only feasible but also possible. Frankly, I find that terrifying.

—**Judy Kahler, RN**, Kona, Hawaii

CPSIA information can be obtained
at www.ICGtesting.com
Printed in the USA
LVHW070740060721
691958LV00009B/85/J

9 781953 537577